"Exsequors. It's Latin for *avenge*. Punish. Step on the pope's sandals and they step back. Very hard. *Exsequor* exsequor. To follow to the grave, or the ends of the earth. Dates back to the old days, when the Jesuits first started flexing their muscles."

Parlow twisted and turned in his chair as he searched through his pockets for an envelope. "Here we go," he said, dropping a packet on the table. "Take a look. One former exsequor, and another who is still alive and kicking."

Tobias was about to pounce on the crouched figure when a voice from behind him said, "Leave the boy alone. Pick on someone your own size."

Tobias spun around, knife slashing the air. He squeezed his eyes until they were almost shut, straining to see the man in black.

"Get out of here," he shouted. "This is none of your business."

The man moved slowly, directly toward Tobias. When he was within fifteen feet, Tobias was able to make out his face and clothing. A Roman collar. A priest . . .

He stepped around a coagulated pool of blood that lay at Paco Ramiro's feet, which, like his arms, were bound with rawhide strips to a heavy wooden chair.

"What caused those circular wounds all over his face and skull?"

"A corkscrew," Garate said with grim satisfaction.

"I've never seen anyone executed in that manner be-fore...."

"The priest finds many uses for that corkscrew."

Other books by Jerry Kennealy

The Forger
The Suspect
The Hunted
The Other Eye
Chasing the Devil
The Vatican Connection

The Carroll Quint Mysteries

Jigsaw
Still Shot

The Nick Polo Mysteries

Polo Solo
Polo, Anyone?
Polo's Ponies
Polo in the Rough
Polo's Wild Card
Green with Envy
Special Delivery
Vintage Polo
Beggar's Choice
All That Glitters

THE
VATICAN
CONNECTION

SPEAKING VOLUMES, LLC
NAPLES, FLORIDA
2013

The Vatican Connection

ISBN 978-1-62815-075-9

THE
VATICAN
CONNECTION

Jerry Kennealy

For my wife, Shirley
Siempre

Prologue

Paris, April 1942

Jago Roldan leaned back in the luxurious upholstery of the midnight-blue Rolls-Royce Phantom and looked out the window at the streets of Paris. The Germans had done nothing really drastic—yet. Joseph Goebbels, the minister of propaganda, had assured the city's residents that France would be kept relatively intact—"an enlarged Switzerland"—a desirable destination for German tourists, as well as a convenient source for fine wines, agreeable women, and high-quality courtiers.

The morning's weather was dismal. Gritty wind-driven clouds blotted the sky. The streets were filthy, clogged with debris and pocked with potholes. Traffic moved in erratic jerks and starts. Even the trees seemed to be affected by the Nazi occupation—no leaves, no blossoms. It was as if spring had decided not to make an appearance this year. Jago was so close to the window that his breath clouded the glass. He grasped his father's knee and pointed out the imposing bulk of the deserted Louvre.

Carlos Roldan had somberly informed Jago that even if they could gain entry to the famed museum, they would be cheated of its full glory. Many of the finest works of art had been shipped to the Fatherland, stored in gloomy vaults in a forest in the Bavarian Alps.

The streets were jammed with every size and shape of military vehicle imaginable—including several menacing tanks, their turrets popped open, German soldiers leaning out and taunting the nervous civilian pedestrians who kept their eyes trained on the sidewalks—the look of a defeated land.

Last night Jago had talked his father into taking him to dinner at Maxim's. The food was marvelous, and Jago had joined in with the drunken Germans as they sang patriotic songs in their native language. His father had tried to persuade him to leave, but Jago was having too much fun. A tall, dashing blond German colonel had invited him to their table. While Jago drank beer and sang, Carlos Roldan sat alone, his shoulders hunched, his head bent down, trying to make himself invisible.

Jago despised his father for his cowardice. He would never amount to anything more than what he was—a poorly paid curator at the Prado Museum in Madrid, temporarily assigned to work with the Spanish ambassador. He had been sent to Paris to pick up a shipment of confiscated paintings for *Generalíssimo* Francisco Franco's personal collection.

The Rolls drew suspicious scowls from the uniformed traffic soldiers. The scowls were quickly replaced by a stiff military salute when they saw the black-shirted SS officer behind the steering wheel.

Jago wondered whom the Rolls had belonged to. Possibly one of the Sephardic Jews, wealthy Spaniards who had foolishly made the mistake of thinking that their money and factories in Spain could guarantee their safety in France. Now they were rotting in prison camps, and the Nazis were enjoying the fruits of their labor. *Which is as it should be,* Jago thought. *To the victors go the spoils of war.* And the Germans were definitely victorious. He only hoped that he could help in some way. Help Spain. And help himself.

The Rolls purred to a stop at the Ritz Hotel's majestic entrance on Place Vendôme. A stocky soldier wearing a field-gray uniform opened the door and frowned as the occupants climbed out.

"I am from the Spanish ambassador's office. I have an appointment to see *Reichmarschall* Göring," Carlos quietly informed the soldier.

They were ushered through the hotel's revolving doors. The lobby was full of uniformed soldiers and attractive, garishly dressed women, *anschaffens,* Parisian housewives and office workers whose only means of earning money now was prostitution.

The entire Vendôme side of the Ritz had been taken over by Hermann Göring and his henchmen. The ornate double-hung Regency doors leading to Göring's personal suite were wide open, and Jago could see a number of soldiers, most in shirtsleeves, packing framed paintings and statues of all sizes into stout wooden crates.

Carlos Roldan nervously presented his credentials to a stone-faced sentry. The man stamped his rifle butt on the parquet floor with one hand and gave a smart salute with the other before bellowing out a loud *"Heil* Hitler!"

"Jawohl, Herr Ambassador. Wait here, please."

Jago looked up at his father and grinned. He was enjoying all of this immensely.

In less than a minute an officer hurried out to meet them. He clicked his heels, gave the stiff salute, and introduced himself.

"Hauptsturmführer Waller at your service. *Reichmarschall* Göring asked me to inform you that he has been called back to Berlin. He ordered me to extend you every courtesy."

Captain Waller was a heavyset, powerful-looking man. His balding head was egg-shaped, small at the top, broad at the chin. He was not wearing his uniform cap, but a red line was scored across his forehead where the cap usually rested. He had a clipboard clasped under one arm.

Jago was disappointed. He had looked forward to meeting Göring. He could see his father was greatly relieved. The frightened old man had told him how much he feared dealing directly with the notorious *Reichmarschall*.

Jago had done his homework. He had studied everything he could find on the Nazi command and had received a detailed briefing from his friend Domingo, the son of a Spanish general, who had met most of the high-ranking Germans. According to Domingo, Göring was immensely fat, with bulging cheeks and a drinker's nose. A glutton who dribbled food and champagne over the rows of medals studding his specially designed pale blue uniform.

Captain Waller was pleased that the Roldans spoke such fluent German, as his Spanish was not good. He took Jago's hand and patted him lightly on the shoulder, admiring the teenager's black leather jacket, made in the style of an SS officer's.

Though fifteen, Jago could easily pass for eighteen or twenty. He was already taller than his father. They shared a slightly hooked nose and brown eyes, but Jago's eyes had a dark, arrogant cast—hunter's eyes—while those of his father were pale, timid, his posture that of a man who was afraid of stumbling over his own feet.

They followed the captain down the hotel's spacious halls. The delicate apricot-pink brocade walls were showing signs of wear: fingerprints, scuff marks, crude graffiti written in pencil.

They made their way down a circular iron stairway to the basement "caves," where the wine was stored, then to the laundry rooms. Waller stopped in front of a battered wooden door, extracted a large iron key from his uniform pocket, unlocked the door, then stood aside and waved an arm, gesturing for Carlos and his son to enter.

The room was square-shaped and smelled of strong soap and disinfectant. A web of electrical wiring hung from the ceiling, and someone had smashed fist-size holes in the plaster walls. Haphazard stacks of framed paintings and tapestries were packed in so tightly that Jago had to get in front of his father and push his way through them.

"The *Reichmarschall* had these Spanish items separated from the others," Waller said. "You may take what you wish, but"—he held up the clipboard in front of him—"I am to keep a record."

"Naturally," Carlos Roldan replied with a bowed head. He took off his jacket, folded it carefully, placed it on a rickety cane-seated chair, and began examining the works of art.

It was a stunning collection. Jago quickly located four oils that his father verified were by Velázquez. They found more than a dozen Goyas, several depicting bullfighting scenes. Others featured bloody battlegrounds, for Spain had been at war during the better part of Goya's lifetime.

Captain Waller had paid strict observance at first, but his attention wandered as time went by. He picked up a badly damaged abstract, held it at arm's length and shook his head.

"*Die scheisse.*" He laughed, using a particularly vulgar expression to describe the painting as shit. He poked a finger through one of the holes in the canvas and laughed again. "One of our soldiers was a critic. He used this for target practice."

Jago examined the painting, frowning when he saw Picasso's signature.

Captain Waller went to the hall to bellow an order for someone to bring them food and wine.

Carlos Roldan was staring at a nearly life-size painting of El Cid conquering Valencia in 1094. Jago knew that Franco would love it. The *caudillo* considered himself to be Spain's modern-day El Cid. The hero in the painting was tall, strong, handsome—but Franco would not take notice of that.

Just then Jago's foot brushed against a cracked, stained wooden box with a brass hasp. He knelt down and examined it. Inside were two small canvases of horses racing up the side of a hill. The paintings appeared to be identical. Beneath them was a mass of crushed paper. He pushed the paper aside and found what appeared to be an ancient letter encased in a copper-colored sheet of glass. The stylish scrawl was in Latin. At the top of the letter was a cracked bloodred signet, a profile of a man's head. Jago narrowed his eyes as he read the date—the fourth day before the Ides of March during the consulship of Nero Caesar Augustus.

He rose to his feet and showed the paintings to his father, who studied them briefly before saying, "Worthless."

"What of this?" Jago said, tapping the glass. " Look at the signature at the bottom. Simon Peter. Can it really be him, Father?"

Carlos's fingers brushed across the scratched glass, then drew back as if he'd touched something hot. He gave an involuntary shudder. "The *Professio*," he whispered hoarsely, making the sign of the cross against his chest. "Put it back. We want no part of it."

Captain Waller reentered the room, pushing a common laundry cart before him. "You can place the things you will be taking back to Spain in here. How much longer will you be?"

"This will take some time," Carlos Roldan responded. "And I'm afraid we will need more carts."

Jago and his father began loading the first cart, while Waller dutifully entered a description of each item and the name of the artist on his clipboard. They stopped long enough for a lunch of sausages and red wine, then went back to work. The original laundry cart was loaded, and five more were rolled into the room and quickly filled.

Waller examined his list, then told Carlos to follow him back to Göring's suite. "We will sign the shipping orders." He pointed a pudgy finger at Jago. "You stay here. I'll send someone to help with the packing."

Jago waited until their footsteps were no longer audible, then carefully withdrew the ancient Latin letter out from under a pile of discarded paintings. He examined it closely again, then made a decision. He unbuttoned his jacket, then his shirt. He slipped the glass-encased letter against his bare skin. Looking around the room, he decided that he might as well take a couple of the paintings home with him. He used a crowbar to break away the frame from a small Goya oil, then rolled the canvas up. He was about to slip it under his shirt when he heard someone say, "What do you think you're doing?"

Jago spun around to see a German soldier, barely older than he was, leering at him. His uniform shirt was soiled, and his boots were scuffed and unpolished.

"I saw what you did. Give me that painting, or you'll be on a train to the camps with the fucking Jews."

Jago was mildly surprised that he felt no fear. "*Verpissen sich*," he said, telling the German to piss off. "You don't know what you're talking about."

The soldier's face turned beet red, and he rested his hand on the butt of the Luger pistol holstered at his hip. "Give it to me."

Jago held out his arm and let the Goya fall to the floor. As the German bent down to pick it up, Jago brought the crowbar down viciously on the back of his head. Once, twice, and a third time as the soldier sank to his knees. Jago applied a final blow when the soldier sprawled on the floor, arms outstretched. One of his legs gave a violent twitch; then he was still.

Jago ran out to the hallway. There was no sign of his father or any more soldiers. Using a sense of calmness under pressure that would serve him well for the rest of his life, he quickly returned and checked the German's pulse. There was none.

He laid an empty laundry cart on its side, rolled the soldier into it, then righted the cart and wheeled it into the hallway. He pushed the cart down the dimly lighted corridor, checking the doors as he went, finally finding one that was unlocked. He opened it and wheeled the cart inside. There were piles of old carpeting and broken-down furniture and torn mattresses. The air was damp and musty. He dumped the soldier behind a faded maroon couch, then covered him with several carpets.

Jago dusted his hands, then hurried back to the room with the paintings. He was wiping down the El Cid canvas when Captain Waller and his father returned.

"Where is Grossman?" Waller demanded when he saw that Jago was alone.

"The soldier?" Jago said innocently. "He was here for a minute; then a young girl came for him. I don't know where they went."

"*Verdammter Schweinehund*," Waller said in disgust. "The horny idiot will find his next piece of ass on the Russian front."

Chapter One

Costa del Sol, Spain, the Present

It was Paco Ramiro's favorite time of the day—a little before nine in the morning. The Mediterranean sky was a watery pink, and sepia-tinted mountains shimmered in the distance. The glassy, salt-scented sea lapped softly against the gray, gritty sand. His beach. Or at least his part of it.

Paco's *cabeza de playa* was the size of two soccer fields, running from the cement bulkhead on the promenade right down to the water's edge. He was responsible for maintaining the area—getting it ready for the wealthy sun lovers who rented their small plots of sand by the day, week, or month. Paco was kept busy arranging the green-and-white-striped umbrellas, the beach chairs and chaise longues, then hurrying to the club for drinks and food for his customers.

It was all very hectic but rewarding. He earned much more on the beach than he could working as a waiter or cleaning rooms at the nearby hotels.

Paco's hair was cut short and skinned around the ears, in the fashion of one of his favorite rap singers. His naturally dark skin was baked by the sun. He wore only a pair of black nylon swimming trunks and a canvas fanny pack in which he kept his tips.

This morning he was scraping through the sand with a fine-toothed rake. He wanted to use a metal detector, but his *capataz* would not allow it. His friend Rico, who worked the beach at El Banondillo, had found a gold bracelet that he sold to the fence Giles Dolius for three hundred American dollars.

So far Paco's searching had turned up only common coins and one ring that he'd thought was a diamond, but proved not to be. Still, one never knew. A gold watch, a wallet, a money clip. Anything was possible.

He was on his knees, running the rake under one of the longues, when a movement caught his eye. He brushed his hands and jumped to his feet. A man. No doubt some cheap German tourist who thought that he could sneak a spot on the beach.

He was wearing dark slacks and a white shirt, carrying his suit jacket in one hand, a large envelope in the other. Paco was about to shout a warning when he recognized the man: Señor Sam Alroy. One of his regulars, he had been to the beach many times. Alroy and his fantastic young wife, Daria. What a beauty. A goddess. A Spanish goddess. Tall, silky golden skin, a magnificent body, and enormous pale blue eyes. According to his *capataz,* Daria was a member of one of the most powerful families in all of Spain, the Roldans.

Many beautiful women frequented Paco's beach. Most of them wore skimpy bathing suits and many went topless. Although Alroy's wife wore a modest two-piece suit, there was no way to conceal that body. After swimming her nipples became hard, long and pointed, causing Paco to fantasize about them scratching across his chest as she writhed against him.

Just yesterday she had called out to him when her husband was not there. "Paco, get me a daiquiri." She had been lying facedown in the sand. When she rolled over, one breast fell free. She looked up at Paco as she slowly readjusted the top of her bathing suit. Her eyes were cold, mocking, and a hint of a smile played on her usually scornful lips. His penis was like a cobra, snaking its way up so that the tip was pushing its way out of the top of his trunks. Paco had run down to the beach, right into the water, wading out until he was chest-deep. Then he freed his cock and stroked it while he looked at her and shot his semen into the Mediterranean.

Such a woman. Why did she marry a man like Señor Alroy? Paco watched the man approach. The American was scrawny, with fish-belly-white skin sprayed with freckles. He wore trunks that reached below his bony knees. And he always kept his shirt and baseball cap on, even when he went into the sea.

While his wife sunbathed, Alroy played cards or highstakes domino games with the array of guests they brought to the beach. Or he sat alone, smoking, lighting one cigarette after another with a magnificent gold lighter. He read books and newspapers, or he worked on his laptop computer. Always he had the laptop, but it was not with him today.

This morning Alroy was not wearing his baseball cap. His carrot-red hair was neatly combed.

For all his faults, Alroy always tipped very well, so Paco ran to his side. "*Buenos días,* Señor Alroy."

Alroy wheeled to face Paco, holding the envelope in front of him, as if to ward off a possible attack. "Hey, Paco. I didn't know you were here this early."

"Catch the worms. Isn't that what the Americans say, señor? I will get a lounge chair for you." He hurried away and came back with one of the cushioned chairs reserved for the beach's customers.

"I'm meeting someone," Alroy said. He reached into his pants pocket and came out with a fistful of paper money. He handed Paco a twenty Euro, and said, "Get me some coffee."

"The concession stand does not open until ten, señor. I will have to go across to the plaza. It will take some time."

Alroy draped his suit jacket over the lounge and lit a cigarette with his lighter. "That's all right."

Paco broke into a slow jog, his feet putting fresh prints into the sand. Alroy's car, a beautiful silver Mercedes, was parked between a battered van and a dusty green sedan. As Paco passed it, he trailed his arm across the dust on the Mercedes's hood. Alroy had sent him to the car several times, to retrieve towels or the cards and domino set that were kept in the trunk. More than once Paco had been tempted by other things in the car. Daria's purse—sitting there just waiting to be picked. Or pieces of her jewelry. All very tempting. But he was not foolish enough to steal anything.

He bought the coffee and sauntered back to the beach.

He found Señor Alroy slumped in the beach chair, his head tilted to one side, his arms hanging down, his hands upturned, the knuckles lying on the sand.

"Your coffee, señor," Paco said, noticing that Alroy's envelope was nowhere in sight.

"Your coffee." Louder this time.

Paco leaned down. Blood was seeping from Alroy's open mouth. Paco stepped back quickly, spilling the coffee in the process.

He stared at Alroy; then his eyes swept the beach. It was deserted. No one was walking along the promenade. He could do whatever he liked, if he did it quickly. He knelt down and began going through the dead man's pockets. At last his fingers touched what he wanted, a key ring, which included the big key that started the Mercedes.

Chapter Two

Off the Coast of Florida

"**B**oss, that coast guard cutter is on our tail. He wants us." Dave Chasen said, "I know, Gaucho, I know." He looked over the bow at the welcoming sight of the St. Petersburg harbor. The sea was calm, the sky chamber-of-commerce blue.

The entrance to the harbor was dotted with paper-hat sailboats, sleek party boats, and a few deep-sea fishing vessels like his, the *Breaking Point*.

A beautiful day, if you didn't have twenty cases of prime Cuban cigars in your hold.

The cutter edged closer, its hull cutting through the ocean with a loud kiss and leaving a wake of creamy foam. Chasen recognized the boat, an eighty-two-foot twin diesel that docked less than a mile from his mooring. He recognized the captain, too, Tom Petya, a young New Englander with a Zapata mustache that made him look like a mournful bandit.

One of the sailors, in dungarees and a baseball cap, held a loudspeaker to his mouth. "Captain Chasen. You are to return to your dock immediately. You have an important visitor."

Chasen waved his hand in acknowledgment. When did the coast guard start calling customs agents important visitors?

There was no way to shake loose of the cutter, and no chance of dumping the cargo without being observed. He cut back on the throttle and handed the wheel to Gaucho Ribera, a lean, hawk-eyed Argentinian. Gaucho's eyes were focused on the coast guard cutter.

"Relax," Chasen told him. Gaucho had nine children ranging from six months to fourteen years. "There's no sense both of us going down for this. I'll drop you off before we hit the dock."

Chasen went below deck and looked at the six crates of prime Cuban cigars he'd picked up two hours earlier from an old, rust-smeared trawler in the Gulf of Mexico. He knew exactly what the customs inspectors would do when he pulled into his slip: confiscate his boat, book him for smuggling, then destroy the cigars. One at a time.

He climbed on deck and took the wheel from Gaucho. The coast guard cutter had backed off a hundred yards. Chasen brought the *Breaking Point* into the harbor, hugging the shoreline. When they reached the first docking pier, he cut the engine, then started it quickly, jamming the gear into reverse, churning up a gumbo of root beer–colored mud. He turned the wheel smartly to the left, bringing the stern within a few feet of the dock.

"Jump, Gaucho!"

Ribera said, "Thanks, boss," then gracefully leaped onto the pier.

Chasen eased the *Breaking Point* forward. He held the wheel with one hand, leaned forward, opened the panel marked *Medical Supplies,* and pulled out a bottle of Appleton Jamaican rum. Gaucho claimed he had worked the sugarcane fields for Appleton before landing in Florida, and drinking it gave him an enormous amount of pleasure.

Chasen took a long swig from the bottle and smiled. Considering the amount of rum Gaucho put away, most any kind of booze should have given him an enormous amount of pleasure. His smile faded as he considered what he had in the boat's hold. There were cigars, several unregistered rifles, and a Peruvian warrior's headdress for which he had no bill of sale. More than enough to keep the customs people busy.

He maneuvered the *Breaking Point* to the dock, wondering just who had turned him in. Patricia, his ex-wife? No, an arrest could end the alimony checks. The trawler captain? No reason for that. Another fisherman who also moonlighted when times were tight, as they were now? It really didn't much matter.

The tide was out. He cut the engine and went forward for the bowline.

"Hey, Chasen," a familiar voice called down to him. "Get a shave and a haircut. And some decent clothes. 'GOD' wants to talk to you."

Chasen looked up at the homely face of Paul Bethard, an agent who had worked for him in Berlin another lifetime ago.

"The Company wants you back, Davey boy," Bethard said. "And you look like you need some honest work."

Langley, Virginia

"Right this way, sir," said a tall, broad-shouldered man. "It can be confusing, so keep close, please."

Dave Chasen said, "Sure, sure," and stretched his legs to keep up with his guide, whose lapel had a plastic tag identifying him as C. Baker.

It had been years since Chasen had been to CIA headquarters just outside of Washington, D.C. There had been many changes, including the "greeting" of the Company's personnel. The guides used to be older, harmless-looking guys in uniforms. C. Baker was built like an NFL linebacker with a banker's haircut and a ready-made suit that did little to conceal the Glock semiautomatic holstered at his hip.

Chasen had been frisked and shuttled through three separate metal detectors before he was allowed to enter the building, after which he was taken in hand by C. Baker and strongly advised not to stray off course.

They walked past a wall plaque sculptured in green serpentine stone showing a three-quarter image of former director William J. Casey. Chasen gave Casey a friendly nod and wondered what the old man would have thought of the Company's operations today. Probably about as little as Chasen did.

"This way, please," C. Baker said, holding open the door to a small elevator. Baker pushed an unlabeled button. The elevator took off in a jerk, and in mere seconds came to an abrupt stop, as if it had hit the ceiling.

Outside the elevator was a varnished oak door with the name *Grady O. Devlin, D.D.* in polished brass letters. Chasen wasn't overly impressed, since there were forty-seven deputy directors in the Company when he'd left, and no doubt double that amount now.

Devlin's middle name was reported to be Oran, but Chasen had the feeling that it was a phony, fabricated so that Devlin could initial his internal documents as G.O.D.

Baker maneuvered his back to block Chasen's view, then punched the appropriate code into a pad on the door. It opened without a sound and Baker said, "I'll be back to escort you out when Mr. Devlin is through with you, sir."

Through with you. That didn't sound very encouraging. Chasen had been booted out five years ago after he'd complained vehemently about United States Senator Ronald Lorenzo's restrictive, politically correct rules regarding the CIA's policy on hiring informants. Lorenzo had subpoenaed Chasen and held a behind-closed-doors session of the Senate Intelligence Committee, an oxymoron if Chasen had ever heard one. One of Chasen's informants, Jorge Quezada, had been a drug trafficker fairly high up in the hierarchy of a Colombian cartel. His lengthy record had included arrests for bank robberies, attempted murder, and rape. The man's name and his criminal background were subsequently leaked to the press. Two days later his mutilated body was found in a drainage ditch in Bogotá. Within a few days, Chasen's entire network of nine informants, including Lora, the woman he was living with, had met similar fates. Fortunately Anica, Lora's young daughter, was away at school when the assassins came.

Furious at the deaths of his informants and certain that Senator Lorenzo had been the one to allow Quezada's name to be made public, Chasen leaked the restrictive hiring policy, and its disastrous results, to the press. Lorenzo rightly figured that Chasen had been the guy with the big mouth. Within a week Chasen had been fired.

Grady Devlin's office was outfitted with the standard government equipment: pigeon-gray carpeting, beige walls, cream-colored file cabinets, and a photograph of the smiling president of the United States on the wall.

Carly Sasser was sitting behind her semicircular receptionist's desk, which was bare except for her brass nameplate, a telephone, and one magazine. She kept her eyes focused on the magazine and didn't look up when Chasen entered the room. Her once-dark hair was now the color of weak tea. She was wearing a scoop-necked sweater that displayed a generous décolletage. Her fingernails were polished a fiery red, too long to be of much use on a computer. He remembered that typing and filing had never been her strong points when they'd worked together in Berlin.

"Hi, Carly."

She looked up and smiled, causing fissures to appear in her perfectly applied makeup.

"Jesus, Dave Chasen. The spy who came in from the beach." She got to her feet, walked around the desk, and hugged him. It brought back fond memories to Chasen. Carly was a first-class hugger—pelvis jutted out, breasts mashed against you, a feathery kiss so as not to smear her lipstick.

"I've missed you," Carly said as she leaned back and studied Chasen. "Handsome as ever. Your hair's a little too long, and there's a touch of gray, but you look thinner, damn you." She patted her hips and frowned. "Wish I could say the same. Operating a fishing boat must agree with you. St. Petersburg, Florida. Fresh air, sunshine." She frowned again. "Too much sun. You can overdo a tan, you know."

"It goes with the territory. What's up? GOD was quite cryptic on the phone. You'd think he was a spy or something."

Carly put her fingers to her lips. "I'll let Grady tell you." Chasen followed her to an unmarked door.

"It's Mr. Chasen, Mr. Devlin," Sasser said formally after opening the door.

Devlin's inner office was six times the size of the reception room. The walls were decorated with seventeenth-century astronomical charts and ancient maps. His elaborate Biedermeier walnut desk, positioned near the window for the best view, was cluttered with files and canary-yellow legal-size pads. The computer's screensaver exploded fireworks in dazzling silence. An impressive Gilman Joslin hand-colored terrestrial globe balanced on a brass tripod alongside the desk.

Devlin was standing at a podium thumbing through a voluminous unabridged dictionary. *Nice touch,* Chasen thought. Better than the sitting-behind-the-desk-looking-busy tactic, or talking softly on the phone and waving your guest to a nearby chair.

Devlin smiled broadly. "Dave. Damn, it's good to see you, man."

Chasen smiled back, noting that Devlin had not aged well. His blond hair had thinned and his cheeks were inlaid with a filigree of broken vessels. His striped blue shirt was open at the collar, his tie undone. His suit coat was unbuttoned, revealing a vest with a gold watch chain that stretched from pocket to pocket. Black plastic–framed reading glasses were perched on the top of his head. He shambled over with his hand out, displaying a noticeable limp.

His grip was as strong as ever, though, and he still had the habit of rotating his hand so that his was on top, a subtle way of showing he was in charge right from the start.

"Carly, bring us some coffee, please. Over there, Dave. By the window. Grab a chair. I'll be right with you."

Three chocolate-colored club chairs were spaced around a zinc-topped coffee table. On the table, parked in a cut-glass ashtray, was a half-smoked, extinguished cigar. Next to the ashtray were two legal-size manila envelopes.

"Carly is looking good, Grady."

"You think so? I've been trying to interest her in an early retirement. We've got a hell of a good package now. I think she needs a change of scenery."

Chasen sat down and watched Devlin enter something into his computer before making his way across the room and gingerly lowering himself into one of the chairs. Devlin put a hand to his hip and winced. "Some free advice, Dave. Never play professional football."

"You never played anything more strenuous than golf or checkers. How'd you hurt yourself?"

"Arthritis, damn it. Dear old Mom had it, and now it's in me bones, lad." He smiled at his joke, but Chasen didn't. "I want to thank you for coming on such short notice."

"What is it, Grady? Is Lorenzo still mad at me?"

"You're not keeping up with the news. Lorenzo is dog meat. Cancer of the liver. He won't make it to the end of the year."

Carly Sasser came in carrying a tray with two china cups and saucers and a steaming silver coffeepot. She put the tray down, poured the coffee, and gave Chasen a slow wink before retreating back to her office.

Devlin fidgeted in his chair, took an aluminum tube from his jacket pocket, then reached for the cigar in the ashtray. He unscrewed the top of the tube and inserted the cigar.

"Damn things cost me seventeen bucks. I hate to waste them. You wouldn't know where I could pick up some really good Cuban cigars, would you?"

"They're legal in Canada," Chasen said. He'd passed several *Positively no smoking* signs on his journey to Devlin's office. Grady hadn't changed. He'd always thought that rules he didn't agree with simply didn't apply to him.

"So tell me about yourself," Devlin said. "From what I hear, things aren't going all that well for you. A failed marriage. Alimony to pay. No kids. But you're still sending money to Lora's girl in Colombia. What was her name? Anica, right? Charitable of you, since the kid's not yours. And then there's your boat. The *Breaking Point*. It's expensive owning a boat. Didn't your father ever tell you about the three Fs? If it flies, floats, or fucks—"

"Rent it," Chasen responded.

"Right. I hear the boat needs a complete overhaul. New engine maybe. And there are rumors that you're doing more than fishing. Antiquities from Colombia and Peru. Illegals from Cuba. Naughty stuff. The kind of things that can land a person in jail. That's what they say, anyway."

"They say that falling in love is wonderful, too. You of all people should know that you can't believe everything you hear, Grady. Now, is there anything else *you* want *me* to tell you about myself?"

"I'll be blunt," Devlin said. "I want you back. Working for me. You'll go on the payroll with your full rank. All benefits restored. In a few years you can retire with a hell of a pension. What do you say?"

Chasen sampled the coffee before replying. After all the crap he'd been put through, now he was being welcomed back. With all past sins forgiven. "Why are you being so good to me?"

Devlin picked up one of the two manila folders from the table. He hefted it in his hand for a moment, as if he were assessing its weight, then tossed it toward Chasen's lap.

"There's your employment contract, medical forms, updated pension benefits. The whole enchilada."

"What's in the other envelope?" Chasen asked. "The names of the twenty guys I'm supposed to eliminate in order to get back in your good graces?"

"You never were out of my graces, Dave. But there was nothing I could do for you. You buried yourself with Senator Lorenzo. There was no point in getting my feet in the mud. You were beyond hope by then."

"Understood," Chasen said. Devlin had it exactly right. There was nothing he could have done. The help would have had to come from the director, and he wanted no part of Senator Lorenzo. "I never had any hard feelings your way, Grady. So tell me, what makes me such a hot commodity all of a sudden?"

Devlin ran a hand down the highly polished silver coffeepot, as if admiring its finish.

"Keely Alroy. Remember her?"

Chasen forced a smile and let his gaze wander around the room. It *was* a setup. Devlin and the Company wanted another piece of him.

"Relax," Devlin said. "I'm not recording this. It's strictly between you and me. Keely Alroy was the reporter who wrote those damaging articles on Senator Lorenzo. We know that you gave her the material. Were you screwing her?"

"No."

"Well, she screwed you, buddy. That story made her a star, and you got the ax. But that's water under the bridge. If you'd read the papers instead of fishing or whatever the hell you're doing on that boat of yours, you might have noticed that Keely's brother, Sam Alroy, was murdered. In Spain. On the Costa del Sol."

"I never met the man."

"Neither did I. Sam Alroy was one of those geeky high-tech geniuses. A Boston Irish Catholic. Studied for the priesthood. Went to MIT. Started his own company, got tired of all the taxes that dear old Uncle Sam was making him pay, so eleven years ago he moved to Cambridge, England, lock, stock, and business. His parents had settled there. He produced flight-simulator programs, branched out into space-exploration technology, then made a ton of money with military-related software. His latest toy has all the boys at the Defense Department jumping up and down and saying, 'Get me that.' Something to do with using microwave beams to upgrade smart bombs. Uncle Sam has already lined his pockets with millions of development dollars for the software."

"Who murdered Alroy?"

"We don't know. One bullet, right to the temple, early in the morning on a deserted beach. The police report is in that other envelope. I'm still waiting for the autopsy. The problem is that Alroy's gee-whiz software was on his laptop computer. Now the laptop is missing. I want you to find it."

"There must be plans of his latest technology somewhere."

"Alroy's people say no. Maybe with the right prodding they could put all the genies back in the bottle, but that would take time. Too much time. Alroy's death turned everything upside down and sideways. No one knows for sure who is going to be in charge. Keely Alroy is listed as vice president of Sam Alroy, Inc., but she really doesn't know diddly about the business." Devlin leaned forward and bored in on Chasen. "You speak Spanish. You know Keely. She's in Spain, on the Costa del Sol. She lives there now. Has for the past three or four years. She's no longer a lowly reporter. She produces highbrow television documentaries."

"Keely doesn't owe me anything," Chasen said. "She might not even talk to me."

Devlin gave a wolfish smile. "I'm not entirely relying on your charm and good looks. Also in the envelope is a cover for you. You're an investigator for Fidelity Surety and

Bonding Company, which happens to hold a five-million-dollar life-insurance policy on Sam Alroy through his business."

"Who gets the five million?"

"The attorneys will probably get most of it, because there's no listed beneficiary. There will be a battle royal for the money between Keely and Alroy's wife."

"You didn't mention a wife."

"It's all in there," Devlin said, plucking an ornate pink-gold pocket watch from his vest pocket. Chasen remembered the gesture well. It signaled the meeting was nearing an end.

"Daria Alroy's the wife," Devlin continued. "Formerly Daria Roldan. Gorgeous creature. Her grandfather is Jago Roldan, an old Spaniard who made his early fortune during Franco's time in the black market. He's been into everything—smuggling, illicit arms sales. Jago has construction companies and an electronics firm. The last few years his main squeeze has been leveraging himself into small corporations, then beating the shareholders over the head with the lever, stripping the business, selling the assets, which is just what I believe he was planing to do to Sam Alroy, Inc. Jago has a mansion in Madrid and a huge villa in Mijas, on the Costa del Sol, which he uses during the summer to escape the heat. He was in Mijas at the time of Sam's death. He's still there. Sam Alroy and Daria were living with him while they were having a place built nearby for themselves."

As usual, Devlin was being thorough. Absently tapping the cigar case on the table, he continued. "I'd say that Jago Roldan is the number one suspect in Alroy's death. If he had Alroy whacked, he has the laptop. Maybe Jago's already transferred the files to his computer. He's giving himself a birthday party tomorrow night at his summer villa. It would be a great opportunity for you to get in there and snoop around his office."

"Except that I don't have an invitation, Grady."

Devlin ran his fingers through his hair and rested his hand on top of his forehead for a moment. "Yesterday you sent Jago an e-mail, identifying yourself as an insurance agent with five million dollars in his pocket. You asked for an appointment late tomorrow afternoon or evening. I'm betting you'll be invited to the party."

Devlin gave a small smile. "Keely Alroy will be there. You e-mailed her, too. Told her that you know about the party and suggested that you meet there. Play it any way you think best, but get into Roldan's house. Maybe Sam had another computer, or some papers relating to his latest project are in his room. If so, my bet is it's there now, in Jago's safe."

"Grady, this is hopeless. Hell, any of a half dozen countries could have sicced their bad guys on Alroy."

"That's true. And if so, I want to know which one. Our government is willing to negotiate. If that doesn't work, we'll have to find other ways. We do know that three days before he died, Sam flew to London from the airport in Málaga, on the Costa del Sol. He was in Cambridge at least one day. One of his employees saw him download the new project information to his laptop, then delete the company files."

"This could mean he was going to sell it to someone," Chasen said.

"Why? Alroy's been doing business with the Pentagon for years. He had a contract with us. We pay top dollar. Why would he jeopardize that arrangement?"

"Where did Alroy go after he left England?"

"We don't know. We do know that he arrived back at the Málaga airport, on the morning of his murder, and—"

"From where?"

"We're not certain," Devlin admitted with a sour grimace. "No trace of him on the servicing airlines. He left his Mercedes in the airport parking lot when he flew off to England on a chartered jet. He picked up the car and, as far as we know, drove directly to the beach where he was murdered."

"Come on," Chasen said. "Things can't be that bad around here. You must have access to his passport, his credit cards."

"He could have used cash, or another name, and chartered another private jet, or sailed from England, taken the Chunnel to Paris and gone damn near anywhere before he ended up back in Spain. It's not like the old days, Dave. No passport or ID checks at the borders. They're taking all the fun out of it. The next thing you know, they'll take away our secret decoders."

Chasen finished his coffee and put the cup down. "I guess there's a plane ticket in that envelope."

"You guessed correctly. Ten o'clock tonight out of Dulles, to Madrid, then on to the Costa del Sol. Carly will supply you with seed money and anything else you'll need—credit cards, insurance company credentials. But no weapons or CIA identification. I want you going in dry. Carly will give you a cell phone, and two local numbers in Spain. The calls will be relayed right back here. One number will ring in my office. If Carly or I are out, you can leave a message. The other number is to the emergency switchboard, in case it's vital you contact me. Carly has a room set aside for you down the hall to study the files we have on Alroy and the Roldans." Devlin extended his hand. "Welcome back."

Chasen made no move to shake. "I didn't commit yet, Grady."

Devlin twisted the large Notre Dame school ring on his finger. "You committed the moment you left Florida and that scroungy boat of yours. If you walk out of here, it'll be impounded before you leave the building."

Chasen sighed and pushed himself to his feet. "Who do I have as backup in Spain?"

"No one worth a damn. All of our agents are well known

to the opposition, and since you don't read the papers, you don't know about the screwup that took place when we sneaked a suspected terrorist out the country. As far as the Spanish are concerned, we are not to be trusted. The local cops are useless. The man you'll have to look out for is Sil Garate, of the CNI, the Centro Nacional de Inteligencia. Spain's poor attempt at duplicating our sterling establishment. Garate used to be in our pocket, but now he's in MI6's, so you may be bumping into a British agent or two. Guess who's in charge of the Brits' Spanish desk?"

"I've been gone so long, Grady. I can't even guess."

"Snake Chalmers. You couldn't have forgotten Snake."

Devlin was right about that. Roger Chalmers had been the British Secret Service's top dog in Berlin, and he and Chasen had bumped heads many times. Chalmers was ruthless, petty, conniving, and vindictive. Grady Devlin with a clipped accent and a bad hair transplant.

"The insurance cover, Fidelity Surety and Bonding, won't work. Keely will see right through it. And this Garate won't be fooled, either."

"So be it," Devlin said. "As long as Jago Roldan doesn't catch on right away, you'll do fine. I know it's a long shot, but long shots pay off, and I could use a big win right now. This is a kick-ass-and-break-glass assignment, Dave. What have we got to lose?"

"Just me."

"Like I said. What have we got to lose?"

Chapter Three

Mijas, Spain

Daria Roldan Alroy rapped her knuckles sharply on the door leading to her grandfather's office, then hurried inside. She came to an abrupt stop when she saw Raul Tobias standing alongside Jago Roldan's desk.

Tobias was in his late thirties, with a trim athletic build that he liked to flaunt by wearing tight-fitting clothes. Today he wore white slacks and a black T-shirt. His dark hair was very fine, receding from a high forehead, and tied at the back in a ponytail. In a few years he would be bald. His face was baby-smooth, and he had a fetish about body hair—shaving his armpits, legs, and groin almost daily.

Her grandfather was shuffling through a sprawling heap of documents. Even in the November of his years, Roldan projected an aura of authority, strength, and power. His hair was silver-gray and as thick as ever. A number of carefully planned cosmetic surgeries during the past ten years had removed all signs of a double chin and the sagging jowls that he'd considered an affront to a man of his position. He gave Daria a brief smile, then went back to the documents.

Daria nodded her head as if to say, *I accept your smile,* then turned her attention back to Tobias. Raul was her grandfather's henchman, who supervised security for the various Roldan business enterprises. And he was also the one who performed the nasty jobs, including bribing policemen, intimidating competitors, and the occasional beating or outright elimination of enemies of the family Roldan.

Daria suspected that Sam Alroy had been Tobias's most recent victim, but both he and her grandfather had denied any part in the murder.

Jago tapped some papers into a neat pile, then handed them to Tobias. "Find Paco, the beach boy. He must know more than he has told the police."

Tobias nodded his head in agreement. "He has disappeared, but I'll find him. Inspector Calvino has provided me with some leads."

"What about the intruder?" Jago asked. Someone had gained entrance to the property, but had been shot by one of the guards before he got near the house.

"No sign of him. He was wounded, though. We found blood on the ground. I have checked the hospitals. Nothing. He may be dead."

Jago grumbled in disapproval. There had been poachers on the property before, but this one, coming so close to Alroy's murder . . . he didn't like it.

"*Abuelo,*" Daria said once Tobias had left and closed the door behind him. She always called Jago that, Spanish for *grandfather,* whether she was speaking English or Spanish. "Why are you wasting Raul's time by sending him after the beach boy?"

"Paco Ramiro was the last person to see Sam alive. Raul was able to locate two men at the Mijas airport who saw Sam drive off in his car the morning of his murder. He had his laptop computer with him. It may still be in the Mercedes. The computer must contain the details of his latest research project, which will be worth an absolute fortune. Our fortune, once we control Sam Alroy, Inc. Raul will make sure Ramiro is not holding out on the police. The little *mayate* may not have killed Sam, but he would have taken anything he could get his hands on."

Daria gave a twitch of a smile. *Mayate.* Faggot. From the way the boy looked at her, he was anything but a homosexual. "Sam's company foreman in Cambridge must have copies of whatever he had on his laptop."

Jago shook his head slowly. "I've spoken to him and was informed that they have nothing. That your dearly departed husband had downloaded everything onto his laptop, then erased the files. Apparently he didn't trust them any more than he trusted me. Why would he do such a crazy thing?"

"Sam was strange. I hadn't seen him for three days before he died."

"What did he say the last time you saw him?" Jago asked.

Daria settled into the red leather chair directly in front of the desk. She was wearing a dress of pale yellow silk crepe carved deeply at both the neck and back. She crossed her legs and slowly adjusted her skirt, knowing that Jago was paying full attention. "Sam said, 'Please. Please don't do it.' "

"Don't do what?" Jago asked, exasperated.

"Get rid of the baby."

"You are pregnant?"

She patted her stomach. "For the moment."

"Is it a boy or a girl?"

"It's too early to tell."

Jago lowered his voice into a conspiratorial whisper. "Are you certain the child is Sam's?"

"Yes," Daria said calmly. She'd learned years ago that the best way to handle Jago was not to react to his baited questions. "Who else could the father be? I know what you're thinking, *Abuelo.* A great-grandson. You would love that. But a granddaughter? You'd be happy to be rid of her, no?"

"For your own good, you'd better not do anything to harm the child. Did you know that Sam's sister was in Australia when she heard of the murder? She's back living on her yacht in Torremolinos. We will have to deal with her."

"Yacht," Daria scoffed. "It's an old barge that Sam let her live on, out of pity, and because she pestered him so much. The same is true of that little shack in town where she makes those silly television documentaries about starving people in Africa or the killing of baby seals in the Arctic. Things that no one watches. She is nothing. I'm going to kick her off the boat after the funeral. She is the sister. I am the widow. Everything of Sam's is now mine, *Abuelo*."

Her grandfather glanced at a pile of official-looking files on his desk. "I am sorry to be the bearer of bad news. Keely Alroy is listed in legal documents as the vice president of Sam Alroy, Incorporated, and—"

"It will all be mine," Daria said defiantly. Sam had been in the process of building a home and a business site in Spain, because Daria flat-out refused to live in England. She hated the cold, damp weather and what she considered the cold, damp character of the people who inhabited it. "The business, the properties here and in England, the bank accounts. All mine."

Jago shrugged at the impudent boast. "Did the two of you make out new wills after the marriage?"

"No," Daria said, concern edging into her voice. "I only married Sam because you begged me to."

"I never beg," Jago said coldly. "I only advise. When I saw the fool drooling over you, I let you know that if you did marry him, and stayed with him for a year, you could contribute to the Roldan family's coffers, and become a very wealthy woman."

Jago had considered Sam Alroy an easy mark. Someone to be used, plundered, then discarded. Daria had no problem with that scenario.

"I promised to marry him and stay with him for a year. No longer."

The old man's lips flattened into a mirthless smile. "Unfortunately, Sam was killed after only seven months of wedded bliss. And the marriage taking place in Brazil, that was foolish. It would have been better if you'd married in Spain."

Daria flared up at this. They'd had several arguments about it before the marriage. "Marriage is marriage. In Brazil or anywhere else. Sam was a romantic. He loved Brazilian music. He had fantasies that I was his girl from Ipanema. He had many fantasies, *Abuelo*. All men have them. You know that."

Jago rapped the tip of his cane on the floor, signaling her to keep her temper. Yet when he spoke, his voice was calm. "He was a strange one, your husband. He looked so much like the fool, yet he was an excellent card player, and sometimes beat me at chess."

Always beat you, Daria knew, but she let it pass.

"Perhaps," Jago said, "Sam was gambling. Lost a great deal of money, and that was the reason for his murder."

"Sam never gambled unless he was certain he would win. He didn't go to casinos, or get mixed up with the underworld. Cards, chess, dominos. They were just mind games to him."

"Tell me the truth," Jago said casually. "Did you have anything to do with his death?"

"No! Stop asking me that," she cried. She narrowed her eyes at him. "The better question is, did you have my husband killed?"

"There was no profit in such an action," Jago said.

They stared at each other without blinking for several seconds, neither believing the other. Then Jago leaned on his ivory-handled cane, pushed himself to his feet, and limped over to the display case against the far wall. The case was filled with bullfighting memorabilia: crossed *banderillas,* the spiked sticks used to torment the bull; an *estoques de torero,* the sword made of high-carbon Toledo steel used to finish the animal off; and the *traje de luces,* the gold-colored suit Jago had been wearing the day an enraged bull had ended his hopes of becoming a matador. He'd been a *novillero,* an apprentice. The bull's horns had ripped his right leg open.

On the wall above the case were a half dozen photographs, a shrine to Daria's deceased father. Naldo had been Jago's pride and joy, "A true Roldan in every way." Naldo, Daria's mother, and Jago's wife had all been killed in a fiery explosion when Daria was a small girl. Jago believed that the Catholic Church was behind the tragedy and swore that he would one day get his revenge.

Daria knew that Jago had never fully recovered from her father's death. He'd worshiped Naldo because of his athletic grace, his good looks, and simply because he was a male Roldan. Daria had to prove her worth to the chauvinistic old man time and again.

Jago's only other offspring was Vidal, Naldo's older brother. In his youth Vidal had studied to become a Benedictine monk, and Jago blamed the bastards for ruining the boy, taking the fire from his stomach. Jago had hoped to groom him to take over the family business, but it had not worked out so far. Vidal operated an art gallery in Madrid, had a true expert's eye, and was quite adept at dealing with the dangerous men who trafficked in stolen masterpieces. He acted the role of the loyal son, though Jago wondered how much of this had to do with Vidal's ambitions to succeed Jago when he was gone.

"Your uncle Vidal is here," Jago said. "Have you spoken to him?"

Daria hated Vidal. She knew that Jago held the view that only a man could operate in his murky world. But now Daria had him by the gray hairs on his shriveled *cojones.* If Sam's estate were as big as she was led to believe, it would be Jago who would have to prove himself worthy to her. "Yes," she said. "He will be staying at the house for a few days, until the funeral. When will the police release Sam's body so that we can get that over with?"

"A day or so. Vidal and Sam seemed to get along well."

"It must be the Catholic thing." She folded her arms under her breasts and took a deep breath, pleased that Jago's tired old eyes followed her every movement. "Vidal was in that monastery, and Sam was a Jesuit for several years. The two of them would get together, smoke *maría,* and talk about their times—"

"*María?* Marijuana?" Jago said quickly. "They smoked dope?"

Daria put her fingers to her mouth and made a kissing sound. "Sam loved it. You must have smelled it, *Abuelo.*"

Jago sighed and caned his way back to his chair. Drugs were a weakness, something for the lower classes, certainly not a Roldan. "I'm concerned about Sam's sister. She claims to have a copy of his will. She would not go into details, but since she was Sam's only living relative when the will was written, I assume that she is listed as the beneficiary. Sam had a five-million-dollar life-insurance policy through his company. An agent for the insurance company, a Señor Chasen, is coming to the party tomorrow night. We want that money, but she will no doubt fight for it. I remember her from the wedding reception I held for you and Sam at the Ritz Hotel in Madrid. She's very attractive. It is her good fortune that she looks nothing like her brother." He frowned, considering a possible complication. "Were Sam and his sister close?"

Close? Daria fantasied of Keely and Sam lying side by side in the same grave site. The winding road leading to the mansion was treacherous, and Keely's car going over the cliff would be the best solution. "Very close," she said, a touch of a smirk in her voice. "Perhaps she could have an accident—"

"Stop talking nonsense. Until we find Sam's laptop, until the legalities of the will and the insurance policy are finalized in your favor, I want you to treat his sister with courtesy. Put on your widow's weeds and cry your beautiful eyes out. Tell the bitch that you are privileged to carry Sam's child. We will have to be careful with her for the time being."

Chapter Four

Dave Chasen arrived at Dulles Airport two hours prior to his flight time. Carly Sasser had claimed that there was no way she could book him into first class. "Director's orders, Dave. Everyone flies coach now."

The crowd queued up for boarding passes included a contingent of sloppily dressed teenagers with cases that obviously contained musical instruments. They were laughing and playing grab-ass with each other. Chasen frowned. His seatmates? Not if he could help it.

He went to the lavatory, sat down in an empty stall, and slipped off his right shoe. He then pried up the inner-sole lining and slipped out two plastic-laminated identification cards. One was his old CIA credential, which he had conveniently "lost" just prior to getting kicked off the job. It had saved his sorry butt more than once since he'd left the Company.

The second was a phony, his somber face stuck on an official-looking card identifying him as Agent Dave Chasen of the Department of Justice. That covered a multitude of agencies.

He slipped the card into his wallet and walked around the airport lobby in search of a security guard. He waved the DOJ card in front of the guard's eyes and asked to be taken to the American Airlines operations office.

The guard escorted Chasen through a maze of corridors

to an isolated area of the terminal. He used a key to open the door to a room where a dozen or more employees were hunched over computers, speaking in brisk professional tones through phone mikes positioned under their chins.

The guard leaned into a glass-fronted office at the back of the room. "Mr. Espero. Man to see you."

The room was triangular in shape, without windows. One desk, one computer, one printer, one annoyed-looking Filipino gentleman.

"I'm Joe Espero. What's the problem?" he asked, getting up from behind his desk. He was a slender man with shiny black hair, wearing a neatly ironed dress shirt, but no tie. The shirt sagged to one side under the weight of a half dozen varicolored ballpoint pens.

Chasen showed Espero his Department of Justice ID.

Espero did not seem overly impressed. "What's going on? No one has informed us of a problem."

"It's my problem, not yours," Chasen explained. "I'm on an undercover assignment. I'd like to see the passenger list for flight nine three one, D.C. to Madrid."

Espero grunted, sat down, and pecked about at his computer. "Here it is. You want a printout?"

"That won't be necessary." Chasen studied the names in first-class seatings. "There's my man."

"Who is your man?" Espero wanted to know. "And what's your interest in him?"

Chasen tapped his finger against the monitor screen. "Like I said, he's not a problem for you. Not a terrorist. Not a gun dealer. Strictly white-collar crime. Paper stuff."

Espero held his hands about six inches apart. "Green paper? With the pictures of dead presidents on them?"

Chasen didn't want Espero to start worrying about the man paying for his flight with counterfeit bills. Espero had an earnest, hardworking looking about him. A man who held people to account.

"Creamy white bond paper, gold embossed. Bearer bonds."

"So what do you want from me?"

Every airline held out one or two first-class seats for each flight, no matter how overbooked they were. The seats were reserved for high-profile politicians, movie stars, large stockholders, or a captain or navigator heading for a flight connection. Each airline had a different code name for these seats. On Delta it was "senators." On United they were called "loges." For reasons unknown to Chasen, the American designation was "tigers." At least he hoped that was the right terminology. It had been some time since he'd had to bluff his way up to first class.

"I'm booked in coach. He's in first class. I was hoping there was a tiger available. I'd like to see if he talks to anyone during the trip."

Espero bulged his lower lip with his tongue. "You're undercover, you say."

"Yes, sir." Chasen laid his carry-on suitcase and briefcase on the desk, then opened the buttons of his blazer. "No weapon."

Espero grunted and studied Chasen's ticket. By the way his face relaxed, Chasen knew he was in. Maybe it was the "no weapon" statement. Many airport operations managers, even with the increased security, didn't like anyone—local police, FBI, or CIA agents—boarding their flights with weapons of any kind.

Espero went back to his computer. "I've got one tiger on this flight. You want to sit next to this character or somewhere behind him?"

"Behind would be best, I think."

"Give me your ticket and leave the suitcase. I'll make sure it gets on the flight. What's in the briefcase?"

Chasen unzipped the inexpensive nylon case Carly Sasser had provided. "Just paperwork, Mr. Espero. There's never an end to that, is there?"

*   *   *

Chasen bought a cup of coffee and hunkered down fifty yards from the boarding area for flight 931. He stifled a yawn. He'd spent much of the evening on the phone to St. Petersburg. Gaucho was handling the distribution of the cigars in the cargo hold of the *Breaking Point.* Since Chasen had no idea when he'd be back to Florida, he told Gaucho to have the boat put in dry dock, and for work to begin on the overdue engine repair.

The rest of the time he'd studied the CIA's files on Sam Alroy and the Roldans, as well as the police report, and pored over maps of the Costa del Sol. The Málaga airport was just ten miles from Torremolinos, where Alroy had been murdered, and the hotel Carly Sasser had booked him into. Keely Alroy's boat appeared to be docked three or four miles from the beach, and Roldan's house in Mijas was some ten miles inland, on a steep mountain, according to the map.

The file also contained a picture of Sam Alroy and his new wife, Daria. She was a real beauty.

He wondered what Grady Devlin had omitted from the files. What Devlin wasn't telling him. The Devlin principle: Always hold something back. Send the field agent into a rat hole to grope around in the dark, find out what the rats were doing. If the agent happened to get bitten, or trip over a land mine, so be it. If the agent knew what was in that hole, he wouldn't crawl into it in the first place. So tell him enough so he looks for the rat, but not enough to scare the rat away. The powers that be, the Devlins of the world, who never entered rat holes themselves, called it "spy craft."

Chasen had heard Devlin use that "kick ass and break glass" line dozens of times in Berlin when he, or one of his fellow agents, had to go across the wall into East Berlin without help, the right resources, or a sure knowledge of what was expected of them.

He remembered Devlin sending him over the wall on a

"routine mission" to meet with Eric Othman, an East German scientist, at the Opera House on the Unter den Linden. Othman never showed, but a half dozen members of the Stassi secret police were there waiting for Chasen. Only a dive into the icy waters of the Spree River had saved him. Devlin's backup team had been frightened off by the Stassi. Chasen had had to rely on an old friend, Hal Gevertz, to arrange safe passage for him back to the west. Gevertz had contacts with all the major governmental intelligence agencies, and equal access to the Mafia families in Europe. Chasen suspected that Gevertz was an agent for Mossad, but he could never prove it. If you needed information, a safe room, arms, furniture, fine art, liquor, a tank, on either side of the Wall, or if you wanted to sell arms, furniture, the family jewels, or information, you called on Hal Gevertz.

They had shared a bottle of cognac on the night the Berlin Wall had come down. At the time Chasen had known damn near every inch of that ninety-one-mile, eleven-foot, eight-inch wall.

"They're breaking my rice bowl," Gevertz had complained bitterly. But Gevertz was the type of man who would always find a full rice bowl. He was a tough, one-armed Jew. The exact facts leading to the loss of that arm changed every few months. Grady Devlin hated "the one-armed bandit," because Gevertz had better sources than either the CIA or British Intelligence in Berlin. Devlin did everything he could to discredit him.

Gevertz had saved Chasen's hide more than once, and he wondered if he could be of any help to him in Spain. If he did call on Hal, he'd have to do it without telling Devlin.

Devlin had spent some time and effort uncovering all that information on Chasen: the alimony, the boat in need of repair, the smuggling. The crack about where to find a good Cuban cigar. And his threat: "The kind of things that can land a man in jail." Not so subtle blackmail, though Chasen knew that in Devlin's mind it was just more spy craft.

He was facing an eight-hour flight to Madrid, a two-hour layover at Barajas Airport, then on to Málaga. He intended to sleep away a good deal of the flight, which was why he wanted to be in first class. He yawned again and set his watch to make up for the time difference between Washington, D.C., and Spain.

Chasen turned his attention back to the police report. Outside of the fact that it was written in Spanish, it was much the same format as police reports worldwide. The first two pages were hand-printed by the first officer to arrive on the scene, Ernesto Osana. The follow-up was typed—poorly—by the investigating detective, Inspector Calvino.

One shot, fired point-blank into the side of Sam Alroy's head as he sat in a beach chair. No witnesses. The body was found by Paco Ramiro, who was an employee at the beach, when he arrived for work. There was no mention of a cartridge casing found at the scene. A professional hit man would have used a silencer and picked up the ejected casing.

Alroy's wallet was missing. So was his watch. The killer had left his gold wedding ring on his finger. A half-filled package of cigarettes was in Alroy's shirt pocket. No car keys. No trace of his vehicle, a Mercedes S-500 sedan.

The victim was wearing shoes, socks, underpants, slacks, and a shirt. No jacket. Chasen tugged his earlobe, adding up the facts. What was Alroy doing on the beach at that time of the morning? An innocent early stroll interrupted by a local thug? Was he meeting someone? Who? Someone he trusted, since he let him get that close with the gun. A new client? And why there? Why not at a hotel? A restaurant? Or in his car?

Chasen heard the call for first-class passengers, boarded the plane, and settled into a spacious window seat. An elderly man with a Lincolnesque beard and granny glasses was sitting next to him, already engrossed in a paperback novel.

Chasen waited until the plane was airborne and the pilot had leveled off before taking off his shoes. He slipped a black satin sleep mask over his eyes, placed foam plugs in both ears, swallowed a Xanax, and waited for sleep to come.

Dave Chasen woke slowly. He peeled the sleeping mask from his face and blinked his eyes into focus as he removed the foam ear plugs.

"You must have a clear conscience," said the man sitting next to him. "You slept like a baby. I envy you."

It wasn't the bearded man with the glasses talking, but a younger man, dressed all in black. It took Chasen a few seconds to place his face. He looked very much like the late actor Burt Lancaster, except where Lancaster had a rugged handsomeness, this face was more chiseled and aristocratic. His hair was a tangled mess of brown curls that appeared to have been combed with his fingers. Chasen couldn't zero in on his age. He could have been anywhere from thirty-five to fifty.

"John Fallon," the man said. "Your former seatmate was having difficulty reading his book. You snore a bit. He asked me to change places. I hope you don't mind."

Chasen introduced himself, then rolled his shoulders and stretched his legs. He undid his lap belt, slipped on his shoes, and rose to his feet.

Fallon swung his legs into the aisle to make room as Chasen headed for the rest room. He washed his face, neck, and hands, all the time wondering about his new seatmate. Fallon's name hadn't been on the first-class passenger list. He grimaced at his image in the rest-room mirror. *You've been away from the game too long,* he told himself. Sound asleep. All those CIA files in the briefcase under the seat. Easy pickings. If this had happened to one of his field agents, he would have given him a good chewing-out.

He slid back the rest-room door and was greeted by the flight attendant, a pretty strawberry blonde with a heart-shaped face.

"Would you like something to eat, Mr. Chasen? I didn't want to wake you. Lemon chicken and potatoes au gratin."

Chasen held out little hope for the meal, but he was hungry. "Thanks for your interest. That sounds good."

John Fallon was waiting, a wide smile on his handsome features.

"Could I interest you in a little wine?" Fallon asked, once Chasen was settled.

"I'm interested."

Fallon waved to the pretty flight attendant, who waved back and moments later brought a black leather case, and placed it on Fallon's lap.

Fallon thanked her, opened the case, and removed a bottle of red wine, two Riedel crystal glasses, and a large staghorn corkscrew.

"How were you able to get that through security?" Chasen asked.

"Tools of the trade," Fallon said. "I'm a priest. And promises of eternal life can do wonders. I've always believed that even the most modest wine tastes better if opened with the proper instrument and served in a proper glass."

Fallon waved the big corkscrew in front of Chasen's face. "This is sixty years old. Given to me by a French bishop." He used the corkscrew's four-inch blade to peel away the foil and expertly eased the cork from the bottle. Pouring a small amount in one of the glasses, he took a sip, then rolled the wine around the back of his tongue and almost seemed to gargle.

"Not bad," he said after he'd swallowed. He poured hefty amounts into both glasses and handed one to Chasen. "It's Barolo. The pope's favorite. He drinks it by the thimbleful. That's one of the perks of being one of his kitchen servants. Great leftovers."

Chasen sampled the wine, which was delicious. "Is that your line of work, Father? Kitchen servant?"

Fallon held the glass up to eye level and studied the dark

ruby color of the wine. "Barolo is made from the Nebbiolo grape. It's named after the fog that rolls over the vineyards in the Piedmont region of Italy." He cocked an eyebrow, remembering Chasen's question. "I work out of the Vatican. Art restoration."

"What were you doing in Washington?"

"I had a little project at Georgetown University."

"Are you heading back to Rome?"

"I thought I'd stop off in Spain for a bit. Beautiful country. I visit there as often as I can. It's the birthplace of our order. Ignio de Loyola, better known as Saint Ignatius, was a Basque."

"Then you're a Jesuit," Chasen said. Sam Alroy had studied for the priesthood at some place near Boston. He couldn't remember if it was a Jesuit organization.

"Black-robed devils to the faithless. Ignio was a tough little bugger. All of them were in those days. We Jesuits were hanged in London. Disemboweled in the Sahara, eaten alive by Indians in Canada, flayed to death in the Middle East. They chopped our heads off in Japan and threw us to the wolves in Russia."

"I guess they didn't like the message you were bringing," Chasen said.

"We went everywhere. Places no one else dreamed about. Lived with the Mandarins in China, prowled the halls of the royal courts in Europe, built the first bridges across the Seine and Danube. Engineers, explorers, athletes, dancers, actors, warriors. We did it all."

"I thought you were missionaries, spreading the word of God."

"Indeed we were. And are. Soldiers of Christ."

The flight attendant arrived with Chasen's dinner tray.

Fallon beamed up at her. His voice slipped into a deep brogue. "Ah, Connie. Sure and you get prettier every day, and today you look like tomorrow."

"Wow," Connie said as she leaned over to hand Chasen

his tray. "I've had it spread on pretty thick before, but you're really something, John." She gave a nose-wrinkling smile, then said, "Are you going to be in Madrid for a few days?"

"I certainly hope so," Fallon answered.

She gave him a knowing look, then strolled away.

Fallon swung his foot up over his knee and massaged his ankle. He glanced over, saw Chasen watching him with curiosity. "Did you hear the one about the rabbi boarding the plane? There's just one seat left, so the rabbi takes it. Next to him are two Arabs. They exchange pleasantries; then the rabbi removes his shoes and relaxes.

"After they take off, one of the Arabs gets to his feet. 'Excuse me,' he says. 'I'm going to get a Coke.'

"The rabbi tells him to stay seated. 'I'll be happy to get it for you.'

"As soon as the rabbi is gone, the Arab picks up one of his shoes and spits into it. The rabbi comes back and gives the guy his Coke. A few minutes later the other Arab starts to get up and says that he's going to get a Coke. Again our friendly rabbi tells him to stay put. He goes to get the Coke and sure enough, the second Arab picks up his other shoe and spits into it.

"The rabbi comes back with the Coke and everything is fine until they get ready to land. As soon as the rabbi puts on his shoes, he knows what happened.

" 'Oh, my God,' he moans. 'When will it ever stop? The shootings. The killings, the bombs, the wars, the spitting in shoes. The pissing in Cokes!' "

Chasen laughed, but not as loudly Fallon did.

Fallon swished the wine around in his glass. "What line of work are you in, Dave?"

"Insurance."

"My, my. That's a conversation stopper, isn't it? Sorry, but I'm in need of none."

"I don't sell it. Just investigate claims."

Fallon smiled, without putting much effort into it. "That must be interesting work."

Chasen took a sip of wine before replying, "Not as interesting as hearing confessions."

"That's passé now. A shame. I used to hear the most fascinating things."

Silence took over for a few minutes as Chasen concentrated on his food and wine. He found that he wasn't as hungry as he thought he was.

When the flight attendant came back to remove the tray, Chasen noticed her slip a piece of paper into Fallon's hand before she asked, "Coffee, gentlemen?"

Both of them declined.

Fallon finished his wine, then handed the bottle to Chasen.

"Help yourself. We should be landing soon. I'm going to try and get a few winks."

As Chasen worked on the wine, he took stock of the priest. Fallon's hands were interesting: the fingers long, the nails blunt-cut. His knuckles were swollen, and the edges of both hands were heavily callused. He knew of only one way for a man to develop such calluses: hours of pounding bags of sand, wooden boards, or bricks.

Fallon's jacket was cashmere and had an Italian cut. His turtleneck sweater appeared to be cashmere also. His shoes were expensive-looking basket-weave loafers. The priest's penchant for dressing in black extended to his choice of a wristwatch: a black-faced Rolex diver's watch that would retail for at least four thousand dollars. Why the expensive watch? Was Fallon a scuba diver? Was it a gift from a wealthy Catholic for services rendered? A sin forgiven? A grandchild baptized?

One of the classes at the CIA's training center was titled Know the Man by His Watch. The instructor's theory, which Chasen agreed with, was that men, especially American men, had an infatuation with wristwatches, and their choice of model and type revealed a great deal about their personalities.

A man might be too intimidated to wear jewelry—bracelets, neck chains, gaudy rings, earrings—or submit to body piercing. But an expensive "power watch" was a symbol, a badge used to influence waiters in order to get a better table, impress a date, or just obtain a favorable nod from the in crowd.

Chasen had chased after a drug dealer in Colombia who also peddled phony Patek Phillippe watches. When he finally caught up with the dealer, he was wearing an authentic twenty-six-thousand-dollar Patek on his wrist.

Chasen looked down at his own hands, callused and scarred from handling fishing and boating equipment. The watch on his left wrist was a twenty-year-old Omega Seamaster that he'd inherited from his father. *What does that say about you?* Chasen asked himself. *Sentimental? Loyal family ties? Or just too cheap to buy a new watch?*

He held up a hand to catch the flight attendant's attention and mouthed the word *coffee*. She nodded her head and frowned. Somehow Chasen had the feeling that had Fallon made the same request, he would have been rewarded with a wide smile.

He reached under his seat to retrieve his briefcase, and thumbed through his files. The Spanish police report had been held together by a red paper clip, on the far left side of the documents. Now the clip was closer to the middle of the page. Fallon had gone through the files. He stared at Fallon's closed-eyed, expressionless face, wondering what interest a Vatican art restorer would have in the death of Sam Alroy.

*　　*　　*

Benita Ramiro pulled the pillow over her head, ground her face into the mattress, and cursed whoever was pounding on the front door. She sat up abruptly and called for her mother. When there was no response she flopped back down again and cupped her ears with her hands. It was no use. The *gilipollas* at the door was driving her mad.

Why didn't her mother answer the door? She yanked the pillow away and focused on the bedside clock, then remembered that Mama had gone to Toledo to be with her sister for a few days. The old cow had had another baby. She was forty years old and still having babies.

Benita climbed to her feet and stretched her arms to the ceiling, catching a glance of her taut sixteen-year-old body in the mirror. She liked what she saw and smiled at her reflection. Should she answer the door like this? Naked? Scare the pants off the idiot who was making so much noise?

Now he was shouting. "*Abra la puerta!*" Open the door.

Benita slipped on a red hooded sweatshirt that barely covered her buttocks. She tugged the zipper up halfway, then hurried to the door.

When she yanked the door open, she flinched for a moment. A policeman. One of the ones who patrolled the beach. He was in his twenties, with pimples on his chin. Benita almost laughed. A policeman with pimples. It was ridiculous. His white shirt and pants were spotless and heavily starched. His cap sat squarely on his head.

"Paco Ramiro. Where is he?" the policeman demanded.

"I don't know where my brother is. Probably at the beach. He works there."

"Not today. Where is he?"

Benita saw his eyes drifting down to admire her legs. She tugged the sweatshirt zipper up to her throat, then slowly pulled it down. "I don't know."

"Perhaps he's here. In bed. Or hiding in a closet."

She shrugged and opened the door wide. "Perhaps he is. Come in and see for yourself."

The policeman hesitated a moment, then crossed the threshold. There was one large room, a combination kitchen and living room. The smell of cooking oil and garlic was heavy in the air.

"Where is your father?"

Benita played with the zipper. "We don't know. He left years ago."

"Your mother?"

"At my aunt's house in Toledo."

"Brothers and sisters?"

"Just Paco."

The policeman adjusted the belt holding his nightstick. "You are here alone?"

She glided the zipper down to her belly button. "Yes."

A beaded curtain led to a hallway. The policeman pushed the beads aside. The three small rooms beyond all had beaded curtains rather than doors.

The first room had a neatly made single bed. A large plaster crucifix hung on a wall behind the bed. Poorly painted portraits of the Madonna and the Christ child stood on the bureau and nightstand.

The next room was a jumble of tangled bedsheets and clothes lying on the floor.

"This is my room," Benita said. "Look under the bed if you wish."

The final room was the largest of the three. The walls and ceiling were covered with posters of guitar-playing rock stars and naked women. A clothesline stretched from one wall to the other and held an array of pants, bright flowery shirts, and a leather jacket.

"When did you last see your brother?" the policeman asked as he poked the clothing.

"Yesterday," Benita answered, a note of concern in her voice. "Has something happened to him?"

"We have more questions about the man who was murdered on the beach." He took a business card from his shirt pocket and tucked it into the opening of her sweatshirt.

"Have him call me, Officer Osana, as soon as he returns, little one."

She pulled her shoulders back and raised her head high. "You think I am so little? At least I don't have pimples."

He reached out, grabbed her by the shoulders, spun her around, raised the sweatshirt, and slapped her firmly on the buttocks. "I recognize you. You work the beaches, fucking the tourists for beer and trinkets. One of these days I'll throw you in a cell with the real whores. They don't like you *jambas* giving it away for free. It's bad for business. Have Paco call me or you'll both be in jail."

Furious at him, Benita lay on the bed until she heard the front door slam shut. The bastard, threatening her. Demanding that Paco call him or they'd both be thrown into jail. She popped up and ran to the front window, peering at Osana's disappearing silhouette through a crack in the shutters. When he was out of sight, she ran back to her brother's room. She grunted as she pushed the bed frame back from the wall. She dropped to her knees, her hand skimming the rough wood flooring until she found the crack. She edged her fingernails in and slowly lifted the piece of board. Paco's hiding place. He thought that she didn't know about it.

She found a wad of money held together by a rubber band. She thumbed through the currency and whistled. She reached back in the hole and pulled out a metal box. A computer. She had no interest in such things. She also found a leather briefcase in the hole. Sitting on top of the case was a gold cigarette lighter. She picked it up, clicked it open, and flicked the fire on.

Suddenly a hand wrapped around her neck and she was yanked to her feet. She started to scream.

"Stay away from my things," Paco Ramiro said, grasping one of his sister's arms and twisting it behind her back.

"Paco." Benita gasped. "A policeman was here. I—"

"I saw him," Paco said. He released her arm, then

grabbed her by the hair and dragged her across the room. "Keep your mouth shut about this, or else."

"I will. I promise," Benita said between sobs. "I was only trying to help."

"To help yourself to my things, eh?"

He removed the briefcase from the hole and laid it on his bed, along with the laptop computer. Then he fingered the roll of money. He knew his little sister only too well. Threats would not keep her big mouth shut for long. "Tell no one of this, and when I get back you will be rewarded." He peeled off two bills from the roll and stuck them down the front of her sweatshirt.

Benita plucked the money from her bosom and smiled when she saw that they were American twenty-dollar bills. "What's in the briefcase?" she asked as she smoothed the cash between her fingers.

"An old letter," Paco said. "Nothing of interest to you."

Chapter Five

"Are you crazy?" Paco Ramiro said. "A hundred Euros? A watch like that is worth a fortune."

Giles Dolius tossed the platinum watch back to Paco, who fumbled it, almost dropping it to the floor.

The two men were sitting in Dolius's private office, located in the basement of his bar, El Gato Negro. A bookshelf covered one of the walls. The books were shelved according to size rather than subject. The adjoining walls were a collage of paintings: oils, watercolors, charcoals, the subjects a blur of wild abstracts, distorted portraits, bucolic country scenes, the rainy streets of Paris, or gondolas traveling through the canals of Venice. One painting, featuring a sad-faced clown riding a horse, had been there on Paco's last visit.

Dolius sat at ease behind his canoe-shaped desk. In his sixties, he had a pudgy, rubicund nose and the hoarse, full-chested voice of an auctioneer. He was bald but for some grayish strands combed sideways, like pencil lines, across his waxy scalp. He ground the heels of his hands together, then said, "There was an inscription on the back of the watch, Paco. What did you use to file it off? A hammer and a chisel? You should have let a professional handle it." He jabbed his thumb into his chest. "Me, I am a professional middleman who arranges to buy and sell items in the secondary market, and to condition those items so that they cannot be traced back to their original owner by the police or anyone else. That is what sets the price. You are a very unprofessional thief."

Ramiro rubbed his thumb across the back of the watch where he had filed off Alroy's initials. "Two hundred."

"Not interested."

"You must be interested in this," Paco said, handing Dolius a camera.

Dolius examined it with interest. A Leica. The very best. "A hundred for the camera. What else do you have?"

"What about the computer?"

"Worthless to me," Dolius said. "Keep it yourself. Learn how to play movies or music on it. I'll tell you what I'll do, my ambitious young friend. The watch, the camera, the passport and that briefcase in your lap. Five hundred. Take it or leave it."

Paco's chair legs scraped across the floor as he bolted to his feet.

"Be patient, my handsome young friend," Dolius advised. "The police are not fools. They have been by, asking questions. About the watch and the passport. And especially the Mercedes. I sincerely hope you have it tucked away in a safe place."

"It's safe. And worth a fortune," Paco said.

"Perhaps. But we will have to wait a few weeks before disposing of it."

"How much?"

Dolius rolled his shoulders. "Whatever the market will pay. You know I won't cheat you."

Ramiro knew no such thing. He hoisted Sam Alroy's leather briefcase onto Dolius's desk. "This case is magnificent. Brand new. It alone is worth more than your pitiful offer."

"What's in the case?" Dolius said. "If it's as valuable as you claim, it must hold something of great importance."

Paco unsnapped the locks and raised the lid, revealing the old glass-encased letter.

Dolius dragged the case closer, his face freezing when he saw the contents.

"What do you think of that?" Paco said, a self-satisfied smirk spreading across his lips.

Dolius gently removed the letter and held it up to the ceiling light fixture. "How much do you want for this?"

"How much are you offering?" Paco countered.

Dolius replaced the document with indifference. "It is difficult to set a price. Leave it for a day and I will check into it." He slipped the desk's center drawer open and pulled out a sheaf of bills. He then rose to his feet, wet his thumb with his tongue, then began dealing the money across the desk. "For now, seven hundred for the watch, the camera, the briefcase, and the passport."

As Paco began counting the money, Dolius moved behind him. He patted Paco on the head and let his hand trail down to the back of his neck. "What happened to your beautiful curly hair?" He felt Paco's neck muscles tighten. "Take the money. I'll let you know about the letter in glass. And stay away from the police."

As soon as Paco left the room, Dolius picked up the document. Sam Alroy, Jago Roldan's granddaughter's husband, had been murdered. By Paco? No. The darling little child would steal his mother's wedding ring, but he would not kill anyone.

His hands strayed to the Leica. There was a roll of film in it. He fiddled with the knobs and buttons and was rewarded with the sound of the film rewinding. He'd have the film developed. Who knew what it might reveal? Perhaps even Alroy's murderer. How much might that be worth?

Dave Chasen dragged his suitcase by its leash across the sparkling tile floor of the lobby of the Tropicana Hotel in Torremolinos. Softly played music was piped through speakers concealed in the slow-paddling ceiling fans. The fans were strictly for decoration. The air-conditioning had given the lobby a pleasant chill.

The layover in Madrid had been shorter than expected. Father John Fallon had given him a friendly pat on the back, then disappeared into the maze of the airport. Chasen had held back the urge to confront Fallon about going through his briefcase; he wanted to know more about the man before doing so.

Chasen called Grady Devlin's office from the airport on the cell phone Carly had provided. Neither Grady nor Sasser were available. He left a message, requesting a background check on one John Fallon, Jesuit, reportedly working out of Rome, and asking in particular if they could find anything connecting Fallon to Sam Alroy.

Chasen remembered running into a hard-bitten Mary-knoll priest in Colombia who hated the Jessies, as he called them. "They're spies, Dave. They spy on everyone, including themselves."

The Vatican was the home base of the Catholic Church's famed spy agency. At first Chasen couldn't recall the name; then, halfway through the short flight from Madrid to Málaga, it had come to him, the *Cannoncciale*. Looking glass. He had never knowingly run into one of their operatives, but they had a reputation for being smart, gutsy, and ruthless.

Chasen greeted the registration clerk, a slim, long-jawed man with a neatly trimmed goatee. "Hi, I'm Dave Chasen. I have a reservation."

"Welcome," the clerk responded in accented English. He quickly confirmed the reservation on the hotel computer.

"You have a message, señor."

Chasen read the short, cryptic note. *Nothing exciting on J. F. Works out of the Vatican. No connection to S.A. that we know of. Carly.*

Chasen deposited his passport and the majority of the ten

thousand dollars in seed money Devlin had provided into the hotel safe. He asked the clerk for a mailing envelope, walked to a lobby desk, wrapped a thousand dollars in hotel stationery, and addressed the envelope to the St. Augustine orphanage in Colombia, where Anica seemed destined to spend a few more years. Adopting families wanted babies, not nine-year-old girls.

Chasen's insistence on adopting the girl had been one of the major reasons for the breakup of his brief marriage. That and the fact that his ex-wife, Patricia, had discovered that being married to a shady fishing-boat captain was not as romantic as she'd thought it would be.

The desk clerk assured him that the envelope would go out with the afternoon mail.

A young, slump-shouldered bellboy who introduced himself as Ciro escorted Chasen to his room. Chasen watched Ciro's movements closely: feet and hands fidgeting, shoulders twitching, eyes bouncing around every few seconds. All wound up and no place to go. Probably on uppers. Amphetamines, he guessed, wondering what the drug was called in Spain. In the States it all depended on the color of the pill: white crosses, oranges, black beauties.

Something to get Ciro through his work shift. Just the kind of lad he was looking for.

Ciro opened the door to Chasen's room, set the suitcase on the bed, then opened the drapes to reveal a terrace with a splendid view of the Mediterranean. In Spanish, Chasen told Ciro to get them a couple of beers from the room's minibar, then walked out onto the terrace.

"We are not allowed to drink with the residents of the hotel," Ciro said.

"Relax, son. I don't want you to drop your pants, or provide me with the phone number of your sister. I want to talk business. Get the beers."

Chasen was on the terrace enjoying the view when Ciro handed Chasen one of the opened bottles of beer.

"Your health," Chasen said before taking a slug of the beer.

Ciro hesitated momentarily, then took a pull from his bottle.

"A man was killed on the beach near here a few days ago," Chasen said. "Do you know about it?"

"*Sí, señor.* Everyone knows of it." He pointed to the mass of flesh on the beach. Neatly partitioned plots of sand were staked out by the colors of the beach umbrellas: red, yellow, green. "The area with the green-and-white-striped umbrellas, señor. That is where the tragedy took place."

Chasen waved a hundred-dollar American bill in front of Ciro's fast-blinking eyes. "I'm an insurance investigator. If you find anyone who knows anything at all about Sam Alroy's death, it will be worth money to them. Understood?"

"Absolutely, señor. There is one thing that I have heard. Paco, the beach boy who found the dead man, has disappeared. The police are looking for him."

Chasen handed him the hundred dollars. "I'd like to talk to him before the police do. If you can arrange that, you'll earn another hundred dollars."

Ciro tilted his head back and drained the beer from the bottle. "I know that Paco lives with his mother. And that he has a sister, Benita. I know her a little. She is a *jamba.*" Chasen was unfamiliar with the term, and Ciro used a familiar hand gesture to explain that she was a prostitute.

Chasen went to his suitcase, took out a map of the area, and had Ciro mark the location of Paco's house.

"Is there anything else, señor?"

"Yes. The police station. Do you know where it is?"

"Only too well," Ciro replied with a shy smile.

Chapter Six

With four floors of charcoal bricks accented by a white-columned entry porch, the building could have been an upscale apartment house or a small hotel. The glossy-painted iron grillwork across the front and the second-floor balcony provided decoration, not protection. Softly glowing saffron-colored lampshades could be seen through the bow windows on the ground floor.

Perry Bryce had never before been invited to Boodles, the oldest of the famed London gentleman's clubs. It was over two hundred years old, though the equally understated Brooks Club across the street was of the same vintage, and catered to the same patrons: upper-crust members of Parliament, filthy-rich solicitors, retired politicians, and the snobbish "gentlemen of means" with posh London flats and sprawling country estates who had become antiquated objects of ridicule to the rest of the world.

Boodles was located on St. James Street, a few hundred yards from the political heart of the United Kingdom: the Houses of Parliament, Westminster Abbey, and the ominous gongs of Big Ben. Legend had it that one Boodles member had become enraged at the thunderous chimes and asked Prime Minister Winston Churchill to "turn the bloody thing off at ten o'clock so we can get a decent night's sleep."

Churchill had been a guest at Boodles but never a member. Saving the Western world from destruction was not enough for the old darlings to vote him in.

Bryce wanted to show up exactly on time, noon, for his luncheon meeting with Sir Sedly Parlow, the former head of the British Secret Service. He was a few minutes early and he whiled away the time by staring in the windows of the nearby legendary Lobb's shoe store, where kings, politicians, and movies stars had their tootsies measured to exact specifications, than waited six months for the finished product to be delivered to their door. There were no prices on the glowing black leather oxfords in the store's window, but he was willing to wager that a pair would set him back a month's salary.

He wiggled his toes in his scuffed, loose-fitting suede shoes. His feet were extraordinarily sensitive, and he wondered how they would adapt to sumptuous leather handcrafted brogues. He studied his image in the sparkling glass window. His face was a little too narrow, his nose slightly off center, and his ears were low set, giving him a bit of a lopsided look, and as usual, he was badly in need of a haircut. He had been instructed by his superior officer, Roger "Snake" Chalmers, in MI6 to "dress like a goddamn gentleman for a change."

His rumpled coat and baggy flannel slacks were the best to be found in his meager wardrobe. He was wearing yesterday's wash-and-wear shirt, which was fairly clean, and there were no food markings on the red, black, and gold regimental tie that he'd bought at a street fair, only to find to his delight that the stripes represented the Royal Marine Light Infantry. The tie caused all kinds of admiring looks until word got out that Bryce had studiously avoided any type of military service before being roped into the British Secret Service.

Roped into was Bryce's choice of words, since he felt that he had indeed had a hangman's knot slipped around his skinny neck by Snake Chalmers, who, in the bluntest mixture of nouns and descriptive adjectives possible, explained that either Bryce sign on, or spend several of his most formative years in one of England's sodomy factories known officially as HMP Brixton, a seedy, moldering stone prison built in 1819, and which, according to Chalmers, had resisted any attempts at modernization, including such things as plumbing and cooking facilities, since opening day.

"Even an ugly little pudding like you would be quite a catch to the horny lifers there, Bryce. They'll be calling you Famous Anus by the time you get out, so do yourself a favor and become a British spy."

Bryce's sphincter had tightened to the size of a very sharp pencil tip at the very thought, and he had signed the recruitment document without a second thought. His crimes, which had seemed minimal to him at the time, included burgling a couple of his professors' residences and hacking into the college's main computer. He'd been trying to breach the firewall at Scotland Yard when he got caught.

Pranks to Bryce, but just the skills dear old MI6 was looking for.

As if on schedule, Big Ben began doling out the bongs to let everyone know it was twelve o'clock noon.

Bryce patted the head of the war-bonneted wooden Indian standing guard in front of Robert Lewis's Pipe and Cigar store and headed for Boodles. Mildly surprised that there was no beefy guard in sight, he took a deep breath and entered through the gleaming ebony front door.

A stiff-backed man in a white tie and striped pants greeted him with raised eyebrows. "Can I help you, sir?"

"Perry Bryce. I'm meeting Sir Sedly Parlow."

"This way, sir."

This way turned out to be across a room furnished with low, comfortable chairs and couches covered in olive-green leather. Bryce recognized a few famous faces reading their papers or engaged in measured conversations with their fellow members. The majority of the men were in their thirties and forties. He had expected to see cliques of coughing, myopic graybeards gargling sherry and cupping a hand over their ears to decipher what the barman was saying.

Sedly Parlow was certainly a graybeard. He'd retired as "C," the head of the SIS, three years ago. James Bond's creator, Ian Fleming, had named his SIS character "M." Some wags in the department claimed that Fleming—whom the old-timers considered a bit of a "sissy boy"—used "M" in honor of his mother.

Bryce followed his leader into a midsize room crowded with linen-covered tables and ladder-back chairs. The tables were set with sparkling crystal glasses and polished cutlery. There wasn't a single diner to be seen.

A chair was whisked out. "If you'll be seated, I'll inform Sir Sedly that you're here, sir."

It was a ten-minute solitary wait. Bryce chided himself for not taking the time to venture into Lobb's and, just for the fun of it, get a price on a pair of those nifty shoes.

Finally he heard someone approach, cough out loud, then say, "Ah, Pryce. Good of you to come."

"That's Bryce, sir. Perry Bryce."

"Of course it is," Sir Sedly Parlow said as he abruptly sat down. He picked up a napkin, flicking it out like a flag on holiday.

Parlow had aged since Bryce had last seen him. He must be close to eighty now, with fleshy jowls and large bags under his zinc-colored eyes. His suit jacket was at least a size too small, and the wattled skin of his neck folded over his shirt collar. He still had his hair, though, the color of silver. Old, expensive silver.

Parlow's most noticeable feature was his eyebrows—shaggy gray caterpillars that went up and down like Venetian blinds when he was excited.

"Good of you to come, Bryce. How are things at the Firm?"

"Very good, sir." It amused Bryce that the Secret Service was known as "the Firm," much as the CIA was "the Company" and the FBI was "the Agency." He much preferred the spy novel term for MI6, "the Circus," because it was a much better fit.

The waiter came with a tall drink for Parlow.

"Pimm's and ginger ale," Sir Sedly explained, patting his stomach. "Good for digestion. What'll you have?"

"Water would be fine," Bryce said.

Parlow leaned across the table. "You don't have to be so proper, son. Have a real drink."

"Just the water, thanks."

Parlow waved the waiter away, then pursed bloodless lips. "So you're new at the Spanish desk, eh? A bit quiet now, I'd wager. Not so when I was your age. That was in the sixties, and the Cold War was raging. Spies everywhere. Communists and leftovers from the Second World War. Bloody Americans misplacing their nuclear bombs as if they were stray socks."

The old man warmed to the memory. "All those Germans that you read about, the ones who went to South America— Borman, Mengele, and the like—they had to get as far away from the continent as possible. The others, the ones who were smart enough not to have their names plastered all over the press, migrated to Spain. Decent weather, reasonable food and wine, and close to home when they wanted to sneak back into the Fatherland."

The waiter came to the table with a tray and settled a glass in front of Bryce. "Will you be having lunch, Sir Sedly?"

"Of course. Beef. Pudding. You know the drill. You pick the wine. What about you, Bryce? Can't beat our beef."

"I'm a vegetarian, sir. If I could have a salad, that would be fine."

"Vegetarian? Really? My God." Parlow ordered another

Pimm's, then frowned for a moment, searching for words. "Where was I?"

"Germans were sneaking back to the Fatherland," Bryce responded.

"Yes," Parlow said. "Franco welcomed the Nazis and ex-members of the Vichy militia with open arms. Charged them a bloody fortune for their safe sanctuaries, of course. This went on for years and years after the war." He waved his thick-veined hands. "Black marketeers all over the place. Hundreds of them. One of the most successful was a young miscreant by the name of Jago Roldan. Know of him, Bryce?"

"Can't say I do, sir," Bryce answered, wondering when this boring lecture would finally come to an end.

"A thief and assassin like the rest, but all that time Roldan had something the others did not. An ally that helped him enormously. The Catholic Church."

"How so?" Bryce asked when Parlow paused yet again, long enough to seem lost in thought.

"By helping Roldan to allow certain Germans to gain passage to Spain. Germans who were in prison, or were wanted by the Allies. Influential men: scientists, industrialists, men who had talents that were of use to Roldan, or who paid Roldan a good deal of money for securing their freedom." Parlow took a deep sip of his drink, then said, "You have to understand the Church was in great turmoil at the time. For all their faults, they were, and are, staunchly anti-communist. They had developed escape routes all over Europe."

That reminded him of something else. "My first wife was Catholic," Parlow said, as if he were describing a woman with a life-threatening disease. "She insisted that I accompany her to Rome once. The Vatican, all that nonsense. One of the churches had a display of chains. They were supposed to have been the ones that the Jews or Romans used to bind up old Saint Peter, but they looked like they could have come from a towing garage." He dipped back into the Pimm's, then added, "They probably did. Have you ever heard of the *Professio*?"

"No, sir."

"It dates back to the history of the Crusades. History became legend and legend became myth. It's reputed to be a document, addressed to Nero, the Emperor of Rome, and signed by Saint Peter, denouncing Jesus Christ as the son of God. It was one of the reasons good King Richard the Lionhearted trooped off to Africa. Never found it, of course. For centuries there was no word of the *Professio*, other than rumors that it had made its way to Egypt, then to Rome and on to Spain with the Moors. Then it disappeared. Somehow Jago Roldan acquired it. Or something that looked like it. No one I know has ever seen the bloody thing."

"Is this . . . *Professio* authentic, sir? I mean, do we know it was actually signed by Saint Peter?" Bryce asked.

"What difference does it make? It's probably as real as those silly chains in Rome."

Sir Sedly rubbed his hands, like someone moving closer to a fire. "The fact is that Jago Roldan had it, and used it to his great advantage for years. Then his home in Madrid was blown up. His wife and one of his sons, Naldo, and a daughter-in-law were killed. If anything, Naldo was a bigger criminal than his father. He stretched the envelope in blackmailing the Vatican. Every new church, new school, built in Spain went through a company controlled by the Roldans. The Church had tremendous influence in political appointments—judges, commissioners, civil servants—and Jago and Naldo used that influence to their advantage.

"It was thought the *Professio* was destroyed in the fire. Thought so myself, but the Firm has come up with some interesting information. Roldan's granddaughter's husband, Sam Alroy, was murdered the other day. By Jago. I'd bet my pension on that. Alroy was American, but had his shop right here in England. Made millions on high-tech doodads for the military. Married Roldan's daughter. Snake Chalmers will give you all of that information when you get back to the Firm.

"The interesting thing is that Sam Alroy was a Jesuit before he went straight. And we have information that two of the pope's top exsequors have been—"

"The pope's what, sir?"

"Exsequors. It's Latin for *avenge*. Punish. Step on the pope's sandals and they step back. Very hard. *Exsequor exsequor.* To follow to the grave, or the ends of the earth. Dates back to the old days, when the Jesuits first started flexing their muscles."

Parlow twisted and turned in his chair as he searched through his pockets for an envelope. "Here we go," he said, dropping a packet on the table. "Take a look. One former exsequor, and another who is still alive and kicking."

Bryce opened the envelope and found a series of black-and-white photographs. There were six of them, two of a man who was obviously a corpse—white-faced, eyes closed.

"Who's this, sir?"

"Father Richard Fabiano. Died two days ago, from a gunshot wound, in a Catholic hospital in Barcelona."

The other four pictures featured a handsome fellow with curly hair, walking, either alone or in a crowd. Judging by the graininess of the pictures, Bryce correctly surmised they'd been taken with a high-powered telephoto lens.

The last photo was taken on a street lined with flowering chestnut trees. Bryce snapped a fingernail against the picture and said, "This looks like Paris, sir."

"It is. The man's name is John Fallon. He was there at the same time the Chinese Embassy was burglarized. We don't know what was taken, but eight days later three Catholic priests were released from a Peking jail. We know he was also quite active in Bosnia during the silly mess there. The unspellables killing the unpronounceables. Those Croats are Catholic, you see."

Parlow tapped the tabletop with a thick finger. "Here's the point. Fallon has been making inquiries about the *Professio*. Our information shows he's en route to Spain, the Costa del Sol, where Alroy was murdered, and we're pretty certain that Fabiano was shot trying to break into Jago Roldan's villa. The connection is obvious. Alroy found the *Professio*. Maybe he even had his hands on it before Roldan killed him.

"Father Lichas was the main exsequor in my day," Parlow continued. "Ruthless chap. A Jesuit, naturally; all the exsequors are. I'm sure he's the one who blew up Roldan's house. Be careful if you have to go up against them. They're experts at judo, karate, all those ridiculous things."

"The *Professio*. Would it be worth a great deal of money, Sir Sedly?"

"Millions, no doubt." Parlow's deeply lined face screwed up in a droll grimace. "If I asked you who had the world's best intelligence agency, out of misguided pride you'd say us, then the Americans. Then the Israelis. But you'd be wrong. It's the Catholic Church. Without a doubt. They have people spying for them everywhere in the world. Every intelligence agency in the world, including the Firm, has a few traitors in its ranks. Not only that, but their agents—priests, nuns, laymen—they all work on the cheap. Get paid in prayers and burning candles. And you know why? Because of fear. Fear of their enemy, the devil."

"Ah, the devil."

"Young man, you have to find the *Professio*. We have to get our hands on it before Fallon does."

"I'm still a bit confused, Sir Sedly. Why is it of such importance to us? Because it may be worth millions?"

Parlow's voice quavered with suppressed emotion. "No. So that *we* can blackmail the Church, of course!"

Chapter Seven

Dave Chasen had a sandwich in the hotel coffee shop, then crossed the promenade and headed for the beach. He felt somewhat out of place with his blazer, slacks, button-down shirt, and cheap briefcase.

The dedicated sun worshipers were out in full force, their oiled and glistening bodies ranging from golden brown to cotton-candy pink. The swimsuits stretched from skimpy string bikinis to loose, bulky garments that reminded Chasen of photographs from the 1920s. Several of the women wore only the bottoms of their suits, and the standard rule of thumb for appearing topless in public was in force: Those who shouldn't did, and those who should, did not. He heard a smattering of foreign languages: French, Dutch, German, and Russian.

A well-built young man was positioning lounge chairs under umbrellas. He had heavily muscled shoulders and the rippling washboard stomach of a dedicated weight lifter. Chasen approached him and waved an American hundred-dollar bill in front of his suspicious face.

"I'm not a policeman," Chasen said in Spanish. "I want to talk to Paco Ramiro. He's in no trouble from me. In fact, I can help him." Chasen folded the bill in half, then folded it again and tore off a quarter piece and handed it to the young man. "Put me in touch with Paco, and the rest is yours. My name is Dave Chasen, and I'm staying at the Tropicana Hotel. Room seven-one-four."

The beach boy pocketed the torn money without comment and went back to his work.

Chasen decided to stretch his legs. His shoes made waffle-like impressions in the sand. The promenade's four traffic lanes narrowed to a pedestrian walkway. The line of shops featuring the inevitable T-shirts, sandals, and fast-food stalls made him think of Miami Beach.

The beachfront police substation was a small white adobe building. The officers on duty, three women and two men, were all young, the oldest not yet thirty. Ernesto Osana, the officer who had made out the preliminary report on Sam Alroy's death, was the youngest of the bunch. His handsome, boyish features were marred by a thin stubble of a mustache and several raw, red pimples dotting his chin.

He reluctantly agreed to talk to Chasen, leading him out to a small patio at the rear of the station.

Chasen was getting abrupt yes-and-no answers to his questions until he said, "I know how tough these cases can be. I used to be a homicide detective in New York City."

Osana almost snapped to attention. Chasen had found over the years that claiming you were a New York cop rather than an FBI agent, or telling the truth and showing his CIA credentials, always brought forth a flow of information from young law-enforcement personnel.

Osana began telling him things that weren't on the report: Paco Ramiro seemed suspicious to him that morning—nervous, fidgety. "I should have questioned him more closely, but by then Inspector Calvino arrived and I was sent to direct traffic."

Osana had followed up the investigation on his own and found a German family who rented the sunbathing spots next to the Alroys. Sam Alroy always had a laptop computer with him. And he smoked many cigarettes, lighting them with an expensive gold lighter. "I think that Ramiro stole them. The lighter, the laptop, the dead man's wallet. Everything. Even the car. Ramiro's never been arrested, but only because he has never been caught. He's a thief. I'm certain of it."

"What does Inspector Calvino think?" Chasen asked.

"He thinks I should concentrate on directing tourists to their hotels and handling reports relating to lost purses and cameras and the like," Osana said with a wry smile. "The inspector has a low opinion of the beach patrol. If you talk to him, it would be better if you did not bring up my name."

Heading off, Chasen assured Osana that he would honor his request. He walked out into the sparkling sunlight again. After studying his map, he made his way to the home of Paco Ramiro.

The house was identical to every one of its neighbors: small, whitewashed once a year, black shutters on the windows, the arched door painted a glossy bright red. The only differences in the houses were the size and color of the flower boxes encased in narrow iron balconies over the door. The Ramiros' flower box contained a crimson bougainvillea lush with blooms. The colorful branches spilled from the balcony and trailed down to the windows.

Chasen could hear loud rock music coming from inside the house. He pounded on the door to be heard. In a few moments it opened a crack. One dark young eye peered out at him and demanded to know what he wanted.

"Paco Ramiro."

The door was slammed shut. He pounded on it again and it was yanked open, revealing a teenage girl. She was dressed in torn denim cutoffs rolled up over the cheeks of her butt and a white, skin-thin knit top that made it obvious she wasn't wearing a bra. Her nest of black hair was teased up on her head, and her lips were slathered with shimmering pink lipstick.

"Déjeme en paz. Llamaré a la policía," the girl said in a shrill voice, threatening to call the police.

Chasen pulled out his wallet and went through the routine of tearing off a quarter of a hundred-dollar bill. "I'm Dave Chasen, an insurance investigator. I mean Paco no harm." He told her his hotel and room number. "Are you Benita?"

The girl snatched the money from his hand. "Why do you want Paco?"

Before Chasen could respond, a stocky middle-aged man came to the door. He was naked except for a bright orange towel tied around his waistband. His hair was wet and serrated, as if he'd just combed it.

"*¿Qué carajo quieres?*" the man shouted. "*Chinga tu madre.*"

A charitable translation was, What do you want? Get out of here and go have sex with your mother. The years in South America had provided Chasen with an extensive gutter-Spanish vocabulary, and he let out a string of obscenities that upped the ante on family sexual contact.

The man took a step toward Chasen and the towel came loose, falling to the floor. In his haste to retrieve it, he slipped and fell hard, landing on his bare backside, his hands flailing the air.

Benita giggled, waved the torn currency at Chasen, and firmly shut the door.

Chasen consulted his map and then moved onto the main police headquarters in the center of Torremolinos.

The desk sergeant could have fit in at any precinct in the world. Fat, bored, surly, and looking as if he were due to be relieved an hour ago. Chasen asked for the person in charge of the Sam Alroy homicide. "Oh, that would be Inspector Calvino."

The inspector kept him waiting for close to half an hour before ushering him into his office. Calvino was a boulder-faced man in his late fifties with a stomach bulging with a lifetime of *tapas* and beer.

Calvino straightened out a handful of wire paper clips while Chasen presented his credentials: letters identifying him as a special investigator for Fidelity Surety and Bonding, and the medical and investigation report release forms that implied that Chasen was entitled to everything the police department had relating to Alroy's murder. Chasen was glad that Carly Sasser had had the forms printed in both English and Spanish, as he was sure by the way Calvino studied the English version that he had no idea of, or interest in, what he was looking at.

The inspector was obviously stalling. His eyes drifted to the clock on the wall, and he jumped up and ordered Chasen to "stay where you are," before hurrying out the door.

Chasen got to his feet and stretched, staring directly into the oversize rectangular mirror on the wall, which he was certain was standard-police-issue two-way glass. He knew of several ways to peek at the person or persons unknown on the other side of the glass: light a match and hold it close to the glass, make a fingernail scratch mark in the first-layer etching, or simply stand near the glass, cupping his hands around his eyes to eliminate most of the light from his side of the room.

Instead he opened his mouth wide and gave the watchers a good look at his dental work before returning to his seat and re-forming Calvino's pile of mangled paper clips.

A tall, well-groomed man in his mid-thirties kicked the door open and entered the room carrying a handful of files. He had thick, wavy dark hair and a hard-muscled face. A thin, unlit cigar was clamped between his teeth. He was wearing a white linen suit, white shirt, and solid black tie. He plopped the files onto the desk, took off his suit jacket, and draped it over the back of Calvino's chair before sitting down. "I'm Lt. Sil Garate of the CNI. I assume you know what CNI stands for?"

"Some special branch of the police department?" Chasen said, admiring Garate's buffed leather shoulder holster. Most policeman never wore one because they were too uncomfortable. Wearing a gun was one of life's vastly over-rated pleasures. Especially a large weapon like the combat-grip revolver in Garate's holster. Chasen had always preferred the smallest pistol or revolver he could get his hands on.

Garate tucked the unlit cigar behind his left ear, then asked for Chasen's passport, driver's license, and Social Security number.

"The passport is at the hotel," Chasen explained. He withdrew his wallet and slipped the plastic-coated Florida DMV card from its holder. "And I don't carry a Social Security card. I can give you the number if you think it's necessary."

Garate examined the driver's license and, after copying down the pertinent information, reluctantly handed it back. "You are the David Chasen who is with the Central Intelligence Agency, are you not?"

Chasen brushed his lower lip with a thumbnail. So that was the reason for Calvino's stalling: to give Garate time to check him out. "*Was* with the CIA, Lieutenant. We parted company. I've been with Fidelity Surety and Bonding for several years."

"Really? Their office is in Boston, yet you have a Florida driver's license. If my grade-school geography was correct, there is a great deal of distance between those two locations."

"I'm the southeast manager, Lieutenant."

"Spain is not in the southeast of America. You flew to London from Washington, D.C., where the CIA headquarters are located. From Dulles International Airport, which is named after a famed member of the CIA. Why were you chosen for this assignment?"

"Why is it of any interest to you?" Chasen challenged, putting a little heat into his voice. "I'm here to do a job. Why all the bullshit? If you want Fidelity to use its attorneys in Madrid to subpoena the medical records and the coroner's records, so be it."

Garate puckered his lips and blew out air. "You will have your records. And they will show that Sam Alroy was murdered. They could have mailed in a request for the information. Why are they wasting your valuable time? My understanding of an insurance policy is that his beneficiary will receive payment, unless he or she is the one who committed the murder. Is that your position?"

"I'm sure my boss would be delighted if that were the case. But it's not uncommon for a man who for some reason wants to commit suicide to hire someone to take him out. A professional hit. Then the insurance company is on the hook for the policy. Is that the way you see Alroy's murder? A professional hit? Do you have any suspects?"

Garate shoved his chair back and rose slowly to his feet. "That was good. Very good. The homicide-suicide bullshit. It may even be true. But we both know who you are. And why you're here."

Garate paused at the door, the knob in his hand. "You may examine the files. But I warn you. Stay out of my way."

"Why would I get in your way in the first place, Lieutenant?" Chasen asked politely.

Garate's lips twisted sardonically. "Do you know what we call the CIA in Spain?"

"Cocky incompetent assholes?" Chasen suggested. "I'd have to agree. That's why I quit."

Garate stood statue-still for several moments; then his lips peeled back from his teeth. "You are going to be trouble for me, aren't you? Be careful where you go. Spain can be a dangerous place."

"The entire world's a dangerous place, Lieutenant. I can take care of myself."

Inspector Calvino returned, torturing another pile of paper clips while Chasen went through the police files.

The autopsy report was much more interesting than the original police report. Sam Alroy had been killed by a .22 long rifle bullet. On it were found traces of *ipomoea batatas*, common sweet potato. An "Irish silencer." Simply hollow out a potato, slip it over the barrel of a semiautomatic pistol, and instead of a loud crack, there's a muffled explosion. The technique was very popular all over South America, but the Irish got the credit since they used it first.

There were significant traces of THC, tetrahydro-cannabinol, the psychoactive ingredient in marijuana, in Alroy's bloodstream.

Numerous photos had been taken of the crime scene. Sam Alroy's body was photographed from every conceivable angle: He was wearing a plain white shirt and dark wool, pin-striped pants. His shoes were leather wingtips, business shoes, not for the beach. Suit pants, but no jacket. There was also a picture of Calvino interviewing a young boy wearing a bathing suit.

Chasen tapped the picture and waved it at Calvino. "Is this Paco Ramiro?"

Calvino gave a brief nod.

"Is he still missing?" brought another nod.

"Inspector, the body was stripped of everything of value except Alroy's wedding ring. Is Ramiro a suspect?"

Calvino arched his back and belched loudly before responding. "I interviewed Ramiro at the crime scene, and again the following day. In my opinion, he is not a suspect."

"I've heard he's disappeared," Chasen said.

"Boys that age are always disappearing for a few days. He'll be back."

"The fragments of potato in the head wound. I don't see any signs of a potato in the photographs. Or of a bullet cartridge. The killer was very careful."

Calvino used the tip of one of the paper clips as a toothpick before replying. "Very careful. A professional, no doubt. We have had many violent crimes lately. Too many."

Chasen asked for copies of the autopsy and the crime-scene photographs, and the inspector agreed to have the copies delivered to Chasen's hotel "in the near future."

Chasen had an idea what the "near future" would be. He thanked the inspector, then made his way out to the streets, grateful to escape from the confines of the police building. He wandered around for several minutes, fingering the cell phone in his pocket. The phone Grady Devlin had provided. He had no doubt that every call he made on the phone would be logged and routed to CIA headquarters, and he didn't want Devlin to know anything about the call he was about to make. When he was sure he wasn't being followed, he entered a small tobacconist's stall and purchased a handful of ten-Euro telephone cards, then went in search of a street pay phone.

Berlin, Germany

"Mr. Gevertz. A call for you. A Mr. Chasen."

Hal Gevertz waved his right arm in acknowledgment to his secretary that he got the message. "Take your time," he advised the portly henna-haired woman who for the past fifteen minutes had been examining an 1830 Bavarian wedding cupboard decorated with flower garlands and bouquets. "Just let my secretary, Hilda, know when you have come to a decision," he said before making his way back to his office.

Gervertz's store was located across from the Friedrichstrasse station. Every available inch of floor space was jammed with furniture, rugs, old books, and glass-topped cases of estate jewelry.

Gevertz was a trim, compactly built man with a mop of sandy-gray hair. He favored cashmere cardigans, tucking the sleeve, where his left arm once was, neatly into the sweater's pocket.

He entered his office, nimbly stepping around an ornate

medieval brass lectern that an old man in Tiergarten had used as a birdhouse. Gevertz had picked it up for forty Euros, and was certain he could sell it for a thousand. He dropped into his chair and punched the speaker button on his phone. "David. Have you found some more gold masks for me?"

Sixteen months earlier Chasen had come across a pair of pre-Columbian gold funerary masks. They weren't listed on either the FBI's or Interpol's list of stolen properties, so Chasen had sold them to Gevertz. Several smaller transactions followed.

"No masks, Hal. I need a little help. I'm on the Costa del Sol. Torremolinos. And I'm looking for the best fence in the area."

Gevertz picked up a pencil and began sketching Chasen's face on a tablet. "Spain. What happened to Florida?"

"It's still there. I'm on business, Hal. Company business."

"Really? How interesting." Gevertz scratched in Chasen's hairline on the drawing. "I thought you were through with that bunch."

"So did I. What about the fence?"

"The man to see on the Costa del Sol is Giles Dolius," Gevertz said, starting in on a drawing of Dolius. "He operates out of his bar, El Gato Negro. He's an old *pedik*. He likes his boys very young and his cognac very old, so you should be safe. He's small-time. Buys and sells just about anything, David. Once in a while he comes across a nice painting. If what you want has been fenced in the area, he has it. Use my name. Dolius owes me. And now so do you, my friend. If you have anything really interesting, call me back. I'll give you a better price than Dolius will."

Gevertz ended their conversation with the same advice he had always given in Berlin: *"Ty mne van'ku ne val'aj."* Don't pretend you are dumber than you really are.

He stared at the drawings he'd made of Chasen and Giles Dolius, then tore the paper from the pad and fed it to the shredder alongside his desk.

A glittering array of well-polished vehicles filled the cavernous garage at Roldan House in Mijas. Four Daimler sedans, Daria's yellow Porsche, a Jeep, and three SUVs. The back wall of the building was lined with neatly laid-out tool benches.

Hector Garcia's arms were tied to a rack used to raise the vehicles for servicing. The rack had been raised to such a height that only the tips of Garcia's bare toes touched the cement floor. Raul Tobias danced about, moving in, faking a punch, then slamming his glove into Garcia's welt-reddened body.

Tobias's thinning hair was sweat-plastered across his scalp. He was stripped to the waist and his entire body was sheened with perspiration. His hands were encased in tight leather gloves, which had pockets of buckshot sewn into the areas covering his knuckles.

"No más," Garcia pleaded. *"No más."*

"Mucho más," Tobias said. "Unless you tell me where Paco Ramiro is, I'm going to beat you to death." He feinted with his right hand again. "Or perhaps I'll just keep hitting you until you beg me to kill you, and then feed what's left of you to the pigs. In a few months I'll have the pigs butchered and sent to your mother, your wife, your sons. And when they're finished eating, I'll explain why they enjoyed the meal so much."

Tobias set his feet and pivoted sharply, giving full lever-age to the blow. Garcia's ribs caving in gave a sharp crack-ing sound.

"Just tell me where Paco is; then you can go home."

"He lives with his mother," Garcia said in between gasps for breath. "That's all I know. I sell him drugs sometimes. Others do too. They know more than me. I swear it."

A door rolled open, and Tobias swiveled around. "Oh, shit." He blotted the sweat from his face with the back of one gloved hand as Daria Roldan Alroy approached.

She was wearing knee-length spurred riding boots, tight denim jeans, and a white silk blouse. Her breasts jiggled with each movement. Yellow-tinted Carrera sunglasses shielded her eyes.

"Who is that?" Daria asked, pointing her riding crop at the naked man tied to the service rack.

"Hector Garcia. An associate of the beach boy, Paco. Perhaps we should meet later, when I've finished with him."

"I need to talk to you now." She turned on her heel and walked over to her sports car. "*Abuelo* invited Keely Alroy to his party."

"I already know that," Tobias said.

Daria settled her tight rump on the Porsche's hood. "I don't like the woman. In fact, I wish she were dead."

"She's a young woman," Tobias responded, knowing where the conversation was heading. "She may live for a long time."

"It would be better for me if she had a fatal accident."

"What is it that makes you hate her?"

"She wants my money. *Abuelo* believes that she will try to claim it. Sam's parents died years ago. He had no other brothers or sisters. If Keely is eliminated, there will be no one to challenge my interests."

"What does Jago say about this?"

Daria stood up and brushed the seat of her pants. "He has too much patience for an old man. His age is beginning to cloud his mind. Who knows how much longer he will be able to control things? No one lives forever. Not even *Abuelo*." She took off the glasses and stared directly into Tobias's eyes. "When I am in charge, I will expect total commitment from my staff, Raul. And those who are loyal to me will profit handsomely. You understand that, don't you?"

"I understand everything." Tobias gave her a brief bow. "I will take care of Señorita Alroy. Now, with your permission, I'll continue my questioning of Señor Garcia."

The sharp snap of Daria's boots on the cement caused Garcia to raise his head.

"Please, señora. Help me."

Daria approached Garcia, moving in until she was within a yard of him. She ran her tongue across her lips, then trailed her eyes slowly from Garcia's down his strong, young body, stopping at his penis. She made a soft cooing sound deep in her throat. Gently she circled the tip of her riding crop around his penis.

Garcia felt a stirring in his groin. He couldn't help himself. He was getting hard.

Daria turned to Tobias. "He's not dead yet, is he?"

Tobias chuckled. "There are times when I believe you could indeed raise the dead."

Daria raised her arm and snapped the riding crop down hard on the stirring flesh between Garcia's legs.

He let out a tortured scream and twisted his torso violently back and forth, his face a gargoyle of pain.

"Are you certain that he knows where Paco is?" Daria asked calmly when Garcia's screams had subsided.

"Probably not. But he knows where his friends are. In an hour or two he'll tell me everything he knows. Somewhere in all of that will be a lead to Paco."

Daria sauntered back to her car and leaned against the hood. "I think I'll stay and watch for a while."

Arlington, Virginia
The Pentagon

United States Air Force Lt. Gen. Roy Kirkwood rose to his feet when Grady Devlin was escorted into his office.

Kirkwood jutted his chin at the soldier standing next to Devlin. "Dismissed, Sergeant," he said in a gruff voice. "Mr. Devlin, it's good to see you again."

Devlin said, "Likewise, General," knowing full well that Kirkwood was as unhappy about the meeting as he was. It had been a couple of years since their last meeting. Kirkwood had put on more weight. His double chin hung over the knot of his tie. His unbuttoned blue uniform jacket had three stars on the shoulders and a salad board of decorations on the chest. What was left of his crew cut had bailed out. Devlin figured Kirkwood would never get that fourth star if he didn't shape up. All the four-star generals had to be ready for TV time in the modern military.

"Have a seat," Kirkwood said, settling himself back in the high-backed leather chair behind his desk. "Have you found my laptop?"

"You mean Sam Alroy's laptop. Not yet, General, but we're working on it."

"Lou Hoyt suggested we should get together and share information."

Devlin drummed his fingers on the brick-colored folder on his lap. CIA Director Louis Hoyt had made it an order, not a suggestion. "Get your ass over there, Grady. Keep these military assholes off our back until we come up with Alroy's laptop."

Kirkwood picked up a gold desk pen and pointed it at Devlin's folder. "What have you got in there for me?"

"You show me yours, General, and I'll show you mine. It would help if I knew exactly what Sam Alroy was working on."

Kirkwood gave a theatrical sigh. "I'm not allowed to

show you any of the data. I can tell you that the code name is Tlaloc, the Aztec Lord of Lightning. Basically it involves HPM, high-power microwave. The prototype was the size of an SUV." Kirkwood leaned back in his chair and spread his hands a foot apart. "Alroy got it down to this, and he claimed he could make it much smaller."

"I need more, General. How does it work?"

Kirkwood loosened his tie and leaned his elbows on the desk. "Place Tlaloc on a fighter plane, or a drone, and fire a single magnetic pulse, two billion watts or more moving at the speed of light, at a target from miles away, and that target, be it a nuclear facility, an underground bunker, or a single vehicle parked in a sea of cars, would disappear. The precision guiding ability is extraordinary, far superior than anything used in the Middle East. With further miniaturization Tlaloc could be used in drones the size of humming-birds. The satellite possibilities go way beyond Star Wars." Kirkland clapped his hands together and smiled. "Now, tell me what you're doing to find Alroy's laptop."

"All I can," Devlin said, holding up his file folder. "I'm not allowed to show you any of the data, but trust me, General, the CIA is on top of this. I've got a crack team working on it. One of my men has a friendly relationship with Keely Alroy, Sam's sister, who is also the vice president of Sam Alroy, Inc. That could be invaluable."

Kirkland's hands flexed, then closed into fists. "Why should I trust you, Grady?"

"We're in this together, aren't we?" Devlin didn't wait for a response. "Tell me something, General. With a weapon of this importance, the Defense Department wouldn't put all its eggs into one basket, Sam Alroy's basket. You must have other options, other contractors working on the project."

"We do," Kirkland agreed. "But they're way behind Alroy. Months, maybe a year. And we can't afford to wait that long."

Devlin pulled his gold watch from his vest pocket. "We know that Sam Alroy downloaded the project files from his office computer to his laptop. Then he disappears. He could have made copies of the files, or turned the laptop over to someone. Hell, he could have e-mailed the vital information anywhere. To anyone."

"True," Kirkland responded. "My forensic experts assure me that the laptop's hard drive will have the information buried in it. We can find what we want, and learn if Alroy did e-mail the stuff, and to who."

Devlin pushed himself to his feet. "What happens if some other country gets hold of Alroy's software?"

"We're fucked," Kirkland said. "So let's not let that happen, okay?"

Chapter Eight

Chasen found El Gato Negro at the end of a shady courtyard. A winking neon black cat with an oversize tail sat
above the arched entry door, which was so low that he had
to duck his head to enter the building. Fifties-style jazz was
blaring out of unseen speakers in the purple velvet–covered
ceiling. Track lighting in reds, blues, and yellows blinked on
and off at staggered intervals.

He recognized the quicksilver notes of Charlie Parker's
saxophone coming through the speakers as he edged his way
through a crowd of men ranging in ages from their teens to
late sixties. Many of the younger men were bare-chested,
dressed in shorts or Speedo swim trunks, shower clogs, or
locally made rope-soled espadrilles. The combined smells of
cologne, sun lotion, cigarette smoke, and sexual tension was
thick in the air.

The bar was manned by three busy men pouring drinks
and pulling drafts of beer. Chasen found an open area at the
end of the bar. The bartender who approached was wearing
a black leather vest. His well-muscled arms were a solid
mass of tattoos from shoulder to wrist.

"Una cerveza, por favor."

"One beer coming up," the bartender said in a harsh
Spanish accent.

"I can spot a Yank a mile away," the bartender said,
switching to English when he returned with Chasen's beer.

He tilted his head to one side and studied Chasen. "You look like a Donald, or a Gerald. Tell you what. I'll bet you twenty dollars that I've got your name tattooed on this arm." He slapped a sinew-swelled hand across one arm. "Right there. How about it?"

"Do you really make money on that old con?" Chasen reached out for a cocktail napkin, plucked a pen from his shirt pocket, and printed out the words *your name*.

"Let's double the bet. I say you have this tattooed on the arm."

The bartender rapped his knuckles on the bar and swore. "You're not a virgin at this, are you? What do you want besides the beer?"

"Giles Dolius. Tell him a friend of Hal Gevertz's wants to see him."

The bartender scratched the chest hair riding above his vest. "What's your name, Yank?"

"Dave Chasen."

"I'll see if Mr. Dolius is available."

Chasen watched the tattooed man duck under the counter at the far end of the bar, then nursed his beer. He ordered another beer when a younger bartender placed a plate in front of him filled with *tapas*: olives, chunks of Catalan sausage, prawns, and *boquerones*, deep-fried anchovies. Giles Dolius was no doubt on the phone to Hal Gevertz in Berlin.

The music had switched from fifties jazz to solo flamenco guitar by the time the tattooed bartender came back and told Chasen to follow him.

They went through a series of doors, then down a steep, cramped circular steel stairway. The bartender pounded a beefy hand against a padded red leather door. Someone on the other side yelled out something unintelligible, and the bartender opened the door and stood aside for Chasen.

The dour-faced man sitting behind his desk waved Chasen to a chair, then said, "I'm Giles Dolius. Taric, you can go. See we are not disturbed."

The desk was cluttered with opened books, newspaper clippings, a half-filled wineglass, and, within easy reach of Dolius's hand, a chrome-plated, pearl-handled pistol, the barrel of which pointed at Chasen.

"I called Gevertz in Berlin," Dolius said with a big smile as Chasen settled into his chair. "He speaks highly of you. How can I be of assistance?"

"You can put the gun away, for starters."

Dolius slipped his index finger in the revolver's trigger and turned the barrel to the wall.

"A precaution with first-time visitors. Even those recommended by Gevertz."

"I'm in the market for a laptop computer, Mr. Dolius."

The smile slid from Dolius's face. "There is very little profit in such items. I don't think—"

"This particular laptop belonged to a man by the name of Sam Alroy. He was murdered a few miles from here. On the beach."

Dolius leaned back in his chair, his fingers laced in front of him. "I read about that, of course."

"My company . . . is very interested in that laptop."

"Nothing else?"

"If Alroy had anything else of value, then we're very interested."

Dolius studied his nails. "Can you be more specific? A man such as Alroy undoubtedly had many things of value. I understand that his car is still missing."

"I don't need a car," Chasen said, realizing that he was missing something. Dolius had something specific in mind. What the hell could it be? What had Devlin held back from him? "Any documents, files, correspondence relating to his business would be something we would want to have, and we'd pay top dollar."

Dolius rose to his feet and made a Pontius Pilate washing-of-his-hands gesture. The smile returned to his face. "I believe I may be able to help. I must make some inquiries. I suggest you return here later tonight. Say around one o'clock. I may have some news for you by then." He picked up a phone on the desk and barked out a two-word order. "Taric. Come."

Moments later, the bartender with the tattoos opened the door and waved for Chasen to follow him.

After the American left, Giles Dolius flopped into his chair and blew a long stream of air through his pinched lips. The laptop. He could have had it for nothing from Paco Ramiro. He pounded a fist on the desk in anger, causing a vase with a single yellow flower to fall to the carpet.

Chasen. His "company." Gevertz had told him that Chasen had connections to the CIA.

What the devil was it about the laptop that drew the interest from that bunch? How much would they pay for it? A great deal. He was certain of that. This could turn out to be the luckiest day in his entire life, and he didn't want a CIA agent screwing it up.

Dolius had spent more than an hour on the Internet, searching for facts about the letter Paco had left with him. There was scant information about something known as the *Professio*. It was thought to be a fabrication, a fairy tale. The names, Nero, Simon Peter. Why would someone as rich as Sam Alroy, who was married to Jago Roldan's granddaughter, deal in such a thing?

He would have to dig deeper. He slid his desk drawer open and took out the packet of photographs he'd had developed from the film in Alroy's Leica camera and spread the pictures across his desk. Twenty-four of them. All taken in a small room with gray walls that appeared to be of metal. There were banks of cabinets in the background, with narrow drawers, also made of metal. There were close-up photos of paintings spread out on the floor.

It was not difficult to identify the paintings. Most were on Interpol's stolen art Web site. A Rembrandt, a Zurbarán, two Chagalls, a Ribera. All stolen years ago. There were others that he was sure were Goyas, and two by Matisse that he had not been able to find on the Net.

How many more paintings were in those metal drawers? And were they authentic?

Dolius gave a deep sigh, closed his eyes, and rubbed his temples, trying to put the jigsaw puzzle in place. The American, Chasen. He wasn't sure about the paintings. "Documents, files, correspondence." And he apparently knew nothing of the Saint Peter letter, or he would have mentioned it. He was fishing.

Dolius picked up the phone again, cradling the receiver under his chin as he neatly stacked the photographs. "Taric, come. You have work to do."

Benita Ramiro was sitting on her bed, thumbing through a magazine she'd found in her brother's room. The women on the slick pages were young, gorgeous, most of them nude. Their bodies didn't interest her, but their hairstyles did. She wondered what she would look like as a blonde.

The front door opened, and she jackknifed to a sitting position, then, when she heard her brother's voice, slipped the magazine under her pillow. She was curled up on the bed when Paco stuck his head through the beads leading to her room.

"Stay here," Paco said. "I have business to conduct."

Benita could see a young girl through the beads. "Some business, huh?"

Paco brushed the beads aside with one hand. "This is Emilia."

The girl was a few years older than Benita, and nothing to look at. Short, heavyset. There were two rings in her right eyebrow. Benita wondered if they were painful. "Hi," she said with little enthusiasm.

The girl responded with a forced smile. "Where's the laptop, Paco?"

"Back here," he said.

Benita slipped quietly from the bed and pressed her ear to the wall separating her room from Paco's. She could hear them quite well. The girl was from Fuengirola, a village a few miles away, and was a freshman student at the Universidad Complutense de Madrid. She was heading back to school, and needed the laptop for her schoolwork. She paid Paco forty Euros for the computer, then left the house in a hurry.

Benita was back on her bed when Paco returned. "I'm going out. I won't be back till the morning."

Benita had no intention of being there when he came back. "I like your pants. And the shirt. New, eh?"

"Stay away from my stuff," Paco warned with a shaking fist. "And keep your mouth shut about my business."

Chapter Nine

The hotel registration clerk with the neatly trimmed goatee was still on duty when Dave Chasen returned to the Tropicana Hotel. "You have a message, Señor Chasen. From Señorita Alroy. She stopped by to see you, but had to leave. She said she would meet you at Roldan House at seven o'clock."

"I don't have transportation. Can you arrange to have a taxi—"

"I'll be happy to give you a lift."

Chasen turned to find a smiling Father John Fallon, decked out in full priestly regalia, black suit and clerical collar.

"I've rented a car," Fallon said. "Just give me time to change, and then—"

"Hold on, Father. I'm going to a party at Roldan House, and I don't know if—"

"I was advised by my superiors in Rome to make an appearance, at the very least to express the Church's condolences to the widow. The Roldans have had a long history with the Church, and Alroy was a brother Jesuit. See you in, let's say, half an hour, okay?"

Fallon strode off without waiting for Chasen's response, which was going to be, *What the hell are you really up to, buddy?*

*   *   *

Dave Chasen clamped his hands on his knees as the silver BMW convertible swerved onto a freeway. John Fallon double-clutched and worked his way expertly through the gears, then accelerated down a straight stretch of road. He was out of his priest's garb, wearing a tailored jet-black tuxedo. The floppy bow tie was tied perfectly. A rolled orange silk handkerchief drooped elegantly from the breast pocket. Racing-style, orange tinted wraparound sunglasses completed the outfit.

Chasen grabbed for a door handle as the BMW surged around a slow-moving sedan.

"Have you been to Roldan's place before?" Chasen asked as Fallon yanked the wheel and executed a tight right turn.

"No." Fallon pushed the sunglasses down the bridge of his nose and glanced at Chasen. "The desk clerk gave me excellent directions. It's about ten miles up into the mountains near a little village called Mijas."

Chasen leaned back into the bucket seat and tried to relax. At least the scenery was spectacular. The bloodred sun was an hour from setting and had turned the blue-green Mediterranean a soft, golden hue. There were dozens of high-rise apartment houses and luxury hotels close to the sea. A few miles inland there were rolling hillsides lush with cork and *pinsapo* trees and terraced vineyards. The mountains were sprinkled with tile-roofed villas of every size and shape. Black vultures and sparrow hawks glided on high thermals above the granite-slashed hills.

Fallon threaded his way past construction trucks carrying lumber, cement, tile, and fencing material. They were driving along a narrow road that snaked up the mountain. In spots the asphalt was worn away to bare dirt. The higher up they drove, the more precarious the road became. Just as Chasen looked straight down at a drop of several hundred feet to the jagged rocks below, Fallon beeped the horn at a yellow bus hogging the road ahead.

The bus lumbered around a curve, tilting so far over to

the right that its rear tire was actually dangling over the side of the road. Chasen could see the passengers leaning to their left, like sailors helping to keep a boat from capsizing. When they reached the next straightaway, Fallon gunned the motor, barely skirting the bus's front bumper as he pulled in to make way for a car coming at them in the opposite direction.

Fallon drove as if he were playing one of those video arcade games, where the only thing that happened if there was a crash was that the game ended, and more coins would be fed into the machine to play another game.

Chasen tapped Fallon on the shoulder. "You may be anxious to meet up with Saint Peter, but I'm not. Slow down."

At a turnoff ahead, the BMW fishtailed across the dusty road, then went into a tortuous skid before coming to a halt. Dust swirled around the open cockpit of the convertible. Fallon twisted the ignition key and killed the engine. "Sorry, I'm used to buzzing around Rome. You have to drive like a kamikaze pilot just to survive. What were you saying about Saint Peter?"

"He's the main guy, isn't he? The one who is in charge of the gates to heaven?"

Fallon whipped his sunglasses off and studied Chasen for several seconds.

"You're not a Catholic, are you, Dave?"

"My mother was."

"What was your father?"

"A drunkard," Chasen said.

"Unfortunately, sometimes the two go hand in hand."

"Theirs was more of a hand-into-fist marriage."

"Your father beat her?"

"Oh, no. Pop was a happy drunk. He'd never lay a finger on Mom. But when he came home loaded and smelling of perfume, she'd give it to him with both hands."

"Maybe that's one of the reasons the Holy Father doesn't allow us to marry," Fallon said, grinning. He started the car up and edged back onto the road. "Let me tell you a story. One day God looks down from heaven, sees these three lovely old Irish nuns, and tells Saint Peter to call them home; they've done enough.

"The three nuns pass away quietly in their sleep and wake to find themselves in front of the pearly gates. Saint Peter has had a slow day, so he decides to have some fun with them.

" 'Sisters,' he says, 'you've led exemplary lives. However, before I open the gates to heaven, you all will have to answer one question.'

"The nuns nod their heads. 'Yes, Saint Peter.'

"Peter asks: 'Who was the first man that God created?'

"The first nun says, 'That was Adam, Saint Peter.'

"Ching—the gates to heaven open and the nun walks through them.

"He asks the second question. 'And who was the first woman that God created?'

"The second nun says, 'That was Eve, Saint Peter.'

"Ching—the gates of heaven open up, and in she goes.

"He turns to the last nun and asks, 'What were the first words that Eve said to Adam?'

"The old nun's face scrunches up and she tugs at her habit. 'That's a hard one . . .'

"Ching, the gates of heaven open up again."

Chasen laughed politely. He had heard the joke before. "You know, Father, all of this is quite a coincidence. You happening to be on the plane with me, staying at the same hotel, and now we're both headed to Jago Roldan's house."

Fallon's knotted fingers played with the ribbed edges of the steering wheel. "Indeed," he said briskly. "We should be getting close. Look for a sign. Roldan Road, of all things," he continued, as casual as could be. "What's your association with the Roldans? The insurance?"

"Yes," Chasen said, studying the priest out of the corner of his eye. Fallon had no signs, no "tells," unconscious little gestures—narrowing of the eyes or licking of the lips—when he lied. And Chasen was sure Fallon was lying to him. He had no doubt that Fallon could pass a lie-detector test with ease. The way Fallon answered questions, the way he turned the conversation around, he was an accomplished liar. Not the kind of man to get into a poker game with.

The question Chasen wanted answered was, Why was Fallon lying? Besides the airplane, the same hotel, offering a ride, it was obvious from the way he drove that Fallon had made this trip before.

"There's an intersection just ahead," Fallon said. "This must be the place."

The BMW's engine gave a throaty roar as Fallon downshifted, then made a sharp left turn. A simple black-on-white sign indicated that they were on Roldan Road.

The smooth tarmac was bordered by towering umbrella pines and stretched out as straight as a ruler for half a mile. Fallon eased off the accelerator as they approached a sentry post manned by a heavyset man in a khaki uniform. He wore a military-style combat helmet. A semiautomatic pistol was holstered on his hip, and he carried a cradled shotgun in his hands.

"*Pare,*" the man ordered.

"How's your Spanish?" Fallon said as the BMW closed in on the man.

"Not good."

Fallon glided to a stop. "I'll talk to the cowboy."

Chasen didn't like the manner in which the man approached them. He was walking on the balls of his feet. His finger was curled around the shotgun's trigger. The embroidered tape on his field jacket bore the name Lucio.

"*Buenos tardes,* Señor Lucio," Fallon said cheerfully.

The guard's face remained impassive.

"We are expected," Fallon continued in classic Spanish. "This is Dave Chasen. How do we get to the main house?"

The guard's eyes narrowed and his head tilted to one side. "I have Señor Chasen's name. Who are you?"

"An underpaid servant, much like yourself, ah, Lucio? They put me in a monkey suit, then pay me with bananas."

Lucio shook his head and smiled, showing a matchstick-size gap in his front teeth. He removed his finger from the shotgun trigger, pointed down the road and rattled off directions, and warned Fallon about the dangers of vicious dogs and trigger-happy horsemen on the property. "Someone tried to break into the house a few days ago. He was shot, but managed to escape."

Fallon gunned the motor and switched on the headlights. The sun was setting through the cleavage of two hills directly in front of them. The towering pines abruptly gave way to neatly spaced rows of olive trees. Chasen didn't see any dogs, but spotted several men on horseback. They stared stoically at the BMW and didn't return Fallon's waved greeting. One of the riders was close enough to the road for Chasen to notice his hip holster and rifle scabbard.

The house drew near. It was a rambling Renaissance-style structure with sun-bleached terra-cotta walls, arched windows, and a red clay-tile roof. The brick-paved driveway bordered a good-size pond that fed into cascading waterfalls. Fallon parked alongside a gleaming white Daimler sedan. A young man in a bright yellow windbreaker ran out to greet them. He opened the door for Fallon and said, "Welcome to Casa Roldan," in passable English.

Chasen and Fallon made their way up the cantilevered flagstone steps. The front door was copper, burnished the color of old pennies. Above the door hung an elaborate wooden plaque with the inscription *Mi Casa es Mi Casa* carved in bold script.

Chasen had to grin at the wording: My House is My House.

"I won't be staying long," Fallon said. "I'm sure you can find a ride back to the hotel."

"Father, I'm going to find someone else to drive me back no matter what your plans are," Chasen said. He gave his name to the diminutive butler guarding the door and was ushered inside.

A dozen or more people, men dressed in tuxedos and elaborately gowned women, milled around the room. It was definitely a black-tie affair. Chasen was wearing the dark blue blazer and slacks that he'd traveled in. He wondered how Fallon had heard about the formal dress code.

Keely Alroy was nowhere in sight. Nor was Fallon, who had slipped past Chasen while he was talking to the butler.

The room—he wasn't sure exactly what to call it—was more like a hotel lobby than a living or dining room, massive in size, with a twenty-foot ceiling. The ceiling was frescoed, featuring a colorful Old World map of Europe, complete with balloon-cheeked angels blowing sailing ships out into the Atlantic Ocean and sea monsters bathing leisurely in the Mediterranean. Oil paintings of somber, long-faced men, outfitted in ancient battle dress, were spaced around the walls. The walls and floors were faced with reddish-orange limestone. Glorious Kerman carpets covered the parts of the floor that weren't cluttered with plump nineteenth-century fringed sofas and chairs. A Bosendorfer grand piano sat in one corner, dwarfed by the size of the room. A red-jacketed pianist played flowery arrangements of show tunes.

An olive-skinned woman in a traditional maid's uniform approached with a tray holding a variety of drinks. Chasen chose a glass of red wine, then began circulating, nodding politely to the other guests, eventually making for the arched doors leading to a beautifully designed terrace. Hip-high stone posts topped with fierce-faced animal heads formed an elaborate fence around a rectangular swimming pool. The pool's cobalt-blue water came right up to the top, giving the impression that if just one person dove in, the water would overflow onto the bordering path.

Chasen heard a light tapping noise. He turned to find a distinguished-looking older man with silver hair rapping his cane on the floor and looking at Chasen's half-empty wineglass.

"¿En que puedo servirle?"

Silence followed, and Jago Roldan noticed the embarrassed look on Chasen's face. "You don't speak Spanish?"

"I'm afraid not much more than 'good morning' and 'good night,' " Chasen said apologetically.

"I am Jago Roldan, and I was asking what you would like to drink."

"Dave Chasen, of Fidelity Surety and Bonding." He handed Roldan one of the Fidelity business cards Carly Sasser had provided. "Thanks for inviting me. The red wine is wonderful. I'll stick with that."

A smile put more wrinkles on Jago's weathered face. His teeth were large, perfectly even, and whiter than his starched shirtfront. "I'm glad you enjoy it. It is from a winery I own in Rioja." He turned and snapped his fingers and one of the servants appeared in moments to top off Chasen's glass.

Chasen inhaled deeply. The air was sweet and clean, lush with jasmine and something else he couldn't identify. "You have a beautiful home, Mr. Roldan."

"I enjoy my summers here. Madrid is unbearable at this time of the year. May I ask when my granddaughter will be receiving payment?" Jago upturned a palm. "Not that we are in a great hurry. But there is no reason to let five million American dollars take a siesta, is there?"

"None that I know of. I'm not really sure if your granddaughter or Mr. Alroy's sister is the beneficiary."

Jago's eyebrows angled toward the inner corners of his eyes. "How could you not know? I would think that—"

Roldan broke off as a man with a ponytail tied at the back with a rawhide strip approached them. He moved with an energized, hair-trigger grace, as if he were about to break out into a run at any moment. His lips were large and full and would have been described as bee-stung if they belonged to a woman.

"Did you find Ramiro, Raul?" Jago asked in Spanish.

The man looked suspiciously at Chasen.

"Don't worry about him," Jago said. "He can't understand us."

Raul apparently had his doubts, because he turned his back to Chasen and spoke softly.

Chasen could make out just a few of his words: *festivo,* festival, and *poco riata,* little prick. And a name—Calvino. The police inspector. Calvino was no doubt in Roldan's pocket, and was feeding him information on how the investigation was progressing.

Jago's response was short and bitter. "Find him. Bring him here."

The man gave Chasen a stony look, then moved off, his shoulder brushing lightly against Chasen's.

"He seems to be in a hurry," Chasen said.

"A small matter," Jago assured him.

The servant reappeared with the bottle of wine, and Chasen politely waved her away.

"Now, Señor Chasen. You were telling me that you had no idea—"

"Good evening," said a man dressed in a shawl-collared tuxedo.

Jago didn't appreciate the interruption. "This is my son, Vidal," he said. "Vidal, this is Señor Chasen, an American insurance investigator."

Vidal offered his hand.

There was no doubting the family resemblance: the strong nose, the same widow's-peak hairline. Vidal's hair still had a lot of black in it, but it was carelessly combed. His face was soft and puffy, his eyes magnified by thick metal-framed glasses. In contrast to his father's stiff, military posture, Vidal was slump-shouldered, his body curved in an academic stoop.

Jago was impeccably groomed and was wearing a beautifully cut white dinner jacket. Vidal's tuxedo had wrinkles in the jacket and pants, the shirt was missing a stud just above the cummerbund, and his fingernails were jagged and uneven, the result of constant gnawing.

"I forgot to wish you a happy birthday, Mr. Roldan," Chasen said.

"Thank you," Jago said with a throwaway gesture of one hand. "This may seem inappropriate to you, so close to Sam Alroy's death, but the guests have come from all over the world. It was too late to cancel. And besides, Daria will have an announcement that may soften the death of her dear husband." He shot his cuff and glanced at his watch. "I have been ignoring my other guests for too long. Excuse me. Vidal, see that Señor Chasen is taken care of."

"My father finds it difficult to stand still for very long," Vidal said, patting his right leg. "An old bullfighting injury. He has to keep moving."

"Don't we all," Chasen said, trying to keep it short. He began to wander down toward the pool. He wanted to shake Vidal and sneak upstairs.

Vidal caught up to him. "Did you know Sam Alroy?"

"I never had the pleasure."

Vidal bent his head and pawed at the tile with his foot, like a horse scraping grass. *He's nervous, unsure of himself,* Chasen surmised. *With none of the force or dominance of his father. And he wants something from me.*

"Your investigation," Vidal said. "Is it progressing well?"

"I just arrived this afternoon."

"Ah, I see. If I can be of any assistance . . ." Vidal's head snapped up, and he gave Chasen a measuring look. "Sam and I were friends. We had some common interests."

"Are you in the software business?" Chasen asked.

"No. I operate an art gallery in Madrid."

"Then Sam was interested in art?"

Vidal gazed at the swimming pool. "In certain things, yes. He was—"

The halogen lights dimmed for a second, as did the lights in the house. The pianist muffed several notes from "Night and Day," then started up again.

The brief electrical disturbance seemed to unsettle Vidal. "Excuse me," he said. "I have to go."

Chasen waited until Vidal had entered the house, then strolled, seemingly without hurry. His eyes flicked back and forth, looking for any signs of Roldan's security force. The house itself was interesting. It had to be sixty years old— with wood-framed windows and thick seasoned tiles on the roof. He noted barely visible strands of painted-over cable leading to the lower-floor windows—an old-style alarm system.

He came to a gravel driveway that opened alongside a wall of shrubbery at the side of the house and was rewarded with the sight of one of Roldan's armed men smoking a cigarette while pacing slowly back and forth between a small collection of older small cars and trucks. The servant's parking lot, hidden away from the guests' Daimlers, Porches, Mercedes, and BMWs. Chasen did an abrupt about-face and hurried back to the terrace.

A woman was standing at the arched doors waiting for him. Keely Alroy gave a wide smile and a friendly wave.

He remembered her as a bit of a chameleon. At their first meeting she'd been dressed in baggy khaki pants and the camouflage jacket and hat that reporters in Colombia favored. Without makeup, it was hard to tell if she was a man or woman. When she changed into slacks or a dress and added a little lipstick and mascara she was transformed into a knockout. She had the lithe, wide-shouldered body of an athlete. He could picture her as a serious swimmer or a professional tennis player.

She was in full knockout mode tonight: auburn hair worn short, a wedge cut. Her reddish-brown skin was dusted with freckles. Her eyes were moss green and her high cheekbones gave her a slightly Nordic look. Her azure-blue silk dress was cinched at the waist by a leather basket-weave belt.

"Dave, it's so good to see you. I tried calling during the hearings. And I wrote, after the CIA let you go, but I never heard back from you."

Keely had been working for the Associated Press in Bogotá when Chasen was the Company's station head there. He had liked her right away. She was ambitious, and she could handle herself, be it with her fellow reporters or the crooked politicians who ran the country. Chasen's position was well known to everyone in the area—the press, the politicians, and the drug lords. He had never leaked anything to Keely before his blowup with the senator, but he had set up meetings for her with the powers that be—at least the ones he was certain wouldn't lure her into the jungle and kill her.

Chasen replied, "I went into something called 'Company Debriefing,' a two-week seminar where they made it perfectly clear what would happen to me if I opened my mouth again, or sent anything to the press that could 'further embarrass the Company.'"

This news surprised her. "You worked for the CIA for a number of years. They just kicked you out? No pension? No severance pay?"

"Guillotine operators get severance pay, Keely, not disgraced agents."

Vidal Roldan walked past them. For a moment he looked as if he were going to stop and join their conversation, but he merely nodded and moved on.

"Did they actually threaten you?" Keely asked in a voice full of concern.

Chasen placed his hand on Keely's elbow and steered her down the steps toward the pool.

"Nah, it was all for show. How about you? Did they contact you?"

"Not directly. But my editor, Dean Bagley, was. Dean told them where to put their complaints. I was surprised when I received your e-mail."

Chasen spotted movement in a second-story window. Curtains parted briefly, then quickly closed. "I'm truly sorry about your brother."

A frown formed on Keely's beautiful face. "Here comes Daria," she said in a resigned tone.

Even dressed in a demure, loose-fitting black summer dress, the woman striding purposely toward them radiated sexual power. Her inky-black hair was a mass of coiled braids. When she got closer, Chasen zeroed in on her eyes—almost violet-blue, large to begin with and exaggerated by their almond shape. He suspected she wore tinted contact lenses to intensify their color, but could see no sign of them.

"Hello, Daria," Keely said with little enthusiasm. "This is Dave Chasen."

Daria turned those incredible eyes on him. "My grandfather told me of you, Señor Chasen. I'm anxious to speak to you. But first," she said, turning back to Keely, "we have to talk. Privately. Come with me."

The air was charged with the tension that surrounded a heavyweight championship prizefight. Chasen realized that the two women hated each other. "Ladies," he said, "I'll leave you alone for now. Keely, I need a ride back to my hotel after dinner. Can you help me out?"

"My grandfather will provide you with transportation," Daria said dismissively. "Come, Keely. This is important."

"When will the services be held?" Chasen said, pointing the question at Daria to see her reaction.

She gave him a withering glance. "As soon as possible. When the police release the body."

"Where will your husband be buried?" Chasen asked quickly, noticing that Daria referred to her husband's remains as "the body," not "Sam's body." It seemed, as far as she was concerned, the sooner he was in the ground the better. Not exactly the grieving widow of a murder victim.

Daria flicked a hand in the air as if his question were of little importance. "I haven't decided, and I don't see that it matters to your investigation."

Chasen watched as they moved away, Daria's arms moving about as she spoke, Keely's head rigid, her shoulders pulled back. Fire and dynamite mixed better than those two. He wondered how long it would be before the explosion took place.

Chapter Ten

Perry Bryce picked the lock in a matter of seconds and quietly entered the room. He closed the door and leaned against it, surveying the layout. The windows were blanketed by heavy green curtains. An immense desk housed one phone, a computer, an answering machine, a rosewood box he assumed was a humidor set next to a cut-glass ashtray, and two bronze desk lamps, both of which were on, spilling pools of light that gave him a shadowy view of the room.

Against one wall was a glass case filled with bullfighting accoutrements. Over the case hung a portrait of a handsome young matador. On the wall behind the desk was a blue and red surrealistic oil.

Bryce took a deep breath and tried to calm himself: The same thing happened every time he was involved in a black-bag job. He perspired so intensely that it seemed the light leather gloves would slip from his hands. Though he'd just emptied his bladder, he felt an intense urge to pee.

Bryce made a mental bet with himself: The safe that his boss Snake Chalmers was certain would be there was hidden behind the surrealistic piece of crap. He crossed the room quickly, ran the beam from his flashlight around the painting's frame, then tugged gently. The painting slid back and to his delight revealed an old-fashioned mechanical combination safe.

"Bloody dumb," Bryce said softly. He propped the flashlight under his arm and wriggled the Ormia Nanoscope from one of the bulging pockets of his charcoal-gray safari coat. Dumb of Roldan to have such an ancient safe, along with an outdated alarm system, and equally dumb of Chalmers to think that Roldan would keep anything as valuable as the *Professio* in such a burglar-friendly environment.

He placed the stethoscope-type hearing device in his ears and the Nanoscope's sensitive microphone directly along-side the combination log and began turning the dial. The Ormia, as MI6 engineers had dubbed it, was a technical marvel, owing its super audio power to the research involv-ing the *Ormia ochracea,* a tiny parasitic housefly with the keenest hearing of any living creature. Each click sounded like a one-note castanet samba, and when the tumbler fell on one of the combination numbers, the sound was of a sewer grate falling on a steel floor.

The sequence of numbers turned out to be eighteen right, fifty-two left, and thirty-three right.

Bryce twisted the handle and swung the door open. No *Professio.* No laptop computer. No priceless paintings. No emerald necklaces or diamond rings. Just good old money, in neat stacks, secured with a white band from the Banco de España around each pack.

He placed the money on the desk, then played the flashlight beam around the safe's interior lining, hoping to discover a secret compartment, but there was none.

Bryce swore softly. So far the exercise, which had in-cluded his being bundled up in the trunk of a rented limou-sine that had delivered two guests to the house, had been a wasted effort.

He'd decided to download whatever was on the com-puter's hard drive when cold metal pressed into the back of his neck.

"Take it easy," said a soft, pleasant voice.

A man's voice. In English. Not England English. Ameri-can? A hint of an Irish brogue?

"Keep your hands on the table," the voice advised him. "Thank you for saving me the trouble of opening the safe."

"You're welcome," Bryce said, wondering if this was going to be it. The bastard must have been hiding behind the curtains. He should have checked. Standard MI6 doctrine: Check the room before commencing the exercise.

The voice said, "From the look of your clothes, and that 'bloody dumb' statement, I take it you're British. Which means Her Majesty's Secret Service. What's your name? Just the first name. I don't need the rank and serial number."

Bryce hesitated until the cold metal object was screwed into his neck. "Perry," he said, hoping that his voice sounded calmer to the man with the gun than it did to him.

"Well, Perry. Did the martial arts instructors at Fort Monckton teach you all about *Shime-waza*?"

"No," Bryce croaked. It was a croak. He couldn't help it. The pressure from his bladder was intense.

"It's from judo. Commonly known as the sleep hold. I'm going to put my fingers around your carotid triangle and apply a slow, steady pressure. You'll pass out in a minute or so. When you wake up depends a lot on your body's makeup. It could be five minutes. It could be thirty. But you will wake up with nothing more than a minor headache. Or I could just blow your head off. It's your choice. I'd go with *Shime-waza* if I were in your place."

"Me too," Bryce said, flinching as he felt strong fingers encircle his neck. He thought of trying one of the techniques that his brutish MI6 self-defense instructor had unsuccessfully tried to teach him, but the voice projected a calm, strong confidence, and Bryce was certain the man would have no trouble finishing him off with or without a gun.

His eyelids started to flutter and he felt the darkness of sleep coming on.

"Say good-night, Perry," the voice said.

"Good night, Perry," Bryce answered in a slur just before he went under.

John Fallon released his grip and let the now-unconscious body topple to the floor. He returned the sterling-silver fountain pen he'd held to the British agent's neck to his breast pocket, then examined the safe himself. Empty as the poor box at a rural church.

He dropped into the desk chair, popped the facepiece off Roldan's computer, then took a screwdriver from his tuxedo jacket and used it to remove the hard drive, which he slipped beneath his cummerbund.

Fallon trailed his hands over the stacks of money, taking a few samples, jamming as much as he could into each pocket without making an obvious bulge. He started for the door, then stopped in midstride and turned back to the desk. He flipped the humidor open and smiled when he saw the distinctive Cohiba band on the thick black cigars. He wrapped his hand around a bunch of the cigars, then whispered, "Forgive me, for I have sinned."

Jago Roldan's guests had consumed enough alcohol so that Dave Chasen was able to slip away with little notice. He spotted a waiter pushing his way through a door at the far end of the room, waited a moment, then followed after him.

The tiled hallway led to the kitchen, where a half dozen white-aproned women were shuffling pots and frying pans. How much time did he have until dinner? Chasen wondered. And how was it announced at Roldan House? The banging of a loud gong? The ringing of bells? Or old Jago bellowing, "Come and get it"?

He slipped into a stairway at the end of the hall. He took the steps two at a time. The second-floor landing door opened to a wide, spacious hall carpeted in a rich gold fleur-de-lys pattern. He began checking doors, the age-old "looking for a bathroom" excuse ready at the tip of his tongue. Several were locked. The lock was of a type that he could pick in minutes, but he didn't have those valuable minutes to waste.

An open door revealed a woman's bedroom. The walls and drapes were pale lavender. Over a carved stone fireplace hung a portrait of Daria Roldan Alroy. She was sitting in a red chair, wearing a pale blue dress, which was an exact match to the color of her eyes.

Tempting. Daria's room. Sam's too? Or were they the separate bedroom types? Chasen decided to move on.

More locked doors, then one that swung open. Peering in, he knew that he'd found what he'd been looking for. He also knew someone had beaten him to the punch. The wall safe's door was wide open.

Chasen moved across the spongy rug as if he were walking on eggshells. When he reached the desk, he could see that the computer's hard drive had been removed.

A body was sprawled on the floor. A man in his late twenties or early thirties dressed in burglar's gray. His thin, bony face might as well have had *Made in England* stamped on it. Chasen knelt down and felt his pulse. Strong and steady. Deep breathing, almost a snore. No sign of any obvious wounds.

The man's pockets were full of electronic gadgetry, but no gun, no ID, and no hard drive.

Chasen was reaching for the safe when he heard footsteps. He dropped to the floor and huddled next to the desk.

The door opened wide. He could see a pair of hiking boots with khaki pants tucked into the tops edge into the room. He heard the distinctive meshing of metal parts. The chambering of a cartridge in a semiautomatic weapon.

The boots moved slowly, then picked up pace, heading for the body on the floor.

Chasen leaped to his feet and drove his elbow into the man's spine. When he stiffened up, Chasen slammed the edge of his hand across the exposed middle constrictor at the back of the guard's neck.

The gun fell from his hands, and Chasen hit the slumping figure again before it made contact with the carpet.

The desk phone rang. Two soft chirps; then the answering machine came on. "This is Jago Roldan. You may leave a message."

The caller did just that: "Señor Roldan. I have possession of some items that may have belonged to the late Sam Alroy. Photographs and the *Professio*. I'll call you again tomorrow."

The caller didn't leave a name. He didn't have to, as far as Chasen was concerned. It was Giles Dolius. Yet the message confused him. Why would Jago Roldan want some photographs? What the devil was the *Professio*?

Hearing more footsteps, Chasen wheeled around in a crouch, hands in front of him, bracing for more contact.

Vidal Roldan shuffled into the room, his hand stuck in the pocket of his tuxedo. He jutted his chin at the unconscious figure of the guard. "Did he see you?"

"I don't think so."

Vidal fingered the computer with his free hand, then shoved his arm into the empty safe.

"Do you think it was there?"

"What was there?" Chasen said, after peeping out in the hall to see if the unconscious guard had a backup. "When I got here the safe was open and the computer was already gutted. Whoever did it left the money on the desk."

Vidal wagged his head. "You really don't know, do you?"

"I know your father isn't going to be too happy when you tell him what happened here."

"I think I'll let him discover this for himself," Vidal said. He pointed to the unconscious burglar. "Who's this?"

"I haven't a clue," Chasen answered truthfully.

Vidal sidled over to the guard's body. He nudged him with the toe of his shoe, then brought the shoe back in a soccer kicker's arc and aimed a savage kick at the man's head.

"Arturo. One of Tobias's men. I hate them all. Is he dead?"

"He will be if you give him another shot like that," Chasen said.

Vidal looked longingly at the stacks of money for a moment, then said, "We'd better go. Father will notice if we're late for dinner. We have to talk. Where can I meet you later?"

"Do you know El Gato Negro, in Torremolinos?" Chasen said.

"No. But I can find it."

"I'll be there at half past one." Chasen reached across the desk and punched the erase button on Jago's answering machine.

"What was that?" Vidal asked sharply.

"Wrong number. Let's eat."

Chapter Eleven

Raul Tobias leaned over the second-floor railing and stared at the street below. A dozen strong-armed young men carried a symbolic, empty, flower-draped coffin through the narrow downtown street of Torremolinos. A cheering, chanting throng of revelers followed the procession. The thick-pressed sidewalk crowd was in a festive mood, many clutching glasses of beer or wine in their hands.

The parade directly behind the coffin consisted of school-girls wearing chalk-white bouffant ruffled dresses, teenage boys in tight black pants, red shirts, and bullfighters' hats, and a string of long-robed priests holding gleaming brass crucifixes close to their chests.

Tobias dragged his eyes from the girls and surveyed the crowd. Ramiro would be there somewhere. The young *pelotas* never missed a saint's-day parade. There were too many beautiful women tourists in attendance, hoping to sample the local talent. Too many drunks with wallets sticking out of their back pockets.

"Come, Paco," Tobias whispered to himself. "We have much to talk about."

Paco Ramiro stretched on his tiptoes, peering over the crowd, searching for Julian, a drug dealer. Hector Garcia, his regular supplier, was nowhere to be found, and now Julian was proving to be equally unreliable.

Sam Alroy's passport and wallet, containing nearly two thousand dollars, plus several credit cards, had been in his suit jacket. The tailor-made jacket had his name stitched above the inside pocket. Paco had cut the jacket into small pieces and burned them. The money he'd made from selling Alroy's watch, passport, camera, and briefcase to Giles Dolius, along with the cash and items he'd bought on Alroy's credit cards, had provided him with enough capital to go into business for himself. The drug business. No more raking sand and fetching drinks for rich tourists. He was his own man now.

Dolius was right about the Mercedes being too hot to move. It was stored in a garage. In a few weeks Dolius would either sell it to a *tienda corta*, where the car would be chopped up, the parts sold separately, or have it smuggled out of the country, to Morocco or Algiers. The Arabs loved Mercedes.

Then there was the mysterious letter in the glass. What could that be worth? Dolius had acted nonchalant about it, but Paco had seen the gleam in his eyes. It was valuable. Dolius would no doubt cheat him, but what other option did he have? None, Paco knew. He'd have to take what the old Greek gave him.

He'd also been tempted to sell Alroy's gold cigarette lighter, but had decided to hold on to it. It would give him some class, like the new cashmere sweater and leather pants he was now wearing. He pictured himself offering his customers a free taste of *maría*, or some fine Moroccan *rakiff*, and setting it afire with the gold lighter.

Someone bumped into Paco from behind and he turned around and swore. It was a bulldog-faced Anglo. The man smiled apologetically and continued on his way.

Paco glanced at the parade's coffin. Who was it today? It seemed that every week there was a celebration for one saint or another. A long, drunken celebration, the casket carried through town and to the local church, which would be ablaze with candles.

Luckily for the makers of candles, and the sellers of beer and wine, there were more than enough saint's-day celebrations to go around. It wasn't bad for the *maría* business either, if only he could find Julian.

Where the . . . There he was. Across the street. Paco waded into the crowd, one hand circling over his head to catch Julian's attention. *"Acá,* Julian," he shouted, his voice swallowed up by the cheers of a group of drunks on the veranda of a coffeehouse.

Out of nowhere a strong hand grabbed him by the shoulder. Paco spun about to find a man with a ponytail. "Let go of me," he yelled.

The man's grip tightened. "I want to talk to you, *culero,"* Tobias said, digging his fingers into Ramiro's shoulder.

Paco recoiled. *Culero.* A petty drug dealer who smuggled hashish in from Morocco by hiding it in his rectum. Who was this bastard? An undercover policeman? He had heard tales of crooked drug cops who shook down small dealers such as Julian.

"Come with me," Tobias said, dragging Paco toward the sidewalk.

"Please," Paco whined. "Don't hurt me." He moaned in pain and sagged his knees.

When the man's grip lightened, he slashed out at his leg, stabbing the pointed tip of his new snakeskin cowboy boot into the man's shin.

Tobias let go and cursed sharply.

Paco broke free and started running. In another moment he could hear the man's footsteps thudding right behind him, then winced from a flash of pain in his left arm. He continued running, stumbling, then regaining his balance. His heart was pounding so hard it wanted to burst free from his chest. He cloaked himself in the crowd, then veered into a side street. Clouds shrouded the moon. It was almost pitch-black. He suddenly felt light-headed. His arm ached. He grabbed it with his other hand, and his fingers came away smeared with blood.

He continued running, zigzagging through the dark cobblestone street, eventually turning in to a narrow dirt path. He leaned against a wall and tried to control his breathing. He closed his eyes and prayed. He could hear footsteps, amplified by the emptiness of the streets.

He peered around the corner of the building. The ponytailed *hombre* was standing in the middle of the street, studying the ground, his eyes moving left and right.

The moon broke through the clouds, so bright that it threw shadows under the sycamore trees bordering the alley. *Turn right,* Paco prayed, his hand going to the wound on his bloodied arm.

The man started to his right, but then changed his mind and began striding up the hill.

Paco walked on his tiptoes, looking for an exit. The alley dead-ended into a rough cement wall. The footsteps were getting louder. He realized he was trapped. *Save me, God. Save me!*

The footsteps halted. Then a menacing shadow appeared at the entrance to the path.

Paco bit his lower lip to keep from screaming.

Raul Tobias crouched down on one knee and dipped his finger into the fresh blood spots on the pavement. He stood up, wiped his finger on a handkerchief, and snapped the knife blade open, holding it alongside his pants leg.

"Paco," he crooned into the alley. "I want to talk to you. Don't worry. I won't hurt you."

Ramiro ground his back into the cement wall, trying to make himself invisible.

"Let's talk like men, Paco. Face-to-face. I just want to ask you a few questions about the American, Sam Alroy."

Tobias spotted the hunched, frightened figure at the far

end of the alley. He checked for windows, for doors, for any possibility of an exit or a witness. There were none. The young fool could not have picked a better place for his execution.

"You have no reason to fear me. I apologize for harming you in the street," Tobias continued in a voice heavy with regret.

Ramiro tried to shout, but it emerged only as a strained whimper.

Tobias was about to pounce on the crouched figure when a voice from behind him said, "Leave the boy alone. Pick on someone your own size."

Tobias spun around, the knife slashing the air. He squeezed his eyes until they were almost shut, straining to see the man in black. "Get out of here," he shouted. "This is none of your business."

The man moved slowly toward Tobias. When he was within fifteen feet, Tobias was able to make out his face and clothing. A Roman collar. A priest. "Get out, or I'll kill you, too."

John Fallon shrugged himself free of his windbreaker, holding it in one hand. He withdrew something from his pants pocket, then said, " 'Too'? You told the boy you would not harm him. Now you admit you were going to kill him. You've added lying to your long list of sins."

"I'm going to kill you first," Tobias promised, lunging at Fallon.

Fallon flicked his jacket at Tobias's face, then slashed at his arm.

Tobias leaped back. He'd been cut. "Get ready to meet your God, priest." He crouched down and waved his knife back and forth slowly, moving on the balls of his feet in the manner of a man who knew exactly what he was doing.

"You're in the way, priest. You should stick to fucking altar boys. Not fighting with men."

Fallon's posture and body language mirrored Tobias's—
in a crouch, outstretched hand in constant motion.

The moon made its presence known again, and Tobias
saw the weapon in the priest's hand: a curved blade at one
end, and sticking out between his fingers was a spiral of
metal. A corkscrew.

Tobias's confidence rose. He feinted, laughing as Fallon
jumped back. He feinted a second time, and the priest
backed away, clumsy in his movements.

"I'm going to cut your balls off, priest. And shove them
down your throat."

"I was thinking of doing the same to you," Fallon said.
"But I don't think the good Lord was kind enough to bless
you with a proper set."

Stung by the insult, Tobias roared and lunged forward.
Fallon snapped the windbreaker in Tobias's face again, then
drove his right foot into his groin.

Tobias gasped in surprise. As he stiffened Fallon kicked
him again, taking his time.

Tobias doubled over. The knife fell from his hands, and
he dropped to the hard-packed dirt path. He fell face-first,
landing with a cracked-ice sound.

Fallon was on top of him in a flash, his knees on Tobias's
shoulders. One hand yanked back his ponytail. The other
twisted the needle-sharp tip of the corkscrew into the side of
his head.

"Who are you? Who do you work for?"

Tobias struggled to get his breath.

Fallon jerked his head back. "Tell me!"

"Raul Tobias. I work for Jago Roldan."

"What's your interest in Paco?"

"He was there when Alroy died."

Fallon twisted the tip of the corkscrew deeper into Tobias's flesh. "If I shove this in an inch, just an inch, I'll be
inside your brain. You'll be spending the rest of your life in

a wheelchair drooling and babbling. Now tell me what you want from Paco."

Tobias's entire body shivered. The crazy priest meant it. "We think he stole the car. The Mercedes Alroy was driving. There are some things in the car that Jago wants."

"What things?"

"Alroy's laptop computer. It should have been in the car."

"What else?"

"That's all," Tobias answered quickly.

Fallon twisted the corkscrew handle. "You're lying. "

Feeling the intense pain, Tobias shouted, "Alroy downloaded some files from his office in England onto his laptop. Jago wants the computer. That is all. I swear."

Fallon relaxed his grip. He slid his right hand down to Tobias's neck. He began firmly applying pressure with his fingers to the two carotid arteries. Tobias tensed, then tried to buck Fallon off his back.

Fallon kept the pressure steady. Tobias shuddered once; then his body slackened and he began breathing steadily through his nose.

"Are . . . are you really a priest?" Ramiro asked in a frightened whimper.

When Fallon didn't answer, Ramiro said, "Are you going to kill him?"

"Yes and no. I am a priest, and I'm not going to kill him." He stretched out and picked up the knife Tobias had dropped. It was a military combat-style model with a half-serrated blade. He used it to cut through Tobias's ponytail, then tossed the hair casually over his shoulder. He rolled Tobias over on his back and went through his pockets. He scanned the wallet before slipping it into his jacket. Tobias's ring of keys quickly followed.

Fallon then used the knife's blade to saw through the laces on one of Tobias's shoes.

He climbed to his feet and heaved the shoe up toward the roof of the nearest building.

Ramiro was sitting in a crouch, his arms wrapped protectively across his chest, staring at Fallon. His mouth opened to form a perfect O. "Why did you do that?"

"Do what?"

"Cut off his hair."

"It's a lot easier than cutting off his balls, and serves much the same purpose," Fallon said.

"And the shoe. Why just the one shoe?"

"A man can run faster barefoot than he can with one shoe. When Tobias wakes up he'll have to make a choice: Either take off after us with one shoe, or run in his socks. Either way, it takes time. Come on; let's get you out of here."

Ramiro stood up unsteadily and said, "Please, Father. Hear my confession. I have sinned greatly."

Fallon wrapped an arm around Ramiro's waist and steered him past the motionless figure of Raul Tobias. "We all have, son. Did you steal Sam Alroy's stuff?"

"Yes. The car. The jewelry. The camera. The briefcase. I did that."

"What about a document? In Latin," Fallon asked as they reached the street.

"Sí. The one in glass. I left it with Señor Dolius this morning. I will take you there."

"And the laptop computer? Where is that?"

Paco was starting to feel better. His strength was returning. And his courage. "I sold that too, Father. Just a few hours ago. To a student who is going back to Madrid. Is it important to you?"

"Perhaps." Fallon moved his arm up around the boy's shoulder and gave him a friendly hug. "Tell me more about this Giles Dolius fellow, Paco."

Chapter Twelve

The ride back in Roldan's Daimler sedan was much more relaxing than the trip up the mountain had been with John Fallon. Chasen eyed the chauffeur through the glass partition dividing the car. Keely Alroy seemed content to sit there and smoke, lighting one cigarette after the other with a vintage brushed-chrome Zippo lighter.

Chasen was happy to escape from Roldan House intact. He wondered about the two unconscious men he'd left in Roldan's office. Which would wake up first? The guard or the burglar? That led to other questions. Who was the unlucky burglar, and who had knocked him out? Also, what was Chasen to make of Vidal? That kick to the guard's head could have done serious damage. There were all sorts of balls in the air. Vidal had assumed he knew what was missing from the safe. And Giles Dolius's cryptic message for Jago Roldan. What was he to make of that?

Chasen's thoughts drifted to dinner. That had been an interesting affair. Jago sat at the head of the table, Daria on one side, a flustered-looking Keely Alroy on the other. Vidal was a half dozen chairs away, not exactly a seat of power.

Chasen had been sandwiched between two attractive middle-aged women, both of whom spent the evening pressing their legs against his and occasionally dropping their hands onto his lap. He had been tempted to somehow get them to shake hands, but the opportunity never arose.

His pretense that he didn't speak Spanish allowed him to pick up all kinds of juicy gossip about Jago, who, despite his age, was still considered a man who was *mas puta que las gallinas*, as horny as they make them. Innuendoes were also dropped about Jago and Daria being more than just grandfather and granddaughter.

The scuttlebutt on Vidal was that he was *grifo*, usually high on marijuana, and a *maricón de la playa*, a homosexual who preferred young boys.

Just before dessert was served, Jago had risen to his feet and tapped his knife against his glass, causing all talk to stop. He thanked everyone for coming, ordered them to say a silent prayer for Daria's devoted late husband, then made an announcement while beaming down at her. "It is my pleasure to tell all of you that my beautiful granddaughter is with child." He turned his smile on the guests and added, "A boy, we all hope," before sitting down to a ringing round of applause.

Daria had accepted the applause with a bemused smile, and Chasen could tell she was not as happy about the pregnancy as Jago Roldan was.

Keely sat quietly during the elaborate meal, while Jago kept up a nonstop conversation with her. By the end she appeared tired. She was more than willing to accept Chasen's offer for company on the drive back to her boat.

The chauffeur lowered the window, twisted his head around, and asked, "Do you wish to go to the hotel first, or the boat?"

"The boat," Keely said. She leaned back in the seat and blew a plume of smoke up toward the headliner.

"Good dinner," Chasen said, just to make small talk.

Keely said, "The best I've had in a while. I've been in Australia, working on a new project." She leaned forward and ran her hand down her calf. "Rough area. I was bitten by a snake. A death adder. The name alone was enough to damn near scare me to death."

"Was it serious?"

"Not life-threatening, but I was sick as hell for a few days." Her shoulders shuddered. "I hate snakes. I shot the miserable creature."

The car had traversed the mountain and was now tooling along the highway bordering the beach.

"I have to confess, I haven't seen any of your documentaries," Chasen said.

"Unfortunately, you're in the majority."

They drove in silence for another five minutes; then the driver slowed and pulled into a well-lit marina. Chasen could see close to a hundred boats, ranging from impressive masts that swayed rhythmically back and forth like clock pendulums to beaten-up commercial fishing boats with rubber tires for skirts.

"The jet-setters and billionaires keep their boats down the road a way, Dave," Keely said when they'd both exited the limousine.

"Come on aboard and have a drink," she invited as she led Chasen down a wobbly mooring dock.

"I'll have to pass," Chasen said, looking at his watch. "Reluctantly. I've got to meet with someone."

Keely didn't try to hide her displeasure. "Someone? A woman in every port?"

"No, a man. Purely business."

Keely paused at a gangplank leading to a boat with the name *Gypsy Queen* neatly stenciled on the bow. She slapped her hand against the hull, then said, "Home sweet home. I've found it's more convenient to live on the boat. The mooring fees are cheaper than paying rent, and I can take it with me on some assignments."

Chasen studied the vessel, a sturdy, forty-foot wooden hull, center-cockpit ketch. "Did you sail it to Australia?"

"No. I'm not that adventurous. To England a few times. France, Italy. I have a small studio here in Torremolinos for all my business materials, so the boat gives me plenty of living room. Come on, Dave. One drink. There's something we have to discuss."

"You talked me into it."

Chasen approved of the boat. The salon had teak walls with built-in glass-fronted cabinets filled with books and bric-a-brac in the main cabin. The port side included a compact galley with a two-burner stove, grill, oven, and a double sink. A J-shaped settee curled around a large oak-plank table in the center of the room. The portholes and fittings were all bright chrome.

While she fished an ice tray from the compact freezer, and two glasses from a cabinet, Keely said, "I transformed the original sleeps-six living quarters into one big room. King-size bed and all."

Chasen eased himself onto the settee. "I really am very sorry about your brother. Tell me about him."

She drizzled Johnnie Walker Red into the glasses, then sat down next to Chasen and lit up another cigarette. Keely inhaled deeply and blew out the smoke before responding. "Sam was . . . Sam. A wonderful, brilliant, loving guy. A genius at anything he put his mind to. Surprisingly enough, he originally wanted to be a priest."

"A Jesuit?" Chasen said.

"Right. What else? They're the big Catholic honchos. Sometimes I wish he'd stayed in the priesthood. Sam never had much to do with women. I just can't imagine him as a family man."

"He married Daria Roldan."

"And regretted it almost immediately. And now she's pregnant. Sam never mentioned that to me. Tonight was the first time I'd heard about it. In a way, I blame myself for the marriage. I talked Sam into moving to Spain. He was fed up with the governmental interference in England. Sam was always uncomfortable around women. Unsure of himself. He was a tiger when it came to business, a pussycat with the ladies." Her face turned sour as she related the next part of the story. "Sam met Jago Roldan at a business conference in Madrid. Jago introduced him to his granddaughter, and Daria stalked him. Sam didn't have a chance. She batted those baby blues, waved those knockers of hers in his face, and he was hooked. Two weeks later they flew off to Brazil and were married. Sam didn't mind flying, yet he couldn't handle being on board a boat, even for a short time. He had Ménière's disease, a form of vertigo." She fiddled with the watch on her wrist, turning it around in one direction, then the other. "So Daria's pregnant," she said, rambling on. "Believe me, the last thing I thought I'd ever be in this life was an aunt. God, I feel sorry for the poor child. Can you imagine having Daria as a mother? Did you see her trying to act like the grieving widow? That dress. That hairdo. She looked like Medusa on a bad snake day."

Chasen laughed lightly. "You don't think she loved Sam?"

"She married Sam for his money. His business. Her grandfather probably talked her into doing it. Jago has quite a reputation when it comes to hostile takeovers. Sam married Daria for the sex."

That reminded Chasen of something, and he said, "A wise man, I think it was my father, told me that marrying for sex was like buying a seven forty-seven for the free peanuts."

Keely gave out a lusty laugh. "Your father *is* a wise man."

Chasen took a sip of the Scotch. "Pop was a wise man. A writer. Historical novels filled with sex and hard living. 'Textual intercourse' is how he described his books. My mother claimed that he did too much personal research." Chasen shook his head, warding off old memories. He focused on Keely, holding her gaze. "Who do you think killed Sam?"

Keely frowned. "Someone hired by Daria. Or Jago." She spun her lighter on the table. "I'll be going back to the lion's den tomorrow morning with my attorney to talk to them about Sam's estate."

Keely's guess might well be right, but Chasen couldn't tell on such limited information. He decided to probe in a different direction. "A priest by the name of John Fallon gave me a ride to the Roldan house tonight. The kind of priest that women look at and say, 'What a waste.' Though in Fallon's case I'm not sure he's wasting it. Tall, curly brown hair. Likes to tell corny religious jokes. Did you happen to see him?"

"No, I'd remember seeing a priest."

"He was wearing a tuxedo. He's a Jesuit."

"Probably an old friend of Sam's," Keely offered.

Chasen checked his watch again. "I'd better get going."

She put her hand out like a traffic cop, not letting him rise. "Dave. Now that I've bared my chest to you, so to speak, don't you think it's time you leveled with me? You can start with your e-mail from Fidelity Surety and Bonding. I know there is such a firm, and that Sam had a life-insurance policy with them. But I couldn't believe you'd hooked up with them. It's just an old reporter's instinct, I guess. I had to check you out. I called Dean Bagley, my old editor. He looked into it, and said that you've been running a fishing boat out of St. Petersburg for the last couple of years. So what's the story? Who are you really working for?"

"I told Grady the cover wouldn't hold up," Chasen said.

"Devlin? You're back with the Company?"

"For the moment." A good-sized vessel must have entered the harbor, because the *Gypsy Queen* rose dramatically with a swell, then dropped just as quickly. "Keely, your brother was working on a software program that the Department of Defense has a great interest in. For some reason, Sam downloaded all the information onto his laptop, then wiped his office computer systems clean. Devlin thinks Sam had the laptop when he was murdered."

"And you're supposed to use me to find it."

Chasen rattled the ice in his glass. "If it weren't for the fact that we know each other, Devlin never would have called me. He thinks Jago Roldan is responsible for Sam's death. He also thinks Jago has the laptop."

"I'm glad to see Devlin hasn't gone senile. It was a Roldan who killed Sam. Jago or Daria," Keely insisted. "Or someone they hired." She stood up, barely giving Chasen room to slip past her. She grabbed his arm and said, "That lady you were living with in Colombia."

"Lora."

"Yes. I felt bad about her. Is there . . . anyone else now?"

"No. How about you?"

"No one," Keely said, moving in closer. She placed her hands on either side of his face and drew him to her. "Do you really have to go?" she said in a husky voice.

Chasen shrugged his shoulders in a hopeless gesture. "What about tomorrow? Dinner?"

Keely rapped her knuckles on the oak table. "It's a date. I'll pick you up at your hotel at nine o'clock."

The crowd at El Gato Negro was larger than it had been earlier in the day. The live music was heavy metal, the volume loud enough to make Dave Chasen wince. The bodies pressed together on the dance floor were so close that they seemed to move in unison.

Chasen elbowed his way through the crowd, most of whom were bare-chested, their bodies glistening with oil and sweat. The bar was three deep, and Taric, the man with all the tattoos, was busy making drinks and popping the tops from bottles of beer.

Chasen caught sight of a handsome man with curly hair for a brief second. John Fallon? The figure disappeared, swallowed up by the dancers, many of whom had their arms raised over their heads, clapping their hands in an effort to match the unmerciful beat of the drummer, who was doing his best to be heard over the screech of the electric keyboard.

Chasen followed the path Taric had taken him on earlier in the day to the stairway leading to Giles Dolius's office. He pounded on the padded red leather office door. There was no response. He twisted the knob and entered the room. Déjà vu all over again. Giles Dolius was slumped in the chair behind his desk, head cricked to one side. There was a small, scorched hole in front of the fence's right ear. The exit wound on the opposite side of Dolius's head was the size of Chasen's fist. No need for an Irish silencer this time. The loud music upstairs would have drowned out the gunshot.

Chasen carefully placed his thumb and forefinger on Dolius's chin. There was no stiffness, no sign of rigor mortis, which didn't tell him much except that Dolius had been dead for several hours.

The room seemed to be in the same condition as it had been earlier in the day. No overturned furniture, no open desk drawers. And no sign of Dolius's pearl-handled revolver. Whoever killed Dolius knew just what he was after, and where it was.

Chasen went through Dolius's jacket pockets: a comb, a small mirror, coins, breath spray. He decided to skip checking the dead man's pants pockets. Like every human being who met his maker, Dolius had completed his final bowel movement, and the stench filled the room.

Chasen dropped to his knees and looked under the desk. Nothing.

Suddenly the music upstairs stopped. He remembered a line from an old Western, John Wayne or another Hollywood cowboy saying that when the drums stopped beating, it meant the Indians were getting ready to attack.

Quickly he exited the room and was about to start up the stairs when the door above opened.

Chasen ducked away, scrambling down a dark hallway cluttered with cases of liquor. Boots thudded down the stairs. "*Pare*," a voice cried. Chasen found a side exit door that was secured by a piece of pipe slotted into metal brackets. A gunshot boomed, the sound magnified by the close quarters. Another shot fired as Chasen fumbled with the pipe. The window above the door fractured into frosted lace. Chasen pulled the pipe free and kicked the door open, as another bullet whizzed by his head.

He found himself in a slippery footpath littered with garbage cans. Cats and what he assumed were rats darted out of the way as he knocked over the cans. Digging in his toes, he started climbing an eight-foot chain-link fence. The sleeve of his sport coat caught on the top of the fence and made a loud ripping noise as he jumped to the ground on the other side. An incline led to a winding street. Bursting out in the open, he found himself shoulder-to-shoulder with night revelers.

More shouts followed as Chasen melted into a crowd of wide-eyed pedestrians jabbering away in excited Spanish.

He immediately found a small half-filled *taberna*, and made for a table in the rear, next to the door leading to the kitchen. A plump teenage waitress with reddish-brown hair that gleamed like polished copper was about to clear the table when Chasen approached and handed her a twenty-Euro note. "Leave it, please. Bring me a *café solo* and a large brandy. And a newspaper, if there's one around."

The waitress gave him a strange look, then shrugged and took off for the bar.

Chasen slipped out of his sport coat, rolled it into a ball, and placed it under the table between his feet. He took off his necktie, dropping it next to the coat, then rolled up his shirtsleeves. He had unbuttoned the top four buttons of his shirt and was ruffling his hair when the waitress returned with his coffee, brandy, and a wrinkled copy of the *Costa Blanca News*.

Judging from the dirty dishes, the previous diner had

feasted on oxtail, prawns, and flan, caramel custard. Chasen's stomach was rumbling, but it wasn't from hunger.

Minutes later two officers in dark blue uniforms entered the restaurant. The taller of the two had a droopy mustache and a rifle strapped over one shoulder. The shorter one had his hat on square, his tie tightly knotted and his gold badge well shined.

Mutt and Jeff, Chasen thought.

Chasen gave them a brief curious glance, then went back to his cognac and newspaper.

He noticed the plump young waitress looking from him to the policemen. She started to say something, but Chasen picked up the custard plate and beat her to the punch:

"Señorita. Dame otro de esos, por favor." I'll have another of these.

The tall policeman patted his partner on the shoulder and jerked his thumb in a gesture indicating it was time for them to leave.

"Gracias," Chasen said when the waitress brought the custard.

He waited twenty minutes before he left. He dropped the torn, bundled-up sport coat and tie in the first garbage can he passed.

Chapter Thirteen

Daria Roldan Alroy strode uninvited into Raul Tobias's bathroom, which wasn't all that unusual. She had visited his quarters at least a half dozen times in the past six months. Always at night, when Raul was in bed. Sometimes she'd give him notice of the visit—by a look, a word, a hand dragged across the back of his pants. Other times she'd just barge in, pull the sheets from the bed, and straddle him. Foreplay was nearly nonexistent. Just looking at her gave him an erection. She would never say a word on these occasions. She would ride him like one of her horses, her head tilted toward the ceiling, her throat making soft moaning sounds, her magnificent breasts waving in his face. As soon as Daria climaxed, she slid off him and left with not so much as a backward glance.

This morning she was wearing an oyster-colored silk robe that reached to her ankles. The sash was tied loosely, allowing a gap that showed a good portion of her breasts. "Raul, where were you when— What happened to your hair?"

Tobias glared at her reflection in the mirror, then concentrated on his own. When he'd regained consciousness in the alley, his car keys and wallet were missing, along with one shoe. Luckily he had a spare key taped under one of the fenders of his car. Not until he'd gotten back to Roldan House did he realize his ponytail had been cut off.

"I was tired of long hair," he said, staring back into the mirror. He appeared somehow older. His receding hairline now more obvious. "I told your grandfather that if he hadn't sent me out chasing that useless beach boy, I'd have been here, and the burglary would not have taken place."

Tobias rinsed the remains of the shaving soap from his face and dropped the razor into the sink. The knife wound to his forearm wasn't deep enough to require stitches. A long-sleeved shirt concealed the injury.

It had been a long night. And an early morning. Jago Roldan had been furious when he saw what had taken place in his office. The safe open, more than fifty thousand Euros gone, along with his precious cigars and the hard drive to his computer. Jago blamed him for the entire fiasco, even though he wasn't there at the time. He castigated the way the men were trained, the way the property was protected. All of it the fault of Raul Tobias.

Tobias had made no mention to Jago of the altercation with the priest in the alley. All he said was that Paco was nowhere to be found, and was thought to have moved to Portugal, possibly Lisbon. Still, Raul was very careful when he lied to Jago Roldan, because the old man had an uncanny way of finding out the truth. That meant that he would now have to kill Paco Ramiro and the man dressed as a priest.

Arturo, the guard who had been found unconscious in Jago's office, had suffered a severe concussion, and was taken to the hospital. He told Tobias that when he entered Jago's office, he found a body on the floor. A second burglar knocked out by his partner? A decoy? A car belonging to one of the servants had been stolen, obviously used by one of the thieves as an escape vehicle. Raul would have to wait until later in the morning to interview Arturo properly.

At least he had interrogated Lucio, the guard at the gate, and the young idiot who had been in charge of guest parking, and found some useful information.

There was one uninvited guest—the man who drove the

American insurance investigator to the party. Lucio had been severely disciplined for his stupidity in letting the man onto the grounds. He had described the driver, through a mouthful of broken teeth, as being fluent in Spanish, with curly brown hair. Wearing a tuxedo. If not for the tuxedo, the description would have fit the bastard in the priest's costume. Could it be the same man? Why a tuxedo at the party and the priest costume later? It made no sense. But he was obviously involved in the burglary, which meant that the American, Dave Chasen, was also.

The thief had entered Jago's and Daria's private rooms, and had passed up the opportunity to steal some priceless works of art and Daria's jewelry. Diamond necklaces, ruby pins, and valuable rings were scattered all over her room.

"He was in my room," Daria said, as if reading his mind. "He went through everything, including Sam's clothing."

Tobias filled her in on his interrogation of Lucio. "It had to be this Chasen's driver. They were in it together."

"Chasen? The American insurance man? I spoke to him briefly. He and Keely Alroy seemed very friendly."

"I'll go and see Chasen as soon as I straighten up a few things."

"No, I will handle him," Daria said firmly. "What about Vidal? Do you think he could be involved? He was talking to Chasen at the party."

"Your uncle?" Tobias scoffed. "Don't be ridiculous. He wets his pants every time one of my men comes near him."

"Don't be too sure about Vidal. He has his eyes on *Abuelo*'s money. One day we will have to deal with him. But for now I want you to concentrate on Keely Alroy." She removed a diamond bracelet from her wrist and draped it over the towel rack. "She will be here in a matter of hours to meet with *Abuelo*'s attorneys."

"I can hardly do anything to her in the house," Tobias protested.

"No. But on the road back to town. An accident, her car

over the cliff. That you could do. You need a friend, Raul," Daria added, loosening her robe sash, then slowly tying it in a knot. "*Abuelo* was talking of getting rid of you. He is especially concerned about the stolen hard drive. What do you think was on it?"

"All of your grandfather's secrets. Both business and personal. The thief made a wise decision in taking it."

"I calmed *Abuelo* down," Daria said. "For the moment." She gave his hair a sharp tug, where the ponytail had once been. "Take care of Sam's sister, and I will take care of you."

Tobias watched her stride arrogantly out the door. What a family. Why did he ever get mixed up with them in the first place? He knew the answer before he finished asking himself the question. Money. But the Roldans hadn't acquired all their wealth by spreading it around lavishly on others. His salary was barely above that of the household help and gardeners.

He picked up Daria's bracelet from the towel rack and held it to the light. He was in the mood for a killing. The phony priest and Paco Ramiro for certain. For now, he might as well settle for Keely Alroy.

Vatican City

Father John Fallon's shoes clicked rhythmically on the polished travertine marble floors of the west wing of the Apostolic Palace. Although he had made this walk hundreds of times, it had never ceased to fascinate him. The bright morning sun blazed through the stained-glass windows, showering the thirty-meter-high walls with a kaleidoscope of colors. He couldn't help but glance upward at the lacunar ceiling with its rich, gilded decorations. The sweet, flowery scent of hundreds of flickering candles, the magnificent statues of the apostles placed in the niches of the pilasters, and the low-toned tapestries depicting fierce battle scenes from the Crusades always gave him the feeling that he was visiting another time—a far better time.

The Swiss Guard in his impressive uniform, designed by none other than Michelangelo, with its red, yellow, and blue stripes, along with the red-plumed helmet, added to the effect. He knew most of the Swiss Guards by sight. They all fit a carefully prescribed mold. They were required to be Roman Catholic, unmarried, between eighteen and twenty-five years of age, over 1.74 meters tall, and, last but not least, good-looking, another tradition allegedly initiated by Michelangelo.

The young man guarding the door today was unknown to Fallon. He rapped the butt of his halberd, a long-handled ax blade crowned with a spearhead, on the marble floor, then asked, "Your business, sir?" in Tuscany-accented Italian.

"To see Father Jerolin." Fallon showed his credentials, and the guard swung open the arched, iron-rimmed door for him.

It was like entering another world. The modern world. White walls and matching doors stretched down a white linoleum floor for some thirty yards. The only spots of color were the brass doorknobs.

The doors were unmarked, but Fallon knew the one he was looking for. He knocked sharply with his knuckles before entering an immense, low-ceilinged room furnished with a hodgepodge of gray metal file cabinets and desks, each desk holding at least one computer screen. Fallon recognized most of the casually dressed young men and women pecking away at their computers.

The booming voice of Father Jerolin roared from the back of the room: "Ladies and gentlemen. Especially ladies. Hold tightly on to your valuables, be they man-made or God-given. John Fallon has just slipped past security and entered our humble domain."

Fallon made a wide, theatrical bow amidst the laughter and calls of welcome. He stopped to shake a few hands and kiss the backs of others as he made his way to Father Jerry Jerolin's office.

Jerolin was slumped in the chair behind his desk. He made no effort to rise or to extend a hand toward Fallon. Jerolin was a hunch-shouldered, heavyset man in his late forties. He wore a black robe made of heavy wool. Fallon knew that under the robe was a hair shirt, fashioned from the coarsest of goat hair in order to inflict a high degree of discomfort.

Jerolin's hair was cut so close to his scalp that it wasn't possible to determine its exact color. His square-jawed face was smooth, except for a V-shaped scar on his left cheek. Fallon knew the face before the scar, since he had been the one who carved it there years ago during a fencing match. Fallon had no fear in facing Jerolin with a rapier, but would have readily conceded defeat had they been paired off with broadswords.

Jerolin picked up an evil-smelling, twisted rope of an Italian cigar from a sardine can ashtray, clamped it between his teeth, and said, "We're busy, John. Very busy. What do you want?"

Fallon slid a bulky, plastic-lined envelope across Jerolin's desk. Jerolin kept his eyes fixed on Fallon as he opened the envelope with his free hand. He took a peek, then tossed it back to Fallon.

"A hard drive. I can get you a new one for less than thirty dollars."

"I like this one. I want to know what's on it."

Jerolin leaned back in his chair and tapped the tips of his fingers together. "Come back in a week or two and I'll see what we can do."

Fallon perched a hip on the edge of the desk. "Now, Jerry. Right now."

"Not possible. We're working on something at the moment that takes precedence over your meddling cabals."

Fallon had never been sure just what had come between

himself and Jerolin. The scar wasn't the cause. Jerolin had won the match and wore the scar as a badge of honor. They'd been close once, lived in the same monklike dormitories, survived the fasting and boot camp training course in the African desert that made the Marine Corps' equivalent seem like a summer vacation. They had been drinking buddies, and no one, Fallon included, had ever left a poker table with more of Jerry's money than he'd lost himself.

Perhaps it was the job. He and Jerolin had worked hard in order to be assigned to the elite corps of exsequors, but Jerolin hadn't lasted long. Rumors circulated that he had killed two men, in self-defense, but the experience soured him. While Fallon thrived in the dark, dangerous corners of the outside world, Jerolin had migrated to the fluorescent-bathed offices of the *Cannoncciale*—the spy glass. He held tight rein over the Vatican's widespread interests in obtaining and analyzing intelligence on anyone, or any country, considered to be a threat to the Church.

"This is no game," Fallon said. "You can pick up the phone and call the man with the three-cornered red hat if you don't believe me."

Jerolin's hand moved toward the phone on his desk, but he pulled it back reluctantly. Fallon wouldn't dangle the name of Cardinal Bertita at him if he didn't have Bertita's full backing.

He climbed to his feet, the chair squeaking as he rose, and picked up the envelope containing the hard disk. "Give me a clue. What are you hoping to find on this?"

"From my lips to your ears and no further. The whereabouts of Simon Peter's *Professio*."

Jerolin was so startled he dropped the envelope, gracefully catching it before it hit the ground. "Peter's declaration? What are you talking about? It was destroyed years ago. It was a fraud to begin with. The only one of us to actually see it was Bishop Sebastian, and he was not the most reliable of sources."

Sebastian had been the Vatican's presence in Madrid and had been well known for his fondness for sacramental wine—throughout the day and night.

"It's surfaced," Fallon said. "With the Roldans. And fraud or not, I have to find it."

Jerolin said, "Fuck."

"Saying the F-word is a venial sin. You should remember that."

Jerolin clamped a hand on Fallon's cashmere-sheathed bicep. "And doing it is a mortal sin. *You* should remember that."

The ginger-haired, freckle-faced man towered over Hal Gevertz. A red felt-tip pen had bled into one of the pockets of his denim shirt. His accent was pure Berlin. "I will take ten thousand Euros. No more or no less."

Gevertz examined the collection of black-and-white paintings strewn across his desk: a pregnant woman jumping out of a window; a bedraggled beggar with a Hitler-style mustache holding out a tin cup with a swastika on it; narrow, enormous-eyed skeletal-faced women screaming in pain while children played soccer or watched television. Men in wheelchairs being pursued by police cars on the Autobahn.

"These are very interesting, Rutgar," Gevertz said. Rutgar was developing a reputation for his works depicting resurgent fascism. As unappetizing as the paintings were to Gevertz, he knew that in a year or less the dreck could bring in a small fortune.

"Leave them with me, and I'll see what I can do."

"Ten thousand," Rutgar said stubbornly.

Hilda, his secretary, came into the office. She was a full-figured woman in her mid-forties with straw-colored hair tied in a waist-long braid. "A phone call, Herr Gevertz. A Mr. Chasen."

"Thank you," Gevertz said. He made a quick decision.

"Provide Mr. Rutgar with ten thousand Euros. And be sure to get a receipt."

When Hilda and Rutgar were out of the room, Gevertz punched the speaker button on his phone and said, "How's by you, David?"

"I have some bad news," Chasen said.

Hal Gevertz wasn't at all surprised to hear of the death of Giles Dolius. "In this business, you must always expect the unexpected, David. Giles wasn't bright enough to consider that."

"Maybe he was just unlucky," Chasen suggested.

"Luck is a matter of preparation meeting opportunity. But you didn't call me just to tell me about Giles. What do you want?"

"Information. A few hours before he was murdered, Dolius made a call to a man by the name of Jago Roldan, saying that he had some photographs, and something he called the *Professio*. Does that ring any bells with you?"

Gevertz began drawing a likeness of Giles Dolius on a scratch pad. "Jago Roldan. It's hard to believe that old *mamzer* is still alive. Be careful of him, David." There was a long pause; then Gevertz said, "*Professio*. Something is tickling my little gray cells. I'll call you back. Give me a number."

Chasen supplied him with his room number at the Tropicana Hotel. "What can you tell me about Jago's son, Vidal? He operates a gallery in Madrid."

"A nebbish. Deals in junk and forgeries. Don't trust him."

"Would he have done business with Giles Dolius?" Chasen asked.

"Why not? Hell, I've done business with Dolius. I'll call when I have something for you."

Gevertz was lost in thought, pondering what interest Chasen and the CIA had in Jago Roldan, when his secretary startled him. "You paid that *schlump* ten thousand for that *bupkis*?"

Gevertz dropped his pencil. "Forget about Rutgar, Hilda. Are you busy?"

Hilda's hand kneaded her braid. "Around here, I'm always busy."

"Well, stop whatever you're doing and find out what you can on something called the *Professio*. "

"What is it?" she asked. "A painting? A statue? A book? What?"

"I don't know," Gevertz admitted. "But somewhere, sometime, I've read about it, or heard about it. And I have a feeling it will turn out to be very valuable."

Hilda trailed her hand across Rutgar's painting of a woman jumping to her death. "At least I never get bored working here."

Chapter Fourteen

Keely Alroy had a splitting headache. She tilted her sunglasses up on top of her head and pinched the bridge of her nose with her thumb and forefinger. She had been sparring with Jago and Daria's four attorneys all morning. The spacious room set up for the conference had delicate plaster work on the walls and ceilings. Alano Duarte, the local lawyer she'd hired to represent her, had been overwhelmed by the opposition. It was like going to a gunfight with a knife. She was going to have to find a high-powered law firm to compete with Roldan's attorneys.

Everyone in the room, with the exception of Alano, smoked. The ashtrays were filling up with cigar and cigarette stubs. Keely lit a cigarette every few minutes, took several puffs, then angrily ground it out. She had expected a civilized meeting with Jago and perhaps one attorney in attendance. This had turned out to be a civil lynching. Jago had never made an appearance.

Daria had cornered Keely in the hallway before the meeting started. "Don't fight me on this. Cooperate, and I will see that you are taken care of. An adequate settlement. A monthly allowance. You may retain the boat Sam provided for you. Possibly his home in England. But resist us, and I promise you I will drag this out and by the time you receive one single dollar, you will be a wrinkled old woman."

Keely's response had been short and to the point. "Fuck you."

When Alano presented the Roldans' attorneys with a copy of Sam's will, which named Keely as the lone beneficiary, they waved it away as being insignificant. The five-million-dollar insurance policy was certainly intended for Sam's wife. Every time Alano submitted a request, his opponents would caucus for several minutes, then bombard him with counterproposals.

Finally Keely had had enough. She told Alano to carry on without her. As she stalked out of the room, the attorneys chorused in with a bewildering wave of excited Spanish.

She found her way to the first floor. Waist-high stacks of expensive leather suitcases were parked near the front door. Jago Roldan drummed his cane on the floor to attract her attention. "Ah, Señorita Alroy, you are leaving. Was the meeting to your satisfaction?"

"No, it was not. Your attorneys are playing hardball, Señor Roldan."

"Attorneys. Life would be so much simpler without them. Allow me to summon your driver."

Jago picked up a nearby phone and made a brief call. When he turned back to Keely, he said, "I wish you had not retained counsel. Then we could have settled this as a family matter. Have you spoken to Daria? I hope the two of you can become friends. She is *encinta*. With child. Soon there will be a young Alroy coming into the world, my grandson. We must think of him."

"Him? She's had tests already?"

Jago spread his hands apologetically. "A figure of speech. Boy or girl, what does it matter? A child is just what Daria needs. We must think first of his . . . or her future. I'm sure we could arrange for you to see the child often."

The front door slapped open and a uniformed chauffeur called out that the car was ready.

Jago shouted out a string of obscenities, causing the driver to back away, nearly tripping over his own feet. "I'm sorry," he apologized. "We are all quite upset today. There was an incident last night at the party. One of my men was badly injured. Señor Chasen, is he known to you?"

"I've met him before," Keely said. "What happened to your man?"

"An altercation. Señor Chasen, he did not arrive with you last night?"

"No. He came with a priest, I believe."

"A priest?" Jago grimaced and closed his eyes, as if in some sudden pain. "You are certain of that?"

"That's what Chasen said on the drive back last night." Keely pointed to the stacks of luggage. "You're leaving?"

"Yes, I'm returning to Madrid," Jago said.

Keely started for the door, Jago hurrying at her heels. "Did Chasen tell you the name of this priest?"

"If he did, I can't remember it."

"I saw no priest at the party." Jago placed his hand on the doorknob. "Tell me, Señorita Alroy. Your brother had a computer, the laptop kind. It may have some information on it that will be beneficial to us. Both of us. To his company. To whatever settlement we finally arrive at. It seems to have disappeared."

"I certainly have no idea where it is," Keely said impatiently. Her head was throbbing and she wanted to get the hell out of there.

Jago stood back and opened the door. "Remember the child. We must not forget Sam's child."

Keely wearily nodded her head in agreement, then skirted around Jago. The driver was waiting, holding the door of the same gleaming white Daimler DS420 seven-seater limousine that had picked her up at her boat that morning. She watched Jago standing in the doorway as they drove off, his face frozen in a tight, mirthless smile, one hand waving his cane in her direction.

Keely snapped open her purse and extracted a pack of cigarettes and clicked her lighter. She leaned back, closed her eyes, and drew deeply on the cigarette, going over her conversation with Jago. He seemed to be dangling the baby in front of her like a prize. *Cooperate with us, and you will be able to see the baby.*

For a moment she had thought the old man was going to have a stroke when she told him the man who drove Chasen to the party was a priest. What did Dave say his name was? Fallon. John Fallon. To hell with Jago. Let him learn the priest's name from someone else.

After she stubbed out the cigarette, the car felt stuffy. The glass window divider between her and the chauffeur was in place. She leaned over and pushed the buttons that lowered the Daimler's rear windows. The wind felt refreshing against her skin.

She could feel the big car slow, then make a right turn. Her eyes felt heavy. She leaned her head into the cushion, closed her eyes, and tried to figure a way to keep the Roldans from squeezing her out of Sam's estate. There had to be a way to—

A jarring impact startled Keely. Her head snapped up. She stared at the driver, who was focused on the rearview mirror. His lips moved, but she couldn't make out what he was saying. He seemed confused, not frightened.

She swiveled around just as the Daimler lurched violently forward. The car slewed and yawed as the squeal of the brakes echoed off the hillside. She caught a glimpse of a dark-colored vehicle, but couldn't see the driver.

Keely searched frantically for her seat belt as there was yet another impact—louder than the others. The limo suddenly swerved off the road. It barreled through a low split-rail fence and into a free fall. Keely's head bounced against the car's roof; her knees banged into the built-in liquor cabinet. She saw brief flashes of blue sky and trees streak past the window. Her screams mingled with the driver's as the big car tumbled down the steep cliff. It came to a bone-jarring halt. The Daimler was upside down. Keely was lying on the headboard. She got cautiously to her knees, and felt the car shifting under her, groaning like a wounded animal.

She peered into the driver's compartment. The chauffeur's head had been forced back against the dividing window by the air bag. His neck was tilted at an awkward angle.

"Are you all right?" she shouted as she inched her way toward the right-side door.

More metallic groaning came from outside and the Daimler teetered like a child's seesaw. She yanked at the door handle, but it wouldn't budge.

A loud creaking noise followed and she felt the metal move under her. At any moment the car was going to fall the rest of the way. She slithered through the open window, wildly clutching rocks and small scrubby plants to pull herself free. Finally she was clear of the car altogether.

She lay on her back for a moment, catching her breath. The Daimler had come to rest on a scattering of jagged rocks—a narrow ledge anchored by a gnarly, rough-barked tree with misshapen branches.

The motor was still running, the wheels spinning aimlessly in the air.

She had to get the driver out too. Keely edged closer to the vehicle, her sandaled feet slipping in the loose-packed earth. She looked down and immediately felt dizzy. The drop was several hundred feet straight down, to a thicket of large rocks and pine trees. She took several deep breaths, then put her hand on the driver's door and gently, cautiously pulled the latch. The door rasped open, a portion of the pillowlike air bag spilling outside.

"Are you all right?" she called. She groped for a hand-hold. Her fingers found an inch-thick branch of the tree. The Daimler rocked sideways and she leaned back in alarm, waiting for it to settle before approaching again.

The chauffeur's left hand poked out from the air bag, his fingers clenched in a fist, pounding the bag helplessly. She could hear his muffled screams.

"*¡Ayúdame! ¡Ayúdame!*"

Keely grasped his flailing hand in hers, and immediately she was pulled toward the car.

She pounded her free hand into the air bag. It was like punching a heavy canvas pillow. "How can I deflate this damn thing?" she screamed helplessly.

With a grinding noise, the Daimler wobbled, then began to roll over.

Keely used both of her hands to yank the driver's arm, but it slowly, steadily slipped from her grasp.

The big car let out one final, deathlike groan, then tipped over on its side and began careening out of control down the mountainside, bouncing off rocks and trees before coming to rest at the bottom of the canyon. After a long, eerie silence the Daimler burst into flames.

Keely watched in horror, her eyes fixed on the burning car. It took her a moment to realize that she was slowly, inch by inch, sliding down the incline.

She dug her heels into the rock-laced earth, then reached out for what was left of the tree stump. When her feet began losing traction, she risked a lunge, grabbing the tree with both arms. She hung on for dear life for several moments, then wrapped her legs and thighs around the stump, squeezing them tight, like a nervous rider on a strange, unsettled horse.

She twisted her neck around and looked back up to the top of the cliff. Someone must have seen them go over the side. Someone must have heard the crash. She squinted her eyes against the sun. There was someone. Just a shadow. She waved her hand frantically.

"Ayúdame! Help me!"

A good-size rock hit the hillside and rolled straight down toward her, picking up additional rocks on the way.

Then another rock, bringing a wave of debris with it. A boulder struck the tree stump inches from her head. She screamed for help again.

A rock slide. Someone was trying to start a rock slide!

Chapter Fifteen

Dave Chasen slipped his card key into the hotel lock. Despite a very short night's sleep, he felt fine. He was one of those rare individuals who didn't suffer from jet lag. He'd read an article about it once. It was an admirable trait that he shared with, of all people, Henry Kissinger and Frank Sinatra.

Chasen had already had a busy morning. After his call to Hal Gevertz he ventured out to the streets of Torremolinos. First he'd waited at the door of an upscale men's store until it opened for the day's business. He'd purchased a dark blue blazer as close in style and color to the one he'd torn when scaling the fence outside of El Gato Negro last night. The store's tailor had somewhat reluctantly agreed to remove the coat's Spanish labels and to replace the bright brass buttons with plain black ones. Hopefully even the sharp-eyed Lieutenant Garate wouldn't notice the difference.

He found nothing in the morning paper about Giles Dolius's death.

Then he spent an hour staking out Paco Ramiro's house. There'd been no sign of the young beach boy.

As he opened the door, he saw something that made him instinctively drop to one knee.

His right hand darted for the twenty-five-caliber Baby Browning pistol usually holstered at his ankle. All his fingers touched were his sock and a bit of hairy leg. The gun was resting in a drawer in his apartment in St. Petersburg. Grady Devlin had been firm on his "no gun" order. The quickest way to get booted out of Spain was to be found carrying a weapon.

Someone was waiting for him out on the terrace, in a lounge chair. He slammed the door against the wall, ready to take on the intruder. Then the beautiful face of Daria Roldan rose above the lounge cushion and gave him a bemused smile.

"The bellboy let me in," Daria explained as she slowly came to her feet. She was wearing a red-and-white vertical-stripe dress, belted loosely at the waist with enough cleavage to reveal a black lace bra.

Chasen wondered if she wore the black bra to show that she was still in mourning for her husband.

"I hope you don't mind," Daria said. "I didn't feel like waiting in the lobby, and the bellboy was so understanding."

Actually, Chasen did mind. He minded a lot, but he saw no point in expressing his displeasure. He had stripped the file folders of everything with a CIA connection, so Daria wouldn't have learned anything she didn't already know.

"Can I get you something to drink?" he asked, pointing at the room's minirefrigerator.

"No," Daria said, smoothing out the wrinkles in the lap of her dress.

Chasen shrugged out of his new sport coat and dropped it onto the bed. The red message light on the phone was blinking, but he ignored it.

"I wish you had called to let me know you were coming," Chasen said, wandering out to the terrace. He rested his hands on the iron balcony, then said, "What can I do for you?"

Daria moved alongside him, her hip bumping lightly into his. "How is your investigation going, Mr. Chasen? Have you satisfied yourself that Sam was murdered?"

"There's no doubt of that. I would like to talk to the last

man to see him alive on the beach. Paco Ramiro, however, seems to have skipped town."

"What could he possibly tell you that would make a difference? Surely a young beach attendant didn't kill my husband."

"You know how insurance companies are. They want all the facts before they release the money."

"We never had a chance to talk last night. You went home with Keely."

"We took the same car," Chasen said, turning to face her. Daria's hair was brushed back, worn long and straight, as if she'd ironed it. Her lipstick was bright red and thickly applied. She was incredibly beautiful, and he found it difficult to focus on anything other than her icy blue eyes.

"But you didn't arrive at *Abuelo*'s house with Keely. You came with someone else, no?"

"Someone else, yes. Why is that of any interest to you?"

Daria lowered herself slowly onto the lounge, as if immersing herself in a too-hot bath. "One of *Abuelo*'s guards was badly injured last night, and, quite frankly, no one invited to the party had any reason to attack him. They were all longtime friends of my grandfather. With the exception of you and your driver." She crossed one long leg over the other and pressed her lips into a kiss of worried disapproval. "You appear to be a man who could be dangerous. You didn't hurt that poor guard, did you?"

"I have no reason to. I'm here to investigate the circumstances of your husband's murder. Lucio, the guard at the gate to your grandfather's house, mentioned that someone had been shot on the grounds a few days before the party. A burglar? Maybe he came back. Or sent a friend. There must be many things in the house that would interest a burglar."

"Lucio talks too much, " Daria said, dismissing the idea. "What about your friend? The one who drove you to the party. Could he be the guilty party?"

"The driver isn't a friend. I don't really know the man.

His name is John Fallon. He's a priest, and he's staying here in this hotel."

Daria raked her fingers through her hair. "A priest? I saw no priest last night."

"No one seems to have seen him," Chasen said amiably. "Apparently he didn't stay long. Maybe he didn't like the music. He told me that he was going to extend the Church's sympathy to you for your husband's death."

Daria held out her hand, like royalty expecting a kiss. Chasen grabbed it and pulled her to her feet. Standing inches away, she turned her eyes on full beam as she stared at him.

"I have to go now," Daria said, her tongue running across her lower lip, "but I do want to talk to you again. Soon. Perhaps I can locate the beach attendant for you."

"I must come and wait in your room next time," Chasen said with a light smile.

Daria didn't smile back. Seduction time was over. The information about Fallon seemed to have troubled her. She walked to the door and let herself out without so much as a good-bye.

Chasen went to the phone and punched the replay button. A message from Vidal Roldan. "I have to see you. Did you hear what happened last night? I'll call back."

Chasen flopped on the bed and stared at the ceiling, wondering what Daria Roldan had thought about her uncle's message. And why she never brought up the robbery. Not a word about the open safe or the cannibalized computer in Jago's office.

There was a light rap on the door. Chasen rolled off the bed and peered through the door's peephole. Paco Ramiro's sister, Benita, looked back at him through the fishbowl lens.

She was waving a piece of paper in her hand. It was the portion of the hundred-dollar bill he'd given her.

Chasen opened the door, waved the girl inside, dragged a chair over, and propped it against the door to keep it open.

Benita was wearing low-slung denim jeans that afforded

a good view of the gold ring in her navel and the Day-Glo orange top of a bikini. White plastic earrings the size of curtain rings dangled from her ears.

She stared at him curiously. "Are you afraid of me?"

Any man who wasn't afraid of being caught alone in a hotel room with a sixteen-year-old girl dressed like that was crazy, in Chasen's estimation.

"What do you want with Paco?" Benita asked.

"I mean your brother no harm. I just want to talk to him about the man who was murdered on the beach. If he's helpful to me, he will be greatly rewarded."

Benita's mood turned sultry. She wandered slowly around the room, rolling her hips, her hand trailing across the bed's mattress. "This is a beautiful room. Expensive, no?"

"Expensive, yes. Where is Paco?"

She waved her hand in front of her face as if it were a fan. She motioned to the refrigerator alongside the TV. "I'm warm. Buy me a beer."

"Not a chance. You're too young to—"

"The legal drinking age here is sixteen. We're not like you Americans, who—"

"Where's your brother?"

"I'm not sure where he is. But . . . it is possible that I can find out."

Chasen slipped his wallet from his pants pocket and plucked out the rest of the hundred-dollar bill. "This is yours when you take me to Paco."

She tried to snatch the snippet of money from his hand, but she wasn't quick enough.

"All right. Be at Monjils, a bar in the La Nogalera district here in town, at six o'clock this evening. I will take you to Paco."

"I'll be there," Chasen promised. "When I see Paco, you get the money."

Benita moved slowly toward the door, pausing at the bed,

her hand again trailing across the bedspread. She leaned over and pushed on the mattress with both hands. "It is soft, no? I could stay with you until then. For a hundred dollars, I could—"

Chasen grabbed her lightly by her shoulder and steered her to the door. "I'll see you at six tonight."

He tried reaching Hal Gevertz in Berlin, but, in a tone that only the Germans could get away with, the stern-voiced woman who answered the phone said that speaking to Gevertz at the moment was *"diese Moglilchkeit ist nicht"*—not possible.

He used the cell phone for the call to Langley, Virginia. Carly Sasser sounded glad to hear from him. "Grady's unavailable."

"I have to talk to him," Chasen said. "Things are coming to a boil over here."

"I'd rather boil on the Costa del Sol than in Washington. The weather's terrible here. Hot and muggy. How is it over there?"

Chasen peered down from the balcony at the sunbathers on the beach. The sun was a butter-yellow ball. The sea had taken on a bluish hue from the cloudless sky. "Not bad, if you have the time to enjoy it. I asked for a background check on John Fallon, allegedly a priest who works out of the Vatican. It came back negative. Have someone dig deeper, and tell Grady to call me as soon as he can."

"He's meeting with the director as we speak, but I'll give him the message."

Chasen ended the conversation with, "See you soon. I hope."

The cell phone screen flashed a blinking battery sign, indicating that it was hungry for a charge.

Langley, Virginia

At one time Grady Devlin had been certain that the CIA director's office would be his. That was before the Homeland Security mob had stomped their boots all over the various United States intelligence communities. Brains, guts, devotion, years of service, ability, all that went by the wayside. Connections counted now more than ever before. And Louis Hoyt, the current director of the CIA, had those in spades.

Hoyt was a small, terrier-like man with a deceptively soft face, two weeks away from his fifty-second birthday. His "height deficiency," according to a piece in the *New York Times*, had never held him back from achieving his goals. Barely five-foot five, Hoyt had picked up the nickname Yellow Pages because of his penchant for sitting on a phone book when being interviewed on the morning TV shows.

Hoyt had taken to doing his exercises indoors after someone had taken a potshot at his limo as it was leaving the CIA parking lot. He was on a treadmill, wearing striped underpants and a T-shirt, when Devlin entered the room.

"Come over here, Grady, so I can see you," Hoyt ordered.

"Good morning, sir," Devlin said, admiring the view of the rolling Virginia hillside through the bulletproof glass.

"What's happening on the Alroy case?" Hoyt said brusquely.

"My man is making progress, sir. I think that by—"

"I read Dave Chasen's file, Grady. Why the hell did you pick him for the job?"

"Chasen was the best operator I had in Berlin. He ran the Strauss network almost single-handedly, and brought in some—"

"Before my time," Hoyt said irritably. "What the hell was the Strauss network?"

"Seven East German agents, all with access to economics intelligence. Chasen kept them together through some rough patches. And he was doing a hell of a job in Colombia before—"

"Before he fucked up royally. That's the trouble with you Cold War warriors. You can't forget the good old days. Get over it. Different times, different crimes. " Hoyt pointed to the chair alongside the treadmill. "Hand me that towel."

Devlin scooped up the towel and passed it to Hoyt. "Chasen has a unique connection to Sam Alroy's sister. She's the vice president of Sam Alroy, Incorporated. That could be invaluable in the future if she inherits the company."

Hoyt scrubbed his neck and shoulders with the towel. "What we need is Alroy's software now, not in the future. Devlin fucked up once; he could do it again. If he doesn't turn up something in the next forty-eight hours, get rid of him. Results, Grady. That's what we need, not some crony of yours whose only claim to fame is that he's screwing Alroy's sister. I've got a lot on my plate, and I want this thing taken care of quickly. Get it?"

"Got it," Devlin said.

"Good." Hoyt stepped off the treadmill and stared up at Devlin. "You're putting on some weight, buddy. There's a treadmill in the basement gym. Feel free to use it."

Chapter Sixteen

Madrid

"*Excusa, pardon,* sorry," Perry Bryce said as he pushed his way through the cosmopolitan crowd at Madrid's Barajas Airport. Actually, *cosmopolitan* was too kind a word for the mob that stood between him and the chained gate some thirty yards away, where Lt. Sil Garate was waiting to escort him directly out to the wonders of Madrid.

"*Leche mon cul,*" a portly, beet-faced Frenchman swore at him when the edge of Bryce's suitcase made contact with his hip.

Bryce's response to the suggestion that he kiss the man's ass was "*Va te faire foutre.*" Fuck off. However, he said it with a smile to show that there were no hard feelings.

The tall, swarthy Spaniard, wearing a white suit and Sinatra-style straw hat, was motioning to him from a doorway. He took one of Bryce's suitcases from his hand. "Smooth flight?"

"I barely had time to fasten my seat belt and gulp down a cup of coffee."

Garate flashed his ID card to the airport security guard, and Bryce followed the slim Spanish agent to his waiting car. They spoke about the weather and stock market until Garate's driver had deposited them at a pleasant glass-walled restaurant with outdoor seating near the Palacio Real, the former Royal Palace, which was now a major tourist attraction.

They settled down at a tree-shaded table that had an excellent view of the street. "Chalmers tells me you need more help," Garate said after they'd been served their drinks, coffee for Garate and a Virgin Mary for Bryce.

Bryce inhaled the warm Madrid air and took notice of the stream of young women parading by, all dark haired, high-breasted, athletic-looking, and trim. He studied Garate's rough, swarthy face. He must know where all those lovelies disappeared to after nightfall.

Bryce poked a finger into his glass, bumped the ice around, then licked his finger dry. "I'd like to get into Jago Roldan's house here in Madrid."

"You didn't find what you were looking for in Roldan's safe last night?"

Bryce wasn't sure just how much information Snake Chalmers had provided the Spanish policeman. The *Professio* was off-limits. "Keep him happy, but keep him stupid," was dear old Snake's sage advice to Bryce.

Bryce slipped the envelope Chalmers had provided from his coat jacket and passed it to Garate under the table. He had taken the opportunity to steam open the envelope and count the money. Eighteen hundred and fifty Euros. Why the unusual amount? Was Garate on a monthly stipend? And what did Garate do with his ill-gotten gains? Did he spend it on good food, or one of those lovely señoritas stretching her long legs around the streets of Madrid? Did he turn it over to his superior and play the age-old double-agent game? Or did he divert the funds to his personal informers? Bryce figured that it was a little of all of them, because that was exactly what he did when those all-too-rare opportunities came about and he had the chance to pocket some loose coin of the realm.

"Getting into Jago's Madrid mansion would be a major undertaking, especially now that he is returning to Madrid."

Garate accepted the envelope without bothering to count the money. "It's a fortress. The security is much more modern and efficient than the house in Mijas."

This news was unexpected. "I thought he stayed at his country place till the end of summer."

"My information is that he threw a temper tantrum after the party last night." Garate removed his straw hat and placed it in the center of the table. "One of his guards, Arturo Nunes, was badly injured. A severe concussion. Inspector Calvino was able to persuade Nunes to talk at the hospital. Nunes said the safe in Jago's office was wide open. Stacks of money were piled on Jago's desk. A man in gray clothing was lying on the floor. Then Nunes was hit from behind and rendered unconscious. When he woke up, the man on the floor was gone, and so was the money."

Bryce's hand unconsciously went to the back of his head. "Quite a party, wasn't it?"

"Was it?" Garate snapped. "I wasn't there. But I did help you gain access to the villa in the trunk of the rented limousine." He leaned forward, wanting information. "I can't help you if I don't know what's going on."

Bryce thought for a moment, one finger brushing his lips. "I was in Jago's office. I opened the safe. What we're looking for wasn't there. Someone sneaked up on me, put me under."

"Someone who?" Garate wanted to know.

"He spoke English and knew judo. That's all I'm certain of." Bryce saw no purpose in informing Garate that the man, just by hearing Bryce's mumbled curse, had zeroed in on him as being a British spy. That was why he'd flaunted his knowledge of MI6's training facilities at Fort Monckton. The bastard had to be working for an intelligence agency, but which one?

Garate pushed himself to his feet. "Wait here," he ordered.

Bryce watched the policeman stalk off in the direction of

his car. He jerked his legs when he caught sight of a rodent scurrying by the boxwood hedge separating their table from the street. The rat stopped to gnaw a piece of bread left by a prior customer.

Garate returned and dropped a stack of photographs in front of Bryce. "One of these men is the one who knocked you out."

Bryce shuffled through the photographs depicting two men in a convertible. The driver was easily recognizable— the man in Sir Sedly Parlow's pictures. The other was a stranger. "The driver is a priest. John Fallon. He works for some hard-ass outfit in the Vatican that—"

"*Cannoncciale,*" Garate said excitedly.

"I don't know the other man."

"Dave Chasen. He's with the CIA, though he claims to be an insurance investigator looking into Sam Alroy's death. I want you to—"

Garate's cell phone buzzed. He stood up again and wandered around the restaurant while he spoke. When he came back this time, there was a hard edge to his voice.

"That was Inspector Calvino. Señorita Keely Alroy is in the hospital. The car she was in, one of Jago's limousines, was pushed off the road this afternoon. The driver died, but she survived."

"An accident?" Bryce said.

Garate measured sugar, almost to the last grain, into a spoon, then dumped it in his coffee. "The driver had made that trip hundreds of times. Firemen had to rescue Alroy by pulling her off a cliff. And last night, after Jago's party, a man by the name of Giles Dolius was murdered. Do you know the name?"

Bryce gave a negative wag of his head.

"A fence. Murdered in his own establishment. A shot to the head. The same as Alroy. I don't mind helping Chalmers out when I can, but this is becoming dangerous. For me. Alroy, Dolius, Jago's driver, all dead. One of Jago's guards in the hospital. The CIA and the *Cannoncciale* involved. It's becoming much too complicated. Either you or Chalmers have to tell me just what is really going on, or you're on your own."

"Quite right," Bryce said, knowing a demand for more money when he heard it. "You should be in on it. It's a laptop computer. Sam Alroy's laptop."

"A laptop?" Garate picked up his hat, leaned back in his chair, his fingers drumming on the hat's brim, and digested the information. Bryce could see he wasn't buying it. Which was too bad, because it was the truth. Chalmers had expressed great interest in the laptop, but Sedly Parlow claimed Alroy's latest software was just a lot of "electronic gallimaufry that some Hindu in Bangalore will render obsolete in a few months."

"This is obviously rather hush-hush," Bryce said. "Chalmers believes Alroy had some information regarding his latest software stored on the laptop."

"You're full of shit," Garate said bluntly. "What would the Vatican want with Alroy's laptop computer?"

Bryce quickly evaded the issue. "Let's go with your theory that either John Fallon or Dave Chasen knocked me out. And Jago's guard, too. Maybe they're working together on this. When I woke up in Jago's office last night, the guard was lying next to me. His head was bloody. Jago's desktop computer had been ripped open. The hard drive missing. MI6 wants Alroy's laptop because it has some of his business applications on it. Chalmers thought it was in Jago's safe. He thinks it was Jago, or one of his goons, who killed Alroy. The CIA would love to get its hands on that laptop before we do." Bryce clasped his hands in front of him. "Why the priest? I don't know. Maybe he's been CIA all along. A double agent. Being a priest isn't a bad cover. He could get into places someone like me—or you—couldn't."

Garate searched Bryce's deadpan face for several moments. "All right," he finally said, "I'll go along with you.

For now. But if I find you've been lying to me, you're going to see the inside of a Spanish prison."

Bryce brushed this threat aside. "Inspector Calvino," he said. "I assume he's in Roldan's pocket."

"You assume correctly," Garate said. "I tell him only what is necessary, of course. He knows nothing of you, or of Chasen being a CIA agent."

Bryce signaled for the bill. Another threat of prison, he thought sourly. It must be inscribed in some clandestine civil servant manual somewhere. Agent doesn't cooperate, threaten him with prison. At least Garate hadn't gone into all of the sexual innuendos that Chalmers had.

The waiter came and placed a saucer with the bill in front of Bryce. "A rat just ran by my foot a little while ago," Bryce complained.

"Impossible, señor. We have no rats here."

"Is that right?" Bryce said as he laid down paper money and coins totaling up to the exact amount on the bill. "Well, I saw one, and he ran off with your tip."

Chapter Seventeen

While Benita Ramiro didn't appear to be strong enough to hurt the proverbial fly, Dave Chasen had no idea where she was leading him, and who might be there, so he wasn't going unarmed. He rummaged through his suitcase and pulled out a Ziploc bag filled with a variety of travel-size sundries: first-aid remedies, aftershaves, and deodorants. He selected a can of spray deodorant, barely bigger than a tube of lipstick. He discarded the cap, then took a long-sleeved light blue shirt from the closet, taped the can to the outside of the lower left sleeve, carefully slipped the shirt on, then rolled the sleeve back three times, securing it within the folds.

He shook his arm several times to make sure it wouldn't fall loose, then draped a dark blue sweater over his shoulders. He transferred some money from his wallet to the innersole of his shoe, gathered his keys, and made his way to the hotel lobby.

Chasen approached the desk clerk and asked for directions to La Nogalera. The clerk circled the area on a map of the town. "The area is a maze of passageways and courtyards."

"I'm meeting someone at a bar called Monjils. Do you know it?"

The clerk's hand went to his mustache. *"Sí, señor."* He

coughed into his hand. "You realize Monjils caters to the . . . gay life."

"Is it near El Gato Negro?"

"Near, but on . . . the opposite side."

Chasen started to move away, then came back to the counter. "Can you tell me if John Fallon is still a guest?"

The clerk's fingers flew across the hotel's computer keyboard. "Fallon. We have no guest by that name, señor."

"A priest. Maybe he checked out."

The clerk went back to the computer, clicked more keys, then said, "We haven't had a guest by that name. Not in the last month. I can inquire further if you wish."

"No. That won't be necessary."

The walk from the hotel to Monjils took less than fifteen minutes. The area, dominated by whitewashed Andalusian storefronts, was teeming with shoppers and sightseers. Chasen passed the usual array of boutiques and souvenir shops, many displaying the sought-after Lladró porcelain statues.

He found Monjils wedged in between a flower stall and a clothing store whose display window featured faceless female mannequins in motorcycle leathers.

Once he was inside, he realized what the hotel clerk had meant by the place being "on the opposite side" of Giles Dolius's establishment, El Gato Negro. It was a lesbian bar. He was the only man there, and his presence brought looks of curiosity, contempt, and outright "get the fuck out of here" from the dozen or more patrons. The name should have been a clue—*monjils* meant nunnery.

He found an open table close to the door. A swaggering fortyish woman wearing a Pepto-Bismol-pink rubber skintight jumpsuit with a silver zipper that ran from her crotch to her Adam's apple approached him. She had a skull-close haircut, and her pasty white face was highlighted by heavily applied mascara and eyebrow liner.

"Are you sure you're not lost?" the woman asked.

"I'm meeting my niece, Benita. Think you could find me a Jack Daniel's while I wait?"

"We get a lot of men in here looking for their 'nieces.' Usually they want to watch them going down on someone else's niece. There's no floor show here."

Chasen shrugged and upturned both palms. "Do I look like a pervert?"

"You're a man, aren't you?" the woman said. "One drink. That's all you get."

Chasen nursed his drink while listening to a recording of a dry-voiced singer lamenting "Her Last Cigarette."

Two customers at the bar took turns giving him hostile looks. The older one had purple-tinted hair that stood up with the firmness of a garden broom. She looked like she'd been ironed into her camouflage military fatigues. Her drinking partner was Benita's age and wore oversize slacks and a man's-style one-button blazer.

At last a slender young man with jaw-length hair and badly chapped lips slid onto the seat next to Chasen. "Benita sent me. Let's go."

"What's your name?" Chasen said.

"Turi," the man said impatiently. "Let's go."

Chasen followed him out of the bar. Rapidly they wended through a confusing maze of streets so narrow that he had to hug the wall when someone approached from the opposite direction.

Turi fast-walked, with his head tilted back, snapping his fingers to a tune in his head. He wore baggy jeans that with each step threatened to slide off his narrow hips, and a black T-shirt displaying the silver emblem of the Oakland Raiders. He glanced over his shoulder several times to make sure that Chasen was keeping up with him.

Chasen checked over *his* shoulder an equal number of times to make sure no one was coming up from the rear.

Finally Turi turned onto an unpaved street. It was lined with an uneven assortment of small homes, all in need of paint and repair. He stopped in front of a two-story affair that was set back a few yards from its neighbors. The stunted garden was a jungle of weeds and unpruned shrubs, protected by a weather-beaten picket fence. Curtains fluttered like angels' wings from the upstairs windows. A tiny garage, its doors locked by a rusty chain and shiny new padlock, hugged the side of the building.

A pair of dust-coated mongrel dogs lay in the shade of the garage. They looked around, turning their necks like sightseers.

Turi pushed his way through the sun-blistered front door, waving for Chasen to follow him. Once inside, Chasen paused long enough for his eyes to adjust to the darkness. The bare wood floor was gritty and scuff-marked. The walls were blanketed with spray-can graffiti slogans, a few of which advised Americans to do unpleasant things to themselves with their nuclear weapons. A ceiling fan, black with grime, turned in endless circles.

The furniture consisted of a moldy tobacco-brown couch, chipped and bruised wooden chairs, and a white plastic table with a hole in the center for the placement of a shade umbrella.

"Where's Benita, Turi?"

"She'll be here. Don't get—"

A door opened with a raspy groan, and a beefy, bare-chested young man with sideburns that narrowed down to a point at his jawline strolled into the room. He was holding a large pistol with both hands.

"I'm Paco Ramiro. What do you want with me?" he said in slow, carefully enunciated English.

"You're not Ramiro," Chasen said. "Where is he?"

The man turned to Turi, and in Spanish asked, "Did you check him?"

"No, Rico. I didn't—"

"Do it!" Rico commanded, waving the gun at Chasen and ordering him to raise his hands.

Turi's hands pawed over Chasen.

"He has no weapon."

"Get his wallet."

Turi tugged Chasen's wallet from his pants pocket, flipping through it with nervous fingers as he walked toward Rico. "There's not much here." He pulled out the two torn hundred-dollar bills and a few tens and ones. "Just this."

Chasen slowly lowered his arms, folding them across his chest. It was obvious to him that Rico was wired on some kind of drug. Drugs and loaded guns were a lethal combination. "Put the gun away, Rico, and we can talk business. Like gentlemen."

"Benita told me he was rich," Turi whined. "Where's the money?"

"Do you think I'd be stupid enough to come here with a wallet full of money? But we can still make a deal. Where's Paco?"

Rico waved the gun wildly around in a circle. "Fuck Paco. He's in Madrid." He scratched the top of his head with the gun barrel, then looked at Turi. "What do we do now?"

"We will be in much trouble," Turi responded as he started edging toward the door.

Chasen began advancing on Rico. "Where in Madrid?"

"He and the priest."

Chasen's fingers wrapped around the spray can under his shirtsleeve. "What priest?"

Rico didn't respond. His eyes bounced nervously from Chasen to Turi.

"Did they take the Mercedes?" Chasen asked. "Or is it still in the garage?"

Outraged, Rico rushed at Chasen, thrusting the barrel of the huge revolver into his stomach. "How do you know about the car? How?"

Chasen kept his voice low and calm. Rico might have his stash of drugs in the garage. "I'm only interested in seeing the car. Nothing else. The lock on the garage door is brand-new. You should have rubbed some mud on it. When did Paco leave?"

Rico's eyes glittered dangerously. He was right on the edge of pulling the trigger. "You know too much. How do—"

Chasen slipped the deodorant can from his shirtsleeve, spraying Rico directly in his eyes.

Rico screamed and dropped the gun to the floor.

Turi pounced for it, but Chasen's foot got there first. He kicked the revolver across the room, then landed an elbow on the side of Turi's head. Turi stumbled, fell to the floor, then did a fast crawl out the door.

Chasen picked up the gun and hefted it in his hand. It was a monster. He recognized the make and model. A Webley-Fosbery, a one-of-a-kind eight-shot automatic-revolver, made famous in John Huston's movie *The Maltese Falcon*. It was the same type gun used to kill Humphrey Bogart/Sam Spade's partner, Miles Archer, and the only true weapon that could be called an automatic-revolver due to its unusual design, which incorporated a revolving cylinder not linked to the gun's hammer, which was automatically cocked via the weapon's recoil action.

It weighed more than three pounds and fired a cartridge the size of Chasen's thumb. This gun was pitted with rust, the bluing worn down to bare metal in spots. The checkered wooden grips were split and scarred. He found the gun's stirrup latch and broke it open. Four of the chambers were loaded. It had to be close to a hundred years old.

Rico was on the floor, knuckling his eyes.

"You're lucky you didn't fire this, Rico. It would have blown your hand off."

"*¡Chupe mi pinga!*"

"I'll let Benita take care of your dick." Chasen reversed his grip on the Webley, held it by the barrel, and rapped the heavy butt on top of Rico's scalp. Not enough to knock him out, but enough to show how much harder it could get. "Relax. I'm not going to call the police." He hooked his foot around a chair leg, then sat down. "Tell me about Paco. And the priest. And what was in the Mercedes. Then you get your money."

Raul Tobias watched Keely's eyes flicker. She seemed to have trouble focusing.

Dr. Eva Bialba smiled down at her and said, "How are you feeling?"

Keely's mouth opened. She tried to speak.

"We believe you've had a reaction to the medicine you were given after the accident," Dr. Bialba explained. "Have you been on any other medication?"

Keely's eyes flickered again, then closed as she began breathing heavily.

Tobias clamped his hand on the doctor's elbow and led her away from the bed. "I have to talk to the señorita, Doctor. How long before—"

Dr. Bialba jerked her arm free of Tobias's grasp. "It could be an hour, four hours, or tomorrow morning. I have no way of knowing."

Tobias thrust his hands into his pockets and tried to conceal his anger. "I understand, Doctor. Send the bill to Jago Roldan's attention and it will be paid immediately."

Tobias watched Keely as her eyes again struggled to open. She had been very lucky. The Daimler had started a fire at the bottom of the canyon, sending up black smoke that could be seen for miles around. A passerby had caused him to stop his attempts at starting a rock slide. The fire department arrived, spotted Keely clinging to the tree, and rappeled down the mountainside in dramatic fashion to rescue her.

Tobias's Jeep SUV was banged up, the bumper bent, the grille crushed from hitting the limo. He'd have to get that repaired in a hurry. And then there was—

The buzzing of his cell phone interrupted his thoughts.

He pulled the phone from his jacket pocket and barked, "Who is it?"

"What the hell went wrong?" Daria Roldan asked in a voice throbbing with anger. "*Abuelo* is furious. One of his drivers dead. He told me that Keely is still alive. Is that true?"

Tobias cupped his hand over the phone. "I'm at the hospital now. The doctor says she will probably recover."

"Probably is not good enough."

"It was pure luck, a miracle she got out of the car," Tobias explained weakly. "The car landed on a ridge just long enough for her to—"

"Luck," Daria said harshly, "is something you are running out of."

"Calm down. I will take care of her for good tonight."

"In the hospital?"

"Why not?" Tobias said. "People die in the hospital all the time."

"I'm holding you to your promise, Raul," Daria said before breaking the connection.

Tobias put the phone away and surveyed the area. There was plenty of activity in the hallway—doctors visiting patients, nurses pushing wheelchairs or gurneys. No one was paying him any attention. Sometime during the night he would be able to finish the job.

Jago Roldan hobbled up the brown-veined marble staircase ascending to the second floor of his Madrid mansion. Flavio, the caretaker, was at his heels. Jago paused for a moment to catch his breath when they reached the second landing. There was an elevator, but today he preferred to use the stairs.

"Tell me again, Flavio. Have there been any incidents or breaches of security?"

"No, señor. None at all."

"Have you hired anyone new?"

"I would not do so without your permission, or on orders from Señor Tobias."

Jago pointed the tip of his cane toward Flavio's chest. "Visits from strangers? Especially priests?"

"As I told you on the phone. No such visits. The only persons allowed into the house were my staff and Señor Alroy, who was here for a short time."

Jago stabbed the tip of his cane into Flavio's stomach. "You didn't tell me about Alroy. When was this?"

"The very day before he died, Señor Jago, " said Flavio, licking his lips nervously. "I saw no reason to mention this to you, since the señor has—"

Jago ordered him to shut up. He marched down the wide carpeted hallway, taking no notice of the fact that, since he was not expected to return for several weeks, the carpets had not been vacuumed and the statues and paintings were coated with a fine film of dust. Jago pushed through the doors to his bedroom, then went directly to the door that led to his "treasure room." He removed a key ring from his pocket and thumbed through it until he had the right key.

Flavio hung back nervously. Neither he nor any of the staff were allowed into that room without Señor Jago's permission.

Jago went to the ceiling-high vault. It was manufactured by the same company that supplied the major Spanish banks. Three feet thick, solid stainless steel. The provider had assured him it could withstand the equivalent of a ton of dynamite. He entered his code onto the electronic pad, then yanked the L-shaped handle. The massive door swung open easily on its oiled hinges.

Jago gasped when he saw the wreckage. He stared with an open mouth. The vault's floor was littered with paintings. His masterpieces. He heard his knees crack as he bent down and picked up a small black plastic container. Alongside the container were the torn remains of a cardboard box. Kodak film. Someone had taken photographs of his paintings.

He used the cane to lever himself upright, then went to the humidified cabinet containing his most valuable treasure. He slid the drawer open slowly, fearful of what he would find. Nothing. Except the red velvet pouch that had held the *Professio*. It was gone!

Jago leaned his head back and let out a loud, half-sobbing scream.

Sam Alroy. How had he opened the vault? No one but Jago knew the code. And only Daria and Vidal knew that the *Professio* still existed and was secured in the vault.

Jago screamed again, causing Flavio to approach him, his lips quivering, his hands clenched. "Are you all right, Señor Jago?"

"Go call Mijas. Tell Tobias I want him here immediately. And Daria. And Vidal. Get them all here at once!"

Chapter Eighteen

Dave Chasen stopped for a much-needed drink at a bar with the uninspired name of El Toro, and went over everything he had learned from Rico and from rummaging through Sam Alroy's Mercedes in the garage next to the house.

The car had been picked clean, except for a small piece of paper that he'd found wedged between the driver's seat and the gearshift. It was a receipt from the Ritz Hotel in Madrid, dated August 18, the day before Sam Alroy's death. One day's lodging, meals, wine, and a driver—the total was sixteen hundred and forty-one dollars. What confused Chasen was the name on the receipt: John Clayton. Who was John Clayton?

Rico had been hesitant to talk about his good friend Paco Ramiro, but once he realized that Chasen had no intention of turning him over to the police, the young man spilled everything Paco had told him. What interested Chasen the most was that Paco had been at the beach when Alroy arrived, carrying an *envoltura grande,* a large envelope. Sam then sent Paco away for coffee. When he came back, Alroy was dead. Paco hadn't mentioned the envelope to the police, because he didn't want them to know he was on the scene before the murder took place.

Paco had taken Alroy's suit jacket, which held his wallet and passport. He had removed Alroy's money clip, car keys, and gold cigarette lighter from the dead man's pants, then drove off with the Mercedes.

The Mercedes was the real *tesoro,* Rico claimed. A treasure by itself, but inside the trunk had been a suitcase that contained Alroy's clothes, a camera, and a briefcase that held an ancient letter encased in glass bearing the names of Nero and Simon Peter. "That's Saint Peter," Rico had explained. "Paco was too stupid to know that."

"What about a laptop computer?" Chasen had asked.

Yes, the laptop was there, but of little value. Paco sold it to a student who attended a university in Madrid. Paco himself was now in Madrid. Rico had not been sure of the address, but, with the help of another hundred-Euro note, had given Chasen an approximate area in Madrid. "Just ask around. You'll find him, señor."

The camera, watch, briefcase, and ancient letter had been placed in the hands of Giles Dolius. Sam's jacket had been destroyed, the suitcase and clothes dumped into the Mediterranean.

Chasen made interlocking rings on the tabletop with the wet bottom of his whiskey glass. The killer had no interest in Alroy's personal possessions or the laptop. Whatever was in the envelope was worth more to him than anything else. The ancient letter had to be the *Professio* that Giles Dolius mentioned in his message to Jago Roldan the night of the party. Was that what was in the missing envelope?

Chasen finished his drink and headed back to the hotel. He spotted Ciro, the bellboy, smoking a cigarette in front of the hotel. "Ciro, I don't want you allowing anyone in my room when I'm not there. Understand?"

"*Sí, señor.*" Ciro quickly dropped his cigarette to the pavement. "But I had no choice this time. The police are in your room now, waiting for you. They do not appear to be very happy. They asked me many questions."

"Did you tell them Daria Alroy visited me?"

"No, señor. I acted dumb." Ciro smiled widely. "I am good at that."

Chasen's first thought was to get out of there fast. However, he'd have to talk to the cops sooner or later. The possibility of their arresting him was small. Even if someone had spotted him at El Gato Negro last night, there was no way to tie him to the murder. Keely Alroy would back him up. He'd found Dolius's body within twenty minutes of leaving her boat, and Dolius had been dead at least an hour prior to that. He handed Ciro the Ritz Hotel receipt he'd found in Alroy's Mercedes. "Hold on to that for me until I'm through with the police."

A uniformed officer was pacing back and forth in front of the elevators. The desk clerk must have given the policeman a signal of some kind, because he immediately asked to see Chasen's identification, then escorted him into an elevator. Another uniformed officer was waiting for them on the seventh floor. The two of them herded Chasen toward his room.

The door was open. Inspector Calvino was pawing through Chasen's suitcase. His clothes had been pulled from the closet and thrown haphazardly across the carpet. The message light on the phone was blinking. "What's going on?" he demanded.

Ernesto Osana, the young beach patrol officer, was standing at the far side of the room, an embarrassed expression on his face. Osana was wearing khakis and a denim shirt. Calvino's suit jacket was undone. His tie stopped short of his stomach. One of the buttons on his shirt was missing, exposing a slash of pale flesh.

Calvino's head hooked around and he glared at Chasen. "Where have you been?"

"What business is it of yours? And what do you think you're doing here?"

"I don't think. I know what I am doing." Calvino jerked his hand violently toward the bed. "Your pockets. Empty them."

"Not until you give me a damn good reason."

"I am the detective in charge of a murder investigation. You will do as I say, or you will answer my questions from behind bars."

"Who was murdered?"

"Miguel Alvarado," Officer Osana said, earning him a withering stare from Inspector Calvino.

Miguel Alvarado's name meant nothing to Chasen.

"Empty your pockets, or I will have you strip-searched," Calvino threatened.

Chasen went through his pockets and dropped the contents onto the bed. "Who is Miguel Alvarado?"

"Who *was* Miguel Alvarado," Calvino corrected. "He was a chauffeur in the employ of Jago Roldan. The car he was driving was forced off the road this afternoon. Señorita Keely Alroy was a passenger in the car at the time."

Chasen was shaken by the news. "What—"

Calvino held up a hand. "She was not seriously injured. She claims that the car was pushed off the road. She is presently in the hospital, as a precaution."

"What hospital? Where—"

"All in good time. First tell me where you were this evening."

"Nowhere. Just wandering around. Playing tourist."

"The desk clerk told me you left a note for Señorita Alroy, advising her that you would be late for your dinner engagement, and that you wanted directions to La Nogalera, our notorious homosexual district."

"I was shopping. Someone told me the stores in that area have the best prices."

"You have no packages. Your trip was unsuccessful?"

"Inspector, I want to see Miss Alroy. Unless you have a damn good reason to hold me, I'm leaving. Right now."

"Oh, I have the damn good reason. Last night you went to Señor Roldan's house."

"Is that a crime? Many people were there."

Calvino's fingers stroked the beak of his nose. "After the party you were driven by Miguel Alvarado, the man who was killed this afternoon. You were driven to Señorita Alroy's boat. Did you spend the night there?"

"That's none of your business," Chasen said.

"Incorrect," Calvino said. "Because late last night Giles Dolius, the operator of El Gato Negro, was murdered in his office. In the same manner as Sam Alroy." Calvino formed a gun with his hand, placing his index finger against his temple and pulling the imaginary trigger. "Bang. One shot to the head. You had been to Dolius's office earlier in the day."

"Who told you that?" Chasen asked.

"I have my sources, señor."

"I'm an investigator, Inspector. I learned that Giles Dolius was the most successful fence in your little precinct. If someone stole Sam Alroy's possessions, Dolius was the obvious buyer."

Calvino obviously didn't appreciate the "little precinct" remark. His face reddened and he threw out his arm in the direction of young Officer Osana. "And who told you that Dolius was a fence? Was it that officer?"

"No. I asked around the streets. Everyone knew about Dolius."

"And what did Dolius tell you at this first meeting, Señor Chasen?"

Nice try, Chasen thought. "There was only the one meeting, and he told me that he knew nothing about any items that may have belonged to Sam Alroy. I assume he told you the same thing."

Calvino picked up Chasen's sport coat from the floor. "A man was seen leaving Dolius's place last night. A man your age, your height, wearing a sport coat of this color."

"It wasn't me, Inspector."

"There has been another murder since you arrived in Tor-remolinos. A man by the name of Hector Garcia. A petty thief, an acquaintance of Paco Ramiro. What do you know of him?"

"Nothing."

Calvino swiveled on his heel to face Officer Osana. "You spoke to this officer before you spoke to me. Why?"

"His name was on the police report," Chasen explained.

"And Officer Osana chose not to inform me of this meeting." Calvino turned back to Chasen. "Which was very unwise of him."

He stopped short, staring at Chasen. He let the silence stretch out. Chasen breathed slowly through his nostrils. It was one of the oldest interrogation techniques in law enforcement: Be quiet and let the suspect sweat. If the Spanish detective was expecting him to be intimidated by the silence, he was in for a long wait.

Osana caught Chasen's eye and frowned. Chasen had put him in deep trouble with his commanding officer.

Calvino walked to the nightstand and picked up the hotel phone. "You have a message. Who is it from?"

"I'd have to listen to it first, Inspector."

Calvino grunted, then clicked on the phone's speaker. "David. *Halt din zoken. Zuruckfrufen.*"

"That's a friend of mine in Berlin, Inspector. He wants me to call him."

"An exact translation is what I want," Calvino insisted.

"Hold on to your socks and call me."

Calvino's brow furrowed. "What does he mean by that? Who is he?"

"Max Muller," Chasen said, pulling out an old standby from his time in Berlin. The CIA had determined that Muller was the most common surname in East Germany. "He's an insurance representative in Berlin who does work for my company."

Calvino wasn't satisfied. "What does he mean with the socks?"

"It's an old American expression, a joke."

"It doesn't sound funny to me," Calvino said. He began to examine the items Chasen had removed from his pockets and placed on the bed. He thumbed through the wallet, pulling out a picture of an attractive blond woman wearing a swimsuit. "Who is this?"

"My ex-wife."

Calvino came out with another photograph—a dark-eyed young girl.

"Your daughter, señor? She does not have the coloring of yourself or the woman you claim was your wife."

"Her name is Anica. She's an orphan in Colombia, Inspector. The daughter of an old friend."

Calvino shook his head and grunted, conveying his disbelief of Chasen's explanation of the pictures. He studied the cell phone, then picked up the small spray deodorant can. He held it cautiously under his nose and pushed the spray button, his nostrils wrinkling at the result.

He dropped the can to the bed and gestured for the uniformed officer who had escorted Chasen up from the lobby to leave. "You are not to leave Torremolinos without my permission. Is that understood?"

Chasen ignored the demand. "Where is Keely Alroy?"

"At the Costa del Sol Hospital in Málaga," Calvino said, marching briskly to the door. "You may go and see her. Your friend Officer Osana can no doubt provide you with directions."

Dave Chasen wrapped his arms tightly around Ernesto Osana's waist as the motorcycle zoomed in and out of traffic en route to the Costa del Sol Hospital in Málaga, some eight miles from Torremolinos. Osana had insisted on providing Chasen with the ride. He was obviously upset, worried about being demoted, or perhaps losing his job.

Osana wheeled the bike into the hospital's parking lot. He booted out the kickstand and removed his helmet. "I hope that your friend is all right," he said to Chasen.

"Thanks. What's with Inspector Calvino? I can understand him trying to hammer on me, but he seems upset with you, too."

"The inspector says that I was out of order when I spoke to you. That I should have cleared it with him first. One of my coworkers obviously agreed, because he informed Calvino of our meeting."

Chasen was anxious to see Keely, but he felt responsible for the young man's troubles. "What do you call informers here? In America we call Spanish informers *bañeras*."

Osana's face registered confusion. "Bathtubs?"

"Yes. Because a lot of their information goes down the drain."

Osana laughed loudly, then said, "Here they are *reclamos*. Decoy birds. As used in hunting ducks."

"Well, I'm going to be your *reclamo*. Under the usual conditions. That what I tell you is confidential. You didn't get it from me. Do you know where Monjils is?"

"Yes. It is . . . well known."

Chasen started walking toward the swinging doors leading to the hospital's emergency entrance. "You leave the Monjils. Turn left. You're walking through some narrow alleys, moving in a westerly direction. You walk fast for three minutes and forty seconds. You come to a street with a red, barnlike house on the corner. Two houses down is a run-down two-story place with a small garage on its north side. It's the only house on the block with a garage." He reached into his pocket and came out with a key. "This opens the padlock on the garage door. Inside you'll find the Mercedes that Sam Alroy was driving the day he was murdered."

Osana's eyebrows arched. "How can you know this? How did you obtain the key?"

Chasen patted Osana on the shoulder. "Don't ask your *reclamos* too many questions, or you'll never see them again. Just keep my name out of it. There's nothing of value left inside the Mercedes. Good luck, *amigo*."

A nurse gave Chasen directions to Keely Alroy's room. He spotted Roldan's man, Tobias, leaning against the wall in the hallway.

Rico had told Chasen how the *sacerdote loco*, the crazy priest, had saved Paco Ramiro by besting Tobias in a knife fight. What had impressed Rico even more was that Fallon then cut off Tobias's ponytail. Father John Fallon—wine connoisseur, burglar, and skilled street fighter. Chasen wondered what other talents the shadowy Jesuit possessed.

As Chasen placed his hand on the doorknob to Keely's room, Tobias unfurled himself from the wall and said, "Don't go in there."

"Shut up, or I'll cut off the rest of your hair," Chasen responded harshly before opening the door and quickly closing it behind him.

Keely was asleep, breathing deeply. An intravenous tube dripped its contents into her left arm. He placed a hand on her forehead. It was cool to the touch. She shifted her weight and moaned, but her eyes remained closed.

Chasen scanned the room, noting the one bed, a metal set of drawers. A door led to a small toilet with shower. The closet held her tattered clothing and scuffed sandals. The fourth-floor window overlooked the parking lot. The window could not be opened.

He sat down next to the bed and placed his hand on Keely's. Her eyes suddenly popped open. Her pupils were constricted from the medication. She stared at him blankly for a moment, then said, "Dave," in a weak, quavering voice.

"How are you feeling?"

Her fingers became claws and dug into his arm. "They tried to kill me, Dave. Don't leave me. Stay with me."

"I will," he assured her. "I will."

Gradually her grip weakened, her eyes closed, and she began to snore lightly.

Chasen went back out to the hallway. Tobias was nowhere in sight.

It was a sadistic thing for Fallon to do, cutting off the man's hair like that. A ponytail was usually worn by men to compensate for a receding hairline. Fallon's scalp job was like putting a brand on the Spaniard, and he'd no doubt want revenge.

Chasen spotted a janitor mopping the floors in the hallway, passed him a combination of American dollars and Euros, and asked him to stay in front of Keely's room and not allow anyone other than the nurse or doctor in until he returned.

Chasen found a cafeteria in the lobby and loaded up with ready-made sandwiches and cartons of milk. He used a pay phone in the lobby to return Hal Gevertz's call.

"My friend, you may have stumbled onto something extremely interesting," Gevertz said. "The *Professio*. There have been vague rumors about just such a document, allegedly signed by Simon Peter, in which he denounces Jesus Christ as the son of God."

Chasen remembered his car ride with John Fallon. The Jesuit had nearly run his sports car off the road when Chasen jokingly mentioned Saint Peter.

"What's it worth, Hal?"

"It's an old legend dating back to the Crusades. There is no documentation whatsoever. Nothing remains of Simon Peter's writings. The paper, the ink, could be dated, of course, depending on the condition. The odds are it's a hoax, a fake."

"Someone wanted it awfully bad. Bad enough to kill Dolius for it. I found someone who did see it. A kid who had no idea of what it was worth. He did say that the names Simon Peter and Nero were on it, and it was encased in glass."

Gevertz fell silent for a few moments and Chasen could almost hear his little gray cells grinding away.

"It is hard to set a price," he said at last. "There would certainly be interest from museums, foreign governments, church haters. Depending on the condition and how authentic it looks, I could see it bringing in several million dollars. Whether the document is real or not, the Catholic Church would be the party most interested. It would create a scandal, and the Church certainly doesn't need another one of those."

"You think the Church would come up with a few million bucks?" Chasen asked skeptically.

"Probably not. But I'm certain they'd agree to an exchange. The Vatican library's secret archives have some absolutely fantastic artifacts. Galileo's maps that nearly cost him his life. Leonardo da Vinci's sketches, his engineering drawings, and God only knows what else is secreted away in those dusty old vaults, and all worth vast sums of money."

A note of cunning entered his voice, one Chasen had heard before. "Another suggestion, my friend. If you do come into possession, bring it here, to Berlin. By train. Don't risk going through an airport. I would be most happy to handle the negotiations. I have many contacts in the Vatican."

"I have one myself," Chasen said. "A Father John Fallon. And he may have beaten us to the punch on this thing."

"If you get it, David, bring it to me. I can understand why Giles Dolius called Jago Roldan about the *Professio*. Do you remember that wave of museum thefts back in the seventies?"

"Before my time, Hal."

"Excuse me, young man," Gevertz said sarcastically. "There were some very, very fine old masters stolen. Prime stuff. Rembrandt, Daumier, Modigliani, Cézanne. Rumors were that Jago sponsored the thefts, and that he keeps the paintings locked up in a vault somewhere. Let me know if you come across something like those. *Tihe be cesher*."

"I hope to see you soon, too," Chasen said, breaking the connection.

Chasen relieved the janitor of his temporary guard duty, peeked in and saw that Keely was fast asleep, then wiggled the cell phone from his pants pocket and, even though it was the middle of the night in Washington, D.C., called Grady Devlin.

The CIA operations officer wasn't thrilled about waking Devlin up, but Chasen convinced him it was urgent.

"What the hell blew up?" Devlin grumbled nastily. "Couldn't this wait till morning?"

"Whoever handled my info request on John Fallon screwed up, Grady. We've got major problems."

Chasen could hear a voice in the background—a woman's voice complaining about the lights being switched on. The voice was too young to be Carly Sasser's, and besides, Carly was too savvy to complain about early-morning wake-up calls.

"Have your girlfriend put some coffee on," Chasen suggested. "This is going to take a while. Have you ever heard of something called the *Professio*?"

Chapter Nineteen

John Fallon pounded the door with the heel of his hand. The screeching wail of an electric guitar instantly stopped, and he could hear scrambling feet and furniture being hastily moved about. The aged wooden door had a thick coat of varnish. Deep gouges next to the white enamel knob suggested that someone had recently tried to break in.

"*¿Quién es?*" demanded a reedy, fear-struck voice.

"It's John Fallon. Open up."

The latch scraped softly out of its notch, the door opened, and one of Paco Ramiro's black eyes stared at him. Fallon entered to find a pair of chest-high amplifiers bracketing the redbrick fireplace. The furniture—a salmon-colored chenille couch with fringed pillows, a few wooden chairs, and some bronze-toned lamps—was grouped together at the end of the room near two tall windows. There were shades on the windows but no curtains.

"Sorry for the mess, Father." Ramiro had a garish purple-and-white guitar draped over one shoulder.

"Do you want a drink? Beer? Wine? Vodka? Whiskey? I've got it all."

"How's the arm?"

Ramiro flexed the arm that had been slashed by Raul Tobias's knife. "It's fine. No problem."

A plume of blue-gray smoke rose languidly into the air from a hand-rolled cigarette in a seashell-shaped glass ashtray. Next to the ashtray was a laptop computer and a gold cigarette lighter.

"I'm sorry about the laptop," Paco said. "That's not the one I sold to the girl. She told me she was a student the Universidad de Madrid, but I was out there all day and couldn't find her."

Fallon wasn't surprised. The Universidad was the largest state institution in Spain. "You told me her name was Emilia."

"Yes. I don't know her last name. The computer there. It's exactly like the one I sold her."

Fallon brought the burning cigarette to his lips and inhaled deeply. He let the smoke out slowly and waved it away with the back of his hand, then picked up the lighter. There were initials engraved on the bottom: *S. A.* For Sam Alroy.

"Did you hear what happened to Dolius?"

"Yes," Paco said, averting his eyes and drumming his fingers on the guitar.

Fallon realized the boy thought that he had killed the Greek fence. "Dolius was dead when I got to his club. The letter you gave to Dolius, the one in glass, was gone. Whoever killed Dolius has it, and I want it. Check with your friends in Torremolinos. See what they know about Dolius's murder. And forget about the girl at the college. I'll find her."

Fallon examined the G4 laptop. There were a few scratches on the titanium case, but no initials. "You're sure this is exactly like the one in Sam Alroy's car?"

"*Sí.* Exactly the same."

Someone turned on the shower in the nearby bathroom. Fallon could hear a voice, a young woman singing a sad love song in Portuguese.

Fallon held the gold lighter up to the ceiling. "Is this for sale?"

"Take it, Father. A gift for saving my life."

Fallon's wallet was fat with the money he had taken off Jago Roldan's desk and from Raul Tobias's pockets. "A worker is worth his hire, Paco. Saint Paul said that. I doubt that he meant it to apply to a thief, but you never know. How about a hundred dollars?"

Dave Chasen untangled himself from the blankets on the floor in Keely Alroy's hospital room when he heard her moving about.

Keely opened her eyes, blinking them into focus. "How long have I been here?" she said nervously.

Just then the attending doctor came by and explained that the fire rescue crew had given her a sedative after pulling her from the side of the cliff and that it had caused a reaction with the medicine she'd taken for the snakebite in Australia. "There's no reason to think there will be any more problems."

Keely felt dry-mouthed and slightly nauseous, but she wanted to get out of the hospital as soon as possible.

They took a cab to her boat, and, while Keely changed, Chasen brought her up-to-date on what had taken place: Giles Dolius's death and the fact that Inspector Calvino considered him a prime suspect.

Keely jumped on the information that Dolius had been shot in the head. "The same man who murdered Sam must have killed Dolius."

Chasen didn't believe that, but didn't press the point. "I'm going to Madrid to find Paco Ramiro."

"I'll go with you. You don't know Madrid. I do. And besides, I don't feel safe here. First Sam, then this Dolius character and the attempt on my life. I know Daria and Jago Roldan are behind it. They're worried that I'll inherit Sam's estate, and that's what I plan to do. I need a really good lawyer to fight them, and Madrid is just the place to find one. Let's take the bullet train rather than flying. It's almost as fast, and it will give us some time to talk."

Chasen had to agree that her knowledge of Madrid would be a plus, and she would be safer with him than on her own.

When Keely's bags were packed, they cabbed over to Chasen's hotel. She waited in the cab while he picked up his passport and money. For Inspector Calvino's benefit, Chasen assured the clerk that he was not checking out.

Ciro stopped Chasen as he was walking back out to the cab. "Señor. This time I didn't let her into your room. Paco's sister is out on the patio, by the pool, waiting for you."

Benita was sitting on the side of the swimming pool. She was wearing white shorts and an orange tank top. Her slender tan legs dangled in the water. She got to her feet when she saw Chasen. "I had nothing to do with what happened yesterday. I swear. It was Rico's fault, not mine."

"It doesn't make much difference now," Chasen said, looking at his watch. "Rico told me your brother is in Madrid. Do you have his address?"

"No," Benita said, balancing on one foot and dipping the other into the water. "Did Rico tell you anything about the laptop?"

Chasen felt certain that the little bitch had spoken to Rico, and knew exactly what had taken place. "You set me up, and now you're wasting my time."

He started to walk away. She ran to keep up with him. "I know the name of the girl Paco sold the computer to. And the school where she goes. Is that worth anything?"

Chasen removed his wallet and peeled a fresh one hundred Euro. "What's her name?"

Benita latched onto the bill, but Chasen held firm. "Her name and the name of the school."

"Emilia. She is in her first year at the Universidad de Madrid. That's what I know."

Chasen didn't release the money. "What does she look like?"

Benita stomped one bare foot on the damp cement. "She's short, fat, and has two gold rings, right here." She slapped her right eyebrow with her free hand. "That's all I know. Can I have my money now?"

Chasen released his fingers and Benita gave him a dazzling smile. "If you want to give me another one of these, I'll go to your room with you."

Chasen didn't bother to reply. Keely Alroy was dozing in the backseat when he returned to the waiting taxi.

Dave Chasen gazed out the window of their small, neatly appointed private compartment on the sleek Talgo 2000 bullet train as it sped across the plains toward Madrid and said, "I don't see any windmills."

Keely Alroy folded her arms across her chest. She had napped for nearly an hour after they boarded the train. The side effects from the medication she'd been given were gone. "There are a few left in La Mancha, but they're just there for the tourists to gawk at."

The train took a curve at high speed, and the coffee cups on the table rattled. Chasen dunked the last piece of croissant in the now-lukewarm coffee, then took a bite. He'd been debating just how much he should tell her. Keely knew he was holding something back. And he needed her help. "What do you know about a man by the name of John Clayton?"

Keely's stern look was replaced by a bemused smile. "John Clayton? Where did you turn that up?"

"I found Sam's Mercedes. Paco Ramiro stole it and stashed it in a garage. It was stripped of everything except this." Chasen rooted through his jacket pocket and came out with the receipt from Madrid's Ritz Hotel. "The date is one day before Sam was murdered. Who is Clayton?"

Keely examined the paper, tears welling up in the corners of her eyes. "I guess you could say it was Sam's alias. Sam's joke. Whenever he wanted to be by himself, to get away from everyone, to rent a cabin, or check into a hotel, he'd always use the name John Clayton." She looked up at Chasen. "Does Lord Greystoke mean anything to you?"

It did, but Chasen couldn't make the connection.

"As a kid, Sam was a major Edgar Rice Burroughs fan. John Clayton became Lord Greystoke, who became Tarzan, king of the jungle. Some joke, huh?"

"Some joke. Why was Sam in Madrid, at the Ritz Hotel, the day before he was killed?"

Keely also knew the reason for that. "The Ritz is where Sam and Daria's wedding reception was held. They stayed in Jago's Madrid mansion after they came back from their honeymoon. I remember Sam telling me the house was like a mausoleum. He hated it."

Keely used a book of matches provided by the train to light a cigarette. She exhaled a long plume of smoke, then turned to him. "I've leveled with you, Dave. When are you going to level with me?"

"Okay, you know I'm back with the CIA. Now, the rest of this is off the record, right?"

Keely refolded her arms across her chest and leaned back in the seat. "Where have I heard that before?"

She sat perfectly still for the next twenty minutes while Chasen told her most of what he knew regarding Sam's death, Father John Fallon, Giles Dolius, Paco Ramiro, and the burglary at Jago Roldan's house, the importance of the missing laptop computer, and what he had learned from Hal Gevertz regarding the *Professio*.

The mention of the *Professio* was what broke Keely's silence.

"God, is it real? Do you have any idea what kind of an impact a documentary on that would have? It's fantastic. How did Sam get his hands on it?"

"I was hoping that John Clayton could shed some light on that," Chasen said dolefully. "There are a couple of other wrinkles. Your brother came to the beach that morning carrying a big envelope. He sent Paco away for coffee. When the kid returned, Sam was dead, and the envelope was gone. Do you have any idea what was in that envelope?"

"No. How could I? Can you believe the beach boy, Paco? Could he be lying about the envelope?"

"Not for any reason I can figure out," Chasen said.

"What's the other wrinkle, Dave?"

"The guy I found on Jago Roldan's carpet. I'm pretty sure he's MI6. Someone else to look out for."

"MI6. British Intelligence. They want Sam's laptop, too."

"And the *Professio*. So does Grady Devlin. He got all hot and bothered when I told him about it. He sees it as a tool to blackmail the Church, which is probably what Jago Roldan had been doing."

Over the years, Devlin had had numerous skirmishes with the Church's spy agency, and turned nearly giddy at the chance of going after the *Cannoncciale*.

Keely reached her hand across the table and stroked Chasen's wrist. "Tell me. Why did you decide to go back to the CIA?"

Chasen interlocked his fingers with hers. "It's what I do, Keely. It's what I'm good at."

Chasen could have added that if he hadn't agreed to work the Alroy case, Grady Devlin would have dropped the dime on his occasional smuggling episodes.

"So, Agent Chasen, what's your next move?"

"Check into the Ritz. Talk to the driver Sam hired. Maybe that will shed some light on that envelope, and where Sam picked up the *Professio*. Then find Paco Ramiro and Emilia, the girl he sold the laptop to. His beach buddy, Rico, claimed he didn't have Paco's address in Madrid, but said he's living somewhere on the Calle Atocha. Do you know it?"

"One-star hotels, sex clubs, drug dealers, and scads of very young, very beautiful prostitutes imported from South America."

"That sounds like Paco's kind of place. I have one other

contact: Vidal Roldan, Jago's son. He has an art gallery in Madrid. He says he and Sam were friends. Did Sam ever mention Vidal to you?"

"No," Keely said. "I remember seeing Vidal at the party. My impression is that Daria hates him. What about this John Fallon character? The *Cannoncciale*. The pope's spy. He sounds fascinating."

"Fallon's the joker in the deck. He's after the *Professio* for obvious reasons."

"Do you think he'd kill for it?" Keely asked.

Chasen rubbed his forehead. "I don't know. We're dealing in probabilities, Keely. Did Sam take the damn thing from Jago in the first place? Or did he buy it from someone else? An unknown? I'm betting that he took it from Jago, but I want to pin it down. We know it was in his car when he was murdered. And Vidal, is he working with his father or against him? Everybody seems to want to get their hands on the *Professio*."

Chasen turned his gaze to the passing scenery. "Look at that. A windmill."

Chapter Twenty

The number of armed soldiers surprised Perry Bryce. A half dozen or more of them were standing, decidedly not at attention, at the entrance to the Centro Superior Información de la Defensa. Real soldiers, not glossy marionettes with patent leather knee boots and beehive-shaped hats. These guys wore baggy dark green uniforms with patches featuring slashed lightning bolts on their sleeves. They had the hard-eyed look of men who knew how to use the menacing-looking nine-millimeter Patchett-Sterling submachine guns cradled in their arms.

The interior halls of the buildings were swarming with them, clustered around stairwells, elevators, and the doors leading to where Bryce sat nursing a cup of really lousy tea in the canteen. His casual clothes drew looks of suspicion from the soldiers, but they kept their distance, loading up their trays with ham, runny scrambled eggs, and hard-bread toast, then settling down in groups of threes and fours and wolfing the food down in big gulps. It all made Bryce homesick for MI6's headquarters, where everyone dressed in civilian clothes and ate Chinese takeout.

Bryce pushed the food around on his tray with a fork, re-arranging it rather than actually eating. He'd been waiting for over half an hour. Another nine minutes, he told himself. If Garate didn't show up by then, he was getting up and leaving. Going back to London, if Garate was going to continue with his high-and-mighty attitude. Of course, he had given himself the same timetable fifteen minutes ago. If the Spaniard didn't help him break into Jago Roldan's mansion, what was the point of it all?

A shadow loomed over his shoulder. Garate had finally made an appearance, literally looking down his bony nose at Bryce. Garate motioned for him to come with a two-fingered gesture.

"Yes, master," Bryce whispered, wondering if he should bark and roll over. The Spaniard was deadly serious, though. Bryce had to hurry to catch up with Garate in the hallway.

"You can stop thinking about breaking into Jago's place," Garate said as they approached his office. "Jago had a visitor a few minutes ago. The car's license plates were traced to the Solvente Security Company. They're the ones who installed his vault fifteen years ago. I have the feeling that someone has beaten you to whatever it was you were after."

"The laptop," Bryce said.

Garate responded with a skeptical raising of one eyebrow. "I've received a call from Inspector Calvino. Keely Alroy and Dave Chasen have left the Costa del Sol. Their train will arrive here in Madrid shortly. I have men waiting at the station to follow them."

"What about the priest, John Fallon? I'm betting he was the bastard who knocked me out in Jago's house."

Garate pushed the door to his office, barely wide enough for him to pass through alone. "No sign of Fallon. I'll keep you posted."

"That's quite charming of you, you miserable asshole," Bryce whispered to the closed door.

Gilbert Fenalda made a clucking sound with his tongue, of the kind used to encourage horses. "Not possible. Just not possible at all, Señor Roldan."

Fenalda, a short man with cupped ears and sparse brown hair, had been the chief of security for Solvente Security for more than twenty years. He had been the man in charge of the installation of the vault and the entire security system at Roldan's house.

He used the vault's locking handle to help pull himself to his feet, brushed his knees, and inserted a magnifying glass back into its sculptured compartment in his briefcase. "No one has tampered with the locking device, and if they had, they would have met with defeat. I stake my reputation on that. Whoever entered your vault did so by using the code numbers."

Jago Roldan nodded his head slowly, then turned toward the corner of the room where his son Vidal was standing. "You hear that, Vidal? Someone had the code."

"It certainly was not me, Father."

Jago turned his attention back to Fenalda. "Thank you for your time, señor."

"My pleasure. If I may, I would like to leave some information for you regarding our new vaults. The technology has greatly changed. Rather than going through the bothersome chore of changing the code every few months, as we have advised in the past, we now have eye scanners, fingerprint scanners, making it absolutely certain that you, or whoever you so appoint, would be the only ones allowed entrance. If I can—"

"No. You can't," Jago said. "Send me the information with your bill. Good day."

Fenalda picked up his hat and case and bowed his way out of the room.

Jago placed the tip of his cane against the vault door and pushed lightly. The door closed with a loud, solid thunk.

"Sam had the code, Vidal. He stole my *Professio*. How? Who gave him the code?"

"Who knew the code?" Vidal countered. "Not I. It has been four or five years since you allowed me into the vault."

Jago slashed the air with his cane. "Only I knew the code!" He chastised himself for not changing the numbers, but, in reality, what difference would it have made? "Alroy was a genius in many ways. He must have found a way. Some way that even Fenalda could not comprehend."

"Have you questioned Daria?" Vidal asked.

"Questioned me about what?" Daria stood in the doorway, one hand on her hip, posed as if expecting someone to take her photograph.

"Where were you?" Jago said. "I told you to be here twenty minutes ago."

"Looking for Raul Tobias."

"Never mind Tobias. He has work to do."

Jago ran the tip of his cane through the curled fingers of one hand. "The vault wasn't broken into. Sam had the code. I want to know how he obtained it."

"*You* dare accuse me?" Daria said sharply.

"It wasn't me," Vidal protested. "I would be happy to take a lie-detector test to prove that."

"Tests," she hissed at him. "They are worthless. As worthless as you. How can you even—"

"Silence," Jago shouted. He glared at Daria. "Your husband was responsible for this. You should have at least known of his intentions."

Daria looked Jago squarely in the eye, her own icy blue eyes shimmering with anger. "How are you so sure it was Sam? Someone broke into your safe in Mijas and stole the hard drive from your computer, *Abuelo*. Someone who wanted to know all your secrets. That wasn't Sam, because he was dead. It could have been the one who is parading as a priest. Chasen told me the man's name was Fallon. John Fallon. Find him, *Abuelo*. He's your thief."

Jago sighed theatrically and studied the two of them. His family. Vidal. Not the strong successor he'd hoped for, but he was clever, crafty—tougher than he looked or acted. Daria, challenging him. She had fire; he had to give her that. But she was too impatient, too hotheaded.

"Enough of this," he said. "Concentrate on finding the

Professio. That is all that matters. Then we will find who was responsible for the theft in Mijas. Go. The two of you. I want to be alone."

Vidal was the first to move. Glad to be away, Jago knew. What was he hiding?

Daria came to him, picked up his hand in hers, and bestowed a slow, lingering kiss, trailing her tongue across his palm. "I'm sorry for what happened, *Abuelo.* Believe me, I had no part in it."

Jago watched as Daria strode confidently from the room, her short skirt swishing around her taut thighs with each step. He knew in his heart that if one of them was the traitor, it had to be Daria. Vidal would never dare to cross him, but Daria . . . she was a true Roldan—ready to pounce at the first sign of weakness. And old age was certainly a weakness.

He remembered their times together when the vault had first been installed. She had pretended to be fascinated with the paintings—to please him. She had pleased him in so many ways back then. He had tried to instruct her in the true value of the paintings. The genius of the artist, the uniqueness of the colors, the textures, the breathtaking majesty of what man could do with a simple brush and piece of canvas.

And he had told her of his own courage, of how he first came into possession of the *Professio.* How he had killed for it. How it had changed his life. Her life. But none of that impressed Daria. Her question was always the same: "How much is it worth, *Abuelo*?"

"Señor Roldan."

Jago snapped out of his reverie. It was Flavio, the servant.

"You have a call, Señor Jago. The man claims it is urgent. Something about hearing your confession."

Chapter Twenty-One

The reception clerk at the Ritz Hotel turned up his narrow-tipped nose when Dave Chasen informed him he wanted a room. A room without a reservation "was simply not possible" until Chasen mentioned Jago Roldan's name, and that his companion was the sister of Daria's late husband.

Chasen and Keely were treated to a complimentary al fresco lunch on the Ritz terrace while a "suitable accommodation" was made ready.

As Chasen toured the pale blue-and-apricot suite, he paid little attention to the elegantly furnished rooms, the Spanish-knot carpeting and coffered ceiling, the Regency bracket clock set into the center of the gilded, rococo-framed mirror over the marble fireplace mantel, the vases of fresh-cut flowers, the overflowing fruit baskets, or the view of the nearby three-hundred-acre Retiro Park.

His interests were the windows and the small bedroom balcony, which was separated from its neighbors by a good twenty yards. Whoever had made the attempt on Keely's life might try again, and Chasen wanted to be prepared.

He stood on the balcony and looked skyward. The suite was on the hotel's top floor, which meant that someone could drop down from the roof. There wasn't much he could do about that, other than to arrange the balcony furniture so that anyone trying to gain access from above would make a hell of a racket. He examined the lock on the sliding glass door leading to the balcony. It could easily be broken open with a screwdriver.

He found what he wanted in one of the spacious closets: wooden coat hangers. He brought four of them over to a circular marble-topped table with ball-and-claw feet and freed the round dowel used to hold a pair of pants from each hanger, then brought the dowels over to the sliding glass door's track. He dropped to his knees and slotted three of the dowels into the track, then scored a mark on the fourth dowel with the edge of the balcony railing, broke it off, and placed it so that it fit snugly against the other three.

"That should do it," he said.

Keely, who had watched the whole operation in silence, curled her tongue against her teeth and whistled softly. "I wonder what the maid is going to think about all this."

She yawned widely, then said, "I need a shower. And so do you. There's a razor in the bathroom. You could use a shave."

Chasen ran his hand across the stubble on his chin. He'd found it difficult to sleep at the hospital last night; then there was the hurried run for the train. He did need a shower, and some fresh clothes. "You go first. The hotel's chauffeur who drove Sam around Madrid is downstairs waiting for us. We'll see where he took Sam after we clean up."

He checked the telephone book, found a listing for Vidal Roldan's art gallery on Hermosilla, and placed a call from the bedside phone. Vidal wasn't in, and Chasen left a message with the sultry-voiced receptionist asking Vidal to contact him at the Ritz Hotel at his earliest opportunity.

Keely called out, "It's all yours."

Chasen stripped out of his clothes, grabbed a white terry-cloth robe from the closet, and entered the steam-filled bathroom.

Keely had a towel wrapped around her and was using the blow-dryer on her hair. There were scratches on her arms and legs as a result of her cliffside rescue. She gave him a demure smile as he slipped out of his robe and entered the large, circular-shaped shower. He was lathering his hair when the shower door opened and a naked Keely joined him.

"You missed a spot," she said, taking the soap from Chasen's hand and circling it slowly across his chest. The soap clattered to the tile floor as Chasen reached out for her. They kissed slowly at first, then more passionately, tongues exploring, hands feeling everywhere. Chasen braced himself against the shower wall as Keely reached down for his penis and guided him into her. They bounced against the wall, almost falling into the glass door before they disengaged. Chasen kneed the door open, picked her up in his arms, and, without breaking their kiss, carried her into the bedroom, where they fell in a tangled heap, feet kicking at the bedcover, elbows and knees slip-sliding on the silk sheets.

The phone rang and the voice mail kicked on. Chasen thought he heard Vidal Roldan's receptionist's voice as he trailed his lips across Keely's breasts.

Perry Bryce adjusted the volume on the cigarette pack–sized receiver and closed his eyes, concentrating on the unmistakable sounds of two people having sex filtering through his earphones. You really had to hand it to the Japanese, he thought. Their banking system was a mess. Gangsters ran the country, and, from what he recalled of his one and only visit there, they lived on a diet of whale blubber, raw fish, and those dreadful McDonald's burgers that tasted like anything but beef. Considerably worse than the indigestible meat that Britain produced, which had started him on the road to becoming a vegetarian.

In spite of all that, they somehow managed to stay on the top rung of the ladder when it came to manufacturing cheap and reliable clandestine electronic devices, such as the ones he had inserted throughout Chasen's hotel suite.

Lieutenant Garate's men had been waiting at the train station when Chasen and Keely Alroy arrived in Madrid. They'd notified Garate of the couple's destination the moment the cabdriver radioed it to his dispatcher.

Garate was well known at the Ritz Hotel and had no difficulty convincing the manager to stall Chasen at the reception desk until his men arrived and were lodged in the room directly below Chasen's. The delay gave Perry Bryce ample time to place the listening devices.

At least one mystery had been cleared up in Bryce's mind: Chasen's voice was definitely not that of the man who had assaulted him in Jago Roldan's office, which meant his guess was right, it had been Fallon. He leered up at the doleful face of Lt. Sil Garate. "They're playing honeymooners."

The CNI lieutenant plucked the earphones from Bryce's head, placed the receiver next to his ear and looked up at the ceiling. *"Van a desvencijar a la cama."*

Bryce's puzzled frown made it clear he didn't understand.

"They're going to wear out the bed," Garate translated.

Jago Roldan ordered the waiter to bring him another *café solo.* He'd been waiting at a streetside table at Cerveceria Alemania for more than thirty minutes. Enough time to draw the attention of a brazen, spindly-legged prostitute. She had stood over him, hands planted on her snakelike hips, and promised him an afternoon he'd never forget. And today she was giving a *"precio reducio por mayor de edad."*

Jago was insulted at the whore calling him an old man, and pitied the poor fools who were desperate enough to accept her offer.

He ran his thumb across the sapphire crystal on his watch, hating the fact that his time was at the mercy of a Vatican assassin and thief. The phone call from the man who wanted to "hear his confession" was no doubt the so-called priest, John Fallon—the burglar who had stolen Jago's hard drive. "Go to the Cerverceria Alemania, Señor Roldan. I have something that belongs to you. Come alone. Remember, you are being watched."

Jago had come alone, leaving his driver parked several hundred yards away. Raul Tobias was out chasing down Paco Ramiro, and he certainly didn't want either Vidal or Daria for company.

Jago took off his sunglasses and held them over the coffee cup, steaming the lenses. He was polishing them with a bar napkin when a man in a black jacket dropped into the chair opposite him. He had a shiny titanium-skinned laptop computer in one hand.

"Waiting long?" John Fallon asked. He waved the laptop in front of Roldan's face, then tucked it under the table. "Are you ready to deal?"

"What is it you want?"

"I removed the hard drive from your office in Mijas. I can describe the room. Dark paneling, some bullfighting memorabilia, a very nice flattop red mahogany desk, Cuban mahogany would be my guess, and a well-stocked humidor. Oh, by the way, the Joan Miró oil hanging over the wall safe, *Blue Sun*, is a forgery. The original is in a storage locker in Berlin."

"You're Fallon. The priest," Jago said.

Fallon whisked one of the Cuban Cohiba cigars he'd taken from Jago's humidor from his jacket pocket and held it out to Roldan.

Jago slapped the cigar from Fallon's hand and half rose from his chair. He settled back down, then said, "I do not like dealing with thieves, señor."

Fallon produced another cigar and took his time lighting it. He toasted the end, making sure that Roldan got a good look at Sam Alroy's gold lighter.

"I've always thought that even a so-so cigar tastes better when lit with a proper lighter."

He blew a perfect smoke ring and slid his finger through

the hole. "Don't talk down to me. You deal with thieves and murderers every day of your life."

Jago's eyes were riveted on the lighter. If Fallon had Sam's lighter, then the laptop must also be Sam's.

The waiter came and Jago waved him away with an angry jerk of his hand.

"What is it you want?" he repeated.

"A cup of coffee. Mind if I borrow yours?" Fallon dragged Jago's cup across the wobbly white plastic table. "And Saint Peter's *Professio*."

Jago's eyebrows rode up above the sunglass frames. "What are you proposing in return? The laptop? My hard drive? How do I know that they are not fakes? Or that you have not damaged them?"

"They're not fakes, I assure you. I can tell you exactly what is on your computer, Jago. Letters to your most prestigious clients. They make interesting reading, since it proves that you have been cheating them for years. There's a list of all your holdings. I'm sure the Spanish government would be interested in those, especially since you haven't been paying taxes on many of them." Fallon paused for another slow puff on the cigar, then said, "For a man your age, you're not in bad shape. You look good. Good enough for an open coffin."

Jago raised his cane and slashed it across the table. Fallon caught the cane easily in one hand and yanked it from Jago's grasp.

"Don't try that again. I don't turn the other cheek. Take a few deep breaths, Jago. You wouldn't want to have a heart attack. How could you be sure I'd give you your last rites?"

Jago studied the man closely. The jacket he was wearing could have come out of his own personal closet. The shirt also. The *sacerdotes* were criminals: rapists, sodomites, molesters of children, petty thieves who stole from the collection box. This one was different only in that he was a bigger criminal than the others.

"What do I call you? Father Fallon? Or are you a bishop? A cardinal? What?"

"John will do for now." Fallon placed the cane on the table, then said, "The sooner you deliver me the *Professio*, the sooner you get back your hard drive." He tapped his foot against the computer under the table. "And Sam Alroy's laptop."

Jago's hand moved slowly across the table. He picked up the gold lighter and examined it. There was an inscription on the bottom: *S. A.* Sam's initials.

"Perhaps we can come to an arrangement. I would be willing to pay—"

"I know you have enough money to air-condition hell. And in your case, that might not be a bad idea. But I don't want money. I want the *Professio*. I figure your man with the bad haircut killed Giles Dolius for it."

"I will need some time," Jago said. "A day or two."

Fallon stood up and tapped an inch of cigar ash into the coffee cup. "Then you don't have it. That's very disappointing. You'd better find it, old man. And soon."

Jago watched as Fallon walked out to the plaza, the laptop swinging rhythmically at his side, like a man without a problem in the world.

The priest was too confident. Too cocky. Still, he had revealed more information than he had obtained. The Church did not have the *Professio*. As for Giles Dolius, he was a small-time criminal. How did he get his grimy hands on it? Who killed him? The same person who killed Sam? None of it made any sense.

Fallon's statement "your man with the bad haircut" referred to Tobias. He had cut his hair, but how did Fallon know of this? What was the bastard's real reason for mentioning it?

Jago snapped his fingers for the waiter. "A fresh *café solo*," he ordered. "And send a glass of wine to that skinny whore over there."

The impudent priest thought he knew something about art. The Joan Miró hanging over the safe in Mijas was no forgery. It was one of the few works of art that Jago had purchased legitimately through Vidal, and was therefore able to put on display.

The waiter came with the coffee. The prostitute waved at him with her glass of wine, mistaking his generosity as a sign that he was interested in what she had to offer.

"Go away," Jago said bluntly when she approached his table. He rose to his feet and when he walked right by her, she hurled an insult at his back.

"Pajero!"

Jago turned around, poised to slap her sun-bitten face. Then he laughed it off and continued on his way. *Pajero.* Street slang for someone who would rather masturbate himself than have sex with another person. He could not recall when the last time was that he had been reduced to engaging in self-gratification, but there was no doubt in his mind that that would have been his choice if the only other option was sleeping with this whore.

Arlington, Virginia

Carly Sasser was surprised to see the door open to Grady Devlin's office when she arrived at her desk a few minutes before eight in the morning. The smell of cigar smoke verified that he was there. She leaned into his office and saw him sprawled out on one of the chocolate leather chairs, cigar in one hand, the telephone in the other.

Carly mouthed a silent "good morning."

"Yes, sir," Devlin said into the phone, ignoring her.

"I want some goddamn action," Director Hoyt said. "I thought I made that plain yesterday."

"You did, sir." From the way Hoyt was speaking, Devlin figured the little prick was on his treadmill. He was nearly out of breath. "There have been some new developments.

When I arrived this morning there was a message from Dave Chasen. He's in Madrid. There was an attempt on Keely Alroy's life, and—"

"And tell someone who gives a shit. I want the laptop. Alroy's software. What have you done about that?"

"We've identified the young woman who we believe has it. A student at the University of Madrid."

"Well, then, go and get the damn thing."

Devlin gnawed on the end of his cigar. "So far we've only got a first name, Emilia. There are one hundred and fifty thousand students, and we're trying to—"

"Don't complain and don't explain, Grady. Just do it. I have to fly up to Canada and consult with our loyal allies on the expanded border patrols. Those lefty bastards don't want to contribute a dime, of course. I want this Alroy matter cleared up by the time I get back. Get it?"

"Got it, sir. Have a nice trip." Devlin dropped the phone on its cradle and called to Carly. "Get me Chasen on his goddamn cell phone."

Devlin fumed and puffed on his cigar while he waited. Hoyt was really holding his feet to the fire. If this didn't come off, it would give the director all the ammunition he needed to have Devlin taken down a notch. It was beginning to look like Chasen had been a bad choice after all. The Ritz. Why the hell couldn't he stay at one of the hotels the Company had contracts with? The *Professio*. Now that was an interesting development.

Carly Sasser came into the room, carrying a fresh cup of coffee. "I have Mr. Chasen on line one," she said.

Devlin pointed two fingers at the coffee cup. "Brandy," he said, then snatched up the phone. "Why the Ritz, buddy?"

"Sam Alroy stayed here the night before his murder," Chasen said. "Under an alias, John Clayton. Clayton was Lord Greystoke," Chasen explained. "Tarzan."

Carly leaned over and poured two fingers of brandy into Devlin's coffee cup. He nodded his thanks. "Great. The guy was a comedian. What's the significance of his night at the Ritz?"

"That's what I'm working on. I've got a meeting set up with the limo driver he hired while he was staying at the hotel. I want to retrace his movements, learn who he met with. He could have shared the files from the laptop with someone while he was in Madrid. I'd like to find just who he met with while here in Madrid."

Devlin studied the frayed end of his cigar. "The laptop, son. We know who has it. Some kid at the University of Madrid."

"I was hoping you could do the groundwork on that, Grady. There can't be too many freshman students named Emilia. I don't want to scare her away. She bought a stolen laptop, and if I go around asking for her, she may go underground. You must have someone who can access or break into the school's record center, pick up a last name, what classes she's taking. In the meantime, I have a good lead on Paco Ramiro. He may know more about Emilia than his sister Benita did, and I'd like to hear his version of what took place on the beach the day of Sam's murder. We only have Rico's word that Paco told him Sam had an envelope with him, and that the killer must have taken it. What was in the envelope? Where did Sam pick it up? Why was it so important to the killer?"

Devlin sampled the coffee. "The *Professio* interests me, too. I don't figure Sam Alroy for a thief, and he has no history as an art collector. Don't lose sight of it. How's the grieving sister doing? Is the CIA paying for two rooms at the Ritz, or just one?"

Chasen ignored the second question. "She's hanging in there," he said.

"I've been given orders from above, Dave. You pull this out of the fire real quick, or it's back to St. Petersburg." He hung up, then held the cup up to Carly. "You make great coffee, kid."

"I thought you were stopping by last night," Carly said, returning the brandy bottle to Devlin's desk drawer.

"Blame Hoyt," Devlin responded, draining his cup. "He's got me working around the clock. Maybe tonight."

Perry Bryce rewound the cassette and listened again to Dave Chasen's telephone conversation. It was a shame that Chasen hadn't used the hotel phone, so that he could have heard both sides, but the other man had to have been his superior at the CIA, Grady Devlin.

Chasen's schedule for the day was interesting—hiring the hotel limo driver who had driven Alroy. Why had Alroy found it necessary to use an alias? Tarzan, of all things. The most interesting bit of information was the envelope Alroy may have had with him when he was murdered. Would Alroy trust an envelope to hold anything as valuable as the *Professio*? And then there was the student, Emilia. *"She bought a stolen laptop."* Emilia, a freshman. Where? How many schools were there in a city the size of Madrid?

Sil Garate would certainly know the answer to that, but Bryce had no intention of sharing any of Chasen's conversation with the Spaniard. He pushed the recorder's erase button and rewound the tape.

Chapter Twenty-Two

"I'm ready," Keely Alroy said, snatching up her purse and giving herself a final once-over in the hall mirror.

Dave Chasen eyed himself in the mirror also, knowing that Grady Devlin and the bean counters at CIA headquarters would have a conniption fit when they saw the bill for the shirts, tie, and underwear he'd purchased from the Ritz in-house boutique. Devlin's call had come in just as he'd returned from his short shopping spree.

At least he'd be well dressed for dinner tonight. Vidal Roldan's receptionist had left a message on the voice mail. Señor Roldan wished to meet with Señor Chasen at Sobrino de Botín at eight-thirty.

Midafternoon Madrid greeted them with a blanket of heat and an odor of leaves, grass, and freshly turned earth. Tiny beige-and-white birds were hopping from branch to branch in the elms and old magnolia trees encircling the Ritz Hotel's driveway.

"Señor Chasen?" said a plump white-haired man with a professionally ready smile. He was neatly dressed in a tan poplin suit, white shirt, and brown-and-white pin-dot tie. His immaculately groomed mustache matched the snowy color of his hair. He wore a pair of gold-framed sunglasses. "I am Felipe Marcario, your driver."

Chasen shook his hand and introduced Keely. "You drove her brother, John Clayton, some days ago."

"The hotel has informed me that you asked for me purposely. I am honored that Señor Clayton found my services adequate."

Felipe led them to a vintage black Cadillac, polished to mirror brightness, of the style no longer produced—sharkfin fenders and lathered with chrome. He held the back door open for them. The interior smelled of old leather and pine spray, which did not completely mask the lingering scent of tobacco.

When Felipe was situated behind the wheel, he turned to look at his passengers. "And where may I take you today?"

Chasen edged forward, the leather squeaking as he moved. "There has been a tragedy. Señor Clayton was murdered. The very morning I assume you drove him from the hotel back to the airport."

Two deep clefts formed between Felipe's eyebrows. He made the sign of the cross against his chest. "I am truly sorry."

"What we'd like you to do is drive us to the same places you took John."

Felipe turned over the engine and lowered the sun visor as he merged into traffic.

"I first met Señor Clayton when he arrived at the Cuatro Vientos Airport on the afternoon of eighteenth August."

"That's not the main airport, is it?" Chasen asked.

"No, señor. It is a civilian airport. Cargo and small private planes."

"Did he have any luggage?"

"One suitcase and a computer. The portable kind. Nothing else."

"Did you take him right to the Ritz?"

"No, señor. He wanted to make a purchase. A briefcase. 'A good sturdy briefcase' was what he wanted. I suggested Loewe's, our finest leather store. Señor Clayton was in Loewe's for a short time. When he came out, he had a beautiful leather case."

The Cadillac motored slowly along a broad, tree-lined boulevard. The air conditioner whined and kicked into action.

"Okay," Chasen said. "I don't think we have to go there."

Keely leaned back into the rolled-leather seat and lit a cigarette with a Ritz matchbook. "Where did you take him next?"

Felipe maneuvered the Caddie back into traffic. "Señor Clayton then told me to drive him to an address in Puerta de Hierro, an area of magnificent private residences."

"Let's go," Chasen said.

Puerta de Hierro was Madrid's answer to Beverly Hills: stately Spanish colonial–style mansions with red-tiled roofs of low pitch or flat roofs rimmed with battlemented parapets, walled off by well-groomed privets and blossoming oleander hedges.

There was very little traffic. Felipe stopped the Caddie in front of a wrought iron gate with the figure of a peacock in the center. "This is the address. Señor Clayton used the telephone there on the post. A man came in a car and let us in the gates. I drove to the house and parked in front. He went inside. I waited."

"Did my brother take the laptop computer or briefcase with him?" Keely asked.

"Just the briefcase, señorita. The computer was placed in the trunk along with his suitcase when I met him at the airport. He was gone thirty, perhaps forty minutes. I had the feeling that he was not expected. That no one was expected. The man who let us in the gate got into an argument with two other men who were dressed in swim trunks. One stayed with me. The other returned in minutes, tucking his shirt into the trousers.

"I was told not to leave the car, which I had no intention of doing. There were dogs. Five, six, I don't know. Big dogs. One of them tried to eat the tire. I had to sound the horn to get him away from the car."

"Did he still have the briefcase with him when he left the house?" Keely asked.

"Oh, yes. He hugged it to his chest as if it were a child."

Chasen climbed out of the Cadillac. He could hear dogs barking. He leaned his head into the car window and looked at Keely.

"Want to take a guess at who lives here?"

"Jago Roldan," she said.

The barking was becoming louder. Chasen picked up the gate phone. There was a hum; then a male voice came on the line: *"¿Quién vive?"*

"¿Está Señor Jago Roldan en casa?"

Two sleek gray-brown Dobermans pounded against the wrought iron gate at the same time the man on the other end of the line said, *"No. ¿Quién vive?"*

Chasen clicked the receiver into its cradle and climbed back into the Cadillac.

One of the dogs had his jaws locked around the gate's ironwork. He gnawed on it as if it were a bone.

"It's Jago's place, all right. Let's get out of here, Felipe. Where did Clayton go next?"

"Urbanización Azca, our finest business district, which is known to many as 'Little Manhattan.' "

"Let's take a look at it," Chasen said.

The trip took less than ten minutes. They passed dozens of dreary towers of redbrick buildings crowned by gray slate roofs and spires. Then they came to an area with clusters of modern skyscrapers. Chasen spotted the names of major United States companies on the buildings: IBM, Shell, and Proctor and Gamble, along with the usual groupings of American and international banks. There was a resemblance to Manhattan, except that in Madrid the buildings seemed to top out at fifty to sixty stories.

Felipe pulled up in front of twin silver-tinted office buildings consisting of tall sheets of reflecting glass—like vertical lakes. "I parked here. Señor Clayton was gone close to an hour."

"Did he go into one of those buildings?" Keely asked.

"I am not certain, señorita. He could have visited the buildings down the street. I did not notice exactly where he went. He took the briefcase with him."

"What about the computer?" Chasen asked.

"That remained in the trunk."

Chasen grabbed the door handle. "Let's take a look."

Twin buildings, twin lobbies, each with a spacious ground floor of shops and restaurants. The lobby register listed hundreds of offices housing accountants, attorneys, Realtors, and engineers.

Keely waved a hand angrily in the air. "This is hopeless. Sam could have gone anywhere."

Chasen agreed.

When they were back in the car, Felipe said, "When he returned, Señor Clayton had an envelope."

"Describe it," Chasen said.

"Tan." Felipe held his arms shoulder width. "It did not appear to be heavy."

"Did you see any writing on the envelope?"

"No, señor."

"How did Clayton treat it? As if there were something valuable inside? Something fragile? Did he put it in the new briefcase?"

"No, señor. He simply tossed it on the seat as he was getting back in the car."

"Did he ever place the envelope in the briefcase?"

Felipe thought about that for a second. "No. Never. "

Keely said, "What was your next stop?"

"Señor Clayton told me to drive him to the Ritz. I did so, and did not see him until very early the following morning, when I drove him back to the Cuatro Vientos Airport. Where may I take you now?"

"The Calle Atocha," Chasen said. "We've got some time

before dinner. Let's spend it trying to run down Paco Ramiro."

The limo ride had turned out to be a worthwhile investment, Chasen thought. Sam Alroy arrived in Madrid at a private airport, and his first move was to purchase a briefcase. The briefcase was a no-brainer. Sam bought it to hold one item only—the *Professio*. He wasn't in Jago's house very long, so he must have known where the *Professio* was kept. Jago wouldn't leave it lying around as a desk ornament. It had to be under lock and key.

Chasen looked at the car's window, catching his reflection from the hazy glare. The dissatisfied expression on his face stared back at him *You're missing something, pal,* he told himself. *Something big.*

The evening had cooled down to a pleasant, windless eighty-five degrees. The streets of Madrid were filled with pedestrians, the majority being young Spaniards, men in jeans and sweatshirts, women in tight-fitting casual clothes of bright colors.

The crowd in front of Sobrino de Botín was mostly well-heeled tourists, decked out in denim and cashmere, waiting patiently to gain entrance to Botín, reputed to be the oldest restaurant in the world, and the place Ernest Hemingway made famous in the final two pages of his novel *The Sun Also Rises.*

Vidal Roldan was there waiting for Chasen. He seemed annoyed when he saw that Keely had come also, but he made a quick recovery. He bowed and bestowed a kiss on her hand in a continental manner. "I'm sorry I didn't get to speak to you at my father's party. I loved your brother very much. I miss him."

"I do too," Keely said.

Vidal seemed nervous and hesitant to talk. Chasen broke the ice. "We didn't get to meet at El Gato Negro."

"By the time I arrived, the police were there. The owner had just been murdered," Vidal said.

"Giles Dolius. Did you know him?"

"No. Do you think his murder was related to Sam's death?" Vidal asked. "Possibly the same killer?"

"Dolius was a fence. Whoever killed Sam may have been using Dolius's services. What has your father said about the murder?"

"He is as confused as everyone," Vidal responded, stretching on his toes to look over the crowd. "I made reservations, but Botín is always mobbed."

"Your niece, Daria, visited me at my hotel in Torremolinos," Chasen said. "In fact she persuaded the bellboy to let her in while I was out shopping. She may have heard the message you left for me."

"Daria is excellent when it comes to persuading men to help her," Vidal said sardonically.

One of the waiters called out a table seating. The name wasn't Roldan. Vidal looked at his watch and scowled.

Someone slapped Chasen on the back.

"Dave. Good to see you." Father John Fallon took Keely's hand and brought it to his lips. "You must be Keely Alroy. My condolences on the loss of your brother. A mass will be served in his memory at the Vatican every day for a year." He released her hand. "I'm John Fallon. Is everyone hungry? Connie and I were expecting some friends, but they had to cancel at the last moment. Why don't you join us?"

At first Chasen didn't recognize the blonde at Fallon's side. She looked much more attractive out of her flight attendant's uniform. She was wearing a jade-colored tank dress and matching three-inch heels. She flashed bright teeth at him and said, "Nice to see you again."

Fallon was dressed casually—dark slacks, a black polo shirt, a fashionable black sport coat. The tips of several cigars peeked out above the coat's breast pocket.

"Are you going to keep wearing black until they make

something darker, Father?" Chasen said. "Say hello to Vidal Roldan. I think you're familiar with his father."

"I had coffee with Jago this afternoon," Fallon said.

Vidal reluctantly offered his hand to Fallon, who squeezed it hard enough for Vidal to shake it lightly as it was released. He glanced at his watch again. "I have reservations."

"Then why are we standing out here?" Fallon smiled. "Follow us."

Fallon gently pressed his way through the crowd, whispered something into the maître d's ear, and was led to an empty table at the back of the main room that provided a view of the open kitchen, charcoal hearth, and immense tile oven used to roast whole suckling pigs.

Vidal stood stiffly by his chair. "I had specified a table upstairs."

Fallon waved him to his seat. "Where Jake Barnes and Lady Brett dined in *The Sun Also Rises*? It's stuffy up there, and all the Hemingway junkies treat it as a shrine. If he were alive and working on the book now, he'd want this very table."

One of the white-hatted chefs hurried over, and Fallon shook his hand vigorously. Chasen spotted Fallon passing a small envelope to the man, who beamed at him before returning to the kitchen.

Fallon settled himself next to Keely. Connie sat on the other side, while Chasen chose the seat to Fallon's right, which gave him a good view of the bar and front entrance. Vidal scraped the chair legs across the tiled floor as he scanned the area with a frown. It was obvious he felt intimidated by Fallon.

"Please allow me to suggest the bill of fare," Fallon said. "And to take care of the check." He began speaking in Spanish to a hovering waiter.

Almost immediately platters of *tapas*—mushrooms, salads, baby eel, shrimp, and mussels—were bused to the table.

Another waiter came from the bar carrying a tray with old-fashioned glasses. Each one had a single sugar cube sitting in a pool of emerald green liquid. The waiter placed a glass in front of each of them, and then used a carafe to drizzle water into the glasses. As the sugar cube crumbled, the green liquor turned milky.

"Is that what I think it is?" Connie asked.

Fallon picked up his glass. "If you're thinking of the green goddess, absinthe, then you're right."

Keely leaned over and sniffed the glass. "Absinthe? I thought that was illegal."

"It was," Fallon said. "Still is in some places. They bottle it in France, but it can't be sold or used there. It can be exported to certain countries, and Spain happens to be one, so enjoy."

He noticed Vidal's hesitancy in sampling his drink. "Give it a try. Hemingway loved it. So did Toulouse-Lautrec, Gauguin, and Van Gogh. You own an art gallery, don't you, Mr. Roldan?"

Vidal said, "Some people think that absinthe is what drove Van Gogh to kill himself."

Fallon waved the thought away with his hand. "Nah. Lead in the water pipes. That's what did Van Gogh in. The prohibitionists of the times used absinthe as a whipping boy." He raised the glass to his lips and took a sip.

Keely was the first to follow suit. She outdid Fallon by taking a much bigger sip than he had, then ran her tongue across her lips. "It's good."

"A hundred-forty proof, so don't get carried away," Fallon cautioned.

After another round of absinthe was poured, the Jesuit took his large stag-horn-handled corkscrew from his pocket and, amid much discussion with the wine steward, uncorked several bottles. They sniffed the corks, sampled the wine, and nodded with each other in agreement.

"Wonderful people, the Spanish," Fallon said, raising a

glass. "You have to hand it to them. Look at this place. It dates back to seventeen twenty-five. Now, that's tradition. And they've had their hard times. As recently as Franco. Any country that could survive the *caudillo* deserves our applause. A bumbler, a fool, a racist, a coward. He was conned into thinking that Spain had vast oil wells, so he sank a fortune into drilling for them, and came up dry every time." He warmed to the tale, drawing in everyone at the table with his gaze. "Franco's personal chauffeur hoodwinked him, claiming he had a process that could make gold out of iron ore. An Austrian persuaded him that by mixing water with distilled water and some secret ingredients, he could produce synthetic gas superior to the real thing. Franco swallowed it all—hook, line, and sinker. If stupidity were an art form, he could have been Michelangelo. He was without question the most fortunate man of his generation."

"Tell me, Father," Keely said, "who do you consider the most fortunate man of *this* generation?"

"Oh, that's easy. William Shatner."

Keely's eyes widened. "William *Shatner*? The actor?"

Connie aimed a half-eaten shrimp at Fallon. "You mean the *Star Trek* guy?"

"Yep. An absolutely terrible actor, with that guaranteed-not-to-get-him-laid toupee and a quart-of-bourbon-a-day puss, yet he stumbled into high-paying movie and TV roles and commercials one right after another. God does indeed move in strange ways."

Connie laughed so hard she drew looks from the nearby tables.

Chasen leaned toward Fallon, and said, "You're a knowledgeable guy, John. What can you tell me about an ancient document? The *Professio*. Ever heard of it?"

Fallon gave him an appraising look. "Indeed I have. Let me tell you a story."

"I'm not interested in one of your stories," Vidal said.

"You'll like this one," Fallon assured him. "It's about

Saint Peter. The time is thirty-four years after the death of Jesus Christ. Simon Peter. Now, there was a real man. Brilliant. Strong. Tough. He had to be. He continued preaching the word of Jesus all over Israel and Egypt. Then onto Greece, and finally Rome, the capital of the world at that time.

"Nero was the man in charge. A real psychopath. He had his mother murdered supposedly because she didn't applaud loud enough at one of his concerts. Nero considered himself to be a great singer, musician, and poet. Think of a druggie rock star as the president of the United States." He smiled at the analogy.

"Nero was into orgies, plundering the treasury and starting fires. To keep the locals from coming after him, he decided he needed a great enemy. He settled on the Christians. The streets of Rome were kept alight with Christians nailed to crosses and set afire. Fire did something for Nero. He believed it inspired him to write his poetry and ballads. But the fires got out of hand. A good portion of Rome was destroyed. So he blamed the Christians again. Rounded them up and brought them to his Circus Maximus, on the Tiber, near Vatican Hill.

"It was a magnificent structure for its time: two thousand feet long, three hundred feet wide, three-tiered. There was standing room only when they dragged the Christians out.

"The more merciful death was to be wrapped in animal skins and thrown to the wild beasts. Thirty thousand drunken Romans were in the stands yelling, 'Make them dance,' as Christians were covered with pitch and set on fire.

"We know all this from documented history archives. After that it gets pretty murky. One story, and a lot of this stuff comes from stories passed on from generation to generation—"

"Like the Bible," Chasen said.

"Exactly," Fallon responded. "We do know that Saint Peter was captured. There are several versions of what took place next. One is that he, his wife, Naomi, and his daughter, Jepthanaia, were thrown into prison with hundreds of condemned Christians. Peter was their leader. The other prisoners looked up to him. Worshiped him.

"Another story has it that Nero wanted to punish Peter in a much more devious manner than just throwing him to the lions or the dogs, or burning him on a cross. He wanted to destroy Peter's faith, and the faith of those who believed the message he preached. If Peter would sign a document proclaiming Christ was not the son of God, and that Nero himself was a god, then Peter and his wife and daughter would be set free.

"Peter was quite old by now. So was his wife. But his daughter was still a young woman. So, the story goes, he signed the document. The *Professio*."

Keely reached for the wine bottle. "Where is it now, Father?"

"Good question. Getting back to Saint Peter, we do know that he was in fact crucified. If we believe our story, Peter, his wife and daughter were released from prison. Once Peter's family was safe, he returned to the Circus voluntarily, and was promptly tied to a cross upside down, covered with pitch, and set afire."

"What happened to the *Professio*?" Chasen said.

Fallon took a long sip of the wine before replying. "The Roman Empire brought wonders to the world: paved roads, aqueducts, basilicas. They were also masterful forgers: Greek and Egyptian artifacts, coins, and every possible kind of letter and document. The Church's position is that the *Professio* is a fake. Paper, papyrus, was hard to come by in ancient Rome. It was encased in glass for protection. Glass was another of the Romans' great achievements. I've never seen it. Have you, Mr. Roldan? Your father is the last person I know of to have possession of the *Professio*."

Vidal cleared his throat, like a man coming down with a cold. "I deal in modern art, not antiquities."

Keely said, "Authentic or not, it would make a wonderful documentary."

"An Inspector Calvino asked who drove me to Roldan's house for his birthday celebration," Chasen told Fallon. "I gave him your name."

Fallon shrugged his shoulders indifferently. "I'll be glad to talk to him."

The absinthe and wine seemed to embolden Vidal. He said, "I don't know how you continue to serve the Church, Father. There are all those pedophiles, and stealing from the collection box." Vidal's eyes drifted over to Connie. "And celibacy has become a joke. Sex is still a sin outside of marriage, isn't it?"

"No," Connie said. "It's not a sin. It's a crime. A misdemeanor. The more of it you miss, the meaner you get."

That brought a roar of approval from everyone except Vidal, who waited for the laughter to die down before pronouncing, "And what of the other commandment you and your kind flaunt so casually—'Thou shalt not kill'?"

"Actually," Fallon said, "that's a King James version mistranslation of the original Hebrew. The correct reading is, 'Thou shalt not murder.' There was a lot of killing going on in those days. Killing for a moral purpose—to prevent a death, or to get rid of Israel's enemies—was readily accepted. And the death penalty was used for all kinds of offenses, including adultery and burglary."

Chasen said, "It's a good thing you weren't born back then, John. You wouldn't have lasted long."

Vidal bundled his napkin into a ball and tossed it to the floor. "The Catholic Church is corrupt, and I'm glad I'm out of it."

Fallon composed his handsome features into a frown. "Left the Church, have you? Well, I'm truly sorry to hear that. We shall miss you. I know you studied with the monks at Santa Domingo de Silos. Let me make a suggestion. Find another religion. A perfect religion. But remember," he added lightly, "after you join, it will no longer be perfect."

As the women laughed, Vidal pushed himself to his feet, his body rigid, his forehead laced with perspiration. He glared at Fallon. "I do not need lectures from a priest. My mother, brother, and sister-in-law were murdered by the likes of you. If there truly is a hell, I hope you rot there for eternity."

Vidal gave Keely and Connie a solemn apologetic bow, then said, "Señor Chasen, perhaps we can continue our discussion tomorrow."

There was an uncomfortable silence as Vidal strode from the table and out the restaurant door.

The waiters came with the main courses, roast suckling pig and *cordero asado*, baby lamb, and everyone concentrated on the food for a while. Fallon excused himself for a brief visit to the kitchen to compliment the chef.

When he returned, Chasen said, "How did Jago Roldan get his hands on the *Professio* in the first place?"

Fallon seized the chance to get the conversation going again. "I've no way to know if this is true or not, but Jago supposedly bragged that he found it in a cellar of the Ritz Hotel, in Paris during the war, and hid it under his shirt. A German solider saw him, and Jago, a tender youth at the time, killed the man. He and his father, Carlos, who had been a curator at the Prado museum before the war, flew back to Spain in a cargo plane provided by the Luftwaffe, loaded with old-master paintings for Franco. Jago claimed that the plane was so cold, the glass protecting the *Professio* nearly froze his skin."

Chasen picked up his wine. "Proving that crime does pay. Which is why there are so many rich criminals. Well, for the rest of us sinners, may we be halfway to heaven before the devil knows we're gone."

"Well stated," Fallon said. "You should be a Catholic."

"Does that mean I won't be allowed into heaven?"

Fallon's lips quirked. "Legend has it that those who are not baptized will spend their eternity in Limbo. Legend also has it that all the really good-looking women end up there, too, so you should enjoy your time there."

Chasen saw that Keely and Connie were engaged in an animated conversation. He turned to the priest and lowered his voice. "How's Paco Ramiro?"

"How would I be knowing that?"

"You saved his life by taking on Roldan's bodyguard, Tobias. With that fancy corkscrew of yours, and in the process gave him a new hairstyle. He's not a happy camper. I'd keep an eye on my back if I were you."

"My back appreciates your concern."

"I'd like to talk to Paco. I went looking for him this afternoon, but it seems he's disappeared again."

"I'll be happy to pass along the message," Fallon said blandly, "if for some reason I should happen to run into him."

"Cut the innocent act, Fallon. I know you took Jago's hard drive. I give you credit for being a first-class burglar and a damn good street fighter. Did you know that someone tried to kill Keely yesterday?"

"No," Fallon said, surprised. "What happened?"

"She was coming back from Jago's place in Mijas. The limousine was pushed off the road. The driver died. Keely was lucky to survive." Chasen's voice dropped to a near whisper. "Let's stop playing games. You're after the *Professio*, and I want Sam Alroy's laptop computer. And I want to know what was in the envelope he had with him on the beach the morning he was murdered."

"Are you suggesting that we work together?" Fallon asked.

"I'm telling you I know who has the *Professio*."

Fallon squinted as if trying to look into a bright light. "Do you really know?"

"Swear to God," Chasen said, wondering if the priest was as good at reading lies as he was at telling them.

"Then you know who killed Sam Alroy."

"I know who killed Giles Dolius. Do we have a deal?"

"Certainly. Tell me who and—"

"I was born at night, Father. But not last night. When you deliver the laptop, we'll talk. But first, tell me how you caught on to me so fast. Sitting next to me on the airplane was no accident."

Fallon swirled the wine around in his glass, making a whirlpool. "In fact, it was. I'd been in Washington, D.C., at Georgetown University, a Jesuit establishment, examining a painting that was thought to be a forgery. I was flying to Spain and saw you in the plane. Your face was familiar. And I—"

"How would my face be familiar to you?"

"My vocation at the Vatican includes access to the files of the top intelligence agencies in the world."

"The *Cannoncciale*," Chasen said.

"Exactly. Your work in Berlin and in South America is well documented. Especially after your squabble with a United States senator. I couldn't remember your name." Fallon nodded his head toward Connie, who was talking to Keely in hushed tones. "She was good enough to provide me with it, and to arrange for me to change seats. It's as simple as that."

Chasen didn't believe any of it. "I think you'd better . . ."

"Better what?" Fallon said.

Chasen had spotted a familiar face at the bar. The burglar he'd found lying on Jago Roldan's office carpet. "There's a man at the bar. I believe you've run into him."

Fallon twisted around and spotted Perry Bryce, who immediately turned his back on them, but not before Chasen spotted the wire leading to his right ear.

"Since you've been opening up to me, I'll return the

favor," Fallon said. "His name is Perry Bryce, and he works for the British government. MI6."

The waiter brought dessert, strawberries with whipped cream.

Fallon seemed to welcome the distraction. He stood up and held out his glass.

"Give one of your beautiful toasts," Connie urged. "I just love the way this man talks."

"I know the type," Keely said in a tone that made it obvious to Chasen that she had been enjoying the wine. "He can tell you to go to hell in such a way that you'd enjoy the trip."

Fallon rose to his feet and raised his glass. *"Salud. Dinero y amor y tiempo para disfrutarlos."*

"To health, money, and love and the time to enjoy them," Connie translated with a giggle.

As soon as Fallon sat down, Keely popped up, glass in hand. "May the devil cut off the toes of all your foes, so you'll know them by their limping."

Fallon clapped his hands in applause. "Well done, Keely. That reminds me of a joke," he added, ignoring Chasen's groan. "Moses comes down from the Mount after negotiating with God over the commandments, and tells the Israelites that there's good news and bad news."

Chasen paid little attention to Fallon's joke, which brought a deep, lusty chuckle from Connie. He excused himself and wandered over to the bar to take on the MI6 agent.

Chapter Twenty-Three

The British secret agent had his elbows on the bar and was staring down at his glass when Dave Chasen approached him.

"Can I buy you a drink?" Chasen asked.

Perry Bryce looked into the mirror behind the bar and frowned. "Thanks, but I don't really drink." He picked up his glass and shook the ice cubes. "Mineral water."

"I thought all you guys at MI6 were hardcore Scotch drinkers."

Bryce straightened up and faced Chasen. "Has someone been squealing on me?"

"Are you wired?" Chasen said. "A few minutes ago you had a plug in one ear. I'm betting that there's a directional microphone hidden somewhere under that ratty jacket of yours."

Bryce unbuttoned his jacket and removed a harmless-looking black object the size of an expensive fountain pen. A single wire trailed from one end of the device and disappeared at the back of Bryce's neck.

"Ratty jacket, you think, huh? It's a shame we're not paid anywhere near what you CIA jokers are."

Chasen caught the attention of one of the busy bartenders and ordered a Calvados. "Royal, if you have it. And another mineral water for my thirsty friend." He pulled the wire from Bryce's directional microphone. "Any more of these?"

"Hundreds," Bryce said, "but not on me."

The bartender placed a small snifter in front of Chasen and refilled Bryce's glass.

"The queen," Chasen said, bringing the glass to his lips.

"Up yours," Bryce said.

"Ah, that dry British wit. You didn't look very funny lying on the rug in Jago Roldan's office the other night."

Bryce ran a finger down the side of his face, hard enough to leave a red mark. "You were there?"

"You're lucky you woke up before Jago's men found you."

"One did, apparently. I had company when I came around. Was that your doing?"

Chasen drained his glass. "You owe me, Mr. Bryce. I'll settle for this drink for now."

Bryce watched as Chasen strolled back to his table. Without his long-range microphone, all he could do was watch while they all had a fine time with dessert and coffee. The priest and the pretty blonde were the first to leave.

Bryce had known from the first sentence out of Fallon's mouth that he was the same man who had used the judo hold on him in Jago's house in Mijas. He plugged the microphone back together and said, "Garate, Fallon's on his way out."

Chasen gave him a friendly wave as he exited the restaurant with Keely Alroy.

Bryce handed the bartender a ten Euro. "That should handle it."

"No, no," the man said. "Thirty-four Euros, and tax."

"For water and one drink?"

"Your friend had Calvados. Brandy made from apples. Royal. The very best."

Bryce cast a panicked look at the departing American couple. By the time he had provided the necessary money and made his way to the street, Chasen and Keely were no longer in sight, and Lieutenant Garate's car was gone.

*　　*　　*

"Don't get too close," Sil Garate instructed his driver. They were following the taxicab that John Fallon had hailed a block from the Sobrino de Botín.

The cab sped through the crowded traffic lanes, but Garate's man had no trouble keeping up with him. When the taxi pulled up in front of the Anaco Hotel, Garate was prepared to call it a night, figuring that Fallon and the sexy blonde would stay put until morning.

But the priest surprised him. He exited the cab, held the door for the woman, and when she was standing beside him, Fallon took her hand, kissed it, said something, then hopped right back into the taxi. The blonde stared at the back of the taxi, stamping one well-shod foot on the pavement in frustration, before turning on her heel and marching into the hotel lobby.

"Stay with the cab," Garate told the driver, making a mental note to contact the woman tomorrow. The beauty appeared to be frustrated, and Garate knew from long experience that frustrated women were often eager to give up their secrets.

The taxi went back to its nearly racing-car pace, finally pulling up in front of an ancient square-towered church. Fallon leaped from the cab, ran up the front steps, and disappeared into the church.

"Stay here," Garate ordered. "I shouldn't be long."

The street lighting was poor, and he came close to slipping on the timeworn brick steps leading up to two massive ironbound oak doors that protected the vestibule. One of the doors was open just wide enough for someone to slip through. Garate edged his way inside the church. The only lighting came from the flames on the numerous stands of head-high brass candleholders.

It was eerily dark. The floors were pebbled marble. There were no pews. A life-size Christ figure hung on chains that disappeared into the ceiling. There was a pungent, musty smell of incense and candle wax.

Garate narrowed his eyes and held his breath. Footsteps. A door opened on the side of the altar. He spied a slice of light, the briefest glance of a figure; then the door slammed shut.

Garate strode purposefully toward the door. His rubber-soled shoes made no noise on the marble flooring. He reached the knob, hesitated a moment, then opened the door slowly. Darkness. No streetlight, and no sign of Fallon.

He stepped outside—and instantly was hit on the back of the neck. The pavement seemed to jump up at his face before he passed out.

Garate had no idea how long he'd been unconscious. He rolled on his side and gently placed a hand on the back of his neck.

The beam of a flashlight licked over him. Garate held his hands over his eyes. "Who is it?" he barked.

"It's me, Lieutenant," Garate's driver said. "What happened?"

"Slipped and fell," Garate grumbled as he made his way unsteadily to his feet. He made an inventory of his suit, finding his revolver, wallet, and keys all in place. He started to walk, then cried out in pain. His foot—his bare right foot—had landed on something sharp.

"Play that light around," he ordered. "I seem to have lost a shoe."

Daria Roldan straddled Raul Tobias, closed her eyes, and lowered a breast to his mouth. She rode him hard, her knees digging into the mattress, her hands wrapped around the bars of the brass headboard. After a few minutes she straightened her back and tilted her head to the ceiling, awaiting her first climax.

Tobias sensed the moment. He grabbed her by the hips

and rolled her over until he was on top. She lay there motionless as he thrust himself into her. Finally he tensed and she could feel his release.

She watched without saying a word as Tobias slipped out of the bed and padded to the bathroom. When the door closed, she reached into the pocket of her silk nightgown and withdrew a prerolled marijuana cigarette and a black Chinese lacquered lighter. She lit up, then adjusted the sheet so that her breasts were barely covered.

When Tobias returned, he was still naked, flaunting his hairless, well-muscled body at her. There was a six-inch strip of yellowing white bandage on his right arm. He stood before her, an insolent smirk on his face.

"Are you proud of yourself?" Daria said.

Tobias rolled from one foot to the other, his semihard penis hovering just above her face.

She inhaled deeply, letting the smoke seep out around her lips. "Get back in bed. We have to talk."

Tobias slipped under the sheet and lay back with his hands behind his neck. "Your grandfather is not pleased with you."

"*Abuelo* is not pleased with anyone at the moment. Especially you. He talks of finding a replacement. After all, you are in charge of security. The robbery in Mijas you may have survived. But not the loss of his precious *Professio*."

Tobias twisted his head into the pillow. "I'd never heard of the thing. He can't blame me for that. Your husband just walked in and took it."

"My deceased husband," Daria said. "If you value your job, and your life, you had better find it for *Abuelo*."

"What's so special about this *Professio*?"

"It was the foundation of *Abuelo*'s wealth. He had been using it to blackmail the Church. But he went too far. The pope sent his people for it. They ended up killing my grandmother, my father, Naldo, and my mother. But the *Professio* survived. *Abuelo* pretended that it had been destroyed. He no longer made demands of the Church." Her voice softened as she told the next part. "He would get drunk, invite me to his vault, and tell me all about how he had acquired the *Professio* as a young man, in Paris. How he had killed a German soldier for it.

"*Abuelo* would boast of his grand plans. On his deathbed, he would release the *Professio*. Embarrass the Church. Exact his vengeance from the grave." She took another hit on the joint. "He won't admit it, but *Abuelo* was always frightened that the Church would find that he still had the *Professio*, and come after it again."

"How do you think Sam was able to open the vault? Jago claims that no one knew the code but him."

Daria had known the code since the age of twelve, when Jago first took her there to show off his prize possessions. By the fifth or sixth visit to the vault, she had the code. And the old fool had never bothered to change it. The numbers included the month and year that his precious son Naldo was born, and the date of his death. Daria held the cigarette out to Tobias.

Abuelo had it figured out. She was sure of it. The way he spoke to her, looked at her. He blamed her, not Vidal. Yet Vidal was as much at fault as she was. He'd told Sam about the *Professio*, which fascinated him. Sam wanted to see it. He had to see it. Just once.

She vividly remembered the day she'd shown it to him. They had been alone in the mansion. *Abuelo* was off somewhere on a business trip. They'd been smoking dope and drinking. It was the only way Daria could endure having sex with Sam, with his pale white body, his ugly hair, his bland Anglo face. She'd smoke up and drink champagne and close her eyes as he went through his amateurish attempts at what he liked to call "making love."

That afternoon, after much drinking and dope, she agreed to show him *Abuelo*'s *Professio*. They'd carried a magnum of champagne to his treasure room and she'd opened the vault for him. She'd been careless. Sam had been hanging over her shoulder, nuzzling her neck when she punched in the code. Drunk as he was, he'd seen the numbers and memorized them.

Tobias leaned over and blew a stream of smoke into Daria's ear. "I asked you how Sam was able to open the vault."

"Vidal must have helped him," she snapped. "My dear gay uncle and Sam were friends. Probably lovers. Have you watched him trying to get back in *Abuelo*'s good graces? It's pathetic. He's telling him that I gave Sam the code. I'm sure of it."

"What if Jago believes Vidal?"

Daria inhaled with cheek-sunken concentration, holding the smoke in her lungs for a long time, then letting it come out between her teeth in a luxurious hiss. "That would not be good. For either of us." She reached over and rubbed the glowing end of the cigarette back and forth against the wide lip of an ashtray.

"You failed to kill Keely," she said sharply. "I still want that job done. And for your sake as well as mine, you had better do something about Vidal."

Tobias reached over and ran the palm of his hand lightly over the extended nipple of her breast.

Daria raked her nails across his bandaged arm. Tobias let out a howl of pain.

"Take care of them," Daria said as she slid off the bed and picked up her nightgown. "And do it very soon or I'll tell *Abuelo* you raped me. The thought of you even touching me will sicken him, Raul, so do as I tell you."

Chapter Twenty-Four

Dave Chasen opened one eyelid as he searched for the telephone beside the bed. Five-twenty-six in the morning.

Lt. Sil Garate's message was short and direct. "I'm in the lobby. Be here in ten minutes, or I'll come and get you."

Chasen and Keely had been out until two o'clock searching for Paco Ramiro, without results. They'd found plenty of people who were willing to sell them drugs, guns, and the sex of their choice, but no one who knew Paco's current whereabouts. Chasen had resisted the temptation to purchase a gun. If Garate found one on his person or in the hotel room, he'd use it as an excuse to throw him into jail or out of the country.

He walked into the Ritz lobby in a foul mood and badly in need of a cup of coffee. Garate was waiting with his arms folded across his chest and a don't-ask-me-any-questions scowl on his face.

"I need coffee before I do anything," Chasen said.

"There is a thermos in the car. Let's go."

"Where to, Lieutenant?"

"A place unknown to tourists."

Garate didn't say a word during the trip, his face a mere silhouette in the dashboard lights. They drove through the high-rises of Madrid and out to an industrial area where the landscape was dominated by ugly flat-roofed buildings circled with eight-foot chain fences and fortresslike structures with towering smokestacks polluting the air, which was the color of used bathwater. *Just the type of place where they'd build a prison,* Chasen thought.

Garate guided the car to a smooth stop alongside a flock of blue-and-white police cars, their emergency lights revolving endlessly in the black of the predawn, exposing a football field–sized lot jammed with battered steel drums. Garate kept to his macho, strong-and-silent attitude as they exited the car, jerking a thumb at Chasen, an order to follow him.

Walking down a set of damp concrete stairs, they passed several uniformed policemen who saluted Garate without saying a word. Chasen was getting the feeling that he was dreaming, that he was in the middle of a Federico Fellini fantasy movie scene filled with silenced actors, when Garate suddenly pointed at the floor and said, "Watch your feet there."

Garate worked his fingers into a pair of rubber gloves, snapping them at his wrists. He handed Chasen a pair of the gloves, then said, "Not a pretty sight, is it?"

"They never are," Chasen said dryly. He surveyed the area. What a dismal place to end one's life. Smoke-blackened walls. A low, mold-encrusted ceiling. A paint-smeared cast-iron sink against one wall. Greasy, rainbow-tinged puddles of heavy oil on the concrete floor. He took his time putting on the gloves. They were typical one-size-fits-all police issue. He stepped around a coagulated pool of blood that lay at Paco Ramiro's feet, which, like his arms, were bound with rawhide strips to a heavy wooden chair.

"What caused those circular wounds all over his face and skull?"

"A corkscrew," Garate said with grim satisfaction.

Chasen edged closer to the dead body, pinching his nostrils and waving the flies away as he examined Ramiro's face. Paco's eyes were wide open. *Tache noire,* thin black bands of discolored sclera, had formed under the irises.

"I've never seen anyone executed in that manner before. I count, what . . . four, five, six wounds that appear to have been made by the corkscrew. Looks like Ramiro bit off part of his tongue while being interrogated."

"Any ideas who did this?"

"No, Lieutenant. I haven't a clue."

Garate sucked in his lips so that they virtually disappeared. "I have all the clues I need. Inspector Calvino told me that you . . . interviewed one of Ramiro's friends, Rico. Did Rico tell you that your friend Father Fallon used a corkscrew to defend himself against Raul Tobias?"

"Fallon's no friend of mine."

"No? He drove you to Jago Roldan's party. You had dinner with him last night, and you say he is not a friend. I find that hard to believe. At dinner Fallon used his own corkscrew to open the wine. The priest finds many uses for that corkscrew."

"Is the medical team through examining the body?" Chasen asked.

"They're finished."

Chasen put a gloved hand on Ramiro's chin and tilted it back and forth, examining the depth of the circular wounds.

Garate leaned over his shoulder and Chasen could smell garlic on his breath.

Chasen stepped back and stripped the rubber gloves from his hands.

"Where is Fallon now?" Garate said.

"I have no idea."

Garate moved in close, so that his face was just inches from Chasen's. "Fallon is no ordinary priest, is he? He's an exsequor. One of the pope's troubleshooters. Some would say he is an assassin."

Chasen took a step back, not out of fear or intimidation,

but to get away from the garlic breath. "You know more about him than I do."

"Last night you and Fallon discussed an ancient document, the *Professio*. That's what this is all about, isn't it? Paco stole Samuel Alroy's vehicle. In the vehicle was the document, which he passed along to Giles Dolius, who was also murdered. What else did you discuss with Fallon at dinner last night?"

"You know what was discussed. Your friend Perry Bryce was there recording it all."

"Not all. You and Fallon were in a whispered discussion. What was said?"

"He was hearing my confession."

Garate's hands bunched into fists, and for a moment Chasen expected the Spaniard to hit him. Alone, in a deserted basement with a squad of armed policeman nearby, there wasn't much he could do about it.

The moment passed. Garate's fists unclenched.

"You and Señorita Alroy went looking for Ramiro after dinner; then you went back to the hotel and enjoyed each other's company. Fallon has disappeared. Find him and notify me immediately, or I will have you sent back to Washington. Is that understood? You may go now. I would suggest a taxi. It's a long and dangerous walk."

One of the uniformed policeman used his radio to summon a taxi. While Chasen waited he called Devlin's office. It was close to one in the afternoon in Washington, D.C., and according to Carly Sasser, Devlin was "probably on his third martini at the Old Ebbett Grill." She did have some good news. They had turned up a freshman student by the name of Emilia Maceda at the Universidad Complutense de Madrid. "She's enrolled in a sociology course. There may be more Emilias, but that's what we have so far, Dave."

The cab arrived. The driver had bushy white sideburns and wore thick glasses that distorted his eyes. An unlit cigarette dangled from the side of his mouth, Humphrey Bogart–style. He introduced himself as Berto. Chasen asked to be taken to the Universidad Complutense de Madrid, which had been Americanized to the University of Madrid and more often simply referred to by its initials, UCM.

He called Keely at the Ritz and filled her in, but left out the gory details regarding Paco Ramiro's death. "Garate is certain that Fallon is the killer."

"What about Sam? Has he found out anything about my brother's murder?"

"If so, he's not letting me in on it. I have a lead on the girl Paco sold the computer to, so I won't be back to the hotel for a few hours."

"I've got plenty to do. Replace my ID that went up in flames with Jago Roldan's limousine. I have to pick up a new passport, go to the bank, and notify the credit card carriers, and, most important, find an attorney with enough guts and brains to take on the Roldans."

"Maybe you should wait until I get back," Chasen suggested.

"I'll be fine," Keely assured him. "Felipe will drive me. No one would try anything here in Madrid in broad daylight. I'll see you no later than cocktail time."

When Chasen finished the call, the driver turned and smiled, displaying gold molars that blended in with the rest of his tobacco-stained teeth. "American, *sí*?"

"*Sí*. Do you know the university, Berto?"

"Very well, señor. It is one of my favorite destinations. I drive many students, their families, and the teachers."

"I'm looking for the sociology department."

The driver swerved, barely missing a small black dog. "That I do not know."

"The administration office?"

"I am not familiar with that, señor," Berto said sadly.

Chasen tugged at his earlobe. "Just what is it about the university that you know so well?"

"The cafeteria, señor. The food is very good, and cheap. Every year I get older, but the new crop of students gets younger and more beautiful." He pulled his hand from the steering wheel and shook it as if he'd touched something hot. "Those young girls. Ah, to be twenty again, eh?"

Chasen had to smile at Berto's enthusiasm. "Okay, let's go to the cafeteria. I'll buy you breakfast."

Vidal Roldan walked slowly, quietly, as if visiting a sick friend in a hospital room. He peered into the den. His father was seated at an eighteenth-century rosewood chess table. One hand was massaging an ivory knight.

Jago appeared tired, his wrinkles deeper, his military posture gone, shoulders slumped, back bent. His hair had been combed but not sprayed in place. There was a small razor nick on his chin. He looked like an old man, Vidal realized.

Daria was sprawled in a maroon leather club chair, her long legs stretched out, her cream-colored skirt well up above her knees, revealing her thighs. She was wearing a blue-and-white polka-dot blouse cut low in front and tied at the midriff. Her hair was clenched in a ponytail. The outfit brought just one image to Vidal's mind: slut.

Raul Tobias was leaning on the burled walnut billiard table, his feet crossed at the ankles.

Vidal was ten minutes early for the meeting, but he had the feeling that his father thought that he was late.

"A policeman interrupted my breakfast this morning," Jago said. "Lieutenant Garate of the CNI. He told me that the body of Paco Ramiro was found. Here in Madrid. Garate believes that Fallon, the priest, is the killer. Ramiro died a slow death. A corkscrew was used."

"I saw Fallon last night, Father," Vidal said. "I had dinner with the American insurance man, Chasen, and Señorita Alroy. Fallon barged in. He has his own corkscrew. He used it to open the wine."

"What was the purpose of the dinner?" Jago said.

"Chasen is investigating Sam's murder. I thought I might find out something of interest. We were at Sobrino de Botín. Fallon arrived, with a young blond woman, and joined us. Uninvited. I asked him to leave, and when he would not, I did."

"So you learned nothing," Daria said.

"On the contrary. Chasen asked Fallon what he knew about the *Professio*. And Fallon recited its history. He fashions himself an expert on everything: Spain, Franco, movie stars, wine. A truly obnoxious son of a bitch."

"Did he mention my name?" Jago wanted to know.

"Yes. He said he'd met with you earlier in the day. He's a pompous one, this Fallon. The way the woman clung to him, it's obvious they're having an affair of some kind. I told him what I thought of him, and that he and his ilk had killed my mother and brother. Then I left."

Jago slammed the chess knight on the board, rattling the other pieces. "Chasen came right out and asked Fallon about the *Professio*? So he knows of it. That damn policeman Garate knows." He turned his glare on Daria. "A short time ago only three of us knew of its existence. Your husband stole it, and now the world knows. Garate told me something else, something you should have discovered by now, Raul. Giles Dolius, a gangster in Torremolinos, was killed. According to Garate, Dolius was doing business with the likes of Paco Ramiro. Garate claims that Ramiro stole Sam's car and sold the contents to Dolius."

Tobias said, "Inspector Calvino told me he had spoken to Dolius. That he was a small-time crook, a notorious homosexual, and nothing to worry about."

"Did you know him, Uncle Vidal?" Daria asked in a mocking tone.

"No. Did you?"

Tobias said, "The priest, Fallon, he must have killed Dolius. And he must have the *Professio*."

"No. Vidal is right," Jago said. "I met with Fallon yesterday. He had Sam's laptop, his gold lighter, and claims he has the hard drive from my computer. He wanted to trade them all for the *Professio*."

"That was yesterday," Daria said. "He may have killed the beach boy, thinking he had the *Professio*."

Jago used his cane to lever himself to his feet. "Anything is possible." He narrowed his eyes at Tobias. "Fallon also knew about this crook Dolius. And he suggested that you killed him for the *Professio*, Raul. 'Your man with the bad haircut.' You've met with Fallon."

"No," Tobias said, ready to call the priest a liar if he told Jago anything about the fight in the alley. "He must have spotted me when I was looking for Ramiro."

"I should hire Fallon. You couldn't find Ramiro, but the *sacerdote* did." Jago turned his attention to his son. "Fallon said something very disturbing. That the Joan Miró hanging behind my desk in Mijas is a fake."

"The man thinks he's an expert on everything. The painting is authentic." Vidal hoped that his voice didn't betray his nervousness. The Miró was a very fine forgery that had easily passed his father's inspection. The miserable priest did indeed have an expert's eye.

"It had better be authentic," Jago snapped. "Can you get in touch with Chasen?"

"He and Keely Alroy are staying here in Madrid," Vidal said. "At the Ritz Hotel."

Jago ambled over to the billiard table. "This Garate was a fountain of information. He claims that Chasen is not what he claims to be. That he's an agent of the American Central Intelligence Agency."

Daria jumped to her feet. "What about the insurance? The five million dollars?"

Jago rolled a red ball across the deep green felt directly at Tobias. "Always the money, eh? Don't worry. The insurance is real. My attorneys have verified that. Vidal. What about Señorita Alroy? How did she behave?"

236

"She and Chasen were quite friendly with each other, Father."

"He's fucking her," Daria said. "She's a whore."

"A whore, perhaps," Jago said. "But one I told you to be polite to. You've turned her into an enemy, Daria. The attempt on her life accomplished nothing but the loss of an excellent chauffeur."

Tobias edged away from the billiard table. "Inspector Calvino's investigation indicates it was an accident, Señor Roldan."

Jago picked up another billiard ball and hurled it against the wall. "Don't treat me like an idiot!" He wagged a finger at Daria. "No more foolishness. I make the decisions in this family. No one else. I want Fallon found. And brought to me. Here."

There was a long, painful silence, broken by Vidal. "I will draw a sketch of Fallon for Tobias, Father."

Jago took several long breaths before responding. "Excellent. You've done well. Come upstairs; I want to show you something."

Daria watched the two Roldan men leave the room. When she was certain that they were out of hearing range, she swept her hand across the chess table, knocking the pieces to the floor, then turned her anger on Tobias.

"Did you see? I told you Vidal is dangerous. The spineless queer is trying to make up to *Abuelo*. You had better take care of Vidal and the whore, or you're finished." She slashed her hand under her chin in a cutting motion. "Finished."

Chapter Twenty-Five

Dave Chasen had to agree with the cabdriver: The university's cafeteria provided good, inexpensive food, and the majority of the young female students were quite attractive. What Chasen wasn't prepared for was the overwhelming size of the campus. There were more than five hundred acres of broad, tree-lined streets with well-maintained parks, soccer fields, swimming pools, and, according to the information kiosk in front of the cafeteria, a hundred and seventeen campus buildings: a mixture of graceful, gingerbread-laced baroque buildings and long stretches of modern three-story brick-and-glass structures that doubled as classrooms and student dormitories. There were also five additional cafeterias spread throughout the area.

Chasen found a map of the campus that listed the location of the sociology department. He used a pretext, telling the students he spoke to that he was a visiting professor from the University of Miami. His longish hair, fishing-boat suntan, morning stubble of beard, and casual dress—sport coat, shirt, no tie—helped him project the image.

"I'm looking for the niece of one of my fellow professors in Miami. Emilia Maceda."

The usual response was *"Yo no la conozco,"* I don't know her, followed by questions about college life in America, especially spring break.

He finally found a middle-aged sociology professor, with

Einstein finger-in-a-light-socket-style hair and a large condor nose, on his way to the faculty lounge. He checked through the briefcase under his arm and found that Emilia Maceda was a student in his eleven-o'clock class. He gave Chasen directions to his classroom and then bombarded him with questions about the University of Miami: tenure, salaries, faculty comforts, and the like.

Chasen thanked the professor, then checked his watch. Forty minutes to eleven. He wandered around, searching for a stocky young woman with two rings in her eyebrows carrying a laptop.

He had just settled on a bench across from the building housing the sociology department when a familiar figure trooped by.

Chasen jumped to his feet and ran to catch up with Father John Fallon. He jabbed a finger into the priest's back. "What the hell are you doing here?"

Fallon pivoted around in a *neko ashi dachi* karate stance: feet apart, a sitting-on-horseback posture, hands raised, ready to strike. He relaxed and smiled when he recognized Chasen. "You shouldn't scare people like that."

"I don't believe anyone has ever scared you, Fallon. What are you doing here?"

Fallon took off in a loose, casual gate. "Not that it's any of your business, but I'm here to assist in the restoration of a Caravaggio, *The Calling of Saint Paul*. It's on loan from the Vatican, and unfortunately has been mistreated. I'm glad you spotted me. I have something for you."

This was the second time that Chasen had seen Fallon wearing his Roman collar. "Just come from serving Mass?"

"The clergy gets a discount in the food halls."

"You've never paid retail for anything in your life. You said you have something for me."

"I do indeed." Fallon handed Chasen a gold lighter. "It's Keely's brother's. I was afraid it might upset her. I'll leave it to your judgment whether or not she would want it."

"Paco Ramiro gave you the lighter, didn't he?"

Fallon nodded at a trio of nuns in long black habits and white cowls who bowed to him as they passed by. "He's sorry he took it in the first place."

"Is he sorry about the car, Sam's wallet, the laptop, and the *Professio*, too?"

"He confessed his sincere remorse." Fallon held out his hand.

Chasen ignored it.

"Why the hostility?" Fallon asked genially.

"I know why you're here. Don't get in my way."

Fallon spread his arms as if he were granting benediction. "I told you why I'm here. The Caravaggio. I admit I'm interested in the *Professio*, and I'm offering you the same practical advice: Don't get in my way."

"You know about Ramiro, don't you?"

"What should I know?"

"He's dead," Chasen said. "Someone took his time with him. Twisted a corkscrew in and out of his head."

Fallon pinched his nose between his thumb and forefinger and closed his eyes. "Has Paco's mother been notified?"

"I wouldn't know," Chasen said.

Fallon scanned the surrounding crowd, and Chasen had the feeling he was looking for the police. The priest took off, the length of his stride increasing with each step, Chasen right on his heels. "Do the police have any suspects?" Fallon said.

"Lieutenant Garate has only one. You."

Fallon's face hardened and his right eyebrow lifted slightly. "Did you bring anyone along with you this morning?"

"Just the cabdriver."

Fallon's eyebrow slipped back in place. He patted Chasen's arm firmly, not a friendly good-bye gesture. More like an athlete or soldier thanking a comrade in arms.

Chasen pushed the arm away. "If you're here for the laptop, forget about it. It's mine."

"I'm sure it is. Excuse me. I have to get to that painting. See you in church," Fallon said, then took off in a fast walk, skirting a group of young women who looked at him with wide, appraising eyes, and giggled together when Fallon was out of sight.

Chasen considered going after Fallon, but it was close to eleven, time to get back to the sociology class and Emilia Maceda.

He leaned against the handrail leading to the building, scanning the students as they came by. He spotted her walking alone, her eyes on the pavement, a bright red backpack looped around one shoulder, a shiny titanium laptop in her hand. She had a plain, oval face, and the rings above her eyebrows looked out of place, too exotic an accent.

"¿Perdóname, Señorita Emilia Maceda?"

The girl looked at him with fearful deer-in-the-headlights black eyes. She clutched the laptop to her chest. *"Yo soy Emilia."*

"I'm afraid I have some bad news," Chasen said. "A friend of yours has been killed."

Emilia took a step backward. "Which friend? Who?"

"Paco Ramiro," Chasen said, seeing the look of shock fade from her face. She'd been afraid she would hear another name. A boyfriend? A loved one?

"Paco. He is not a friend. I barely knew him. I only met him—"

"When you bought that computer," Chasen said. "You knew it was stolen, didn't you?"

The girl clutched the laptop to her ample chest. "I did not," she said.

Chasen gave a serious frown. "We know that you did not commit a crime," he assured her. "But the laptop is of great importance to the owner. He has authorized me to buy you a replacement. Is there a place on the campus that sells such things?"

"No, no," the girl protested. "It is too late. I already gave Paco's laptop to the priest." She held up the computer in her hands. "He provided me with this one."

"Shit!" Chasen said in English, startling Emilia. She scuttled sideways to the opposite side of the stairs, then darted inside the building.

Chasen was in a foul mood when he got back to the Ritz. John Fallon had been two steps ahead of him all the time, and he now had Alroy's laptop. The slippery bastard would use it to barter for what he really wanted—the *Professio.* Which meant that somehow Chasen had to beat him to it. Keely was still out, replacing her passport and hiring an attorney. He shaved, showered, and ordered lunch from room service.

As he drank the last of the coffee, he thought about Lieutenant Garate's statement that he and Keely had returned to the hotel and "enjoyed each other's company." The Spaniard had been listening in.

He turned the TV onto an English broadcasting station and began searching for listening devices. In twenty minutes he had located seven "tack-bugs," minielectronic marvels that looked exactly like ordinary thumbtacks. They operated on built-in batteries that lasted up to a week. Their one drawback was that the transmitting power was limited to fifty feet.

He carefully eased one of the tacks from the bed frame and dropped it into a half-finished glass of orange juice. Chasen picked up the room-service delivery tray and slipped out the door.

Holding the tray up in front of the peephole of the suite adjacent to his, he knocked. The door was opened by a grumpy man with the puffy face and sunken eyes of an alcoholic.

Chasen apologized for coming to the wrong room. There was no answer to his knock on the door on the opposite side of his suite. He didn't think the Ritz would allow Perry Bryce or Lieutenant Garate's men to camp out on the roof. That left the floor below.

"It's open," Perry Bryce called out in response to Chasen's knock.

Chasen placed the tray on the floor and entered the room. "Did anyone ever tell you that you're not really cut out for this line of work?" he said to Bryce, who greeted him with a face lathered with shaving cream.

"It wasn't my idea. Mother wanted me to be a dentist," Bryce said sarcastically.

Chasen took the glass of orange juice to the bathroom, dumped out the ice in the basin, and picked out the tack-bug.

"I found seven of these in my suite. How many did I miss?"

Bryce used a towel to clean his face. "You have them all."

"Was this your idea or Garate's?"

"It was a mutual decision. I bugged your room. He's working on bugging Jago's Madrid mansion."

There was a knock at the door, and again Bryce called out, "It's open."

A waiter wheeled in a food tray. Bryce signed the bill and poured himself a cup of tea. "Help yourself," he said.

"How did you get into this racket?" Chasen asked.

Bryce sat down and started on his meal. "It wasn't entirely voluntary. A man by the name of Chalmers at MI6 talked me into it."

"How is Snake? Has he done anything with his hair? He had the worst transplant I've ever seen when I knew him in Berlin."

" 'Toothbrush head' is what we call him. Though not to his face. He didn't mention he'd worked with you."

"They never tell you everything, Perry. You should know that by now."

Bryce cut into his eggs and watched the yolk leak into the fried potatoes. "What is it you want? You're smart enough to have played with us, used the bugs to send us off on wild-goose chases. And you're too sharp just to be showing off."

" 'Us.' You and Garate? He was in the Company's pocket before he jumped into yours."

Bryce chomped noisily on his toast. "It's his country. I have to play along."

"That's what I want us to do," Chasen said. "Play along, together. What does Chalmers want? The laptop? The *Professio*?"

"Both. The *Professio* first and foremost."

"Why?"

Bryce studied Chasen for a few seconds to see if that was a serious question. "Jago Roldan has been blackmailing the Church with it for years. Chalmers wants a turn at it."

Chasen took a chair and sat astraddle it, leaning his elbow on the wooden back, his hand propped under his chin. "Sam Alroy took it from Jago to blackmail the old man and Daria. The marriage wasn't a happy one. The Roldans made life miserable for Alroy. They were after his company. That's why he downloaded his latest software. To keep it away from them."

Bryce blotted up the egg yolk with the remains of his toast. "That's plausible, but it doesn't get me any closer to the *Professio*."

"You and I helping each other out is plausible. Let's work together. Snake Chalmers never needs to know."

"He always seems to find things out."

"If you were working for me, I'd suggest you find another line of work. You're not happy being a spy. Why not quit?"

"It's not so simple in London. You leave without their permission, and the best job you'll find is mucking out horse stalls. The only comfortable way out is to win the lottery or marry a rich old duchess." Bryce steepled his fingers and smiled benignly. "You can't just walk away and end up with a cushy job at Fidelity Surety and Bonding."

"Touché," Chasen said. "Garate got me out of bed this morning. Drove me way the hell out to the edge of town just to show me the mutilated body of Paco Ramiro."

"I know. He called me. I declined the invitation. Garate has Father John Fallon's name on the murder docket, or whatever they call it here."

"Fallon didn't kill Ramiro," Chasen said, getting to his feet.

"Who did?"

"Raul Tobias, Jago's henchman. Fallon wouldn't be dumb enough to carve Ramiro up with a corkscrew."

Bryce nodded his agreement. "Since you're solving murders, who killed Sam Alroy and Giles Dolius?"

"It wasn't Tobias," Chasen said. "Listen, Lieutenant Garate knows about the *Professio*, thanks to you. It won't be easy for either one of us to get out of Spain with it."

"We couldn't very well split it in half. Garate's a very unlikable man. Reminds me of Chalmers in a way. He's already put the bite on Chalmers for more money."

"Time is running out," Chasen said as he made his way to the door. "I spoke to a man who deals in items like the *Professio*. He tells me that he could sell it for a minimum of three million dollars. In cash." He smiled. "That wouldn't be hard to split."

"Why should I trust you?" Bryce said.

"Because I'm tired of the spy game, too." He paused, and when he spoke again there was a hard edge in his voice. "And if you tried to screw me, I'd make sure that Chalmers found out that you ran off with all the money stacked on Jago's desk. I didn't take it. Neither did Vidal Roldan. That leaves you, Bryce. Then you wouldn't have to worry about finding a job cleaning out stables. You'd be dead. In Berlin,

Chalmers had a nasty way of getting rid of his agents if he found they were holding out on him, or cooperating with the other side. An acid bath, as I remember. The poor bastards were boiled down to the bone."

Bryce took a long, slurping sip of his tea, then said, "And the CIA never did such things, of course."

"I never did," Chasen said, heading for the door. "Look, Bryce. We're both being used. Too many people are dying for a two-thousand-year-old letter that may not even be real. Let's play it smart this time."

Bryce felt a need to use the toilet, but he wanted to wait until the American was gone. He had a final question. "Since we're going to be partners, tell me about the laptop. I heard you talking to your boss. The girl, the freshman, Emilia. Did you find her?"

"No," Chasen said, mad at himself for not realizing earlier that his suite was bugged. Chasing after Emilia would keep Bryce busy and out of his hair for a while. "Does Garate know about her?"

Bryce patted his lips with a napkin and rose to his feet. "Not from me. I've decided to keep him out of the loop as much as possible."

"Good idea," Chasen said. "Just don't keep me out of your loop from now on."

Chapter Twenty-Six

Raul Tobias leaned back in the seat of one of Jago Roldan's Madrid-based SUV Jeeps that was similar to the one he'd used to run Keely Alroy off the road in Mijas. That vehicle was being repaired at the garage of a friend of his on the Costa del Sol. He stretched his arms out to the steering wheel. He'd been parked across from the Ritz Hotel waiting to see Chasen or Señorita Alroy make an appearance. Or perhaps his luck would really turn, and Fallon would show up.

He was working out a plan in his mind of how he could kill the priest. And the woman. Daria was insistent that he take care of Keely. Now she wanted her uncle eliminated as well. She also hinted that Jago himself had outlived his usefulness. What a family. How had he ever—

A jarring impact to the rear of the SUV snapped his head back.

He cursed and climbed out of the vehicle. A black sedan was nosed against his rear bumper. The passenger door opened, and Lieutenant Garate, the policeman who'd been by Roldan's house earlier in the day, leaned out the rear window and waved for Tobias to join him.

"Get in," Garate ordered though the car's open window. "Put on the seat belt."

While Tobias was struggling with the belt, Garate struck

him directly on his ear with a balled-up fist. "What are you doing here?"

"Hey, I don't—"

Garate hit him again, in the same spot, then said, "Be silent. You say one word and you will lose all your teeth." He leaned forward and told the driver to take off. "The Alcala-Meco jail, Vincente."

Arlington, Virginia

Carly Sasser methodically went through the drawers of Grady Devlin's elaborate walnut desk, searching for clues that might tell her just who Devlin was seeing—her replacement. There were matchbooks from Felix Lounge, a spot he used to take her, and one from a place unknown to Carly, Tryst. *How appropriate,* she thought, slamming the drawer shut.

She leaned back in Devlin's chair, fingering the diamond-studded crucifix hanging from the gold chain around her neck. Devlin had given her the chain for her birthday two years ago. For her last birthday she received a box from Victoria's Secret, filled with lacy lingerie. She wondered what kinds of presents his new paramour was receiving, and, more important, just who she was. There were several possibilities: all ambitious young secretaries in the Company. She suspected it was Patricia something or other, a busty brunette in Technical Services. She lived—

The phone rang, jarring her out of her thoughts. "Mr. Devlin's office."

"Hi, Carly," Dave Chasen said. "Put the man on the phone."

"No can do, Dave. He's in New York. Some Homeland Security–United Nations confrontation. Very hush-hush. I won't be able to talk to him until later tonight. Anything I can do in the meantime?"

"Bad news on the laptop. Emilia Maceda sold it to a

friend at school. I'm chasing her down now. Listen, twice I've asked for a rundown on John Fallon and all I get back is that he's a priest working out of the Vatican. We must have more on him than that. He's a heavy player, always sticking his pretty little nose into things."

"Hold on," Carly said, flicking through the stacks of papers on Devlin's desk. "Grady did order a profile on him. Here it is. Fallon, John. Forty-one years of age. Jesuit. Works for the Vatican's spy agency, the—"

"*Cannoncciale,*" Chasen supplied. "I know that. I want some specifics. Something I can use to put pressure on him. He must have screwed up somewhere along the way."

"I'm sorry," Carly said. "There's nothing here."

"Well, the local cop, Lieutenant Garate, is ready to pin the murder of Paco Ramiro on Fallon. Tell Grady my hunch is that the lieutenant has found out about the *Professio* and wants a piece of it."

"Ramiro? The beach boy?"

"Yep. Tell Grady the kid was murdered with a corkscrew, something Fallon's an expert with. I'll buzz you tomorrow, or sooner if something comes up."

"Take care," Carly said before hanging up the phone. She put Devlin's desktop papers back in order, then rose to her feet, her hand going back to fingering the crucifix. The name of the brunette in technical services suddenly came to her. Patricia Adams. "All tits and no brains," according to one of her supervisors. Unfortunately, that description wouldn't deter Devlin in the least.

Raul Tobias woke with a start as the cell door clanged open. He rolled into a fetal position, bringing his knees up to his chin while pulling his head into his neck like a turtle, peering through one eye at the man standing menacingly above him.

He groaned when he saw it was the same sergeant, a hulking, slant-eyed pervert who had worked him over earlier. They had taken his watch, his clothes. Everything. He'd been hosed down, then beaten with towel-wrapped fists and rubber hoses.

When the sergeant noticed that his legs, genitals, and armpits had been shaved, he assumed Tobias was a *maricón*, a homosexual, and promised to make him the prison's *chocha cuerera*, number one whore.

"No más," Tobias pleaded as he inched his way toward the back wall.

The sergeant tapped an eighteen-inch length of black rubber hose against his leg and smiled. He had a muscular yet flabby build, and his false teeth didn't fit properly, causing him to lisp when he spoke. His gray uniform was drenched with sweat, the result, Tobias feared, of having beaten another prisoner.

"¡Levántese, pedazo de pelotudo!"

Tobias hugged his legs closer to his body and tried to curl into a ball, knowing that if he followed the order to stand up, the bastard would just knock him down again.

The guard snapped the hose against Tobias's bare buttocks. *"Vestirse."* Get dressed.

Tobias cracked open both eyes. His still-damp pants and shirt were lying alongside him. He cautiously unwound his legs, and with some difficulty struggled to his knees and shakily slipped into his clothes.

The sergeant handcuffed Tobias's hands behind his back and shoved him from the cell. He padded barefoot down the clammy cement corridor, the guard poking his buttocks with the tip of the hose and warning him what would happen if he complained about his treatment. His fellow prisoners called out obscenities and made rude gestures with their hands and fingers through the bars of their cells.

He was led to a tennis court–size room with redbrick walls. Concrete oozed out between the bricks. Through the window half-opened blinds gave a striped view of the adjoining building. There were two pieces of furniture: a circular table, scarred from cigarette burns and ballpoint-pen graffiti, and a single wooden chair.

Lieutenant Garate and a thin, horse-faced man wearing a plaid sport coat burst into the room. "Wait outside," Garate told the sergeant.

Garate dropped a black plastic bag on the table, then settled into the chair, leaning back, balancing on the rear legs. The horse-faced man thrust his hands into his pockets and rested his haunches against the windowsill.

"I'm not sure what to do with you, Tobias," Garate said. "You provide me with so many choices. Do I charge you with the murder of Señor Alroy, the old fag, Giles Dolius, or the young beach boy, Paco Ramiro?"

"I am not guilty of any of—"

Garate leaned forward and banged his fist on the table. "Did I give you permission to speak?"

"No, sir."

Garate ripped open the plastic bag, and Tobias's watch, wallet, pocketknife, matches, and half a dozen marijuana cigarettes spilled onto the table.

The policeman picked up the knife, opened the blade, and flicked at the joints. "Dope. A minor charge against you, but strong enough to keep you here in Sergeant Alvarado's tender care for several weeks." Garate picked up one of the cigarettes and ran it under his nose. "Do you think you would last a week in here, Raul? Sergeant Alvarado says that you shave your body like a young girl, and that you will be very popular with your fellow prisoners. I thought that you were fucking Daria, but no. You were fucking her husband. Is that why you killed Alroy? A lovers' quarrel?"

Tobias opened his mouth to protest, but wisely said nothing.

Garate extracted several folded papers from his coat pocket and spread them across the table. Tobias knew exactly what they were. His *ficha*. Police record.

"You've been a busy one," Garate said. "But that's why Jago Roldan hired you, is that not correct?"

Tobias wasn't sure if he should answer or not, since Garate had not given him permission to speak.

"I asked you a question, *chapero*."

"I am not queer," Tobias said with as much indignation as he dared to show. "And I did not kill anyone."

"You are not queer? You are not a killer?" Garate thumped the arms of the chair with his palms. "You know what you are to me, Tobias? A solution. I can hang all of the murders on you and clear up my desk. I can type out a few reports and go home. Unless you can convince me to do otherwise."

Tobias's wrists were swelling up due to the tightness of the cuffs. His body was a mass of welts and bruises. Only his face had been spared the attentions of Sergeant Alvarado's rubber hose. He knew if he didn't tell Garate what he wanted to know, right now, he would never leave the jail alive.

He swallowed hard, trying to put some moisture into his mouth. "I know much about the Roldans, Lieutenant. All of them. I would be pleased to share my knowledge with you."

Garate looked over at the horse-faced man. "Isn't that wonderful, Perry? He is going to share his knowledge with us." The policeman turned his gaze back to Tobias. "And you will tell me about the American, Chasen, and about the fucking priest, Fallon."

"I would gladly kill the priest for you, Lieutenant," Tobias said, his voice hard and belligerent.

Garate brought his hands together in a loud clap. "Proving to me that you are capable of murder. Sergeant Alvarado," he shouted.

The door opened with a slap, and Garate said, "Remove the cuffs from my friend's hands, Sergeant, and bring us some coffee."

Chapter Twenty-Seven

When Dave Chasen returned to the hotel he found a voice mail message from Keely: "Having trouble with the passport; won't be back until six or seven. Don't worry. See you then."

Chasen felt edgy, like a boxer ready to go ten rounds, ready to hit someone. But he was alone in the ring. He could either wait for an opponent to show up, or go out and find a target. Vidal Roldan was a prime target. It was time, in Grady Devlin's vernacular, to kick ass and break glass.

Roldan's gallery was located in an upscale area of Madrid filled with antique shops, silversmiths, and estate jewelry stores. The door to Vidal's shop was open. Light classical music spilled out into the street. The receptionist was a slim young woman with hollow cheeks, sunken eyes, and wine-black hair. Vidal was with a customer, but she promised Chasen that he would be available in just a few minutes.

Chasen roamed around the empty gallery. The once bright red carpet was frayed and stained. The sand in the knee-high chrome ashtrays was littered with cigarette and cigar butts. He stopped before a life-size plaster standing statue of a woman, face and upper body sandblasted, the legs marble-smooth, as if the artist had changed his mind at midpoint during the creation. Next to the statue was a rainbow of crystal butterflies perched on a Lucite tree.

The ceilings were painted hospital white in a shiny enamel that reflected the abstract paintings on the walls below, much as a pond reflected the trees around it. Some of the paintings were such a geometric riot of bright, hard colors that the ceiling reflection took on a soft, muted impressionist feel. All in all, Chasen thought he liked the ceiling versions better.

He heard approaching footsteps and turned to see Vidal Roldan, decked out in a plum-colored velvet smoking jacket and a silk ascot around his neck. "Find anything you like?" Roldan asked.

"I don't see any price tags."

Roldan upturned his palms. "Everything is negotiable. I'm sorry about last night at the restaurant, but I couldn't tolerate Father Fallon any longer."

"Not many people can," Chasen said. "Is there somewhere we can talk privately?"

Vidal led Chasen to a low-ceilinged room illuminated by fluorescent lighting and reeking of chemicals. A workbench was strewn with paintings undergoing restoration. Canvases of all shapes and sizes were stacked throughout the room.

"You've quite an inventory," Chasen said.

"I conduct a good deal of my business on-line and through our catalog. Once you establish a reputation, it's much easier that way."

"Tell me about Sam Alroy," Chasen said. "The two of you were friends, weren't you?"

"I'd like to think we were. Sam was a very nice man. Unfortunately, he made the mistake of marrying my niece."

"You don't like Daria?"

"No one likes Daria. Men may lust after her, yearn for her, but they don't like her."

"Sam included? He was thinking of leaving her, wasn't he?"

Roldan took off his glasses and polished them with the silk handkerchief from the smoking jacket's breast pocket.

"Yes. But there were complications. The pregnancy. Daria is not the motherly type. She threatened to have an abortion. That was devastating to Sam."

"So Sam took the *Professio* and said, 'If Jago ever wants to see it again, give me a divorce, and the kid.' Is that how it went?"

"I'm afraid so, though of course I knew nothing about it until after Sam's death."

Chasen was watching Roldan very closely. "Who do you think killed him?"

Vidal carefully replaced his glasses and the handkerchief. "I would be afraid to hazard a guess."

"Afraid? Your father killed a man for the *Professio*. You're just following in his footsteps. You killed Sam, didn't you?"

Vidal rocked back on his heels. "Of course not. I had no reason to. I was here in Madrid at the time he was murdered. It came as a great shock to me."

"Were you going to meet with Sam? Were the two of you working out some kind of a deal?"

Vidal slipped his right hand into his jacket pocket and took a full step backward. "You have no right to talk to me like this. I want you out of here."

"If you have a gun in your pocket, keep it there, Vidal. That night at your father's house, you had your hand in your jacket, just like you do now. You overheard the phone message Giles Dolius left for Jago. You knew he had the *Professio*. That he was hoping to sell it to your father."

"I never heard of the man," Vidal protested.

"Give me a break," Chasen said scornfully. "How long has Jago had the house in Mijas? Thirty years? You spent your summers there. El Gato Negro is the most notorious gay bar in Torremolinos, and you pretended you didn't know where it was. Dolius dealt in stolen goods. The walls of his office were covered with paintings. Stolen paintings. You two were in business together. But when Dolius realized he had something really special, the *Professio*, he didn't want to deal with you. He wanted to go to the source. The man with real money. Jago Roldan, not his wimpy son. You ducked out of the dinner party early, giving you plenty of time to get to El Gato Negro, kill Dolius, and take the *Professio* before I got there."

Chasen waved an arm around the room. "Where is it? Hidden among all this junk?"

Vidal flinched, as if he'd been slapped. "You are insane. And a fraud. You're not an insurance man. You are an American spy."

"An American spy with a lot of money. I'm willing to pay you more for the *Professio* than you'll get from anyone else. Including the Church. John Fallon is not the kind of man you can negotiate with." Chasen picked up one of the open cans of paint on the table and crept closer to Vidal. "Fallon would be happy to destroy the *Professio*. This gallery could be turned into an inferno. And if you happened to be here, that would be your tough luck. He's not someone like the unconscious guard you almost kicked to death in your father's office, or Giles Dolius. He's out of your league, Vidal. He'd kill you before you had time to say a last prayer."

Chasen could see Roldan was wavering. He was frightened of the priest. "Here's my proposition, Vidal. I have a buyer. A middle man. Your father would never know who ended up with the *Professio*. The sale could never be traced back to you. We'll split the proceeds fifty-fifty, and I won't tell Lieutenant Garate about you killing Sam and Dolius, or Fallon that you have the *Professio*."

For an instant Chasen thought the bluff had worked. Vidal's eyes turned glassy, his breathing loud, uneven.

The spell was broken when the door opened and the hollow-cheeked receptionist strode into the room. "Señor Vidal, your father is on the phone. He says it is most urgent."

*   *   *

"A gathering of the clan," Perry Bryce said as he watched Vidal Roldan's vintage dark green Jaguar sedan pull up in front of the gates guarding Jago's Madrid mansion.

Lt. Sil Garate shifted his weight in the cramped surveillance van parked across the street. "The listening device you placed on Tobias had better work," he warned.

"You'll be able to hear him fart during dinner," Bryce assured him.

"I hope to forgo that pleasure." Garate squirmed in his seat as he added, "I no longer have the patience or kidneys for this type of work."

Bryce, who had frozen his butt off in his own Morris Minor on untold numbers of black-bag jobs for MI6 in London, considered the van a luxury—refrigerator, microwave, even a portable toilet.

He adjusted the volume on the transmitter. There was a dull, beating sound.

"What's that?" Garate asked.

"Raul Tobias's heart."

"If he doesn't come through, I'll cut it out," Garate said with a dry chuckle.

Jago Roldan met Vidal at the front door. He had a small cardboard box clasped under one arm. "In here, son."

Vidal couldn't remember the last time his father had called him "son."

Daria and Raul Tobias were sitting at one end of the dining room table. Neither bothered to look up as Vidal entered the room.

Jago handed the box to Vidal. "This was delivered an hour ago, by a messenger service. Open it."

Tobias moved one of the silver candleholders as Vidal eased a single piece of paper, a cell phone, and two photographs from the box onto the table.

Jago snatched the paper and pushed it to Vidal. "Read it aloud."

Vidal coughed into his hand before starting. " 'Jago Roldan. I have the *Professio*. You have one chance to acquire it. Tonight. Be at the center of the Plaza Mayor, by the statue of King Felipe, at midnight. Have two hundred thousand Euros and the painting in the photograph. I will call the cell phone exactly at midnight and tell you where to go. Be alone. If you try anything, the *Professio* goes to the Church.' "

Vidal handed the paper to Daria's outstretched hand, then picked up the photographs. One was a Polaroid of the *Professio*. The other a crisp close-up of Francisco José de Goya's *Dreams by the Lake,* a muted oil on canvas depicting three voluptuous women, their long gowns disheveled, revealing bare shoulders and long legs, cavorting with two men near a lake. One of the women was holding a finger in front of her lips as if giving a shushing sign to the artist.

"He wants money, and the Goya," Jago said. "Why this Goya, son? Why not the Rembrandt, the Zurbarán, the Chagalls, the Ribera, the Picassos, or another Goya?"

"I don't know, Father. It is magnificent, but worth no more or less than the others."

"The Plaza Mayor," Daria said. "He's a clever one, isn't he?"

The Plaza Mayor was Madrid's main square. It dated back to the sixteenth century, when Arab merchants set up a marketplace on the bed of a dry lake inside the walls of the city. The original plaza had burned to the ground in 1790, and had been rebuilt and expanded through the years. The massive cobbled courtyard was surrounded by a four-story structure capped with spires and towers. There were dozens of *tascas,* bars that served *tapas*, along with elegant restaurants ringing the plaza.

From midnight to three in the morning, the area would be a madhouse.

"Perhaps too clever," Tobias said. "The police avoid the plaza like a plague, especially on a Saturday night. If they arrested every thief, drunk, and dope dealer working there, they would flood the prisons."

Jago gripped his forehead, as if trying to squeeze the problem away. "He wants me to deliver the Goya and the money."

Daria said, "It's too dangerous, *Abuelo*. Let Tobias go in your place. When the thief shows up with the *Professio*, he will kill him."

Tobias scratched his chest where the listening device was taped. What would Garate make of Daria's statement? "He will kill him," said so casually, as if she were sending him out to polish her Porsche.

"No," Vidal said forcefully. "This is a job for a Roldan, Father. With your permission, I will go with you. When the thief calls, we will explain that I have the money and the painting, and that he will have to deal with me."

Jago looked at his son with respect. He was finally acting like a true Roldan. "Yes. That's what we'll do. Raul, I want you nearby. You are not to let Vidal out of your sight."

"This thief is no fool, Father," Vidal said. "He no doubt knows what Raul looks like. I can handle it alone."

"Everyone will be partying," Tobias said. "I can wear a disguise. No one will recognize me."

Jago picked up the photograph of the Goya. "Is there time to make a substitute? A forgery?"

"No, Father. We only have a few hours. I doubt if a reproduction of *Dreams by the Lake* exists. No one has seen it in sixty years."

"No one but me," Jago said. He dropped the photo in front of Daria. "And you, when you were a child. And your husband, of course. Sam took this picture. In my vault. He must have photographed all of my paintings."

Daria sat up straight and squared her shoulders. "It's only one painting, *Abuelo*, and very little money. Give the man what he wants, and get your precious *Professio* back if it means so much to you."

Jago's eyes narrowed to slits, and the lines in his forehead deepened. "You never understood, did you? Never understood what my paintings mean to me." He reached out and grabbed Vidal by the elbow. "Come. We will prepare the Goya."

Tobias went to the liquor cabinet and poured himself a stiff brandy. Daria joined him, holding up an empty glass. He poured brandy until the glass was filled to the brim, so she had to bend over in order to sip without spilling.

"You know what you have to do tonight, Raul."

"I know what I have to do every night." He tipped his glass and drained the last drops of the liquor. "We will talk later."

"We will talk now," Daria said. "This is your chance to finish Vidal—"

"Later," Tobias said, stalking out of the room in the wake of a stream of curses from Daria.

Perry Bryce adjusted the receiver once again. "That is one tough woman."

"I doubt that this is the first time she has volunteered Tobias's services to kill a man." Garate said. "And those paintings Jago mentioned—they're all worth millions. I wonder how many were stolen by the old scoundrel. The Goya the thief wants, what's so special about it?"

"I don't know a whole lot about art," Bryce said.

"Do you know the Plaza Mayor?"

"I believe I had lunch there once, but I don't remember enough about it."

Garate slid uncomfortably from his chair and twisted his neck in an effort to relieve the tension. "My driver will take you back to the hotel. I'll pick you up at ten o'clock. Bring the necessary equipment. New batteries for Tobias's transmitter, whatever is needed, Bryce."

"Who do you think sent the package to Jago Roldan, Lieutenant?"

"We will have the answer a few minutes after midnight." Garate slapped his palm against his holster. "You are to bring no weapons. Gun, knife, nothing. Understood? I don't want any difficulties at the plaza."

"I hear you. But what about the guy with the *Professio*? He may have other ideas."

"He is my responsibility," Garate said, reaching for the van's door. "As are you. If things go as planned, you'll be back in London by tomorrow morning."

Chapter Twenty-Eight

Keely Alroy greeted Chasen with a tight-lipped kiss when he walked into the Ritz Hotel suite.

"Tough day?" he asked.

"You could say that. I was at the—"

Chasen put his index finger to her lips and whispered, "The room is bugged. Let's go down to the lobby."

Keely's head snapped back, her eyebrows raised, and her mouth formed the word *Bugged?*

They were silent on the ride down in the crowded elevator. Chasen steered her to an open seating area in the lobby bar. A waiter came and took their drinks order. Chasen filled Keely in on the listening devices in their suite.

"How long were they there?"

"From moment one," Chasen said.

"Jesus, what next? MI6. The Spanish CNI. It's hard to believe," she said, shaking her head. "What kind of man is Perry Bryce?"

"English," Chasen said, as if the one word were explanation enough. "Tell me about your day."

"The embassy took forever to issue my new passport. They had a copy of the police report faxed from Torremolinos; then there were all kinds of papers to fill out. The bank was just as bad. But the topper was the attorneys. I spoke to four of them, and it wasn't encouraging. It could take years to come to a reasonable settlement if Jago, or Daria, decides to string this out. In the meantime, it's going to cost me a lot of money to go up against them."

"Is the money that important to you?" Chasen said.

Keely pursed her mouth in a gesture of contempt. "They killed Sam, and I'm not about to let them profit from it."

Chasen took Sam Alroy's gold lighter from his pocket and handed it to her. "John Fallon wanted you to have this."

She hefted the lighter in her hand. "How did Fallon get it?"

"From Paco Ramiro. Before he was killed. At least that's what Fallon says. And I believe him on that one."

Keely snapped the lighter on and off several times. "Fallon is everything you said he was. That line at dinner about the luckiest man of his generation. William Shatner. Now, that was funny. And Fallon is one handsome dude."

"What a waste, huh?"

"From what Connie, the flight attendant, said, it is a waste. The lady is in raging heat, but all Fallon does is wine her, dine her, and leave her at the door. Alone. Did you notice those little white packets Fallon was handing out at the restaurant? Rosary beads. Blessed by the pope. Connie says he passes them out as small bribes."

"I left in the middle of one of Fallon's jokes. Moses came down from the Mount with good news and bad news. What was the rest of it?"

"Moses says, 'The good news is, I've got him down to ten commandments. The bad news is, committing adultery is still one of them.' "

The waiter came with their martinis: frosted glasses and a bottle of Grey Goose vodka that had been frozen in a narrow block of ice.

Keely raised her glass above her head. *"Arriba."* Dropped it down to table level. *"Abajo."* Then to chest level. *"Centro."* And finally brought the glass to her lips. *"Al dentro."*

"Up, down, middle, and inside," Chasen translated. "I'll drink to that."

"I have so much work to do on the Australian project, Dave. I've got to get back there and finish it up. There was some good news at the embassy. The police have released Sam's body for burial. Daria told me she doesn't care where Sam is buried. She was happy to drop that little chore into my lap. I want to get that over and done with. I was thinking—"

"Am I interrupting?" Perry Bryce said.

"It's what you're good at," Chasen said, waving for Bryce to sit down. He made the introductions.

Keely stared daggers at Bryce.

The waiter came by and Bryce asked for a mineral water.

"So how was your day?" Chasen asked.

Bryce's eyes bounced from Chasen's to Keely's. "I'm not sure Miss Alroy would be interested in hearing everything."

Keely upended her glass and rose to her feet. "Isn't this the part in the movie where the ingenue tells the boys that she has to powder her nose? I have some packing to do."

Bryce watched Keely head for the elevators, then undid his tie and slipped into the empty chair. "Jago Roldan has been contacted by someone who says he has the *Professio*. There's to be an exchange tonight. Midnight, at the Plaza Mayor, here in Madrid. Next to the statue of King Felipe."

"Plaza Mayor. What's it like?" Chasen asked.

"New Year's Eve in New York City, according to Lieutenant Garate." Bryce plucked the olive from Keely's martini glass and popped it into his mouth. "Garate specified that I be unarmed. He patted that cannon under his arm when he gave me my orders."

"What's the deal? What does Jago have to cough up for the *Professio*?"

"One of his paintings, *Dreams by the Lake*, by Francisco José de Goya. And two hundred thousand Euros."

Chasen scratched his jaw thoughtfully. "The plot curdles. What's the painting worth?"

"I have no idea. I can find out from Chalmers; I'm sure that—"

"Don't bother MI6. I know an expert who'll come up with a price. Two hundred thousand Euros. That doesn't make much sense. Why not a million? Two million?"

"I wouldn't turn my nose up at two hundred thousand," Bryce said.

"Maybe whoever set this up knows how much money Jago has lying around the house. Two hundred thousand is petty cash to Jago. He might balk at handing over a million or two, though."

Bryce looked at his watch. "Garate is picking me up at ten o'clock. Less than an hour from now. I have to get ready."

"How did you develop all of this information? From Garate?"

"Raul Tobias. Garate has him scared witless. I wired Tobias."

"Is Jago delivering the painting and money himself?"

"No. He's going to the plaza, but Vidal insisted on being the bag man. Tobias is going to be there, keeping an eye on him."

Chasen scratched his jaw again. "That's interesting. Vidal, the dutiful son. I just can't picture him putting himself in jeopardy."

Bryce pushed himself to his feet and stretched his neck, exposing his Adam's apple as he tightened his tie. "Jeopardy is right. Daria Alroy more or less ordered Tobias to take care of the thief and Vidal tonight. Nice family, huh?"

"The best," Chasen said. "Garate is being awfully cooperative with you."

"He's being well paid. I picked up another fat packet of money at the British Embassy, courtesy of Snake Chalmers, and passed it on to our dedicated lieutenant this afternoon."

Bryce was halfway to the elevators when he doubled back and said, "You never told me about your day."

"Boring," Chasen said. "Damn boring."

"It doesn't look very promising, does it? Either of us getting our hands on the *Professio*."

"Where's that plucky, never-say-die British spirit, Bryce? There's still a chance."

"You never made your—or should I say our—position very clear. If we do get the damn thing you propose what? A fifty-fifty split?"

"Exactly. The person who'll handle the transaction is very reliable. No one will know we were involved, if we play it right."

"If we get to play it at all," Bryce said. "You'll be there? At the plaza?"

"I'll be there," Chasen promised.

Berlin, Germany

"I'm going home now," Hal Gevertz's secretary told him.

"I'm sorry I kept you so late, Hilda," Gevertz apologized. "Take the morning off. Have breakfast in bed with that lucky young man of yours."

Hilda ran her hand down her golden braid, then flung it over her shoulder. "He's out of the picture. The *shmekel* is married."

Gevertz picked up a pencil and began doodling. Hilda was well known for her strong sexual appetite. "That never bothered you before," he teased.

"Three children," she said bitterly. "One just a newborn."

"If only I were a little younger." Gevertz grinned. *"Ale montik un donershtik."* Every Monday, Thursday, every time you turn around.

Hilda patted her ample hips. "You're old, but you're not dead yet, are you?"

"I can rise to the occasion." He shooed her away. "Sleep

late. Enjoy yourself." He leaned over the desk and began sketching pictures of a naked Hilda in various poses.

He dropped the pencil when his private phone line rang.

"I'm glad I caught you in," Dave Chasen said.

"Anscheiben, David. Shame on you. You don't trust me anymore? Where are you?"

"In a pay phone at the Ritz Hotel in Madrid. And I trust you as much as you trust me, Hal."

"Then why are you shopping around that item we talked about?"

"The *Professio*?"

"What else? If not you, then some *gonif* who wants to know what it's worth?"

"They contacted you?" Chasen said.

"No. A fellow I know in London, who, lucky for us, didn't know dreck about it. So he called me."

"What did you tell your London friend?"

Gevertz's pencil sketched out a crude image of the fat-faced Londoner. "That it was *das geschwalle.* Nonsense. A fraud. I'm afraid he didn't believe me."

"Did your friend tell you who was asking the questions?"

"He's not that good a friend," Gevertz said with a soft chuckle.

"What can you tell me about a Goya painting, *Dreams by the Lake*?"

"First the *Professio* and now a Goya. You are moving in very high circles, David. Hold on." Gevertz dropped the pencil. His fingers flew across the computer's keyboard. Not satisfied, he got up, foraged through a shelf of books, and found one with illustrations of Goya's paintings. When he came back on the line he was in high spirits. "Do you happen to have this Goya in your lap right now, my friend?"

"No. But it's within reach. What would it bring on the underground market?"

"Why underground?" Gevertz asked. "The Goya hasn't been seen in years, David, not all that long after Goya completed the painting. The story is that the great man was un-happy with it, and gave it to one of the women in the paint-ing. The one with the big tits spilling out of her dress. It's not *beutenkunst*," he said, using the term used to refer to known works of art seized by the Nazis. "The provenance is unclouded. I'll have to do more research, but it appears that it's 'finders keepers.' You could sell it through Christie's or Sotheby's, if you wished to. I would advise against that, though. An intermediary, such as myself, would allow you to remain unknown. I'm sure that would be to your benefit."

"I'll keep you posted, Hal."

"You do that, David. And be careful. *Shainera mechen haut me gelicht in drert.*"

Chasen returned the receiver to its cradle, mulling over Gevertz's parting words. "They've buried better-looking people than you." He wondered as he rode the elevator up to his suite why so many words of advice seemed to have something to do with the dead or dying. He knocked on the door and motioned for Keely Alroy to join him in the hall-way.

She listened with rapt attention when he told her about his latest discussion with Bryce.

"Tell me about the Plaza Mayor," he said.

"It's a mob scene," Keely responded. "*La movida,* the in-tense nightlife of Madrid. Whoever planned this knows Madrid well. It's not just the plaza. The parties start there; then the crowd wanders from place to place, street to street."

"I've got to keep an eye on Vidal. My hunch is that this is all a sham. That's he's already in possession of the *Pro-fessio.*"

"That doesn't make a lot of sense," Keely said.

"Sure it does. Vidal knows that if he sold it on the open market, there's a good chance Jago would be able to trace the sale right back to him. Jago has one foot and three toes in the grave. Vidal has been a black sheep, but all of a sudden he becomes a hero. Gets back in Daddy's good graces by rescuing the *Professio*, which, if he does this right, will soon be his, along with all of Jago's estate."

"Daria would never let him get away with that," Keely said.

"Maybe, maybe not. But Vidal has his mitts on the Goya now. And the cash. If I'm right, he'll pretend to make the switch with someone at the plaza, and run right back to Jago with the *Professio*. The cash is a payoff for whoever's in this with him. That's why I've got to keep an eye on Vidal."

"We've got to keep an eye on Vidal," Keely said. "It's almost impossible for someone who doesn't know the area. You'd get swallowed up. My folks vacationed in Spain every summer. I was part of that crowd in my younger years, Dave, and I've been there dozens of times since I moved to Spain. I know what it's like. I'll take my camera. Believe me, they have a good chance of pulling this off. At least I can get a picture or two of him."

"No, Keely. I don't want you in the middle—"

"I've been in the middle of thicker mud than this, Dave. Colombia. The Arctic Circle. And the backlands of Australia wasn't exactly a picnic."

"Tobias will be there, too. And Vidal, and Jago. You'll be spotted right away."

"And you won't?" Keely countered.

"All right. I suggest we get over to the plaza right now. Scope it out and buy some clothes, so that we can blend in with the crowd." Chasen cupped his hand around Keely's elbow and drew her close. "One way or another, you are going to get one hell of a documentary out of this."

Chapter Twenty-Nine

Jago and Vidal Roldan stood side by side in the center of the Plaza Mayor, next to the statue of King Felipe III on horseback. A sea of young men and women were enjoying *la movida*. They swayed to the music coming from ragtag bands or boomboxes, shared bottles of wine and beer, danced, hugged, fondled each other.

Jago felt uneasy as he surveyed those around him. Many of the women—girls actually—were attractive, in a restless, youthful way. Their skimpy clothes, low-cut shorts, and half-buttoned blouses showed off their hard bodies to good advantage. The males appeared to be an unkempt lot, scraggily beards, their shirts stained from beer, food, or God knew what. A few were dressed in gruesome costumes: ghosts with white masks, devils in skintight red outfits and painted faces. Others had political slogans painted on their bare chests and backs.

It was the way that they looked at him that angered Jago. The males smirked. One joked out loud at *el viejo verde buscar flete*—literally a horny old man out looking for a piece of ass.

Jago, who had made love to more women than these *pendejos* could ever dream of, would have welcomed the opportunity to beat some respect into the lot of them. But he was forced to stand there, like the King Felipe statue, and wait for the cell phone to ring.

"It's almost midnight, Father," Vidal said.

To Jago, his son looked almost as foolish as the young celebrants. Vidal was wearing a loose-fitting yellow nylon jacket and a long-billed royal blue hat, of the type fishermen wore to protect themselves from the sun. The colorful clothing had been Vidal's idea. It would make it easier for Raul Tobias to keep track of him. Tobias was there in the crowd somewhere, in costume—a masked ghost with the flowing white beard of a biblical prophet.

There was a loud bang. At first Jago thought it was a gunshot.

Vidal flinched and dropped to his knees, drawing howls of laughter from the scum nearby. Someone on the far side of the square had set off a rocket. It streaked high up into the black Madrid night air and exploded in a shower of sparkles.

The cell phone rang. "Yes," Jago barked.

"Are the painting and the money in the black bag on your shoulder?" A man's voice. Unfamiliar. Harsh, strained, as if he were holding his hand against his throat as he spoke.

Jago flexed his right shoulder. The cheap canvas bag contained Goya's masterpiece and two hundred thousand Euros. Vidal had carefully prepared the painting, removing the frame, wrapping it in silicone-coated parchment paper, then placing it between two sheets of nonacid fiberboard before adding a thick padding of bubble-wrap foil. "I have what you want. You had better have what I want, or I swear I'll track you down and kill you."

"Start walking. Leave the phone line open. Go through the arches leading to Cava Alta or Cava Baja. It doesn't matter which one. Stay with the crowd. Stop at a *tasca*. Then another. I'll catch up with you sooner or later."

"I am feeling ill," Jago said. "My son, Vidal, is standing next to me. He will make the delivery."

"This had better not be a trick," the harsh voice threatened.

"You are exactly right. It had better not be a trick on your part." Jago handed the canvas bag and the cell phone to Vidal, and repeated the orders he'd been given. "Be careful, son."

"Don't worry, Father. I'll bring the *Professio* to you."

Vidal hesitated a moment, took a deep breath, then joined the tide of young people on their *tasca* crawl—traipsing from *tasca* to *tasca*, sampling the wine or beer in each one.

Dave Chasen could hear the soft whirling sound of Keely Alroy's camera as she adjusted the zoom lens. Jago and Vidal Roldan were standing in the center of the plaza. Jago had a cell phone to his ear, and Vidal was moving around from one leg to the other as if he had to go to the bathroom.

The plan was for Keely to take wide-angle shots of the area, hoping to identify the person Vidal was supposedly meeting.

She had removed all of her makeup and was wearing a bandanna knotted pirate-style over her hair, lightly tinted glasses with lenses the size of coffee cups, and a multipocketed black jacket stuffed with photography equipment.

Chasen had found a used-clothing store near the plaza and purchased a black, knee-length jacket and battered felt fedora that could have been used in an Indiana Jones movie.

"Who do you think Vidal is working with?" Keely asked.

"Maybe no one. He certainly wouldn't trust anyone with the *Professio*. It's either under his jacket, or he has it stashed somewhere close by," Chasen said. The apple didn't fall far from the tree. After years of humiliation and disrespect, Vidal was sticking it to Jago, and in a manner that the old man might appreciate if it weren't happening directly to him. What Chasen had to do was get to Vidal without Tobias, Jago, or Lieutenant Garate being any the wiser.

Jago handed the cell phone and the black canvas bag to Vidal. He patted his son on the shoulder just before Vidal plunged into the crowd.

"Keep the camera on the yellow jacket," Chasen said as

they took off after Vidal. "If we become separated, we'll meet back by the King Felipe statue."

Perry Bryce twisted the focus dial on his binoculars, overcompensated, and twisted it back. "Where's Tobias?"

"A ghost's costume," Lt. Sil Garate said. "With a long white beard."

Bryce scanned the crowd, finding Tobias in his white sheet and ghost's mask complete with the chest-length beard. "What's he saying?"

Garate adjusted the earphones, listening to the sounds being transmitted by the microphone taped to Tobias's chest. The only earphones. Bryce would have to take Garate's word as to what information Tobias passed along. What information Garate chose to pass on. It was obvious to Bryce now that Garate was going to make a try for either the *Professio*, the canvas bag, or both.

Garate prodded Bryce with an elbow. "Vidal is on the move. Go. Vidal has never seen you. Get close to him, but don't act until I have given the order."

Bryce was certain that he'd never hear Garate's order. That he was being used by the Spanish policeman in much the same way he was used by his MI6 superiors. Snake Chalmers, after several Scotches in a pub near the Firm's headquarters, had once toasted a fallen comrade, some poor agent who'd bought it in a disgusting cellar in Pakistan—literally skinned alive. "Good man, Stilwell. Tough way to go, but luckily he was expendable."

Not so lucky for Stilwell. Right now Bryce wasn't feeling so lucky himself. Where the hell was Dave Chasen?

The crowds were as predicted. On the plus side, Chasen and Keely had no trouble keeping sight of Vidal Roldan's yellow jacket and bright blue hat.

They left the plaza, walked down a steep flight of uneven, timeworn stone steps, and emerged into an ancient part of the city, with narrow, serpentine streets known as *cavas*. The *cavas* bordering the plaza were originally moats or ditches built along the medieval walls, and were used as escape routes for people in the old walled city of Madrid during those times when battles weren't going their way.

The *cavas* were framed by old stone-faced two- and three-story buildings housing apartments, shops, and numerous bars and food stands. The streetlights were pale yellow smudges in the black night air. Several groups of musicians, dressed up in medieval costumes, were playing guitars, lutes, and tambourines for tips, or preferably a free drink.

Keely stopped every few minutes to film the area. At one point she stepped onto a platform leading to a restaurant at the same time a particularly obnoxious group of young men got into a shoving match that erupted into a full gang fight, Madrid-style, fists, bottles, and the occasional flash of a knife blade.

Chasen found himself in the middle of the battle. When he finally pushed his way around the men, Keely was nowhere to be seen. He climbed up on the base of a streetlight and, balancing precariously, scanned the crowd. No Keely Alroy. Vidal Roldan's yellow jacket was gone, too.

Perry Bryce took birdlike sips of the *chatos*, a small glass of red wine, sold at the first two *tascas* he stopped at while tailing Vidal Roldan. Vidal didn't look like a man carrying a priceless painting and two hundred thousand Euros. He looked like . . . what? Bryce asked himself. A man heading for a poker game. With a stack of marked cards in his pocket. Occasionally he would put the cell phone to his ear, mumble something, and take off again.

There was barely room to move at the next establishment. Hot, sweaty bodies of both sexes writhed to heavy rock music and occasionally bumped up against him. Bryce ordered a beer and drank all of it before moving on with the debauching crowd. He saw several young men passing pills about. Ecstacy and psychedelic drugs, was his guess. It seemed somehow sinful to need the help of drugs to have a good time when all those beautiful girls looked so willing and available.

After a while, it all seemed somehow orchestrated. A stream of drunken, singing, shouting *Madrileños* would decide to leave one *tasca* just as another loud group entered, occupying the same chairs, leaning against the same walls—kissing, drinking, smoking, dancing.

Bryce was beginning to feel like a lone trout groping around in a river of spawning fish.

There was no sign of Garate, but Tobias, in his white-bearded ghost costume, was never far away.

On to yet another drinking establishment, Las Cuevas de Luis Candelas, a cavelike building named after a famous bandit who was reputed to be the Robin Hood of old Spain. A waiter brought a tray of frosty-mugged beers, and one was pressed into Bryce's hand.

The breasts of an attractive teenager with shoulder-length hair and bangs that reached down to her eyebrows brushed his arm. She looked up at him with enormous suction-cup black eyes. Her lips moved, but Bryce couldn't hear over the noise of the crowd. He leaned down and she placed her lips close to his ear and said, "*Hazme una cubana.*"

At any other time, he would have willingly taken her up on her offer to place his penis between her breasts. Bryce shook his head in a negative response.

"*Me he perdido.*" She pouted. "*Tengo sed.*"

She was lost and thirsty.

Bryce offered her his beer. Without warning, his outstretched hand was grabbed in a viselike grip. The girl snatched the glass and splashed the beer in his face.

Bryce used a handkerchief to wipe his eyes. The group around him had backed off and began to laugh and jeer. He looked for Vidal Roldan, but he was nowhere to be seen.

"¡Qué maricón! ¿Qué hay de nuevo?" a gangly eighteen-year-old with a shaven head shouted, calling Bryce a homosexual and mocking him. This brought another round of laughter from his companions.

With as much dignity as he could muster, he looked around for Vidal Roldan, but he was gone. Bryce stalked out of the *tasca,* only to be knocked off his feet by the fleeing figure of Raul Tobias in his ghost's costume.

Dave Chasen glanced at his watch. Almost twenty minutes since he'd lost sight of Keely and Vidal. Then, out of the corner of his eye, he saw it: Vidal's yellow jacket. Chasen picked up the pace, using his shoulders and elbows to clear a path through the milling crowds. The yellow jacket. The blue hat. But the walk. The tilt of the neck, the roll of the buttocks. It wasn't Vidal!

He forged ahead, angering a towering young man wearing a sweatshirt with the sleeves cut off at the shoulders to show off his huge arms.

"¡Jódate y apriete el culo!" the young man swore.

Chasen ignored the insult, but when he tried to edge by, he was grabbed and yanked backward.

The man never saw the short, knuckles-extended punch Chasen landed directly into his solar plexus.

Chasen ran forward. He grasped the sleeve of the yellow jacket and used his free hand to knock off the blue hat. The figure that spun around to face him had hollow cheeks, sunken eyes, and wine-black hair. Vidal Roldan's receptionist.

"Get away from me," she said calmly.

Perry Bryce heard a gunshot. The distinct sound set it apart from the strings of firecrackers and rockets that had been going off all night.

He stood in the middle of a cobblestone street, head swiveling left and right, looking for Garate or, hopefully,

Dave Chasen, and trying to determine where the shot had come from.

Crack. Crack. Crack. Three more shots. Close by. Even the young drunks in the street seemed to realize that those weren't firecrackers. A thick-bodied man with a face contorted in pain stumbled out of an alley, hands clutching at his stomach. Blood was seeping through his fingers. He tottered for several seconds, then lurched back into the darkness. *Who the hell is he?* Bryce wondered as he cautiously entered the pitch-black alley. There was a brief flash of light at the end of the alley, then another shot.

Bryce dropped to the ground and tried to remember a prayer.

Dave Chasen heard the gunshots, then a series of whistles. He began running, going in the general direction of the shots. He spotted Lieutenant Garate and two men outfitted in riot gear clustered in front of an alley.

"How did you get here?" Garate said when he noticed Chasen.

A man in a ghost's costume and flowing white beard thudded to a stop near them. Raul Tobias ripped off the beard and rubber mask. His face was sheened with sweat. The strands of his thinning hair were plastered across his forehead.

Tobias was pointing to a motionless body on the ground, lying on its face, arms akimbo, the sleeve of his jacket pushed up near the elbow, revealing a braid of tattoos.

"It's the fucking priest, Fallon," Tobias said. "It has to be him."

Garate knelt down, his hand going to the neck of the man on the ground. He raised the man's head just enough for Chasen to see his face.

"Lieutenant," Chasen said. "I believe you'll find that the dead man has your name tattooed on his arm."

Garate gave Chasen a hard look, then rose to his feet. "What do you mean? You know this man?"

"His name's Taric. He worked for Giles Dolius."

Tobias kicked out at an empty bottle, sending it crashing into a lamppost. "Where's the *Professio*? The money?"

Garate approached Tobias, threw him against the wall, and ordered one of his men to search him. He turned to Chasen, who lifted his arms away from his body. "I'm not carrying a weapon, Lieutenant."

Garate gave Chasen a professional patting down. "The two of you are to accompany my men to police headquarters," he announced.

"Keely Alroy's around here somewhere," Chasen said. "I'm not leaving till I'm sure she's safe."

Garate was about to respond when Perry Bryce showed up, breathing deeply. He bent over at the waist and gulped in air.

"Where have you been?" Garate asked.

"Chasing Vidal Roldan's killer all over this goddamn plaza," Bryce said, his voice hoarse with anger. "I lost him." He jerked a finger to a doorway at the end of the alley. "Vidal's in there, lying next to a crapper, deader than the British Empire."

Chapter Thirty

"**N**ot the place I'd pick for my last communion with Mother Nature," Perry Bryce said, peering down at Vidal Roldan.

The swamper's room was nearly closet-sized, used to store janitorial supplies, brooms, mops, and toilet paper. It featured a lone square window and two rickety wooden doors blanketed with grime and smudged fingerprints, one leading to the *tasca* where he'd been pelted with the beer, the other to the alley where the body of the man with the tattoos had been found.

A single bare lightbulb surrounded by protective steel mesh was the only source of light.

Roldan was lying on his back on the damp, disinfectant-infused cement floor, his head cocked at an awkward angle against a chipped and seatless toilet bowl.

His glasses were dangling from one ear, his legs sprawled out in front of him. He was still wearing the bright yellow jacket, but it was open, as was his blue-and-white-striped shirt. A strip of thick adhesive tape had been ripped from his chest, leaving a raw, red stripe. One end of the tape dangled down to his midsection.

The blue cap was several feet from his outstretched left hand. His eyes were stretched wide, as if he'd been surprised when he'd seen his killer. A single bullet hole was centered in his forehead.

A small semiautomatic pistol lay on the floor near the door leading to the alley.

Lt. Sil Garate closed his eyes and massaged his temples with the heels of his hands. "Tell me again how you found Roldan here."

"I was on the street. I heard shots. One. A break. Then three more. This bloke staggers out into the alley. It was obvious he was shot. I checked the bloke—"

"The bloke's name is Taric," Garate said angrily. "He worked for Giles Dolius, according to Chasen."

"Yeah, well, he's new to me. Since I didn't have a gun, I shouted, '*Policía.*' There was another shot. The door from this dump leading to the alley opened. A man, all in black, with a knit cap, took one look at me and slammed the door."

"What did he look like? Was it John Fallon?"

"I couldn't tell. I was trying to dig a hole in the street and hide, and his face was in the shadows. I ran in here. Saw Vidal Roldan lying just as he is now." Bryce pointed to Vidal. "I could see he was dead, so I took off after the guy with the knit cap."

"What about the canvas bag?" Calvino asked.

"Knit cap had it looped over his shoulder. I chased him. If you had trusted me with a radio, a phone to call you or your men, or a gun, I would have had him."

"You must have gotten some kind of a look at him?"

"Just his back. Curly dark brown hair at the back of the knit cap. About Fallon's size, and he moved like an athlete. I could never get close enough to see his face."

Garate waved a hand angrily in the air. "It had to be Fallon. I never should have gotten mixed up with you people."

Bryce liked that. *You people.* Another highly paid asset of MI6 about to jump ship when a major storm approached. But not while Bryce was still on board, if he could help it. It was time to let the Spaniard know just how much trouble he was in.

"Look on the bright side, Lieutenant. You've got two

dead men. A shoot-out. Vidal Roldan got in the first four shots, killing Taric, but before he dies, Taric shoots Vidal, or knit cap does. Knit cap could be Fallon, or one of Taric's men, and Taric probably has a record worse than Tobias. Another case solved by your sterling detective work."

"What of the missing money, my fine British spy? And the painting? The *Professio*?"

"Knit cap got it all. And if that fails, you've got Tobias on the scene."

"You forget that Tobias was wired. I heard his every move."

"Tonight you did. But not between the family gathering at Jago's house and me resetting his transmitter right here in the plaza. Tobias could have gotten the word to one of his buddies. Or to Daria. She had no love for Vidal. A long night with your sergeant friend at the jail, and Tobias will confess to whatever fits best."

Garate tilted his head to one side and pursed his mouth in a gesture of contempt. "It's going to be a long night for all of us. You included."

Bryce tapped his foot against Vidal Roldan's outstretched arm. "I don't think so. I'm tired. I'm going to bed. That's not some small-time crook with his head up against a crapper. That's Jago Roldan's one and only son. He's not going to be a happy camper. And if he found out that a respected member of the Centro Nacional de Inteligencia had been illegally bugging his house, and using one of his employees as an informant, Jago would be really pissed. I imagine he could swing a lot of weight, even with the CNI."

"Are you threatening me?" Garate said between clenched teeth.

"Just explaining the facts of life, Lieutenant. Which you'd better explain to Raul Tobias. And don't forget the American, Chasen. He was in the area when all this went down. You can never trust the Yanks. I'll stop by and see you in the morning."

*   *   *

Daria Roldan Alroy had kept an apartment in her grand-father's Madrid mansion for most of her life. After her marriage to Sam, they had both moved into the house while their own residence was being constructed. A residence she would no longer need. She'd heard that Vidal was dead, and she was pleased. Raul Tobias had finally fulfilled his obligations. Only Keely Alroy remained to be dealt with.

Jago had been devastated when he learned of his son's death. The *Professio* meant little to him now. The Goya and the money, nothing. Vidal was dead. "The last of the Roldans, Daria. Unless . . ." The old fool had placed his quivering hand on Daria's stomach and begged, actually begged her to have this child.

She breezed into her apartment, her mind dizzy with the prospect of taking control of the family wealth. Of humiliating Keely, buying her off with a few meaningless trinkets—the boat, perhaps Sam's house in London.

She entered her bedroom to find Raul Tobias searching through her jewelry box.

"What do you think you're doing?" she demanded.

Tobias glared at her, then upended the box, stuffing bracelets, necklaces, and rings into his pockets. "I need money. Cash."

Daria crossed the room in three quick strides. "Have you gone mad?" She slapped Tobias across the face. "Get out of here."

"With great pleasure. But not empty-handed."

Daria was genuinely shocked. "I don't understand this. You eliminated Vidal. I was going—"

"It wasn't me," Tobias said. "Because of you, the police have me set up for it, if things don't go their way. I have to get away from Madrid. From Spain." He began going through a chest of drawers, tossing out lingerie and cash-mere sweaters. "Your purse. Where is it?" He grabbed her arm and twisted it cruelly behind her back. "A better idea would be Jago's vault. You have the code, don't you?"

Daria struggled to free herself. She screamed for help and Tobias hit her across the face. She screamed again. Tobias ripped the back of her dress and threw her onto the bed. He started to unbuckle his pants. "One more before I go, eh? My terms, Daria. On top. You don't like that, do—"

"Get away from her," Jago Roldan shouted.

Tobias's head jerked around. Roldan was swaying on his feet, his face beet red, his hair disheveled. He looked a hundred years old.

"*Abuelo*," Daria cried. "He tried to rape me. He killed Vidal."

"Rape," Tobias mocked. "If anyone was raped, it was me. For all I know, that baby in your granddaughter's stomach is mine. Or maybe it's yours, Jago, eh?"

"You killed my son," Jago said woodenly. He closed the door behind him and engaged the lock before turning to face Tobias.

"Are you all right?" he asked Daria. Her face was swollen, and trickles of blood seeped from the side of her mouth. He glared at Tobias. "I'm going to kill you, you miserable excuse for a man."

Tobias withdrew his knife. "No, you're going to open your vault for me."

Jago's back bumped into the wall.

"No place to run," Tobias said, tossing the knife from hand to hand, taunting Jago.

As Tobias lunged forward, Jago twisted the ivory handle of his cane and a sixteen-inch steel blade slid from its wooden sheath. He executed a rusty, ungraceful *balestra*, a tiny hop forward, his stiff arm shooting out, driving the blade straight into Tobias's stomach.

Tobias stiffened, breath whooshing out of his mouth like air from a punctured balloon. He stared at Jago in disbelief.

Jago yanked the blade free. "You young bulls always make the mistake of underestimating the old ones."

Tobias dropped to his knees. He opened his mouth to speak, blood bubbles forming on his lips.

Jago stepped around the pool of blood forming on the carpet, placed the tip of the blade between Tobias's shoulder blades, and in the manner of a bullfighter performing an *estoque*, thrust the knife forward again.

Tobias toppled to the floor and Jago withdrew the blade, wiping it clean on Tobias's pant leg. He stood over his kill for a moment, then looked over at Daria, the expression on his face one of fierce pride.

Keely Alroy raced over to Dave Chasen when he entered the Ritz Hotel suite.

"I've been trying to reach you all night." She wrapped her arms around him and nestled her head against his chest. "I've called the jail a dozen times. All they would tell me was that you were being questioned. Perry Bryce called a couple of hours ago. He told me what happened." She grabbed Chasen's hand and led him to the couch.

"The room's still bugged," Chasen said. "Bryce must have heard you calling the jail and did his Good Samaritan deed of the day. I checked his room. He's gone."

Keely folded her arms across her chest and cupped her elbows in her palms. She was wearing a lacy pink slip that clung to her curves. "What are you going to do now?"

"I need coffee, food, and a shower," Chasen said as he plopped on the couch. "What happened? Where did you disappear to?"

"I got tangled up in the crowd. I couldn't see you, Vidal, anyone. I went back to the plaza. To the statue, like we'd planned. Jago Roldan was still there. A policeman came, talked to him. From Roldan's reaction I knew something terrible had happened."

"Terrible is a mild description," Chasen said wearily.

"Has any of this gotten us any closer to Sam's killer? Bryce told me that Vidal killed a man. Someone who worked for Dolius, the fence you told me about. He must have killed Sam, too."

"The police will probably end up saying he did, but I'm not buying it."

"What about John Fallon? Was he there at the Plaza Mayor last night?"

"Garate would love to pin Vidal's death on Fallon. Bryce told him he saw the killer—a man all in black, about Fallon's size and build, but he didn't see his face." Chasen rubbed his forehead. He had a fierce headache. "The *Professio*, the painting, the money, all up in smoke. And John Fallon has your brother's laptop computer, which is what I was sent to find in the first place."

"I'm going back to Torremolinos," Keely said. "I can't take much more of this. Once Sam's funeral is taken care of, I'm heading for Australia."

Chasen placed his hands on his knees and levered himself to his feet. "I'm stuck here for at least another day. Order me something from room service. Steak, eggs, toast, a gallon or two of coffee." He paused at the bedroom door. Keely's luggage was set neatly alongside the bed. "When are you leaving?"

Keely walked past him and jerked the bedcover down. "After breakfast."

Chapter Thirty-One

Three cars were lined up behind the hearse: one of Jago Roldan's Daimlers, a dusty black compact, and a light-colored four-door sedan with twin spotlights and a whip antenna.

"Park right here," Dave Chasen told the cabdriver. "And wait. No matter how long it takes."

The church, located a few miles south of Torremolinos, was a one-story adobe structure with a bird-bombed tile roof and moisture stains around the windows. The neighboring cemetery featured neat rows of knee-high grave markers in the shape of crosses that stretched down to an abandoned orchard filled with trees that looked like white parasols. A stiff afternoon wind had kicked up, scattering blossoms like dirty confetti. The neighboring hills were clouded with wild mustard and purple lupine.

Chasen's feet made crunching sounds on an orange path of pine needles leading to the burial site.

The elderly, white-haired priest was reading from a Bible in mumbled Spanish over the open grave.

Keely Alroy, wearing a fawn-colored skirt and jacket, and holding a bouquet of crimson-petaled flowers, looked up at Chasen, gave him a brief nod, then cast her eyes back on the raw pine coffin.

Daria Roldan Alroy had dressed for the occasion: a shapeless ecclesiastical-severe dress and a somber black hat complete with a gauzy veil that failed to hide her icy blue eyes.

Jago Roldan was in better shape than Chasen expected: a perfectly tailored gray suit, his hair sprayed in place, smoky-lensed sunglasses, his posture erect, both hands cupped around his cane.

Vidal's burial was to be the following day, in Madrid, at the Basilica de San Francisco el Grande, an eighteenth-century church with a dome larger than that of St. Paul's in London. A far cry from Sam Alroy's final resting place.

Lt. Sil Garate and Inspector Calvino were also in attendance. Garate, head dropping to his chest, looking as if it were he who had lost a loved one. Calvino was chewing gum and jiggling change in his pants pockets.

Two men in dusty pants and soiled T-shirts stood a respectful distance away, shovels in hand, waiting to finish their day's work.

The priest said a final prayer and the two workers dropped their shovels, picked up the thick ropes attached to the coffin, centered it over the hole, and lowered it into the ground.

Keely dropped the flowers onto Sam's coffin and slowly made her way to Chasen. "I need a big goddamn drink," she said softly.

Jago Roldan approached. He addressed Keely, ignoring Chasen. "You are welcome to attend Vidal's services tomorrow."

"I won't be able to make it," Keely answered curtly.

Jago took off his glasses. His eyes were red-rimmed, watery. "If we could talk alone for a moment . . ."

Chasen took the hint and wandered over to where Garate and Calvino were standing.

"I told you not to leave Torremolinos," Calvino admonished right away.

"Inspector, go to the car and wait for me," Garate ordered.

"How goes the investigation?" Chasen asked.

The policeman meandered over to a row of graves. He dragged his fingers across a weathered headstone. "Eighteen hundred and fifty-seven. That is a long time in the ground."

"I think one day would be a long time. Have you found Fallon?"

"No, he has disappeared. I assume he is back in Rome, attending to the sick and poor. Praying for the souls of all sinners."

Chasen's eyes narrowed, making crow's-feet. "Or maybe he's celebrating the return of the *Professio* to the Vatican. Where's Perry Bryce?"

"In London, where he belongs. You have no doubt heard of the death of Raul Tobias."

Chasen looked over to Keely and Jago Roldan, and saw they were still in deep conversation. "Yes. Jago's still a tough old bird."

"Señor Roldan did us a service. Our investigation points to Tobias as the murderer of Vidal Roldan and the thief Taric."

"Isn't that strange? I could swear that Tobias showed up just after you found Taric's body."

"He had an accomplice," Garate said, dusting his hands of the soot from the tombstone. "Eventually he will be found."

"Eventually you could be right, Lieutenant. Are you going to lay Sam Alroy's death at Tobias's dirty feet, too? That would make a nice, neat package."

Garate twisted his head upward to watch a hovering hawk. "Inspector Calvino agrees with that theory, and the murder took place in his jurisdiction. He tells me that Tobias killed Alroy and Giles Dolius. For reasons of his own. There is no involvement on the part of Señor Roldan."

"Calvino will dance to any tune you or Roldan plays, Lieutenant."

Garate's upper lip tightened and rode up over his teeth. "I

want you out of Spain, Chasen. Right away. And unlike Inspector Calvino, I expect my orders to be followed."

"I have a flight booked for tomorrow morning."

"Good," Garate said on a note of dismissal. "And do not return. Ever."

Keely Alroy handed an envelope to the elderly priest, paid the driver of the hearse, then slipped into Chasen's cab. "I think I saw a bar on the road near the turnoff to the church. Let's get that drink."

"There is always a bar near a cemetery," the cabdriver said.

The establishment the cabdriver selected looked to be the sort that catered to a mostly local crowd, supplemented on occasion by those in mourning. Keely ordered a glass of beer and a shot of whiskey, Chasen an Aguardiente, a clear Spanish brandy. When the drinks came, Keely took a long sip of the beer, then poured the whiskey into the beer glass and swirled it around. "Do you know what the trail guides in Australia call this drink? Roo-butt. Because after three or four, it makes the back end of a kangaroo look pretty damn good to them."

Chasen said, "You and Jago seemed to be talking serious business."

"He's really a ruthless bastard. Sam not even cold in his grave, his own son to be buried tomorrow, and all Jago wanted to do was talk business. 'We must come to a just settlement,' " Keely said, parodying Roldan's gravelly voice. " 'A settlement we can both live with.' He warned me that if I try to fight him in court over Sam's business, or the insurance money, I would have to suffer the consequences."

Chasen sampled his brandy. "That almost sounds like a threat."

"There's no 'almost' about it."

"What did you tell him?"

"To talk to my attorney." She took a swallow of her

drink. "Did you see Daria smirking behind that veil? She looked like the cat that swallowed the canary. Vidal gone. She's the one and only now. She'll probably wear a burqa for his funeral so no one will see her laughing."

"What about the baby?" Chasen asked. "Sam's baby."

"Daria's too strict a Catholic to have an abortion," Keely said sarcastically. "My money's on a miscarriage. It will break Jago's heart, but she's too much of a bitch to care."

"The police are going to wrap up their investigation of Sam's murder. Officially Raul Tobias will be the guilty party."

"They're right," Keely said angrily. "He pulled the trigger, but Daria ordered the execution. It's amazing the things you can get away with when you're as rich as the Roldans."

Chasen waved a hand to the cabdriver, who looked as if he were worried Chasen was going to duck out on him. "What's your next move?"

"To put some distance between myself and the Roldans. Back to Australia and work. What about you?"

"I have to get back to Washington. It hasn't exactly been a successful trip as far as the CIA is concerned. No laptop. No *Professio*. I may be back in Florida fishing for tarpon in a few days."

"Would they kick you out again? Just like that?"

"Just like that. I may stop in London on the way home to see Perry Bryce. I'd like to find out what really happened that night in the plaza."

"My guess is that we'll never know for certain," Keely said, pushing her glass toward Chasen. "I've had enough. Let's get out of here."

Keely gave Chasen a tender hug at the dock leading to her boat. "One month from today. Let's make a date right now. I don't care if you're in Washington or Florida. I want to see you." She fumbled in her purse, coming out with one of her business cards. "E-mail me, Dave." Her lips brushed his. "Please. Don't disappoint me."

"It's a date."

Chasen watched her board the *Gypsy Queen*; then he got back into the cab. He had the driver let him off a mile or so from his hotel.

Despite the wind, the beach was jammed. Once again he looked out of place in his jacket and tie among all the sun worshipers. He made his way to the area where Sam Alroy had been shot and stood there for several minutes, oblivious to the parade of oiled bodies, beach balls, and children racing past him.

Someone nudged him on the shoulder.

"I believe there's an excellent bar in your hotel. I could use a drink," Perry Bryce said cheerfully. "Would you care to join me?"

Chapter Thirty-Two

The hotel bar overlooked the swimming pool. Chasen found a table at the far end of the room and positioned himself so that he could monitor the entrance of the hotel, half expecting to have Garate or Inspector Calvino storm in at any moment to arrest him on some trumped-up charge. Trumped up with the help of Perry Bryce.

Bryce was wearing his usual baggy flannel slacks and a red knit shirt with a decal of a smiling sun circled by italicized letters spelling out *Costa de Sol* on the breast pocket.

"Garate told me that you'd gone back to London, Perry."

"Been there and done that," Bryce said. "And in all honesty, it wasn't a pleasant trip. Snake Chalmers is none too happy. I blamed you for all that went wrong, of course."

The cocktail waitress came by for their orders. She was wearing a black satin outfit that reminded Bryce of the type Playboy bunnies once wore. Her long legs were sheathed in black fishnet stockings with a line straight down the back. It was amazing what a simple alteration such as that could do to a man's imagination. He ordered a Pimm's and ginger ale.

"I thought you were a teetotaler," Chasen said, asking for a cup of coffee.

Bryce patted his flat stomach. "I'm told it's good for the digestion."

"Where's the *Professio*, Perry?"

"I told Chalmers that either you or Father John Fallon had it. He seemed to favor Fallon."

Chasen picked up a salt shaker and wrapped his fist around it. "Tell me what happened at the Plaza Mayor."

"Total confusion."

The waitress returned with their drinks, her breasts nearly spilling from her bodice as she leaned across the table to hand Chasen his coffee.

"I was set up in that grubby cavelike bar," Bryce continued. "Grabbed. Beer thrown in my face. Vidal disappeared. He'd been talking on the cell phone, presumably to the man he was supposed to meet up with. Obviously he was talking to one of his accomplices. It worked. Raul Tobias was fooled too. He almost knocked me down running out of the place."

"You scared Vidal," Chasen said. "He hadn't counted on you, just Tobias."

"But Vidal never saw me before. He couldn't know who I was."

"Wrong. He had an up-close-and-personal look at you when you were passed out on the floor in Jago's office."

"Vidal was there? You didn't tell me that."

"I should have," Chasen admitted. "You must have shaken him up. He had Taric all set to waylay Tobias. So when he saw you following him around, he had Taric arrange that scene in the bar to get rid of the two of you."

Bryce sampled his drink. He screwed up his face. "It must be an acquired taste."

"All of the good things in life are," Chasen said. "What happened next?"

"I was out on the streets, wandering around, trying not to appear foolish, when I heard a shot. There was a pause of, oh, fifteen or twenty seconds. Then three more shots in rapid succession. I saw this large man staggering out of an alley. I'd never seen him before. He fell to the ground. I went to investigate. There was a flash of light at the end of the alley.

The door was partway open. The killer must have switched the lights off and on, then immediately another shot."

Chasen rapped the salt shaker lightly on the table. "The man you told Garate you saw, all in black, with the knit cap, that was all bullshit, right?"

"Absolutely. I never saw a soul. I was having a religious conversion, eyes closed, hugging the dirt, denouncing all past sins if God just saved me this time."

Chasen studied Bryce's eyes, wondering if the MI6 agent were as good a liar as John Fallon. "You weren't on the dirt long. Garate must have arrived within a few minutes of the shots."

"I wish I'd had more time. The black sack was lying on the ground, a few feet from the dead man."

"What was in the sack?"

"Just the money. I went to the door at the end of the alley and found Vidal just as Garate did—lying on the floor next to a filthy toilet. Only there was a neatly wrapped package under his back."

"The *Professio*."

Bryce tried the Pimm's again. "No. Though I didn't realize that until I opened the package later. A painting. Not to my liking, but Goya's name is signed on the bottom right-hand corner. It was unframed but well protected."

"Tell me more about Vidal."

"Well, he was lying there, a small pistol near one hand. Cordite, gunpowder thick in the air. His shirt was unbuttoned. There was a piece of tape, the clear type used for wrapping packages, stuck on his chest. It had just been pulled away, by the looks of the red marks."

"That's where Vidal hid the *Professio*," Chasen said. "He'd learned that trick from his father. According to Fallon, Jago smuggled it out of Paris by carrying it under his shirt. Vidal was going to do the same thing with the Goya, tape it to his chest, then carry the *Professio* back to Jago."

"Well, someone certainly spoiled his plans. I scooped up

the painting, shoved it in the sack, and took off through the bar."

Chasen picked up a spoon and used its tip to draw a pattern on the tablecloth. "Taric spoiled his plans. Or maybe Vidal had planned on bumping him off all the time. Vidal needed someone to help him at the plaza—to get rid of Tobias. He had his receptionist out on the streets in the yellow-jacket-blue-cap getup to confuse everyone. Maybe the two hundred thousand Euros was a payoff for Taric. Taric may have known Vidal killed Giles Dolius. Or they could have been in on that together. We'll never know. What we do know is that planned or not, Vidal shot Taric. He wouldn't have to worry about the police. All he had to say was that Taric threatened him. That he wanted the *Professio*, the Goya, and the money. Vidal had to shoot him in self-defense. Who was going to challenge that scenario? It would have worked out perfectly for Vidal, except that someone caught him while he was untaping the *Professio* from his chest."

"And shot him," Bryce said. "Who was it? Fallon? Someone Taric had working with him?"

"I don't see Fallon as the shooting type. Where'd you stash the money and the painting?"

"In the garbage can of a restaurant a block or so away. I was sweating bloody bullets thinking that some drunk or dishwasher would discover it before I could return. But it was still there, amidst a cornucopia of old fruit and soggy vegetables."

Chasen spoke in a metered tone, stressing each word. "Why should I believe you?"

"Because basically I'm a coward," Bryce said genially. "And reasonably intelligent. I'm not a greedy man. Half of the cash, and half of what the Goya will bring, will suit me just dandy, especially if I don't have to worry about you popping up in the middle of the night with a gun, or dropping hints that I'm the bad guy into Snake Chalmers's treacherous ear. Chalmers told me you could be a vicious bastard in Berlin when crossed, but he grudgingly conceded that for a CIA man, you were straight as an arrow with your agents. 'Worried about 'em as if they was family' were his exact words."

"Where's the Goya now?" Chasen wanted to know.

"Safe in London. Along with the cash. The only problem I see now is how to best liquidate the painting. I was hoping you might have an idea." Bryce paused for dramatic effect, then added, "Partner."

Chasen rubbed his chin and sighed. Selling the Goya would be no problem. Hal Gevertz would jump at the chance of handling the transaction. Was Bryce leveling with him? "You make a really lousy spy, Perry. If you stay in the game any longer, you'll get yourself killed."

"Mother certainly wouldn't like that," Bryce said dryly. The third sip of Pimm's wasn't all that bad.

"I'll give you the name of a man in Berlin. Take the painting directly to him. We'll wait a while, three months or so, before selling the Goya. That suit you?"

"Absolutely." Bryce pushed his hand across the table. "What about the money?"

"Give my share to the man in Berlin for now. He's safer than a bank."

Bryce raised his head, looking for the darling in the black satin outfit. "I guess that settles everything."

"Not quite," Chasen said. "There's still the laptop and the *Professio*."

Dave Chasen noticed the thin metal case lying in the exact center of the bed as he opened the door to his hotel room. He checked the bathroom, then the terrace, then returned to the bed and picked up the laptop computer.

The telephone answering machine's red message light was blinking. He punched the *Play messages* button.

John Fallon's voice greeted him. "Dave. The laptop is the

real McCoy. Luckily the student at the Universidad Complutense de Madrid hadn't gotten around to messing it up yet, so all of Sam Alroy's files are intact. Sam protected them with some rather elaborate firewalls, but I'm sure the CIA technicians will be able to penetrate them. We did. You owe me, and you know what I want. See you in church."

Chasen carried the laptop out to the terrace. He sank onto the lounge, staring out at the Mediterranean, the computer in his lap, his fingers drumming on the case.

Mission accomplished? He had the laptop. Fallon's experts in the *Cannoncciale* had certainly gone through it thoroughly and copied the files. To what end? To use as a medium of exchange. For what Fallon wanted—the *Professio*. *"You owe me, and you know what I want."* Fallon didn't have the damn thing, which meant it was still loose, out there somewhere.

He set the laptop on the floor, stretched out on the lounge, closed his eyes, and went through it in his mind from the beginning, starting with his visit to CIA headquarters in Washington. The sun had set by the time he came up with the answers. Almost all the answers. The missing piece of the puzzle was the envelope that Sam Alroy had brought to the beach.

He grabbed the arms of the lounge chair and hauled himself to his feet, cursing Grady Devlin out loud for pulling him off his boat, sending him into the middle of this mess. Smuggling Cuban cigars and South American artifacts seemed like a nice, clean, safe way of life.

Chapter Thirty-Three

The harbormaster thumbed through his docking list.

"*Gypsy Queen.* Here it is. It moved from its regular mooring spot down to the end of the pier by the fueling dock. Taking off for good, tonight or in the morning. Are you interested in her old spot?"

"Not right now," Dave Chasen said.

The *Gypsy Queen*'s idling engine sounded like the magnified buzzing of insects. The virile, meaty voice of Luciano Pavarotti was pouring from the portholes. It sounded like something from *La Bohème*, but Chasen wasn't sure.

He climbed up the gangplank and hopped on board just as the tenor hit a high note.

The door leading below was open. He started down the stairs, hesitating when he noticed the smell of cigar smoke mixed in with the boat's diesel engine exhaust.

"Welcome aboard," Grady Devlin said, waving the bulblike barrel of a silenced semiautomatic in Chasen's direction. A fat cigar was stuck between his thick lips.

"Nice and quiet, Davey boy. From the look on your face, I can see that you're surprised. Hands all the way up. You know the drill."

Chasen's fingers made contact with the low-slung ceiling as Devlin slipped behind him, the gun's barrel stuck firmly against his spine while Devlin used his free hand to search him.

"Unarmed. Good man. Move over there, away from the stove, and keep those hands high."

Chasen followed orders. "Where's Keely?"

"In bed." Devlin waved the gun barrel. "Through that door. Don't try anything silly. I'm not an expert shot, but at this range there's no way I could miss."

Chasen bumped the door open with his knee. Keely's bedroom took up the entire fourteen feet of the *Gypsy Queen*'s beam. There were built-in cabinets, a makeup table, an Exercycle, and a large-screen TV.

Keely was lying on the left side of the king-size bed, her hands stretched over her head, her wrists duct-taped together, then fastened to the brass headboard. There was an open cut over her left eye. Her blouse had been ripped open. The underside of her pale arms were marred with circular burns the size of the tip of Devlin's cigar. A silver slash of the tape was pasted across her mouth. Her legs were taped together at the ankles. On the opposite side of the bed was a piece of sepia-tinted glass the size of a hardback novel.

Chasen scanned the area, looking for something he could use as a weapon. There wasn't much, except for the jars of cosmetics and a long-handled mirror on the makeup table.

Keely looked up at Chasen with wide, frightened eyes, her lips moving silently under the tape.

Devlin went to a stereo unit next to the bed and adjusted the volume. More Pavarotti.

"Did you just drop by for a final kiss, or have you put it all together?"

"I think I've put most of it together," Chasen said.

"Keely and I had a long talk. She told me where she stashed the *Professio*," Devlin said. He leaned over the bed and ripped the tape from Keely's mouth. "Under the sink. Not very imaginative."

Keely coughed and spat at Devlin.

"Temper, temper," he cautioned, keeping the gun aimed at Chasen as he moved to the bed and rapped his knuckles against the *Professio*. "Doesn't look all that impressive, does it?"

"What are you going to do with it?" Chasen said, edging over toward the makeup table.

"Return it to its rightful owner, of course. That is, if Jago Roldan wants it badly enough. How much of it did you figure out?" Devlin asked.

"Almost everything. But not you, Grady. You're right. You were a surprise."

Devlin puffed repeatedly until the cigar tip glowed red. "I'm glad you showed up. I need a good man at the helm." He waved the gun barrel in Keely's direction. "I don't think she's up to it."

"How, Grady? The *Professio*. How did you know?"

"The trouble with all you field agents is that you go off half-cocked. You don't do your homework."

"You didn't give me much time on this one."

"True. But you could have asked questions. Take Keely here. She screwed you once. Screwed the Company with that story on Senator Lorenzo. I wanted to make her pay for that, but those in positions above me forbade it. That didn't stop me from doing a blue line on her."

Devlin turned to Keely and said, "Blue line. Company jargon for a very thorough background check. But maybe you already knew that. Anyway, I ran her inside out. Her parents were well off, but not really rich. They tried making babies, but no luck. So they adopted an orphan. Keely here. Three months later, guess what? Mom gets pregnant. They have a son. Samuel. He became the star of the show. Ugly little brat, but smart as hell. Child prodigy. Left little Keely in the dust. Isn't that how it was, sweetheart? Mom and Dad loved Sammy best?"

"He's crazy, Dave," Keely said. "Help me."

Chasen lowered his arms a bare inch. Devlin was ten, maybe eleven feet away. He had to get closer. A long-ago class given by the CIA's armorer preached the theory that if you could get within six feet of a man with a loaded gun, you could disarm him before he had time to pull the trigger. Chasen hadn't believed it then. He had no choice but to hope it was true now.

"None of that had anything to do with the *Professio*, Grady."

"Ah, but it did. Patience, Dave, patience. That's what you've always lacked. That's why you'd never be a good desk commander. When Momma and Poppa bit the dust in a traffic accident, it was Sam who was left in charge of the family finances. What the hell, he was a brilliant scientist; she was just a newspaper junky. Sam controlled the purse strings, and he didn't open them very wide. He used all the money available to start up his company."

Devlin worked the cigar from one side of his mouth to the other. "He wasn't a complete prick. He let her use this boat. And there was no way she could have made those award-winning, money-losing documentaries without his backing. Then Sam marries Daria Roldan. Bad news for Keely. Really bad news when Sam knocks Daria up. He wants that baby and—Bite down on your lower lip, Dave."

"What?"

The silenced weapon made that soft, throaty sound that the movies somehow never got quite right.

Chasen screamed and grabbed his forearm.

"You were going to try something stupid," Devlin said. "I can read you like a book, pal. I taught you most of what you know, so don't make another dumb move. Where was I?"

"Sam wanted a baby," Chasen said, using his right hand to try to stanch the flow of blood streaming from his arm. The bullet must have hit an artery.

"Daria and old Jago thought they had Sam all wrapped, sealed, and delivered. They thought they could rip off everything of value from Sam's company, then kick him out of the house. But the Alroys didn't raise no dumb chicken. Sam hired a sharp lawyer, had a new will drawn up. Sam Alroy,

Incorporated, liquidated. Everything he owned would go to the child. If Daria had an abortion or lost the kid, then the money went to the Church. Not to his adopted sister. I bet John Fallon didn't know that. He might have killed Alroy himself.

"To cover the bases, Sam stripped the company computers of his new software. He'd start up a new company. To hell with the Roldans. His big mistake was telling his sister about the new will, and the change in the company makeup. She had been the sole beneficiary in the old will, and was listed in corporation filings as the vice president at Sam Alroy, Inc. She knew about the five-million-dollar life-insurance policy. Then Sam told Keely he was going to steal something from Jago. Something tremendously valuable that would give him control over Roldan. A letter, isn't that what he told you, Keely?" Devlin smiled at Keely. "She's a little tongue-tied now," Devlin said, "but twenty minutes ago she was a real songbird. Sam just didn't mention that it was a two-thousand-year-old letter signed by Saint Peter. Keely thought it was a business letter of some kind, something Sam could use to blackmail Jago. If he could, why couldn't she?"

"That's what was in the envelope on the beach, then," Chasen said. "The new will. The company papers."

"Right," Devlin said, flicking an inch of his cigar ash onto Keely's legs. "She thought everything was in the envelope. I'll bet you were pissed when you found out what you left on the beach, huh, kid? The *Professio* and the laptop were sitting there in Sam's car, and you let a dumb beach boy get away with them. As vice president of the company, Keely had to sign off on the new setup. Poor dumb Sam thought she was just going to scribble her name down and thank him for past favors. No one figured that Sam's dear sister was the killer. She said she was in Australia, and everyone believed her. The dumb Spanish cops didn't bother to check. I did. Keely arrived in Madrid the evening before

Sam's murder." He turned to Keely again. "I don't know how she lured him to the beach."

"Sam didn't like boats," Chasen said. "Ménière's disease."

Devlin nodded his head in approval. "Good work. I didn't know that. So she meets him and uses the old Irish-silencer routine. How many poor bastards were wasted like that in Colombia on your watch? Dozens. And you were right there, writing about them, weren't you, Keely? Our little girl here is no stranger to guns. She applied for a concealed-weapons permit in Washington. She was always packing in Colombia. I bet that if the cops dragged this yacht harbor, they'd find the gun she used to kill her brother. Then the Roldans tried to kill her by pushing the car off the cliff. She wasn't about to let them get away with that again, so she gets another gun. Either here or in Madrid when you thought she was out getting her hair done. She was ready to pop Jago or Daria if the opportunity presented itself. Or you, Dave, if you got wise to her. Where'd you dump the gun you shot Vidal Roldan with, honey? Somewhere in Madrid? You wouldn't risk bringing it back here."

Chasen remembered Keely telling him that she'd shot the snake that bit her in Australia.

"Do something, Dave," Keely said. "He's going to kill us."

"Everybody dies sooner or later," Devlin said.

Chasen couldn't stop the bleeding. He was starting to feel woozy.

Devlin pulled his gold watch from his vest and checked the time. "What really burned Keely's butt was when Jago and Daria played hardball with her on Sam's old will. Daria wasn't about to give up the insurance money, and Keely had nothing to stop them. Any half-assed attorney would know she didn't stand a chance against them. She ended up killing her brother for nothing. Then Dave Chasen shows up on the scene. Her hero. She learned that the letter Sam talked about was the *Professio*. If she could grab that, all wasn't lost."

Chasen wobbled on his feet, then fell to one knee.

Devlin shot him again in the same arm, just above his wrist.

The impact spun Chasen around, and he collapsed to the floor.

"Come on, pal," Devlin said. "Don't quit on me now. You're a better sailor with one arm than I am with two, but if you force me to kill you now, I will."

Blood streamed down from Chasen's wrist to his hand. "Why are you telling me all this, Grady? Confession good for the soul?"

"Why?" Devlin took the cigar from his mouth and ground it into an open jar of Keely's cold cream. "Who else am I going to tell? I have to brag to someone about how brilliant I was. Before you pass out, tell me where the painting is. The Goya."

When Chasen didn't respond, Devlin pulled the trigger again. The bullet grazed Chasen's shoulder and buried itself into the mattress. "This gun has a fourteen-bullet clip. And I've got a spare in my pocket. Where's the painting?"

"Garate, the Spanish CNI man, must have picked it up at the Plaza Mayor."

Devlin sighted the pistol at Chasen's head, then slowly lowered it. "I don't think he's that sharp."

"Then Fallon has it. Or the MI6 man, Bryce, because I don't."

"That's a shame, Dave. I was hoping you had it."

"Fallon found Sam's laptop. He left it in my room at my hotel."

"Good for him. That should give my pension a little boost. Did you know that I was being eased out? Those Homeland Security assholes are calling all the shots now. Out with the old and in with the incompetent."

Chasen's vision was getting blurry. He'd have to make a

move soon, or he'd bleed to death. He closed his eyes and moaned. Straightening out his right leg, he struggled to one knee, his hand grasping at the bedspread. "How did you know Keely had the *Professio*?"

"Herb Kessler. A shady London fence who deals in priceless objects. Stolen priceless objects. As soon as you told me about the *Professio*, I started asking around. Someone called Kessler asking about the *Professio*. A woman. It didn't take much to add those two and twos together. Coupled with your report. Who else had an opportunity that night at the plaza? That's what brought you here tonight, isn't it? The process of elimination. If it wasn't Eeny, Meeny, or Miney, it had to be Mo."

"That's still pretty thin," Chasen said, watching his blood pool out on the carpet. He groaned in pain and raised the heel of his right foot off the ground, shifting the weight to his toes, like a sprinter getting ready to leave the starting blocks.

"You're right. The truth be told, I thought you and Keely were in on it together, and you had it all, the *Professio*, the Goya, and the money. That's the only thing that made sense. When I came here tonight, she took one look at me, figured I was on to her. Went for one of those knives in the galley and tried to fillet me." Devlin moved to the edge of the bed and said, "That was a stupid move, kid," then pulled the trigger twice.

Keely's body jerked violently.

Chasen gritted his teeth and lunged at Devlin, aiming his head at Devlin's arthritic hip.

Devlin swore and fell to the carpet. The *Professio* slid off the spread, landing at Chasen's feet. He picked it up and slammed it into Devlin's face.

Devlin fired wildly, three shots whizzing by Chasen's head and burrowing into the paneled ceiling.

As Chasen hit Devlin again, the *Professio* broke apart into shards of glass.

Devlin fired twice more, then threw the gun away, his hands going to his bleeding eyes.

Chasen used his good elbow like a ski pole, dragging himself toward the gun.

"You prick," Devlin screamed as he groped blindly for Chasen. His face was a mass of blood and glass splinters.

Chasen reached the gun as Devlin's hands clamped around his wounded arm. The gun slipped from Chasen's fingers. Devlin buried his bloody face in Chasen's arm and bit down hard. Chasen screamed. The pain was intense, but it kept him from blacking out.

Chasen flung his hand toward the gun butt. His index finger snagged the trigger guard. With a last burst of panic-induced energy he jabbed the barrel at Devlin's chest and pulled the trigger. "Kick ass and break glass," he managed to say before he passed out.

He woke with a strong metallic taste in his mouth. Pavarotti was soaring through "Ave Maria."

"Your arm's a mess," John Fallon said, unbuckling his belt and cinching it tightly around Chasen's wounded arm. "We've got to stop the bleeding."

"Is Keely dead?"

"Very." Fallon slipped out of his coat, bundled it up, and placed it under Chasen's head. "Devlin's still alive, but just barely."

Chasen rolled his head to the side, coming face-to-face with Grady Devlin's bloody face.

Fallon was kneeling over him. "Help is on the way. Just in case they're late, I think the last rites are in order."

He crossed his thumb on Chasen's forehead, then said, *"Sacrum Unctionem infirmorum."*

Chapter Thirty-Four

St. Petersburg, Florida

"Hey, boss," Gaucho Ribera said. "There's a guy coming down the dock all dressed in black. It's too damn hot for black."

John Fallon, in slacks and polo shirt with an upturned collar, waved a friendly hand when he spotted Chasen.

"Permission to board, Captain."

"Ask Gaucho," Chasen said. "He's the captain of the *Breaking Point* now. I'm just a one-armed fisherman."

A dark-haired little girl skipped by Fallon and jumped from the dock onto the bow of the boat.

"Careful, Anica," Chasen yelled.

She smiled the wide, fearless smile of a nine-year-old and leaped back onto the dock, joining a group of kids ranging from four to fourteen, nearly the entire Gaucho Ribera clan.

Fallon stopped to chat with the children. He put his hand on Anica's head, then handed her a white envelope. "A rosary. Blessed by the pope, just for you."

Anica ripped the envelope open and held the beads out to the other children. Their expressions made it plain that candy or money would have been appreciated more.

"She's a beautiful child," Fallon said as he hopped on board.

Chasen used his one good arm to fish a beer from the ice chest and handed it to Fallon.

"You'll have to twist the top off yourself," he said, settling himself into the fiberglass-shelled Sailfish fighting chair on the *Breaking Point*'s stern.

"It's been, what?" Fallon said, cracking open the beer and resting one foot on the side railing. "Three, four months since that night on Keely's boat?"

"Four months, two weeks, and three days," Chasen answered, looking out at the rooster tail left in the teal-green water by a speedboat heading out of the harbor.

"How's the arm?"

"The doctor says I was lucky to save it. It won't be of much use, but at least it's there."

Fallon pointed the tip of his beer bottle at the children playing on the dock. "Anica's yours, isn't she?"

"I'm hoping so. There are always complications with an adoption by a single parent."

"I have friends in high places. I'd be happy to lend a hand."

"I could use a hand," Chasen said, not liking his own pun. "Tell me, what happened to the *Professio*? It was in pretty bad shape the last time I saw it."

"Beyond repair, I'm afraid. What wasn't destroyed by your breaking it across Devlin's face just dissolved into mush when it was exposed to the air."

"Then you don't know if it was authentic?"

"No one will ever know. I read in the papers that a Goya painting sold for seven million dollars at a Christie's auction last week. A source told me that Jago Roldan was one of the bidders, but that he dropped out when it hit four million."

"I guess he didn't want it badly enough."

"That's the key. Wanting it bad enough. What do you hear about Grady Devlin?"

"You have better sources than me, John."

"A rest home in West Virginia. That's the official word, anyway."

"What's the unofficial word?"

Fallon pointed a finger skyward, then reversed it to the boat's deck. "The big fire-and-brimstone rest home down below."

"Speaking of sources, how's Carly Sasser?"

Fallon's forehead wrinkled. "Carly. Devlin's secretary?"

"When we worked together in Berlin, Carly went to church often. St. Hedwigs. She dragged me there one morning, after a long night in her bed."

"Repentance is good for the soul."

"When I asked for a rundown on you, Carly sent back a no-record response. According to her, all the CIA knew about you was that you worked out of the Vatican and dealt in art restoration. Nothing about the *Cannoncciale*, or you being one of the pope's exsequors."

"Have you mentioned this to anyone at the CIA?" Fallon asked.

"No, we're finished now. I keep my mouth shut, I get a pension, and no one bothers me again. I always liked Carly. Still do. But I want to know what happened. You owe me that."

"I guess I do," Fallon admitted. "I was telling you the truth when I said I was in Washington, D.C., at Georgetown University. I was meeting with Professor Tregenza, a fellow Jesuit, and an ancient religious-document expert. Sam Alroy knew Tregenza from his early days as a Jesuit student. He called Tregenza and asked about the *Professio*. From the tenor of his calls, Tregenza felt that Sam had actually seen it. Sam's next call to him was traced to Jago's villa in Mijas. Rome knew that Devlin and the CIA had an interest in Alroy because of his software program."

"And Carly filled you in on everything?"

"She has been helpful to us on occasions in the past. You know the rest."

"Not all the rest," Chasen said. "The night you drove me to Jago's party. The guard mentioned that there had been a prowler at the villa. And that he'd been shot. He was one of your people, wasn't he? Another exsequor."

"Father Fabiano. Unfortunately, the wound proved fatal."

"So when you sat down next to me on the plane, it was all set up by Carly Sasser."

"You made it damn difficult with that move up to first class. Originally you had the seat next to me in coach. Fortunately, I was able to bump up to first class, and Connie, bless her beautiful soul, got me into that seat next to you."

"And how did you happen to show up at Keely's boat that night?"

Fallon placed his beer bottle in the cupholder on Chasen's chair. "Carly again. She passed the word along that Devlin had flown to Mijas. We found the cabdriver who shuttled him out to the marina. I wish I had gotten there a little sooner."

Chasen massaged the numb fingers of his left hand. "So do I, John."

"And what brought you back to the boat?"

"Grady Devlin had it right. A process of elimination. Who had motive and opportunity? Not Jago. I couldn't imagine Daria doing any dirty work herself. No matter how hard Garate spins it, Raul Tobias didn't have a chance to kill Vidal. So it had to either be Perry Bryce or Keely."

"Wasn't I on the list of suspects?" Fallon asked.

"Right at the top, until you left the laptop in my room. That meant you were still after the *Professio*. I'd told Keely that I thought Vidal had the *Professio* on him that night. That the whole switch was a scam. Then Bryce said something about seeing a flash of light in the alley just before the final shot that killed Vidal was fired. He figured the killer flicked the lights off and on before he pulled the trigger. I went back the next morning. The lightbulb in that room is sixty watts and covered with dead insects. Even in the black of night, it wouldn't send out a flash. Keely had her camera with her. I thought there was a possibility she flashed it in Vidal's eyes, startling him, then shot him and took off with the *Professio*.

"I hoped I was wrong. I went to the *Gypsy Queen* just to talk to her. You know the rest."

"Well, I'd better be going," Fallon said. When he was on the dock he turned back and said, "The Goya painting *and* a CIA pension? Isn't that overdoing it?"

Chasen gave a weary smile. "See you in church, John."